A PENGUIN MYSTERY

DEAD MARCH

Ann McMillan, who was born in Georgia, has been a writer and editor for the Medical College of Virginia in Richmond, where she lives.

For Franklin, a Civil War buff—

Ann McMillan

Ann McMillan

DEAD MARCH

PENGUIN BOOKS

PENGUIN BOOKS

Published by the Penguin Group

Penguin Putnam Inc., 375 Hudson Street, New York, New York 10014, U.S.A.

Penguin Books Ltd, 27 Wrights Lane, London W8 5TZ, England

Penguin Books Australia Ltd, Ringwood, Victoria, Australia

Penguin Books Canada Ltd, 10 Alcorn Avenue, Toronto, Ontario,
Canada M4V 3B2

Penguin Books (N.Z.) Ltd, 182–190 Wairau Road, Auckland 10, New Zealand

Penguin Books Ltd, Registered Offices: Harmondsworth, Middlesex, England

First published in the United States of America by Viking Penguin,
a member of Penguin Putnam Inc. 1998
Published in Penguin Books 1999

1 3 5 7 9 10 8 6 4 2

Map courtesy of The Library of Virginia Picture Collection
(altered to highlight points of interest)

ISBN 0-670-88147-3 (hc.)
ISBN 0 14 02.8020 0 (pbk.)
(CIP data available)

Printed in the United States of America
Set in Minion
Designed by Francesca Belanger

In memory of
Charles Hunter McMillan,
a gentle man

Acknowledgments

I would like to thank:

Charlotte Crystal and David Mattern, Ruth Hallman, Ruth McMillan, Mary Ellen and Dick Mercer, and Susan Ober, who read, suggested, and endlessly encouraged; Civil War historians Dr. Sandra V. Parker and Dr. Robert W. Waitt; medical experts Charles L. Cooke, M.D., and Vincent Ober, M.D.; Jonathan O'Neal, M.D., and other reenactors at Gordonsville in 1995; discerning reader Rozanne Garrett Epps; Sharla Fett, historian specializing in African American slave women healers; Dr. Edgar Toppin, historian of the African American experience; Jodi Koste, archivist at the Tompkins-McCaw Library of the Medical College of Virginia, Virginia Commonwealth University; the staffs of the Valentine Museum, Virginia Historical Society, and State Library of Virginia; my agent, Nancy Yost; my editors, Al Silverman and Carolyn Carlson; and my loves, Randy and Hunter.

1. **Hollywood Cemetery**

2. **Chimborazo Heights**

3. **Medical College of Virginia**

4. **Richmond, Fredericksburg & Potomac Railroad Depot**

5. **Exchange Hotel**

6. **Farmers' Market**

DEAD
MARCH

Chapter One

RICHMOND, VIRGINIA
THE FIRST OF MARCH, 1861

A shovel struck the ground, bit deep. Then a second. The two blades set a rhythm, scooping the dirt and dumping it aside, moving in and out of the narrow beam of light thrown across the ground by a bull's-eye lantern.

The diggers were two black men, one old, one young. They worked quickly, their faces glistening with sweat despite the cold. Soon they had hollowed a trench more than a foot deep and large enough for a man to lie down in.

Two white men stood a few paces off in the darkness. "Careful now, Old Billy, and you, Cyrus," came a drawl from the nearer of the two. "There's no coffin."

"All right, Doc Archer," the younger man, Cyrus, called in response. He glanced at Old Billy and spoke, too low for the white men to hear: "How'd he know that? I ain't complaining, mind you. No coffin, don't need no hooks. Might as well be digging up taters."

Overhead the stars were bright in the moonless sky. The air was cold, but not sharply so. In the almost-blackness was visible a jumble of pale shapes that fenced in the scene. After a while Old Billy paused in his work and held his hand up to his companion. "Done hit something."

Cyrus shook his head, wondering. "Whoever put 'em in ain't spent no time digging deep."

Old Billy made no reply.

The shovels moved more slowly now. Soon a fold of dirt-encrusted sacking was revealed. The shovels continued lifting and brushing clods away until they had uncovered an oblong shape, a little under six feet long, wrapped in wide bands of burlap. Through the smell of turned earth came another smell, rotten, repellent. The shovels stopped. Cyrus wrinkled his nose and spoke again.

"Doc said this here stiff was fresh."

"Just put in, that's what he said," Old Billy corrected. "Come on, Cyrus, let's finish it up."

Old Billy and Cyrus stepped back from the trench and dropped their shovels. Old Billy pushed back his sleeves, revealing scrawny arms corded with muscle. Two fingers on his left hand were missing below the knuckles. Despite his grizzled hair, he looked the stronger of the two. Cyrus fingered a string around his neck and avoided Old Billy's eyes. He was strong too, but softer, with rounded shoulders and a wispy goatee.

Cyrus turned his gaze to the two white men.

Cameron Archer, arms folded across his chest, leaned against a carved monument—an angel in the shape of a woman—that gleamed faintly in the darkness. He wore a cape flung across his body and a wide-brimmed slouch hat pulled low over curling dark hair that reached his collar. He was taking in the scene with eager, restless eyes that belied his nonchalant pose.

The fourth member of the party, a man of about twenty, stood slightly behind Archer. He had on a heavy coat, a knitted muffler around his throat; his head was bare. His brown eyes were wide but steady, his lips compressed.

Archer stepped forward, motioning to the younger man.

"All right, let's see the prize for our night's work. Come on, Charley—it's not going to bite you."

The workmen lifted the bundled shape from the trench and placed it on the ground. They fumbled for the head and pulled away the rough sacking. Beneath it the head was wound in a band of fine white cloth. The smell enveloped them then, a physical presence that made their throats close and their eyes water. Archer picked up the lantern and bent down to pull away the cloth. He directed the shaft of light onto the face, examined it for a few seconds, then turned away, leaving the dead in darkness once again.

Behind Archer, Old Billy stared at Cyrus, his eyebrows low over his eyes as if warning the younger man against showing any reaction. Cyrus, mouth agape, was still looking down toward where the body lay at their feet.

"Sack her up, boys." Archer's drawling voice was brisker now.

Cyrus spoke up. "Ain't we going to strip the graveclothes? We always been told not to take nothing from the graves but the stiffs. That way, we ain't stealing."

"Bring it all," Archer responded. He walked away, brushing his gloved hands together.

Cyrus shrugged. "Did you see that, Old Billy?" he whispered. "Stiff's a colored gal, just stuck in the ground with all these dead white folks. Reckon they'd thank us for getting her out of here, if they knowed. Though, now's I think of it, don't none of them smell any better, I reckon, for all that they got their fancy coffins and their stones." He smiled as his eyes sought out the still shapes of the funerary sculptures. "I ain't never thought to be raising up the dead in Hollywood Cemetery."

With practiced economy of movement, Old Billy and Cyrus thrust the bundle into a big burlap sack that enclosed it completely. They picked up the sack as if it had no weight at all, walked with it a few paces, and dropped it into a small cart. They shoveled the displaced earth back into the trench and smoothed it down. Cyrus picked up the bull's-eye lantern and flicked its beam over the place where the earth was raw. A shimmer of white caught the light. Cyrus eyed it, hesitating. It was the cloth that had been wrapped around the dead woman's head. Old Billy cast a quick glance over his shoulder, then picked up the white cloth and thrust it into his pocket. Then he shouldered his shovel and stepped into the lead. Cyrus placed his shovel atop the sack and followed, trundling the cart. The two white men fell in behind, walking single file, not speaking. Only the last in line, Charley Wilson, looked back over his shoulder at the place where they had been.

The darkness swallowed them.

HANOVER COUNTY, VIRGINIA
LATE MARCH

From where she sat on the rough stone bench in the family graveyard, Narcissa Powers squinted against the sun's glare past the top of her father's headstone, up across the sloping meadow to the farmhouse called Springfield. Small white clouds raced across a sky whose blue, after so many days of gray, was startling. She could feel the quickening of spring, though the orchard trees were still bare and tattered brown leaves clung to the oaks that bordered the fields. Green shoots were starting up from the dry, spidery remains of last summer's peonies, the new growth pushing the dead aside in its urgency to be born. Narcissa felt no kindred quickening. The whitewashed pickets that fenced in the graveyard seemed to enclose her life as well. There were the graves of her mother, buried when Narcissa was fifteen, and her father, buried four years later. There was the small stone lamb that marked the burial place of Narcissa's youngest sister.

Gazing at this group of stones, Narcissa saw another grave-yard, not a country burial plot but a formal cemetery, brick-walled and imposing. There lay her husband, and next to him their son, who had died a few hours after his birth. They were buried at Hampden-Sydney College, near Farmville, about sixty miles to the southwest. It was there that Narcissa had met Rives Powers—the young tutor of her brother Char-ley. She and Rives had made their home at Hampden-Sydney for the two years of their marriage, had awaited the birth of their child and mourned his death together. And there, a widow at twenty-one, she had mourned Rives's death from consumption.

When she'd watched Rives's casket being lowered into the ground, Narcissa felt that if she could endure the loneliness she felt then, she could endure anything. Although the two years prescribed for deep mourning had now passed, she was in no hurry to set aside her black clothing for the somber colors of half-mourning. On her last visit her sister Lydia had remarked that, with her black hair and dark brown eyes against her pale skin, she looked ready to enter a convent. Narcissa ignored Lydia's suggestion of adding "just a little color around the face," knowing what lay behind the words: You'll never attract another husband that way, Narcissa.

What of it? She would never marry again. But she knew her sister's concern was meant kindly. Without marriage, there would be no home for her to make. No hope of a child. The pain of this was so deep that she turned away from the thought. There is nothing made by grieving.

Narcissa rose and stood between her father's grave and her mother's, her fingers brushing each arched top. Her still face, its strong jawline curving to the cleft chin, could itself have been carved from marble. Then she turned away, toward the gate and the path that led from the graveyard to the house.

A flock of starlings rose out of the corn stubble and flew above the meadow, so close together that their wings formed a black scarf pulled across the sky between Narcissa and the house. So sudden was their appearance, so dense the fabric of their interlacing wings, that the sight caught Narcissa's breath. She thought of the Romans, finding portents in the flight of birds. At her left—that meant bad luck. Was this the sign of another death to afflict her kin . . . another mourning?

Shaking off the thought, she made her way past the silent stones and out through the little gate. Soon she was taking long strides, the breeze lifting strands of dark hair at her neck and temples. The exertion brought color to her pale face. Her bonnet swung from one hand; with the other, she half-lifted her skirts, already soaked to the braid from the early morning damp.

As she neared the house, her steps slowed. She took little joy in the day's chores—the never-ending round of meals and washdays, the basketful of mending that waited by her chair. They were the work of duty only, not of love.

Before Narcissa left to marry Rives, Springfield was simply home. Its trees would grow taller, flowers would bloom and die, tobacco, wheat, and corn would be planted, tended, harvested. These were her earliest memories. It had never occurred to her that these things would change; and indeed they had not. But circumstances had changed. Springfield now belonged to her half-brother John, his wife, Mary, and the family that would come.

Narcissa thought sometimes of leaving Springfield. Her inheritance from Rives would enable her to pay her keep at one of her sisters' houses. But wherever she went, her role would be the same: the widowed aunt, striving to adapt herself to everyone else's wishes. Darning stockings worn through at the heels by someone else's husband, returning smiles given as an afterthought, suppressing her own inclinations, her own judgment. It was a noble ideal to give of oneself for others. But suppose no one needed what she had to give?

Yes, circumstances were changing. Whenever she visited with neighbors, talk of secession dominated. The words had grown more vehement with the election of President Lincoln. Some of the fire-eaters wanted war. Narcissa found the images stirred her against her will. If Virginia seceded, if war came, men would take up arms and fight. Her brother Charley, closest in age to her and the one she loved best, was finishing his medical studies in Richmond: he would be a doctor, saving lives on the field of battle. But she, who was so much like him, could not follow. Where would she be? What could she do?

She walked on toward Springfield, whose clapboard walls, flanked with twin stone chimneys, and deep-sloping Dutch roof had always seemed to embrace her with warmth and safety. Now she looked for excuses to postpone going inside.

As Narcissa passed the outbuilding that housed the kitchen, Aunt Dodie's voice came to her through the open door that relieved the heat from the cooking fire. Narcissa thought about going in to busy her hands and talk with the old servant. At least there she still felt at home. Then she saw Dru over at the stable, unhitching Samson from the wagon. That meant the mail would be here. Narcissa gave the gray-haired black man a smile and a wave, then quickened her pace for the house. Could there be a letter from Charley? Several weeks had passed since the last one, and she blamed herself. She tried to make her letters to him cheerful, but . . .

Narcissa raked the insteps of her boots over the scraper and then removed them, slipping on low-heeled shoes. She shook out her skirts and stepped inside, hanging her bonnet and shawl on the hall tree inside the back door.

The first floor of Springfield was two big rooms, each with two doors opening into the center hall. The furnishings were so familiar to Narcissa that she barely noticed them from one year to the next. There were the worn Turkey carpets where she and Charley fought battles with his toy soldiers; the straight-legged old chairs and tables, black with age, which she kept polished with a mixture of wax and white sap; the rosewood sofa upholstered in blue velvet, bought new, whose carved wooden legs in front had looked to the young Narcissa like grotesque, long-nosed faces.

The mail would be left just inside the parlor door, on the little rosewood secretary that had belonged to Narcissa's mother.

Mary stepped out into the hall, holding in one hand a stocking she had been mending. The wool stretched over the darning egg, Narcissa thought, looked like the bodice of Mary's dress, pulled tight over her thickening waistline. "There's a letter from Richmond for you," Mary said, handing her a small white packet. "It's not from Charley," she added as she turned back into the parlor. "It looks like a woman's writing."

How like Mary, Narcissa thought, exerting herself just to

vex me. Then the envelope caught her attention and made her forget her bad temper. It was heavy, cream-colored paper, sealed with the imprint of a signet ring. No one she knew used such expensive paper. She slipped her thumbnail under the scalloped border of the envelope and pulled out the folded paper. She glanced at the signature first: "Rachel Hughes (Mrs. Edgar Hughes)," with an address on Marshall Street written below. Dr. Hughes was one of Charley's professors, she recalled. This must be the doctor's wife. She turned to the beginning and read:

> Dear Mrs. Powers,
> It is my sad duty to inform you that your brother Charles is very ill with erysipelas. He is here at our home on Shockoe Hill, being attended by my husband, who is one of Charles's professors at the Medical College. Be assured that my husband and I are giving him every care and comfort. Charles has asked to see you, and I urge you not to delay in coming to us, since your presence may aid in his recovery.

Narcissa stood still, frightened but also puzzled. She read the letter a second time. As a child, her sister Lelia had had a slight case of erysipelas—a kind of blood poisoning that caused painful reddening of the skin—and their driver Dru had had it once. Though she knew erysipelas was sometimes fatal, she had never known anyone who had been very ill with it.

Surely, though, for Rachel Hughes to write in this way, Charley must be—Narcissa tried to call out but could not find her voice to tell what she had read. When I speak, she thought, it will be true.

As Narcissa consulted with Mary and the servants, she turned over the letter in her hands. It had been canceled in Richmond the day before. Dru had picked it up early that morning from the post office at Denton's Tavern. Mrs. Hughes would expect her to arrive this afternoon, Richmond being about four hours away.

Aunt Dodie came in from the kitchen to help pack Narcissa's trunk. Narcissa quickly selected two plain dresses with extra collars and undersleeves, stockings and undergarments, her merino shawl, and other necessities for a few days' stay. She could easily send for more things should she need to prolong her visit. Last of all she placed in the trunk a worn, black-bound Bible and a diary bound in green, gold-stamped leather.

Aunt Dodie's soft, wrinkled brown face was wet with tears. Narcissa was torn between wanting to storm at her old nurse, and wanting to cry herself and be comforted. "Auntie," she said, taking hold of the old woman's shoulders and looking into her face, "please don't take on so. You will quite 'unwoman' me." Narcissa smiled ruefully, and Aunt Dodie returned the smile after a moment. The two women embraced, then returned to their preparations.

When Narcissa came downstairs again, John was there. He had ridden in from the fields and walked into the hall still wearing his boots. Mary, clinging to his arm, frowned at the sticky red mud on his boots but said nothing. Narcissa stopped in front of her half-brother and looked up at him. John's resemblance to their father increased as his dark hair grayed. But his somber look held nothing of affection toward her, or of concern for Charley.

"Narcissa, I hope this sickness puts some sense into Charley. I know Father encouraged his foolishness, but Charley's spent enough time getting educated."

Enough money, you mean, Narcissa thought. John, the eldest, couldn't hide his resentment of the fact that the younger ones, even the girls, had more learning, because their mother—his father's second wife, had valued it. She paid for their education with her own money, and some of their father's as well.

John went on. "He can come back here to Springfield and get his strength back, help with the spring planting and the calving. That's where a son belongs, with the land."

Narcissa kept silent. John was thinking of Charley as a boy, strong enough to work, but without the needs of a man for his own home, his own occupation. Charley would have to shrink to fit back into Springfield—shrink, as I have done, she thought with a flash of bitterness.

Even after the trunk was loaded onto the buggy, it seemed to Narcissa that they would never get away, with Mary's finicking orders to Dru. The time spent in driving Narcissa to Richmond could only be recompensed, it appeared, by errands to the city's stores. Mary fumbled in her purse, calculating exactly the money Dru would need and not a cent more. Narcissa fumed, remembering how graciously her mother had treated these same servants.

Just before Narcissa lost patience entirely and loosed a sharp tongue at her sister-in-law, Mary seemed to recall the urgency of the trip. "Go on, Dru," she snapped, thrusting the coins at him, "Narcissa can't wait for your dawdling." Narcissa and Dru exchanged a wry look as he helped her into the buggy. Then he vaulted into the driver's seat and took up the reins.

As they left Springfield behind, Narcissa felt her heart lift a little despite her fear. She smiled and leaned forward to call to Dru, "Do you remember when Charley and I used to ride with you and Father to take the tobacco into town?" Dru smiled back at her and nodded. Taking their tobacco, rolled into kegs, to the markets in Richmond had meant a joyful excursion. She and Charley were always excited to think that their crop was beginning a journey that could take it all over the world—and excited by the anticipation of a special toy or book that each might be allowed to purchase in town if the crop brought a good price. Lydia and Lelia, her older sisters, had never wanted to come. Even as girls they had stayed close to their mother, worked hard to prepare for their future roles as wives and mothers. Narcissa had never envied their contentment, or deplored her own restlessness, until Charley had gone off to college, leaving her behind.

She felt the sun, warm through the black fabric of her dress, and looked out at land that was so familiar to her and Charley: the thick woods and rolling fields of Hanover. In the fields she saw calves trotting after their mothers, nosing at their flanks, or suckling contentedly. Bluebirds darted in and out of view, too quick often for the eye to catch their heaven's blue but easy to identify by the distinctive scallop of their wings in flight.

The buggy rolled and jolted down the Pouncey Tract road past Denton's Tavern. There the bright day had brought the old men back out onto the wide front porch, where for as long as she could remember they had rocked and talked and spat tobacco juice between the whitewashed rails. The men saluted her, touching their fingertips to the wide brims of their hats. Their eyes followed the buggy until a bend in the road took it out of sight. They would be wondering about the purpose of her errand, Narcissa thought; it was even possible, the way news travels in the country, that they already knew.

The noise of the buggy's approach startled a buzzard from the roadside. Bigger than a wild turkey and graceless on the ground, the buzzard flapped awkwardly away from a torn and bloody bit of fur in the road. Narcissa shrank from the bird's dirty gray wings and pink, shriveled head. On the right—that was *good* luck, wasn't it? But she shuddered. This time she could not shake off the sense of foreboding.

Chapter Two

RICHMOND, VIRGINIA

Judah Daniel stood in her garden, running her hands up and down the length of sacking that served as her gardening apron. The damp earth felt good on her hands. Even the sore place between her shoulders felt good. She looked around her with pleasure. It was a perfect March day in Richmond, warm sun and cool breeze. The trees were bare of just budding; if she angled her eyes just right, she could see from her yard straight down to where the James River winked in the sun.

She stood with her shoulders back, legs braced apart, head high, as if she had conquered more than the soil beneath her feet. Despite her almost forty years, her dark brown skin was taut on her spare frame, and the eyes in her high-cheekboned face were bright. Her full, curving lips, relaxed for an instant from their usual compression, gave her face its only sign of softness. She took pleasure in this garden, which extended about twenty feet across—a little more than the width of her house—and eight feet deep. In that small space grew flowers, herbs, and shrubs of all descriptions. Not much this early to be showing new growth, but she had prepared the rich earth. Many of the plants she grew there would be called weeds, and despised by gardeners, but they were among her most potent medicines, whose power had been known to the Indians: milkweed, butterfly weed, wild geranium, tansy, angel trumpet, horse nettle. By July their growth would be lavish, needing to be controlled rather than nurtured. Other plants, and the bark of trees—dogwood, willow—she would gather down by the river.

It ain't much, she thought as she looked at the ground she tended. But it's work I done for myself, not some master, and it's me that'll get the good of it. Me and them that I doctor. She was respected—and rightly, she thought. Depending on the healer's skill, the plants she used as medicines could cure or kill, ease pain or cause it, calm a madman's raving or drive a sane one mad with terrible visions.

Yet the women who had taught her had not been respected by the white men and women who owned them. Not respected—though they could heal, though they were close to God, who healed through them, though their old wisdom gave them weapons they could have used to kill those who enslaved them. She followed their lead, resisted temptation to take justice into her own hands, though sometimes it was hard. *Vengeance is mine, saith the Lord.*

The sun was getting halfway down the sky, and when a cloud blocked its rays, the sudden chill made her shiver. She had just made up her mind to go inside for a mug of coffee when she sensed, rather than heard, a presence behind her. She turned.

"Yes, child, what is it?" She smiled to soften her brusqueness, lest Darcy mistake her tone for anger and shrink into her shell. Darcy's responding smile was lopsided, drawn by a broad, incised scar on her right cheek. She was skinny, eight years old, and small for her age—she could stand sideways and not make a shadow.

Darcy carried messages to and from those seeking Judah Daniel's help. The girl's small size, her quietness, her swift bare feet and quick brain made her an ideal messenger. And she was as loyal as the best daughter, since Judah Daniel had mended her body, flayed by fire, and her spirit as well. Darcy's eyes sparkled now, her hair was neatly braided close to her head, and her erect posture showed she was proud to be training under the healer.

Judah Daniel stood, hands on hips, and waited to hear where she had been summoned.

"Judah Daniel, Cyrus Roper the sack-'em-up man sent to John Chapman to let you know he be coming to see you tonight, 'in the dead of night,' he said."

This last phrase was repeated from careful memory. Darcy paused, looking into Judah Daniel's eyes, her expression solemn. Darcy knew free blacks weren't allowed to wander at night—that the man would be endangering both himself and Judah Daniel by this action.

Judah Daniel stood still, frowning with thought. Cyrus Roper had consulted her before, a few years back, but not in this secretive and risky fashion. As free Negroes, both she and Cyrus were used to living by a host of laws, written and unwritten, made by the whites to fence them in. And they knew how to get around those fences: where they could go, and when, to carry on their business in relative safety.

With his father, Old Billy, Cyrus made his living by robbing graves for the medical school—so he knew something of moving about the city in the "dead of night." He would know some tricks to be sure he wouldn't be caught—or maybe the leave granted him to do the white folks' nighttime errands could be stretched to cover one of his own.

"What he want to see me for?" she queried Darcy.

"John Chapman say Cyrus not sick in body, but troubled in his mind."

Judah Daniel bent down to pick up her gardening spade and fork. Feeling that twinge from the sore muscle in her upper back, she flexed her shoulders gingerly. Trouble in mind and trouble in body went together. When Cyrus had come to her before, she recalled, she had given him a tonic of red oak bark and pine bark boiled together to drink, and some pieces of the bark ground with black snakeroot into a powder to wear in a pouch around his neck. He had thanked her and paid her in silver coins.

Cyrus might well have troubles, she mused. He and Old Billy (still known by that name, though his firstborn son, Young Billy, had been dead now a year or two) were shunned by the other free blacks because of their traffic in corpses. Cyrus was not overly gifted with brains, but he followed his father's lead.

Except, perhaps, in consulting her. Old Billy was a solitary man who didn't hold with religion. That suited him to his job, since grave-robbing went against the Bible's teachings, African wisdom too, of how the dead should be treated. And lots of folks went further in their dread of the sack-'em-up men, reasoning that anyone capable of digging up the dead to sell their bodies was also capable of killing. Killing was easier work, when you thought about it, and would pay just as well. She'd heard it said that Old Billy had a bag of gold coins hidden in his straw pallet. But who would dare to steal from the sack-'em-up man?

Judah Daniel suspected it was John Chapman's sense of his role as unofficial mayor of the free blacks that made him overcome personal distaste and community disapproval to help Cyrus Roper. For her, it was not a point to debate. She would help anyone who came to her, slave or freedman. But she set the terms, that was understood; and she avoided as much as possible the world of the whites.

Cyrus's dramatic plea for her help had got her curiosity up. She didn't doubt she could help him this time as she had before, whether through medicine, ritual, or simply listening and advising.

Putting her arm around Darcy's thin shoulders, Judah Daniel walked into her house.

>=<

Dru drove the buggy into Richmond close by the line of the Richmond, Fredericksburg & Potomac Railroad, which ran east-west through the city between the two dirt roads comprising Broad Street and down to the station at Eighth. The fluffy white clouds of the morning now had heavy gray bottoms and cast chilly shadows when they raced across the sun.

The roads were churned to mud, and the buggy moved slowly with the tide of traffic. It seemed to take forever to reach the station. Narcissa and Dru pointed out landmarks to each other, but she saw him frown as he clucked to the horses and knew he shared her anxiety. At the station a train was pulled up, taking on and discharging passengers, disgorging black clouds from its funnel-shaped smokestacks. Here she noted more crowds, made up largely of rough-looking men. Drawn to Virginia's capital by rumors of war, she supposed.

From the station, it was a few blocks to the address given by Mrs. Hughes—Marshall Street, two blocks up from where the Medical College of Virginia was located on Shockoe Hill. Here, away from the coal smoke of the trains, Narcissa could smell the tang of tobacco carried from the warehouses down by the river—a smell like strong tea.

In the bustling indifference of the city, Narcissa's fears were mounting. She felt out of place; how little had she known of Charley's life since he had left Hampden-Sydney! His letters more often commented on family news than told his own. She pulled her shawl tight around her and fought down her dread.

At last Dru pulled up the horses and stepped down in front of a white-painted double house, divided by a chimney in the center, with identical green doors and shutters on each side—one of a line of a half-dozen such houses that gave the street an elegant simplicity.

As Narcissa watched, Dru hesitated, hat in hand, wondering which door to approach. Almost at once the door on the left was opened by a neatly dressed maidservant. Close on her heels was a handsome woman in her forties, dressed in rich maroon wool trimmed with black soutache braid. Narcissa noted neatly dressed dark hair streaked with gray, hazel eyes beneath straight brows, and a full mouth turned down at the corners. Rachel Hughes, surely.

The woman spoke a few words to Dru, who hurried back to the carriage to help Narcissa down. As Narcissa stepped onto the porch the woman reached out and took her hands in her own with a brief pressure, then laced her right arm through Narcissa's left as if to support her.

"Mrs. Powers, I am so glad that you have come. Your dear brother . . . I hope that he will know you. . . . I pray that your visit will do him some good." Mrs. Hughes seemed to be near tears. Narcissa felt the shock of her words and leaned for a moment on her supporting arm.

They went in through the open door. Narcissa had a vague impression of the inside of the house as elegant, formal, with dark, polished wood and rich, red-toned brocades. Mrs. Hughes and her maidservant were thoughtful, quickly and quietly helping Narcissa remove her traveling clothes and seeing to her luggage. She was led into the other half of the double house, then down a hallway tiled with squares of rose and gray stone, uncarpeted. They passed a book-lined office, then came to a door that stood ajar.

Rachel Hughes stopped. Rather than rudely pull away from the woman's grasp on her arm, Narcissa halted as well, though she wanted nothing save to get through that door to Charley.

"I can hardly bear to tell you . . ." Rachel Hughes spoke hesitantly. "They thought it best to amputate his left arm. My husband can tell you more; I will send at once to let him know you are here."

Narcissa could not take in the meaning of her words. She could see in her mind's eye Charley's hands, strong to rein in a runaway horse, gentle to bandage a hurt kitten. He was going to be a doctor; he would need both his hands.

Only let me see him, she thought; there must be some mistake. She broke away from Mrs. Hughes and stepped into the room.

It was a sitting room made over into a sick room, perhaps for proximity to the doctor's office, well proportioned but stripped of ornament. The mirror over the fireplace had been covered with a heavy green cloth. Narcissa shuddered; it was like the draping of mirrors after a death.

A deep armchair had been drawn up close to the bed, and a small table stood by with corked bottles of medicine and medical paraphernalia Narcissa did not recognize.

The pungent, oily smell of wood tar could not disguise the stench of dead flesh. The shape in the bed was still, the face turned away, the body so wasted that knobs and ridges of bones showed through the covers. The hair was thick and black, like her own. It was Charley.

Narcissa turned to look at Rachel Hughes.

Mrs. Hughes bowed her head. "I pray there may be some change."

Narcissa nodded acknowledgment, then walked the few paces to stand close to the bed. She knelt over Charley. He was lying on his back, sleeping or unconscious. His eyes were closed, the lashes long and black against the pale skin that sank into a hollow between the high cheekbone and the jaw.

"I will send for my husband," Mrs. Hughes said again. "Phebe will be just outside the door in case you need anything," she added in a subdued voice, then left the room.

Gently Narcissa pulled back the covers and saw that it was true. The loose white cotton sleeve nearest her lay flat against the sheet, empty. Charley's left arm was gone. Now that she had seen him, the disfigurement seemed unimportant, if only he could live. She seated herself in the chair, clutching her shawl around her in the chilly room, and watched. Charley was breathing in shallow, irregular gasps. Every few seconds he shuddered as though chilled. Beads of sweat stood on his face. A bowl of water was close at hand on the table, with a wrung-out cloth next to it. Narcissa dabbed his face with the cloth, called his name, and prayed over and over, "God please if it be thy will let my brother live. Thy will be done. Amen." Now and then Charley would mutter or call out as if trying to speak. Narcissa's heart thumped painfully at the sound, and she would bend over him, touch him, call his name. Then she would sit back, heartsick at the realization that he lay separated from her by a gulf she could not cross.

After a time, she heard footsteps approaching down the hall—a loud, hard-soled tread, not the soft-shod step of a servant. She straightened and faced the door expectantly. It was a tall man dressed in a black frock coat, with vest, trousers, and stock also black.

The man, whom she took to be Dr. Hughes, came up to her and took her hand. Bowing over it, he mumbled, "Mrs. Powers . . . your brother . . . I am sorry . . ." He spoke stiffly. The conventional words of sympathy seemed to make him ill at ease. Then he dropped her hand and turned away. Narcissa opened her mouth to call him back, but she saw that he intended only to draw up a side chair that was next to the door.

Hughes set the light chair next to Narcissa's armchair and seated himself. He looked past her to where Charley lay.

Narcissa gazed at the doctor eagerly, wanting to speak but hesitating. Would he offer hope or confirm her fears? She could not tell. His frown, she thought, could be interpreted as expressing deep thought, or concern for his patient, or sorrow, or annoyance.

She found the doctor a sharp contrast to his wife, who was carrying her lush loveliness into middle age. He was ascetic in appearance and manner, tall and thin, clean-shaven. He wore his pale hair short and brushed straight back. His large, pale-lashed blue eyes were deep-socketed, his forehead and cheeks scored with deep lines.

When at last Dr. Hughes began to speak, the words came out in a measured clip, the intonation flat, as if the course of Charley's illness were the subject of an oft-repeated lecture. More expressive than his face or voice were his hands, with long, tapered fingers that sketched shapes in the air.

It had begun perhaps two weeks before, with a wound— no more than a scratch, really—on the inside of the left forearm. The doctor swept his right hand down along his own left arm to indicate the place. The wound had been bandaged, but it seemed that Charley, caught up in the busy round of medical studies and perhaps lulled by that sense of invulnerability common to young men, had not had the dressing changed often enough. Erysipelas had taken hold.

The treatments, chiefly water dripped into the wound—a fluttering motion of the fingers indicated the drops—had not been effective. Gangrene had supervened.

At first, Dr. Hughes explained in the same dry tone, Charley had refused to hear of the amputation that might save his life. At last the arm had been removed, but it was too late.

"Is there any chance?" Narcissa had to ask, though she knew the answer.

"All that could be done, was done." The pale blue eyes met hers, then slid away. "We are all in God's hands." He looked down at his own hands, now lying still in his lap. He has given up, she thought; but despite his words, he did not seem reconciled. Instead he seemed acutely uneasy.

They sat in silence for a few moments. At last Hughes rose from his chair and asked Narcissa to leave the room so that he could examine his patient. She went out into the hallway. Rachel Hughes's sharp-faced servant—the one called Phebe—was seated near the door. She stood up quickly and moved away several paces. Narcissa took the seat and tried to smile her thanks, but the servant avoided her eyes.

She is expressing as much resentment as a conscientious servant can, Narcissa thought, for the burden Charley's illness has imposed on her household and her mistress. A sudden rush of gratitude to Mrs. Hughes warmed Narcissa momentarily. Then the cold chill returned. Grief, fear, and a bitter guilt. Why had she not known about Charley's injury? How had her brother become a stranger? As children, they had urged each other on to mischief. Later, Charley had passed her in height and entered into experiences she could not share. That had been an awkward time, but they had grown closer again when, after their mother's death, Narcissa had taken the maternal role of cherishing and counseling.

Had she known about his wound, she would have made

sure he took proper care of it. But lately she had been so full of her own concerns. No wonder Charley had hesitated to turn to her with his, she thought sadly.

The door to the sickroom opened. Hughes stood for a moment in the doorway, jotting on a piece of paper that was folded lengthwise to take the pressure of the pencil. He looked inclined to hurry away, but Narcissa stopped him with a hand on his arm. "There is no change," was all he said. She let him go then. At least, alone with her brother, she could summon the memory of their familiar closeness and believe that in some way, though she could not tell it, he was comforted by her presence.

Through the evening servants came and went, stirring the fire and offering refreshment. She took some tea, bread, and soup in the hall, leaving the door to the sickroom open so that she could hear any sound that Charley might make, then hurrying back to resume her post next to his bed. At about ten o'clock, with her feet propped on a stool and the rigid hoops of her skirts arranged as comfortably as possible around her, Narcissa closed her eyes and gave in to weariness.

Suddenly—she had no idea how much time had passed—she awoke, heart pounding. Charley had spoken, she was sure of it. She heard, echoing in the room or inside her head, one word: "resurrection."

Narcissa knelt by the bed, bent her head close to Charley's, and whispered his name. He was silent, his pulse low and irregular. How could I have fallen asleep? she thought despairingly. Now he may never speak again. I can't be sure I heard it . . . But the word resounded in her brain. Whether spoken or not, it had come to her, she was sure—come to her from Charley. Watching him, listening to his faint breaths sigh in the air, she wondered what he had meant. Charley was not religious. Was he trying to tell her, by a word or by an impression of feeling, that he believed? Was he trying to pray? All our senses tell us that the difference between life and death is absolute, she thought, but our hearts will not believe it. I believe in the communion of saints . . . the resurrection of the body . . . the life everlasting. . . . As she heard the familiar words in her mind, she saw her husband's face, her mother's, her father's—all dead. I believe it, she thought, because nothing else is bearable.

She watched then, fighting off her tiredness. Hours passed. Suddenly Charley convulsed as if some force were passing through his wasted body. His eyes opened, but he did not see her. As she reached out to him, he fell back. She knew that he was dead.

Narcissa awoke to light sifting through closed shutters. Her first thought was, I've slept so late. Then the memory of Charley's death, and its curiously flat aftermath, returned to her.

The servant Phebe had been asleep in the chair outside the door. Narcissa had touched her shoulder and asked her to call her mistress. Soon both Dr. Hughes and Mrs. Hughes had come, blinking away sleep but busily efficient, the doctor confirming Charley's death, his wife speaking in low tones to the servants and attending to Narcissa. Mrs. Hughes and a maidservant had taken her up the stairs to a small, daintily appointed room, had helped her out of her garments, into her nightgown, and into bed. After the intense emotions of the day, she had felt only emptiness. As yet, no tears had come.

A knock on the door brought Narcissa wide awake. As she swung her feet onto the floor, the servant who had helped undress her the night before entered the room to offer coffee and toast. The servant, a gentle, middle-aged woman called Jane, eased Narcissa through the routine of dressing. As she was finishing, there was a discreet knock at the door. The maid opened it to admit Rachel Hughes, with Phebe close behind her. Rachel stepped over to Narcissa and put her arm around her shoulder.

"My dear," she said gently to Narcissa, "I am so very sorry." Rachel was dressed somberly in black, and her face was pale and tired. How difficult it must have been for her, Narcissa thought again, and embraced her gratefully. I'm a stranger to her, and Charley little more than a stranger.

"I am . . . so much obliged . . ." Narcissa found that her voice failed her.

"Hush, please don't talk of it," Mrs. Hughes interrupted, tightening her embrace briefly. "It is too early to speak of it, but I hope that you will consider us your friends, and that we will see more of you in the future. That will help to make up for the loss of your brother." Her eyes dropped momentarily, as if her own grief had for a moment overpowered her. Then she looked up at Narcissa, smiled sadly, and took her leave, Phebe and Jane following.

Left alone, Narcissa looked around her. The room was pretty, decorated in light colors. The shutters were open now, and bright spring sunshine flowed into the room. Narcissa felt glad of its warmth.

Her things had been replaced in her trunk, but her diary and Bible were still lying on the small table next to the bed. Narcissa picked up the Bible and opened it at random, as was her habit, to find a message in the first passage her eye fell upon. It had begun as a game, but more than once Narcissa had found herself reading words with an eerie relevance to her thoughts. As she riffled the pages, a small packet fell into her lap. She put down the Bible and picked up the folded paper. It had not been there, she knew, at Springfield, when she had placed the Bible in the trunk.

Narcissa opened the paper. It was blank, but in its folds was another paper, blackened along one edge as if it had been burned. She recognized her brother's handwriting. It is something of Charley's, she thought, saved for me—perhaps pulled from the fireplace. But why was it left in the Bible, where it could have been misplaced? Why not give it to me directly? And why had Charley—or someone—started to burn it?

Carefully she smoothed the blank paper flat and placed the burned paper on it, so as not to damage it any further. The portion that was saved was part of a small, coarse sheet of paper, perhaps torn from a notebook, with writing on both sides. Fire had consumed the top of the paper, and the first few lines had been burned away. She found the signature, then turned the paper over and began to read.

anatomical study. Yet this study necessitates the removal of corpses from their graves. It is an evil, yet I ask myself how holy is the prohibition against grave-robbing, when cadavers are needed for medical study that can save lives? In order to learn, a medical student must perform an anatomy. Yet I fear some greater evil has been done, something that taints us all with sin.

At the invitation of my teacher—almost as a sort of initiation into the brotherhood of medicine—I accompanied him on the digging up of a grave. I wondered at the incongruity of the site and how he came by his knowledge of it, but, trusting him, I asked no questions

Here the page ended. Carefully Narcissa turned it over and read on. The letter resumed as abruptly as it had begun.

and determined that the woman, a young mulatto, had borne a child and suffered from childbed fever. As I continued

the anatomy, I discovered that the subject had met with
a violent death—a rag had been forced down her
throat! I called out; the servants came in, then Archer
and Hughes. They sent me away and shut the door.
They were shouting at each other. I never saw the
cadaver again, and my questions have been met with
silence.

I fear there is some dreadful secret here. I find there is no
one I trust, and I long for your ear and woman's heart.

> *Your loving*
> *brother,*
> *Charley*

Narcissa read the words again and again, until she felt she had puzzled them out as well as she could. Childbed fever was a scourge of womanhood, giving awful reality to the cursed lot of Eve—through an unknown cause, the pain and sorrow of childbirth were followed by the hideous suffering and death of the new mother. The threat of childbed fever, among other dangers, made women prepare for the births of their children by planning for their own deaths, arranging details such as who would inherit treasured possessions and who would care for surviving children. Many women were afflicted, and too many died.

This unknown woman had not died this way, though; she had been killed. When her "violent death" was discovered, why had Dr. Hughes, and the man called Archer, reacted with anger, then silence? Was one of them the teacher who had drawn Charley into the grave-robbing? Their unwillingness to answer Charley's questions proclaimed them guilty, but of what? What was the "dreadful secret"?

Narcissa sat back, suddenly weak. She ran her tongue over her lips. They tingled, and her hands felt cold and stiff. Carefully she replaced the burned paper in its wrapper and the folded packet in the Bible. She went to her trunk, placed the Bible and her diary at the bottom, and replaced the contents so as to conceal them, then closed and locked it. She stood in the center of the room, turning over the key in her hand.

From the paper her brother's voice cried out in loneliness and fear—called out to her. Once more, the knowledge of her own failure overwhelmed Narcissa. If only she had not been so wrapped up in her own concerns. He had hesitated to send the letter, perhaps unwilling to add to her grief with his own worries. Then someone had tried to destroy the paper, and had very nearly succeeded. Or, she thought, perhaps Charley had tried to destroy it himself, then changed his mind or been interrupted.

Yet someone among the household's occupants had left the charred fragment to speak to her with Charley's voice after Charley himself could no longer do so; someone had wished her to know of the evil that haunted his last days. She felt fiercely grateful to that person, whoever it might be. It helped to know that Charley had tried to tell her, had had faith in her. She blinked away hot tears.

But why in this way? Whoever had placed the paper in her Bible, Narcissa thought, had not wanted to answer questions—had wanted his or her identity to remain a secret— had perhaps been afraid. After all, this paper accused the master of this house of concealing a terrible crime. She felt a chill of fear. Then a wave of hot anger drove out the fear. What right had these men to involve Charley in crimes that would so trouble him?

Hearing footsteps in the hall, Narcissa knew that the question beating in her head would have to wait. She placed the key in her reticule and began to prepare for the mourning ritual before her.

Chapter Three

RICHMOND

"Judah Daniel, you recollect my daddy Old Billy and me dig up bodies for the medical school."

She nodded, watching Cyrus Roper's face across the plank table that stood in the center of her house's one room. The tallow candle set between them left the rest of the room in darkness. The candle's flickering glow gave Cyrus's features more animation than they possessed by nature, and carved dark hollows under the high cheekbones of Judah Daniel.

"I can't say as I like it, but my daddy's a hard man to say no to. It's a good living, and he expects me to carry it on. You gave me this medicine bag when I came to you a couple years back, after my brother died." Cyrus tugged at a string around his neck, bringing a tiny leather pouch, shiny from fingering, from under his shirt, and rubbed it between his thumb and forefinger. "The cemetery ain't the healthiest place. First thing was my brother had a cough, and then it poisoned his whole body. He was dead in less than a week. I was scared I was going to get it." He caressed the pouch a moment longer, then tucked it back inside his shirt. "Since you gave me this charm, I ain't never gone without it, and I ain't had no trouble up till now."

"What's happened?" Judah Daniel asked.

Cyrus lowered his eyes, then raised them to meet hers. He spoke in a low voice. "She after us."

"Who?"

Cyrus flicked his eyes again. "One of them dead folks we dug up."

Judah Daniel leaned back, pressing her palms down on the table. "How long you been in this business?" She spoke briskly to dispel the chill she felt coming from Cyrus.

"Old Billy done it from a young man. I been helping him since I got strong enough, thirteen years old, I reckon. I work more since my brother died."

"And what are you now, about twenty-five?" Judah Daniel pursued.

"That's right."

"So this business been going on twenty years and more, and you been doing it a dozen years, and you just now being troubled?" Her tone was deliberately disbelieving. She saw Cyrus pull himself upright a little in response.

She leaned forward, following his motion. It was time to find out if it was true what people said about the resurrection men. "If you come to me for help, you got to tell me straight. You kill anybody?"

Cyrus jerked his head up at that. "How you know about somebody being killed?"

"Suppose you tell me about it."

Cyrus was meeting her eyes now, and frowning. "Old Billy and me, we ain't never killed nobody." His voice was scornful. "I know what some people say about us sack-'em-up men, but you ain't ignorant like they is. We just keep an eye out for the likely ones, poor black folks with no family mostly, the ones won't nobody miss." Then the haunted look returned to his face. "They got souls, though. And now one of them souls is after Old Billy and me.

"It ain't just me," he went on. "I ain't disputing what folks say about me, that I ain't as tough as my daddy. Old Billy tough as an old boot. I ain't never seen him afraid of nothing. He done resurrected more dead folks than you birthed babies." Cyrus twisted his mouth in a smile, but his eyes shifted away from hers. "But now he looking over his shoulder, and I seen him whispering with the doctors and folks over to the medical school. He look at me sometimes like he want to tell me something. I say anything to him, he act like I dreaming it up. But I know I ain't."

There was silence for a moment. Cyrus would talk about the killing in his own time, Judah Daniel realized; she didn't want to spook him. At last she ventured, "Sounds like you messed with somebody got a strong power on them."

"Yes'm, and I reckon I know who. It weren't nothing but trouble going into white folks' burying ground."

"Ain't no white folks put a spell on you," Judah Daniel said with a slight smile. "White folks got other ways to bring black folks to grief."

Cyrus nodded, concurring. "That's right, it was a colored gal. I don't know who she was. But we dug her up in Hollywood Cemetery."

Judah Daniel's eyebrows rose. Hollywood was an elegant park of many rolling acres overlooking the James River, less than a mile away from her own home but in a different world. President Monroe had been dug up from somewhere up north and reburied there with great ceremony only a couple years back, she remembered. It was a favorite place for white city-dwellers to picnic and stroll. No Negro would be buried there; in fact it was against the law. She waited for Cyrus to continue.

"Was a colored gal," he said again. "Just stuck in the ground, no coffin or nothing. The docs said she been sick with the childbed fever. But wasn't that she died of. Somebody killed her, stuffed a rag down her throat."

Again Judah Daniel forced herself to show no reaction.

"I don't know nothing about that," he added quickly, shooting a defensive glance in her direction. "We dug her up and brung her back to the medical school just like always, except it was easier since there weren't no coffin. Then the next day we was cleaning out one of the dissecting rooms when we heard that young fellow Charley Wilson calling. He's the one cut her up and found the rag. Me and Old Billy went in, and we saw it. Then Doc Archer came, and Doc Hughes, and they run us off. Later on they told Old Billy to cut up the body and put it down in the pit, and put quicklime on it. The pit is where we put all the legs and arms the doctors cut off, and the bodies they cut up too."

He shuddered. "The day we put her in the pit, I seen a big black snake out behind the house. I think that was a plat-eye."

Judah Daniel nodded slowly, feeling the fear in Cyrus's words. A plat-eye was a soul that had not received proper burial. It wandered its familiar haunts, changing form at will, bent on evil. A plat-eye was a nothingness, a hole in the wall that separates the dead and the living, capable of pulling a living man or woman into its void.

"Who killed her?" Judah Daniel asked abruptly.

Cyrus shrugged his ignorance.

"What happened to the baby?"

"What?" Cyrus blinked.

"Nobody dies of the childbed fever without they had a

baby. So where's it gone to? I know you know the rites. If the baby wasn't passed over the grave, the mother likely come back to take it."

Cyrus was looking even more apprehensive. He plainly had not considered this last question. "Weren't no baby in the grave." But he had still more on his mind. "And that white boy Wilson, the one who cut her up, he got to looking around like he seeing something that wasn't there. Now I hear tell he died. Seem like the"—Cyrus dropped his voice— "the plat-eye done started with him."

They sat quietly for a moment, thinking their own thoughts.

"Cyrus," Judah Daniel said with a sigh, "you got big problems. My advice to you is to lay low for a while. I'll put some different powders in that bag for you. And it would be a help if you could get me the last thing the dead woman touched."

Cyrus thought for a moment, then replied with hesitation. "There was a white piece of cloth around her face, had some fancy stitching on it. Old Billy kept it, said he might could get some money for it. But ain't nobody going to pay money for it, it been in the ground with a stiff and it ain't never going to come clean. I . . . I think I can get it."

"See if you can," Judah Daniel said, remembering the stories about Old Billy's fondness for gold coins. "If we can bury it with the rites, we might can stop the plat-eye."

Seeing Cyrus's expression lighten with hope, she concealed her own dread. She believed Cyrus was as innocent as he appeared; Old Billy might be a very different story. By his own son's description, he was a greedy man not much troubled by pangs of conscience. He was talking with the doctors, not telling his son what was said. Was he whispering with them about a grave-stained cloth? That cloth might indeed be worth money, to those who wanted whatever secrets it held to remain hidden.

And somewhere there was a baby. It was the woman's love for her baby that was keeping her spirit tied to this world. So the baby was alive, Judah Daniel reasoned, but maybe in danger. And while that was true, the woman's spirit would not rest.

There was evil here, involving the living with the dead. The burial of a piece of cloth might help Cyrus overcome his fear, Judah Daniel mused, but it would not make him safe.

HANOVER COUNTY

On the day Charley was buried, Narcissa stood between her sisters, withdrawn into her own thoughts, not hearing the Reverend Knox as he intoned the familiar words of the service for the dead. The little graveyard at Springfield was beautiful; cascades of yellow forsythia, glowing bright in the gloom of the overcast day, spilled over the fence to glorify the simple white headstones. Branches of forsythia were cut, ready to lay on the bare earth that would be mounded over Charley's grave.

Narcissa was remembering earlier that morning, when she had sought out Aunt Dodie in the kitchen. They had embraced and wept, then dried their tears: there is nothing made by grieving. And there had been much to do. Upward of a hundred people—family, friends, neighbors, and servants, most bringing food themselves—would soon be filling the house and yard at Springfield. Lelia and Lydia, with their husbands and children, and others who'd come a long way would expect to stay a few days at least.

The old servant's hands had trembled as she peeled the

potatoes brought up from the root cellar. Narcissa, picking up a knife to help her, marveled at the ability of those gnarled fingers to pare a smoothly curving spiral of peel while her own young hand slipped, started over, and slipped again.

Charley's death had shaken Aunt Dodie. "I remember when your mama died," she had told Narcissa in a quavering voice. "All the folks came from miles around, black folks as well as white. Mister Sparks from over to Bienvenue brought his house servants in the wagon. They all loved your mama because she nursed them so good through the scarlet fever.

"They brought a half dozen of those cream cakes that was the specialty of Alberta. You mind her? Course they would keep because the weather was cool. We killed a calf and the whole thing was eaten, down to the brains and the calf's-foot jelly, that very day, or next day, any rate."

This had made Narcissa smile. Food—the making, serving, even the memory of food—always cheered Aunt Dodie.

"My own mama was just that way. She died before you was born, Miss Narcissa, here on this very farm. White folks came to her funeral, they did, as well as black.

"Think if Master Charley had made a doctor! Think of how many lives he would have saved! Think how many would have mourned his passing, if he had lived to a full age. I little thought, when he was a baby in my arms, that I would live to see him buried."

Narcissa had listened to the servant's words, thinking, If I were to die now, who would care? And if I live another fifty years, who will care? Charley could have done so much, but there's nothing I can do.

And now, as she stood dry-eyed beside the grave, Lelia and Lydia weeping softly on either side of her, the words still filled her mind. *There's nothing I can do.*

Reverend Knox's voice suddenly grew stronger, breaking

through Narcissa's despondency. " 'Behold, I shew you a mystery; We shall not all sleep, but we shall all be changed.' "

" 'In a moment, in the twinkling of an eye, at the last trump: for the trumpet shall sound, and the dead shall be raised—' "

The preacher's voice was drowned by new voices speaking in her head. A woman had been raised from the dead, not by the angel's trumpet but by Charley and people he had trusted. Trusted, until their actions convinced him they were hiding some guilty secret having to do with that woman's death. Who was she? Why was she killed? What was the secret that Charley suspected, that made him afraid to speak openly to his colleagues, his teachers?

After the burial, Narcissa shut herself away in the little up-stairs room she had shared with her sisters. When she had asked for a few moments alone, Lelia and Lydia had exchanged a look. Narcissa could read their thoughts: they imagined she would be at last releasing the tears that had not come during the funeral.

But still she did not cry. She sat on her bed and pulled to her the bulky packet Rachel Hughes had given her as she left Richmond to accompany Charley's body back to Springfield—Charley's things, his clothes and a few personal items, sent over by his landlady. As she unfolded the shirts—that was her own mending, that patch on the elbow—she thought again of the questions that had haunted Charley before he died, that with his letter he had conveyed to her.

He had longed, his letter said, for her ear and her woman's heart. Despite his death, and the near-destruction of the letter, his words had reached her. And she, with her "woman's heart"—what would he have wanted her to do?

What would she have done for Charley, had she reached

him in time? She would have been a place of safety to which he could retreat, where he need not fear judgment. She would have listened to him work out what he should do to make things right. And then, hardest of all, she would have let him go do it. Charley's was a quiet nature, but wholehearted in defense of justice. He would never have let an evil act be covered up and forgotten.

But now, with Charley dead, she must be her own counselor. What did her "woman's heart" tell her to do?

Narcissa rose, pulled Charley's shirt on over her dress, and fastened the buttons up to her throat. She put her arms into his dark brown sack coat and settled it on her shoulders. Only a little loose. She walked over to the little wood-framed mirror that hung on the wall and looked into it to see Charley looking back at her.

What made a woman, and what, a man? She resembled Charley, both in feature—dark, straight brows, straight nose, strong jaw and chin—and in nature, more than she did her fairer, softer sisters. And yet, she thought, her eyes searching the image in the glass, no one would believe for a moment that she was a man, or even a boy. Her underlip was too full, her cheeks too soft, and as for the rest of her body. . . . It appeared she was marked indelibly as a woman, to do the things that women do.

Well, she had tried. She had been a daughter, a wife, a mother. Already, at twenty-three, those roles had fallen from her as easily as she would take off this man's coat. As a woman, she had nothing left. And nothing left to lose.

Someone had to do what Charley would have done, had he lived. Uncover the truth. There was no one else to do it; nothing, no one, holding her back. She would find a way.

As it happened, Narcissa had no difficulty acting on her resolve. A gentle expression of concern by her sister-in-law Mirrie Powers, Rives's older sister, opened the way. Letters were written back and forth over the next few weeks, and at last it was agreed that Narcissa would come to Richmond to take over some responsibilities in the Powers household. Much of Mirrie's own time was spent in assisting her father, retired as a professor of ancient languages at Hampden-Sydney, in completing his translations and annotations of classical authors. While disdaining marriage for herself, she had happily celebrated the marriage of her brother Rives to Narcissa Wilson, and Mirrie and Narcissa had become good friends despite their differences in age and education.

Now in her late thirties, Mirrie resided with her father, who had lived to old age very much crippled with arthritis but still mentally acute. The Powers home was just west of Richmond, in a house the family had built many years before. After Professor Powers's retirement and Rives's death, the father and daughter had left the college and returned to the family home.

The big old house lent a note of rural simplicity to the neighborhood that had grown up around it. Narcissa took in with pleasure its plain design of stuccoed brick, two stories high and rather more deep than wide, with a small central porch supported by double columns. In the front yard grew a prized cedar of Lebanon, planted when the house was new. The dogwoods were budding, and in a day or two viburnum would scent the air.

Mirrie appeared in the doorway. Though Mirrie and Rives

had not much resembled one another, there was something about the sight of her there—her fair coloring, or the shape of her face—that brought a lump to Narcissa's throat, it reminded her so of her young husband who had died.

Up close, the resemblance faded, and Mirrie was herself again, disheveled as always; unruly red tendrils, now streaked with white, had escaped the tucking-comb, and a smudge of ink marked her cheek. Narcissa hugged her tightly, as if, through Mirrie, she could reach Rives. "Now we have both lost brothers," Mirrie said softly into her ear as they embraced.

Mirrie took Narcissa's hand and led her into the hall. Inside, the house's claim to elegance was its woodwork—hand-carved mahogany mantels, chair rails, and wainscoting, and especially the shuttered screen in the front hall, setting off the graceful stairway. The wood was beautifully polished, and fine Turkey carpets glowed in garnet and ruby tones. Mirrie had filled the house with flowers, and Narcissa, knowing her sister-in-law's lack of interest in domestic matters, felt they were a special gift for her. Shandy, the Powerses' blond spaniel, bounded up to Narcissa, who bent down to let her hand be sniffed, then stroked the dog's silky head.

The back parlor looked more like a library, for the Powerses were omnivorous readers; thick tomes in Latin and German vied for space with the latest novels from France and England and with several weeks' worth of a half-dozen different newspapers. Mirrie swept some volumes off a low sofa and pulled Narcissa down to sit beside her. Shandy settled close to her, nosing under Narcissa's arm.

Mirrie talked about Charley, about her memories of the boy whom she and her father had watched grow to manhood at Hampden-Sydney. Narcissa smiled at the reminiscences. After a few minutes, the family servant Beulah, a freed slave, entered the room. She too greeted Narcissa affectionately, expressing regret over Charley's death. Then Beulah and Mirrie went off to settle some household matters and bring refreshments.

Narcissa looked around the room with mingled joy and sadness. Its familiarity was reassuring—in some ways, this seemed more her home now than did Springfield. The drawing room from the Powerses' house at Hampden-Sydney had been re-created here, the shelves and tables crammed with objects—rocks, arrowheads, and fossils, fragments of antique sculpture, a bust of Dante topped with a Phrygian cap, purported to be a genuine artifact of the French Revolution—all gathered for study rather than display.

Narcissa recalled her first visit to the Powerses' home, where she had stayed when she came to visit Charley at college. She had been eighteen years old, her own formal schooling long since ended. It had come to her as a revelation that there was so much to learn, so much to be discovered in books and newspapers and objects whose history transported her to other worlds.

Soon that excitement had become entangled with the feelings awakened in her by Rives Powers, recently graduated from Hampden-Sydney, further educated at Princeton, and beginning his own career as a professor of antique languages. Her heart would beat faster, somehow even before he entered the room, as if she could sense his nearness. She'd wondered if he felt the same almost painful elation in her presence. It had seemed impossible that he could. After a while, she'd learned that he did. It had been sweet, as his wife, to rest her head on Rives's chest in perfect security and remember that initial feeling.

When Mirrie reentered the room, Narcissa was leaning against the cushions, her lips curved in a slight smile. Mirrie took Narcissa by both hands and pulled her to her feet. "Beulah and I decided to make a picnic. There's cold chicken from yesterday's dinner, and Beulah is making lemonade. We'll eat out on the piazza."

Narcissa followed Mirrie out from the dark, cool house into the bright sunlight. Tall trees, whose shade would be welcome in summer, hung over the slate terrace. Beulah was standing beside a small wrought-iron table with two little round-seated chairs drawn up to it. The table was covered with platters of chicken, biscuits, slaw, and pickles, leaving room only for small yellow plates and snowy napkins. Suddenly Narcissa felt hunger—the first true, healthy hunger she had felt since Charley's death. She ate with pleasure, then suggested to Mirrie that she would like to see the garden.

The two women walked slowly and in silence, watching Shandy follow his nose along unseen paths and enjoying the beauty of the day. Under the still-bare oaks, budding maples, and glossy-leaved magnolias, a brick walk led through a small grass lawn past a tall box hedge. The hedge enclosed garden plots bordered in brick with plantings of fruit trees, grape arbors, and dwarf box. The roses were showing little of their promise, but their lack was made up for by snowdrops, violets, and jonquils.

At length Mirrie said, "Father will be so pleased to see you. He is resting now, but we will dine together if he feels well enough.

"And I should warn you," she continued, "we expect some of Father's friends tomorrow night. Even though he is unable to get about much himself, many of his former students still seek him out, and some of his younger colleagues—they're retired by now themselves! So we have quite a company on Thursday evenings. You don't have to come if you don't feel up to it. But don't fear it would be inappropriate for your mourning. Most of them are so old that they've forgotten I'm female, so they don't expect any charm from me and aren't shocked when I speak my mind—or perhaps they know me too well by now!"

Mirrie wrinkled her nose in the way she had when making a joke, especially one at her own expense. Narcissa asked, laughing, "Who are these charming courtiers?"

"I call them the Frogs, from Aristophanes, you know," Mirrie answered, laughing. "They're great croakers. Some doctors of philosophy, some doctors of divinity—and even some doctors of medicine, since the medical college seceded, as it were, from Hampden-Sydney."

Narcissa felt herself stiffen, and she saw Mirrie's brow furrow in response. "Would it be painful . . . to see people who may have known Charley at the medical college?" Mirrie asked.

I must tell her now what I have come to do, Narcissa thought. I cannot hide my feelings from her, and she must wonder—

She drew Mirrie to a wood-and-wrought-iron bench overhung by sweetgum branches.

"Narcissa, you are pale as a ghost. It's something else, isn't it?"

"I'm sorry." Narcissa smiled and drew a deep breath. "It's funny—I had been burning to tell you, but now that I'm here everything seems so sane, and it seems impossible. I'm afraid you'll think I've taken leave of my senses, but I didn't dream it. I have the letter!"

Mirrie squeezed Narcissa's hand. "My dear, remember who you are talking to. You are quite the sanest person I know. But you are not making any sense. Tell me everything, starting from the beginning."

Narcissa gave Mirrie a grateful smile. She picked up a

prickly brown sweetgum ball that lay on the bench and twirled the stem between her thumb and forefinger. She kept her eyes fixed on it as she spoke.

"I only learned that Charley was sick on the day he died. I got a letter at Springfield from a Mrs. Hughes, the wife of one of Charley's professors at the medical college. She said that he was ill and that I should come at once, so of course I did. When I got there, they told me Charley was dying. Dr. Hughes had taken off his arm!"

Mirrie pressed Narcissa's shoulder.

"He told me a lot of things about what he had done for Charley. I didn't understand much of it, but he clearly wanted me to know that he had done the best he could for Charley and that Charley himself had been partly to blame for being careless.

"I was in the room with Charley, alone most of the time except for servants and the Hugheses' coming in and out. I fell asleep at one point, and somehow I woke up quite suddenly. I was sure that I had heard Charley speak. I could hear the word in my head, 'Resurrection.' He didn't say any more. Finally I fell asleep again, and when I woke up, Charley was in his death agony. There is such a thing, you know. I've seen it before."

Narcissa looked at Mirrie for a moment and blinked away tears. "After he was dead, they took me to a room where they had put my things, and I slept a little."

Again she looked at Mirrie, who nodded slightly.

"When I got up the next morning I opened my Bible, the one I brought with me from Springfield. It was on the table next to the bed along with my diary. In it I found part of a paper—a letter—written in Charley's hand. It was written to me. The top part of it was burned, and it was a small page, front and back, so I suppose the beginning of the letter and the, um, third quarter or so was missing. In this letter, Charley wrote that he had gone along on a grave-robbing. That's how medical schools get cadavers to dissect, the letter said."

"A 'resurrection.'" Mirrie said the word thoughtfully.

"What?" Narcissa's voice was sharp with surprise.

"A 'resurrection' is a grave-robbing," Mirrie explained, "as the medical students phrase it rather grossly. The men who dig up the bodies for dissection are called 'resurrection men.' Of course, what they are doing is illegal, but it's accepted as a necessary evil for students to learn about human anatomy."

"Oh, Mirrie," Narcissa said softly. "He was trying to tell me." She was silent for a moment, then went on. "He said— the paper said that it was the body of a colored woman, and that she had been near death from childbed fever. But when he . . . cut her open, he found she had been murdered, with a cloth forced down her throat!

"At least two people came in and saw the cloth, Dr. Hughes and someone named Archer. Their reaction, the way he described it, seemed so strange. They were angry, and they sent Charley out of the room, and afterward the body just disappeared. They wouldn't speak of it, wouldn't answer Charley's questions. It haunted him; he said he feared 'some dreadful secret.' Those were the words he used.

"Mirrie, someone put that paper in my Bible. Someone wanted me to know. And yet the paper was burned as if someone had tried to destroy it. Whoever put the paper in the Bible must be waiting, wondering what I will do. Of course, I haven't done anything—I don't know what *to* do. But I feel I must do something," she said more firmly, raising her chin, "and I will."

Mirrie thought for a moment. "It had to be someone in the household, I suppose. Who could have gone into your room?"

"Dr. Hughes, Mrs. Hughes, the servants—anyone could have come to the house during the afternoon or evening, I would not have known it. My things could have been lying out for hours. And I didn't pick up the Bible until the next day."

"There was nothing else there besides the paper?" Mirrie asked.

"No, but . . . it occurred to me one night last week, in the middle of the night, that whoever left the paper could have looked at my diary. I got up and lit the lamp and looked through it, but of course there was no way I could tell.

"The diary . . . I burned it," Narcissa continued, tucking a strand of black hair behind her ear and smiling a little. "It seems overdramatic, I know, but I can't escape the feeling that someone had looked through it. It's as if they had been looking at *me*, spying on me through a window. Whenever I opened my diary, I had that feeling all over again." She was frowning now, and she leveled her gaze at Mirrie.

"I am determined to find out the truth of what happened. I know that's what Charley would have wanted to do. Can you help me?"

Mirrie stared out across the lawn, eyes focused on nothing. At last she spoke.

"I know Dr. and Mrs. Hughes and Dr. Archer, Cameron Archer; not well, but we have mutual acquaintances. Hughes is a surgeon, but his appointment is in anatomy, so he would work closely with Archer, who is the demonstrator in anatomy. Yes, that means he would oversee the students doing their dissections.

"As for the rest of the professors, you may be meeting some of them tomorrow night. There is MacKenzie Stedman, professor of surgery. He has been covering obstetrics too this year since Conyers left. Dr. Stedman is a good friend of

Father's. I find him almost unbearably pompous, but his wife is pleasant company. She believes the worst of everyone. Another good friend of Father's and mine—well, I don't *like* him, but he is a good friend—is James Henry. His field is *materia medica*, the preparation of medicines. McPherson does theory and practice, and Fielding is chemistry and pharmacy."

Narcissa's eyebrows rose inquiringly.

"You must remember, Narcissa," Mirrie said with a slight smile, "Richmond is not such a big city as all that. Those with mutual associations—the medical school, for instance—all know each other, just as your neighbors do in Hanover. It's just that, instead of open space between them, they have people."

Narcissa imagined acres upon acres of people, standing close together like stalks of corn.

Mirrie smiled again, rather grimly this time. "I suspect Cameron Archer could be rather a Steerforth to the medical students. He has a reputation for being what is all too commonly termed a man of the world. If Archer, or any of them, got Charley involved in a—a crime, we should do all we can to make them very sorry."

Steerforth, Narcissa thought. But as Dickens wrote it, David Copperfield lived, and it was the charming, cold-hearted Steerforth who died. Blinking back angry tears, she looked at Mirrie. She knew that Mirrie had wealth and, in certain circles at least, powerful connections, and that if she believed a question of justice were involved, she would not hesitate to use them.

"I don't know, Mirrie. It's against the law to steal a body, but it's accepted, and Charley agreed to go along. But, Mirrie—"

Their speculation was interrupted by the entrance of

Professor Powers into the garden. Beulah pushed him in a wheeled invalid's chair, adapted by his own design with a little reading desk across the lap that now held a thick volume, held open by a horn-handled reading glass, with stacks of paper on each side.

The two women rose to greet the old man. He was very thin, his skin white and loose, his head downed with fine white hair. But there was still a lively interest in his blue eyes as his cool, dry hand grasped Narcissa's. "Your brother's death is a great loss, my dear . . . a great loss. He would have been a fine doctor. *Integer vitae*—a rare sort of purity, like a stream that's clear to the bottom. I could see it from the first."

Narcissa kissed his cheek and smiled her thanks. They were silent for a moment. Then the old man smiled up at her. "I'm glad you've come to stay with us. I know Mirrie gets worn down, looking after me." He gave his daughter an affectionate look, which she returned. Mirrie took Beulah's place pushing Dr. Powers's chair, and Narcissa walked beside them, remembering Charley.

That night, as Narcissa was preparing for bed, Mirrie came into the room. She was holding a heavy volume, keeping her place with her forefinger. Her mouth was twisted in an unhappy grimace, and she made no response to Narcissa's welcoming words. Perplexed by Mirrie's expression, Narcissa went to her side. Mirrie sat down on the bed and pulled Narcissa down to sit beside her.

"What is it?" Narcissa asked.

"I did not wish to say anything until I verified my memory," Mirrie said. "This is a volume of famous—or infamous—criminal trials. One of the most infamous concerns Burke and Hare."

At Mirrie's questioning look, Narcissa shook her head. The names meant nothing to her.

Mirrie drew in a breath and began. "Edinburgh has the greatest medical school in the world. The students and professors are constantly in need of corpses on which to conduct their anatomical studies, and the reward for a fresh one is evidently generous. Burke and Hare simply eliminated the tedious waiting for natural death, plus all the work of digging. It's believed they killed as many as sixteen people. If they hadn't been so careless as to kill off the boarders in their rooming house one by one, it's likely they would never have been caught.

"They finally slipped up and killed someone who was missed. There was a trial. Burke was hanged, then publicly dissected by one of the doctors he sold the bodies to. Hare and their two female accomplices managed to pin the blame on Burke, and so went free. Of course many people blamed the doctors as well. If they hadn't been so greedy for bodies, such a crime would never have been invented."

Narcissa nodded slowly.

Mirrie went on. "Burke and Hare suffocated their victims so as to leave the bodies intact for dissection. This kind of murder for dissection has a name—'burking.' I will leave you the book to read for yourself," she said gently, rising and placing the open book on the nightstand.

Narcissa sprang up to stand by Mirrie. She spoke urgently. "Don't you see, this could explain it. Hughes, Archer, the servants . . . they knew the body would be in that grave because they killed her and buried her there. Maybe they even brought Charley along as a witness that the body was dug up, just like a normal 'resurrection.' " The word tasted bitter in her mouth. "But the cloth was left in by mistake. When it was found, and the murder was revealed, they were angry. Something had gone wrong, and put them in danger of being found out. Maybe the servants did the killing, but the doctors must have known. So the body disappeared. Charley must have wondered who among his teachers and his friends knew about the murder and were protecting the killers."

Narcissa and Mirrie looked at each other, not speaking. Charley would have brought them to justice, Narcissa thought. Now—it's up to me.

Chapter Four

RICHMOND
EARLY APRIL

William Grandison Wallace wrote his three names with a flourish in the big leather-bound register of Richmond's Exchange Hotel. He had planned to use his full name as a correspondent—on the model of William Howard Russell, war correspondent for the *Times* of London. But on his journey across the Atlantic, he had acquired a nickname that he was thinking of using instead.

"Brit" Wallace had a ring to it, he thought—it marked him as an exotic here in the States, and at the same time encouraged his readers at home to identify with him as his dispatches in the *Weekly Argus* dissected the various forms of American posturing and pomposity. And if the vainglory of Americans, north and south, should lead to war, he mused, he would surely be in the middle of the action. And then the Brit Wallace name could attain the recognition accorded his idol Russell.

The Exchange Hotel, with its three-story-high white columns topped by perfect Ionic capitals and set between curving bays, made an earnest attempt at elegance that rather gratified Brit, even as it amused him. The hotel seemed to him like a country girl who had donned all her finery in an attempt to win his approval. But after seeing his bags arranged in a pile in a tiny room he would share with two other men, Brit realized he had overestimated his own importance, and underestimated the effect that rumors of war had had on the city. Already the population was swelling to two and three times its normal size, and men of more consequence than an untried foreign journalist were scrambling to find lodging.

Brit dressed with care, donning gray trousers and frock coat and tying about his neck a stock of blue silk. He placed in his coat pocket the note from Dr. James Henry, an old friend of his father's from Oxford, originally from Massachusetts but for some twenty years now a resident of Richmond. The evening reception to which Henry was inviting Wallace seemed tame—who was this Professor Powers? Some doddering old boy retired from obscurity to obscurity, he surmised. But never mind; he would get a good story or two out of the evening, to convey the flavor of this pride-maddened town to his readers. His career as a foreign correspondent was beginning. He smiled at the thought.

As the visitors began to arrive that evening, Narcissa could see that Mirrie had been modest in her description of the "Frogs" and of her own role. Among the guests Narcissa met not only old friends and colleagues of Professor Powers but several younger men and women. Most in the group were clearly frequent visitors who spoke in the allusive style of friends continuing a conversation. They eagerly sought Mirrie's opinions and gave her openings to exercise her wit. Nat Cohen, a tall, comfortably stout man with graying black hair and beard, seemed to be a special friend of Mirrie's. She introduced him with a proprietary air that in another woman might have presaged an engagement, Narcissa thought.

"I'm sure that on some visit to Richmond you've made your obligatory pilgrimage to Cohen and Sons," Mirrie said to her. "It's been a Richmond landmark for half a century. Our rustic visitors have it on their list of attractions to visit, along with Jefferson's Capitol and St. John's Church."

"I am vastly flattered," Cohen responded as he shook hands with Narcissa, the grin rounding his cheeks. He looked like a comfortable paterfamilias or favorite uncle who would always have candies in his pockets. Narcissa had been in the store, she remembered, on Broad at Third Street. They sold fancy goods, household furnishings, china, and glassware in a display of luxury that had awakened her country girl's heart to the pleasures of the city, as Mirrie jokingly suggested.

Narcissa cast around for a conversational opening. "Do you do much traveling in search of beautiful things, Mr. Cohen?" Cohen responded with a warmth and humor that endeared him to Narcissa, easing her into the group and freeing Mirrie to greet her other guests. A few minutes later Narcissa noticed that the buzz in the room had subsided; she followed the gaze of most of the room's occupants toward a newcomer in their midst. The man was in his mid-twenties, with curling black hair cut rather short and a smooth-shaven face emphasizing boyish good looks that she imagined would persist into old age. He was dressed in a dove-gray frock coat of a heavier fabric and slightly more exaggerated cut than the clothing of the other men, accented by a sapphire-colored stock. When he glanced her way, Narcissa noticed the color had been chosen—with a self-awareness almost unbecoming, Narcissa thought, in a man—to match the color of his eyes.

Brit Wallace took note of the woman in black: black mourning dress, black brows over thick-lashed dark eyes, black hair pulled severely from a center part and confined—one could hardly say *adorned*—with what appeared to be black grosgrain ribbon folded into a flat bow and chenille netting. Horrible. But the woman herself was beautiful, he thought, Her still, somewhat haughty expression contrasted with the passionate nature he read in her full underlip, her square jaw, tender flesh over strong bone. She looked like a statue waiting to be brought to life with a kiss. "See, in yon brilliant window-niche how statue-like I see thee stand! The agate lamp within thy hand. Ah! Psyche, from the regions which Are Holy Land!" Edgar Allan Poe, Richmond's adopted son, sprang to mind.

Mirrie led Wallace through the fifteen or so people in the room to present him to her father. After a few minutes, they found their way to where Narcissa and Nat Cohen were standing. "Mrs. Powers, Mr. Cohen, may I present Mr. Brit Wallace. Mr. Wallace has come from Oxford with a letter of introduction to Dr. Henry."

Narcissa extended her hand, and Brit Wallace shook it, his smile growing wider. He explained that his name was William Wallace, "Brit" being a nickname bestowed on him en route to the States. He had landed in Norfolk earlier in the week and just that day arrived in Richmond.

"Mr. Wallace is in Richmond as a correspondent for the *Weekly Argus*," Mirrie continued. "A war correspondent, I suppose! So there's no turning back now; they might as well sign the declaration. We would hate for Mr. Wallace's trip to be wasted."

Brit Wallace lowered his eyes and laughed with enough embarrassment to show that Mirrie's words held some truth. "Of course," he protested, "we all hope and pray that differences within the Union can be resolved without bloodshed. I do not wish for war to break out just to advance my career." Then he added, "Miss Powers and I quickly discovered our shared admiration for William Howard Russell of the *Times*, whose dispatches from the Crimea are so noted."

"I don't believe I know of Russell," Narcissa remarked, smiling to invite his explanation.

"Have you heard of Florence Nightingale?"

"Of course!" Narcissa answered. Her interest was real now.

"William Howard Russell brought her work in the hospital at Scutari to the attention of the British public. Through his dispatches, published in the *Times*, Miss Nightingale drew the nation's attention to conditions in the Crimea. The publicity vastly increased her power to do good. She is revered now as the Lady with the Lamp, but it was Russell who brought the lamp out from under the bushel. The help that flowed to her military hospitals, and the money, was thanks to him. Of course, the military leaders didn't fare so well once he revealed their incompetence and bungling. So many died needlessly."

Wallace frowned at the memory. Then he shrugged off the mood, smiled, and went on. "Russell immortalized the Light Brigade's role in that war as well, don't you know. Lord Tennyson merely put it into verse. 'Thumpety, thumpety, thumpety bumble,' and so on," he added.

"'Half a league, half a league, half a league onward; All in the valley of death rode the six hundred,'" Narcissa quoted softly. So Russell had advanced the cause of Florence Nightingale. If a war correspondent could do so much, she thought, it was indeed a worthy calling.

Wallace felt a little disappointed in meeting his Psyche. Mrs. Powers was beautiful, but more shy than aloof, and he sensed no tumultuous undercurrent of feeling waiting to be kindled, at least not by him.

As Wallace bowed and turned away, Narcissa smiled

warmly at him, not caring if he thought her provincial for admiring the poem. Images of the Lady with the Lamp filled her mind. Florence Nightingale, with her exacting standards of morality and cleanliness, had made it possible for ladies to serve as nurses. She had managed to obtain for them the time-honored respect accorded to nuns who tended the sick; her nurses were even referred to as *"sisters."* But that was in England. If only it were possible here in America, in Virginia. If she could be a nurse, the calling that had given meaning to Charley's life could open up her own—and give her a chance to find out more about the crime that had so haunted Charley in his last moments of life.

"That's Dr. Henry," Mirrie said, tugging on Narcissa's arm, her eyes darting toward a man standing a few yards away. Mr. Wallace's acquaintance appeared to be in his fifties, rather fat and red-faced, with a fading red beard and hair. Narcissa spoke into Mirrie's ear. "Do you think Dr. Henry might know anything about . . . you know . . . ?"

Mirrie whispered back, "Dr. Henry knows nothing of his colleagues' activities. I do not believe that he can perceive humanity in single units. And as his field is the preparation of medicines, it is not likely that he would be involved very much with dissection.

"I had hoped the Stedmans would be able to come. It may be that we will learn nothing tonight. But never mind," she added, giving Narcissa's hand a squeeze. "We will find them out."

When they rejoined the others, the talk had turned to the burning question of the day: secession. South Carolina had led the way, six other states had followed. What would Virginia do? "The Richmond news-papers are without conscience," Mirrie exclaimed, her face flushed with anger. "They are propelling us toward a war that only the fire-eaters want.

They vilify in the lowest possible way the statesmen who want to preserve the Union. The vote is almost two to one against *Virginia seceding, but here they are feeding their readers this run-mad mush.

"Narcissa, did you see the infamous piece in the *Examiner* last month? Wait a minute," Narcissa, Brit Wallace, and Nat Cohen exchanged smiles as Mirrie swept across the room to fetch a newspaper from a side table. She returned, holding the folded paper close to her face and reading. "Abraham Lincoln is orang-outang, Colonel Johnson is the 'sleek fat pony from Richmond who neighed submission.' " Mirrie brought the paper down on the arm of the sofa with a *thwack.* Shandy the spaniel, who had been asleep under the table, looked up to see whether his mistress was displeased with him.

Another speaker, a Mr. Peterson, joined in. "And do you know, just the other day they shot at each other, on Franklin Street, in broad daylight! Colonel Johnson shot at John Daniel—"

"The editor of the *Examiner*," Mirrie whispered to Narcissa and Wallace.

"—and he shot back! The colonel's under bond to keep the peace. Otherwise, they would certainly go out to the dueling grounds, and one or the other would be killed."

The other guests began to gather, many joining in with anecdotes illustrative of tensions in the town. Narcissa felt she and Brit Wallace, as newcomers to Richmond, were offering an occasion for everyone to rehearse opinions they had already expressed to each other many times.

Dr. Henry's booming voice commanded attention. "It's all over slavery, though many would deny it," said Henry. "Anyone who has a conscience knows slavery is wrong and must be ended."

Narcissa looked at Henry with interest, recalling that Mirrie had described him as a friend she did not like. Clearly his abolitionist views would win Mirrie's approval, but perhaps his manner—he was scowling over his pince-nez as if daring anyone to disagree—put her off.

"We southerners will all kill each other," Mirrie responded dryly, "or we'll patch up our differences and kill boys from the North, which will at the least be a diversion from our problems."

"The problem does seem to me a simple one," Nat Cohen said thoughtfully. "How to put an end to slavery. The solution, it seems, no one knows."

"The *problem*," said a black-haired man with thickly curling side-whiskers who, it seemed to Narcissa, was not one of the regulars, "is that the abolitionists think they could run our affairs better than we can. They preach at us southerners and hector us—Miss Powers, the Richmond papers are models of restraint compared to the filth that's coming from the North!"

"They set John Brown up to slaughter us, now make him into a hero! I think they want to kill us all!" The black-whiskered man's wife, a plump blonde wearing a rose gown and beautiful lace, spoke these words in a rush. She blushed and looked down, then raised her eyes again and said defiantly, "I do!"

Dr. Henry's smile was scornful. "If slavery is an affront to God, as I believe it is, then we have ample illustration of its annihilation at any cost: the firstborn sons of Egypt."

The Old Testament reference was met with a second or two of silence. Then Nat Cohen responded quietly, "If there's a war, many sons, North and South, will die."

Mirrie spoke up again, an ironic smile returning to her face. "And for those who say the South would win such a war in a month, well, there are men who believe Bellingham's Stimulating Unguent will make them grow a mustache!" She picked up the *Examiner* and unfolded it to show them the front, where the ointment was extolled in an advertisement running almost the length of the page.

Narcissa saw that some of the guests laughed at this, while others looked ready to take offense. Then Professor Powers held his hand out to his daughter. Mirrie went to him, clasped his hand, and held it. She bent down over his chair, and the two looked into each other's eyes. There was great affection there, Narcissa thought, seeing the intensity of their gaze, but there was also a struggle between two strong wills. The guests fell silent, as if waiting to see which of the two would dominate.

"Whatever happens," Professor Powers said slowly, "whatever the decision may be, do not forget: we are Virginians born. She is truly our alma mater—our nourishing mother. People may speak of the South, or of the Union, but we must always be loyal to her, Miranda—to Virginia."

Narcissa saw several of the guests nod solemnly. Of course he is right, she thought. The sentiments could have been spoken by her own father or mother, had they lived. But the set expression on Mirrie's usually mobile face showed Narcissa that her friend was keeping silent out of respect to her father and against her own inclination.

Narcissa noticed that as the guests broke again into conversation they divided along the lines of their opinions, with Dr. Henry dominating the antislavery talk. Mirrie left her father's side, skirted the arguing groups, and returned to where Narcissa was standing. "A narrow escape," Mirrie whispered to Narcissa. "We could have been stuck listening to Dr. Windy for an hour!"

Narcissa smiled at the nickname. Dr. Henry in full oration,

beard thrust forward and lips pursed, did resemble one of those old map personifications of the North Wind.

After refreshments were served—cold chicken, hot biscuits, and several side dishes—Mirrie, Nat Cohen, Brit Wallace, and Narcissa made a foursome. Mirrie and Narcissa sat together on the low sofa, their wide skirts arranged around them, and the men seated themselves in chairs facing them.

Narcissa, half-listening to the others, reflected on her own opinion about slavery, learned in childhood: that the reciprocal bond obliging their owners to care for them made the lot of southern slaves preferable to that of poor workers in the North. That *should* be true, she thought; it's true in my family and most of the families I know. Perhaps it fails sometimes, but every ideal fails sometimes. . . . How terrible if all the slaves were suddenly freed, with no idea of how to govern themselves and no one caring if they starved. Mirrie's opinion, she knew, was very different from her own. Mirrie hated the institution and had even persuaded her father to free their slaves and employ them for wages as free blacks. There were many free blacks in Richmond, Narcissa knew, but many more slaves.

What about the woman whose murder Charley had discovered? She had likely been a slave. Someone was—should have been—responsible for her. Did they think she had died of childbed fever? How would they feel if they learned she had been killed, for the most coldhearted of reasons?

Nat Cohen spoke to Brit Wallace, drawing Narcissa's attention back to the conversation. "What kind of stories would you like to send back to your readers? Would the kind of writing that we're seeing in the *Examiner* amuse them? Or convince *tout le monde* that we Virginians are all orangoutangs?" Cohen was smiling his comfortable smile, and Narcissa felt again how much she liked him. Here was a man who was at home anywhere in the world, but who chose to live in Richmond. She watched Wallace for his response.

Brit composed his features in a serious expression. "I would say, we British satirize in general terms—the government, the law, and such sources of injustice—more than the personal. When the personal is satirized, it is more for what he or she represents.

"You Americans, or rather you southerners," Brit continued, "cannot bear criticism of your systems, but you love to hear an individual mocked down to his pocket handkerchief. Do you agree?"

"It's certainly true," replied Cohen, "that northern criticism of slavery enrages southerners, even many who wouldn't hesitate to condemn the institution among themselves." He shrugged. "It wasn't so long ago, certainly within my lifetime, that the Richmond papers argued that slaveholding was retarding progress in the South and should be done away with. Now, cotton is king and slavery is defended as a sacred right. 'Progress' is no longer in fashion." His smile was tight at the corners of his mouth.

Mirrie joined in. "Sometimes I think we cannot bear any satire or criticism at all. For instance, that feud between the editor Daniel and the colonel. I hate to admit it, but such a falling-out is not at all uncommon, nor is it uncommon for those who take offense to resort to violence."

Nat Cohen was nodding. He asked Brit Wallace, "Is anyone dueling, now, in England?" Wallace shook his head, bemused.

"But here," Mirrie broke in eagerly, "it's, 'I'll not stand it, sir,' and call for pistols! Among our newspaper editors, especially, it's viewed as a sport. Of course, there are some of them that I would want to shoot myself!" She took aim with her forefinger at the *Examiner* where it lay on the table.

Wallace returned to Nat Cohen's question. "You asked me about subject matter. As to that, I would be happy with some personality sketches, some dramas of daily life. For instance, that duel you mentioned. Who—"

"If it's dramas of daily life you want," Dr. Henry, who had joined the group, broke in, "you should go to a slave auction. You could write about humans sold like cattle, families split apart. Maybe you could shine the light of reason into this benighted country."

Mirrie stared at him for a moment, seeming put out at the interruption. Then Narcissa saw her friend's eyes widen and her jaw grow tense. She knew before Mirrie spoke that the idea had taken hold of her imagination and, lodged there, would not easily be dismissed. Mirrie turned her eyes to Brit Wallace. "I agree," she said in a voice that did not admit of argument. "In fact, I think all of us should go."

Dr. Henry shut his mouth; his face turned so red that Narcissa looked around for a glass of water. He was shocked at the idea, she knew: it was all very well for a man, but not at all proper for a lady.

Mirrie was still talking, arguing her point, though no one yet had spoken against it. "Those of us who live under the cloud should be the first to seek the light," Narcissa heard her say. Brit Wallace was silent, watching Dr. Henry as if seeking some clue as to how he should respond. Nat Cohen was smiling as if the scene amused him, but his eyes lingered on Mirrie with obvious admiration.

Narcissa was silent too, but her mind was filled with images: the firstborn sons of Egypt, blood on the doorposts, the avenging angel . . . Who would avenge a brown-skinned woman, murdered, her body stolen from its unhallowed grave?

Narcissa broke the silence. "I think Mirrie is right; we

should go." As soon as the words were spoken, she found herself wanting to call them back. But at once the scene before her rearranged itself, all eyes suddenly focused on her. Mirrie grinned as if to say, Well done. Dr. Henry transferred his gaze from Mirrie to Narcissa, but he still had not spoken—perhaps, Narcissa thought, his longest spell of silence in twenty years.

Mirrie turned once more to Brit Wallace. "Next week, then? Perhaps Friday?" Wallace nodded.

Still addressing Wallace, but turning to catch the eyes of the group, Mirrie changed the subject. "I hear there is to be a Grand Dress Southern Rights Ball at the Old Market Hall on Tuesday. The local luminaries are leading the effort to raise funds for a 'Southern Rights' flag to be flown on Seventeenth Street. You should go, and hear the opinions of a rather different group than this. Besides," she continued, "you might meet the famous Hardie McDowell."

"Oh?" Wallace responded. "Who is he, some fire-eater spoiling for a duel? Are you trying to get me killed, Miss Powers?"

Narcissa saw Nat Cohen suppress a smile. Mirrie was wearing an earnest, wide-eyed expression that Narcissa recognized as a warning of some prank to be pulled.

"Mr. Wallace, it is only fair that I tell you that Hardie McDowell has brought many a brave man to grief."

Brit Wallace's eyes asked a question, but Mirrie merely smiled. When the young man looked away, Mirrie whispered to Narcissa, "Wait till he finds out Hardie McDowell is a *she!*"

Lying awake in her bed later that night, Narcissa regretted having agreed to go see a slave auction. Whatever had prompted her to do it?

Narcissa sat up, fluffed the pillow, lay down again. She dreaded to go to an auction where humans were bought and sold. It was the kind of thing ladies were protected from—of course, for Mirrie, that in itself would be reason enough to go. But for her . . .

Then she recalled what she had felt when she put on Charley's shirt and coat. She could not become her brother—could not simply put on his clothes and take on his role. But she had taken on Charley's cause, his calling, as if it were an invisible garment next to her skin. A rough woolen garment at that, to judge by the discomfort it was causing her, she thought wryly as she turned onto her left side and pulled her nightgown down over her feet.

She was determined to find out the truth about the unknown woman. She was coming to feel responsible for her. Perhaps the slave auction would prove a source of information. To have come so near to death in childbirth, only to be murdered—the anger Narcissa felt at last drove out her misgivings. But alas, she thought as she rolled onto her back and stared at the moonlight pouring through the shutters, anger doesn't make for a good night's sleep.

At last Narcissa slept. She dreamed that she was standing in a field surrounded by tall pine trees. The sun was hot in a white sky, and the dry-bones rattle of the cicadas beat in her ears. In the distance, she became aware of men shouting and hounds baying.

Suddenly a figure broke through the underbrush. It was a boy about fourteen years old, running into the clearing, running toward her, calling to her.

It was Charley. He was not dead, it had been a mistake; he was coming back to her.

Then she realized the men and dogs were chasing him.

She ran to meet him; as the first man came through the trees, she caught Charley in her arms and thrust him behind her back. The man spoke to her brusquely. "We're chasing a runaway slave, ma'am. You've no call to get involved in this."

"He's my brother!" Narcissa was shouting. The man grabbed the boy's arm and pulled him forward. The boy was black. Narcissa gasped.

She stood as the man dragged the boy back toward the trees. The boy was twisting his head to call to her. "Narcissa! Narcissa!" It was Charley's voice. In the dream, Narcissa stood still, tears running down her face.

She awoke to find her face wet with tears.

Chapter Five

RICHMOND
MID-APRIL

Judah Daniel had arranged to meet Old Billy Roper at John Chapman's bake shop on Main Street. A genial and intelligent man, Chapman kept good relations with everyone, but his white customers probably weren't aware that his shop served as the unofficial meeting place for free blacks.

The front room was kept cool and dark by a deep awning over the door, and the late morning sun threw little light into the cramped and shabby counter area at the front of the shop, but the smell of the pies, cakes, and pastries would be advertisement enough to draw in the most exacting shopper. When Judah Daniel entered, a black woman accompanied by two white children was selecting items; the older girl held the younger one's hand, and both children gazed round-eyed as Chapman whisked aside snowy napkins to display his wares.

John Chapman nodded a greeting. He was a plump, dignified man in his fifties, light-skinned, with a neat beard and short, wiry brown hair. Judah Daniel hung back as though waiting her turn to be served.

As soon as the customers left, Chapman bustled over to her and, putting his hand on her arm, ushered her behind the counter into the kitchen, which made up most of the tiny building. Heat lingered there from oven fires kindled before sunrise. Chapman stopped just inside the door, not crossing to the table where several people were seated. Judah Daniel stopped too, sensing that Chapman had something to say he did not want overheard, and waved a greeting to the others.

Four adults sat on rough stools around the big kitchen table made of planks, now smooth and swaybacked with use, set on sawhorses. They greeted Judah Daniel, who recognized them as family, or as good as. What can he have to say that he doesn't want them to hear? she wondered.

Chapman's father, Honus, who had run the bakery before him, was among those at the table. The old man was bent and frail, but he preserved a good humor. He was very light-skinned and was said to resemble his father, the master of a great plantation on the James, who at his death had freed his son and given him a small inheritance.

The sole woman spending this time of day at the bake shop was Elda Chapman, wife of John's son Tyler. Her work, begun in the early hours of the morning, was mostly over, and she was taking time off from rolling and crimping pie crusts to tend to her child. Her husband, Judah Daniel knew, would be taking their wagon to make deliveries to hotels, eating houses, and private homes in town.

The baby, Young John, whom Judah Daniel had helped into the world about six months back, was his grandfather's pet and pride. Judah Daniel saw a smile spread over John Chapman's face in response to the baby's gummy grin.

"Darcy gave you the message, I see," Chapman said in a low tone. "That girl is steady as sunrise."

"I thought Old Billy would be here," Judah Daniel said.

"He should be here directly." Chapman hesitated. "You know I reverence you, Judah Daniel, and I bear no ill will to Old Billy. But I wonder if you wouldn't mind talking with him out back. I got a couple benches out there. It's just . . . the smell," he said at last, eyebrows cocked as he watched for her reaction. "I reckon after all these years he couldn't wash it off him—"

Judah Daniel smiled with one side of her mouth. "Even if he tried, which he don't. Suits me to talk with him out in the fresh air, truth be known." Her eyes searched Chapman's face. His bright brown eyes always had a calmness about them, she thought, but now they were troubled.

"Cyrus . . . he's a little soft in the head," Chapman said gently. "He never did like going into the business his daddy did." Chapman was delicate in not mentioning grave-robbing. She nodded, and Chapman went on.

"I know Cyrus been troubled. I don't know why. Now I think Old Billy's troubled too. It's almost like he's scared of something."

Judah Daniel's eyes narrowed. It was hard to imagine anything that could scare Old Billy. He was a buzzard of a man—tough, wary, used to pecking his livelihood from death and rottenness. If whatever it was, mortal or spirit, had gotten to Old Billy, Cyrus was right to be afraid.

The bell on the shop door tinkled. Chapman gestured Judah Daniel toward the table. "Tell Elda to get you a piece of cake." Then he disappeared through the door into the shop.

Judah Daniel and Elda exchanged smiles. "I can get it for myself, honey," Judah Daniel said. The marble cake looked good. She cut a slice and wrapped it in a thick cotton napkin. Then she joined the others at the table.

They acknowledged the doctoress with respectful nods. Webb Clark had been a blacksmith, his heavily muscled frame now running to fat. Zed Truesdale, a thin man with clouded eyes, had worked at many jobs, but his calling was to preach—an activity that, in the time since Truesdale's youth, had been made illegal by white lawmakers. The preacher for Richmond's largest black congregation was white. But Truesdale still preached sometimes, brought to some hidden place where believers gathered around an iron pot "to catch the sound," a tradition brought from Africa.

After some general talk—Judah Daniel complimenting Honus's newest great-grandson, and the men asking after her garden—the conversation turned again to war. Elda rolled her eyes at Judah Daniel in a woman's jest at what men find important, then returned her gaze to the dimpled baby on her knee, who was gumming a little gourd rattle.

"It is the fulfillment of prophecy," Truesdale intoned. "Why does a comet appear in the sky just as the armies prepare for war? 'And there fell a great star from heaven, burning as it were a lamp, and the name of the star is called Wormwood. And the angel said with a loud voice, "Woe, woe, woe, to the inhabitors of the earth!" ' "

" 'And in those days,' " the eldest Chapman joined in, " 'men shall seek death, and not find it.' "

"God is dividing the sheep from the goats," Truesdale continued.

"Amen," Clark said quietly. "Change got to come." The men went on in this vein. Judah Daniel savored her piece of cake, then accepted a cup of sweet milk from Elda.

There was a bustle at the back door, and Judah Daniel looked up expectantly, thinking it would be Old Billy Roper. Instead it was Tyler Chapman, returned from making his deliveries. Tyler greeted his wife and son with cheerful affection, helped himself to a piece of pie, and joined the others at the table. He dispatched the piece in three bites, then sat back, eyes sparkling. "I heard President Lincoln's going to give arms to any black man that makes it to the free states."

The old men shook their heads and smiled, expressing amazement, approval, and disbelief at once and all without uttering a word.

Tyler's grandfather gazed at him. "Do you think things is going to be different in your lifetime?" he asked the younger man.

"Well, sir, you know I have a hope. . . . I have a hope. The abolitionists up north know slavery is wrong, and most of them ain't never even been here to see it. When they come with their conquering army, the truth will be known. Won't nobody be able to deny it no longer."

" 'The people who lived in darkness have seen a great light,' " Truesdale said.

Clark shifted in his seat. "I hope and pray that the light will come. But I cannot pray for my country to be overrun with an enemy army."

"Abe Lincoln's army will free the slaves, and strike down the laws that keep us from being truly free," Tyler responded, passion ringing in his voice.

Clark shook his head. His voice was low and sad. "Do you want to see Richmond burn—burn to the ground? I seen a stable on fire one time; we tried to put it out, but we was too late. Two men burned to death, and six horses. I can still hear their screams, and smell the stench of burning bodies. Ain't nothing like that smell." Clark was looking hard at Tyler Chapman. "What about this business that was your granddaddy's, and someday be yours, and your son's, God willing? Do you think the fire know what color you are?"

"We can build it back up," the younger man answered

eagerly, "build it as truly free men. And we can go to the City Council and to the House of Delegates and make our own laws, laws that treat the black man the same as the white. And we won't have to meet in secret to hear Reverend Truesdale preach the word."

The old men smiled at this, torn between amusement at Tyler's naïveté and delight at the prospect of a world in which this dream could come true. Then Truesdale spoke, his blue-white eyes staring as if seeing the future. " 'By these three was the third part of men killed, by the fire, and by the smoke, and by the brimstone. And the rest of the men which were not killed yet repented not of the work of their hands.' "

The words sent a chill through Judah Daniel. The baby Young John, who had been playing quietly straddling his mother's knee, burst into loud wails. Elda bent down to pick up the rattle he had dropped. "Shame on all of you for scaring us half to death," she scolded the men affectionately.

At that moment John Chapman stepped into the room. He had a young boy with him. Chapman motioned to Judah Daniel; she got up from the table and crossed to where they were standing. "Old Billy's waiting for you out back." Chapman gave a coin to the boy, who took it with a smile and ran off on bare feet.

Judah Daniel walked out back to where Old Billy was waiting. As she walked, she let the friendly, companionable feeling drain from her face until it was a mask carved of oak, all planes and angles. Old Billy would be expecting wiles from her; she would show him none. He would read a smile as cajolery, a twitch of her eyes away from him as weakness.

The yard was beaten-down dirt with a faint barnyard smell from the lean-to shed a few steps away, where the cart horse was stabled. Old Billy sat at the farthest end of a wide plank bench. He stood up and bared his head in greeting, then crammed the hat back on and resumed his seat. He stared straight ahead into the yard. Judah Daniel seated herself a few feet away and looked him over, taking her time speaking.

Age had whitened some of the hairs on his head and lined his face with wrinkles, but age had not brought repose. Old Billy was a strong contrast to the men whose company she had just left. She had the impression of a man whose wires were pulled so tight he almost gave off a hum. She doubted if he knew there was a war coming. If he knew, he didn't care. His war was inside his own head.

She continued to sit in silence. At last, he turned to face her. He was angry, but he was keeping it in.

"Well, you wanted to talk to me. Here I is. So talk."

"I appreciate you coming to see me. I want to tell you that Cyrus—"

"That boy fanciful. You ain't helped matters by giving him that damn bit of leather he wears around his neck all the time. And he got no business going to you with what don't concern you none."

"Cyrus asked for my help. That's why it concerns me."

"Fanciful!" Old Billy shot her an angry look, then turned away to spit into the dust. When he turned back around, his face wore a different expression, a smile that creased his cheeks but didn't reach his eyes.

"Look, now, if Cyrus want your help, go ahead and give it to him. Give him another one of them little bags to wear. I hate to see the boy waste money, is all."

Judah Daniel moved an inch closer and held her eyes on his. "I hear tell you made a lot of money in your business."

Old Billy sat up straight, backbone stiff. He read her face a moment. She knew what he was looking for there—any sign that she might be working him, hoping to trick or wheedle some of that money for herself. She made sure he could look right through her face into her soul, where nothing he or any man could do could move her one inch. At last he relaxed and gave a little laugh. "I can't complain none. Business been real good since them boys came back south from the medical schools up north. And we get orders from over to Charlottesville. Yes, ma'am—we can sell as many as we can dig up, and that's a fact."

This was something Cyrus—mind taken up with the plateye—hadn't mentioned. So there was a shortage of bodies for dissection. All the more reason to hasten the death of a dying woman. "From what Cyrus told me," Judah Daniel rejoined, "someone been speeding the harvest. A woman y'all dug up a few weeks back. In Hollywood Cemetery, was it?" She shook her head wonderingly, still holding her eyes on Old Billy's. He looked away. She continued. "What I wonder is, how did y'all know that body was there?"

Old Billy shifted in his seat. "One of the doctors told us. I don't recollect which one."

"Hughes?" Judah Daniel prompted.

"Might have been him." Old Billy nodded slowly as if thinking it over. "Might be the owners called him in to try and save her. Might be they decided to kill her instead, to save the cost of doctoring."

Judah Daniel smiled a little. "Thoughtful of them to let him know where he could find her."

Old Billy shrugged.

"Archer?" she persisted.

Old Billy smiled and put his hand to resettle his hat. Judah Daniel saw where two fingers had been cut off to stumps. The sight made her flesh crawl. She had seen far worse deformities, but this was somehow more than an ordinary mutilation; it was an outward sign of something cut off, stunted, in his soul.

"Doc Archer like to walk up on Hollywood in the company of one or other of the young women he acquainted with. I reckon he make them hang on his arm with his stories about grave-robbing. Must be he seen the body put in and knowed where it was. Yes," he said, nodding faster, "come to me now that that's how it was. Archer took Cyrus and me there, and Charley Wilson."

Judah Daniel saw the blink Old Billy gave right after he spoke the name of Charley Wilson. "That the young man who died?" she spoke quickly.

Old Billy's guard was up. "Yes'm, seem to me I heard he died." He got to his feet. "You tell Cyrus to let them fancies be. When you die, all your strength go with you. Seem to me he ought to know that by now. Don't matter how that woman died. Fact is, she dead, and ain't nobody weeping after her."

"What about her baby?" Judah Daniel asked.

"Weren't no baby in the grave," Old Billy said, echoing what Cyrus had said. "If there was, we'd have got four more dollars."

Old Billy left then. Judah Daniel remained sitting on the bench. She thought she had never seen any black man lie so calmly and with such unconcern as to whether or not he was believed. Might be the dead woman's owners had called in Dr. Hughes to save her life; might be, but not likely. Might be Archer happened to see the woman buried while he dallied with some female companion in Hollywood Cemetery. Again, not likely. The burial must have taken place after dark, and no white woman who was anything but a prostitute would walk alone with a man after dark. And with a prostitute, why spend time walking?

Old Billy agreed to meet her, probably to find out how much she knew. But he lied as if he wasn't afraid of anything she could do to him—and that was just as well, she thought. If he thought he had any reason to be afraid of her, she would have to watch out.

RICHMOND
APRIL 19

When Narcissa and Mirrie had taken their seats for breakfast, Professor Powers pulled a small piece of notepaper from his coat pocket and waved it at them. "I must ask Stedman to what I owe this charming invitation—a doddering old relic like me who has to be carried everywhere!" The professor was enjoying his joke, smiling a facetious smile that reminded Narcissa of Mirrie's when she was in a high humor.

"Of course, it is you ladies who are the desired guests, not this old death's-head casting a pall over the celebrants." His tone was sardonic. "And I hope you will attend. It's not every day that our dear Old Dominion secedes from its Union, and it's natural to want the best view of the festivities. Though to me," he continued, his tone growing more somber, "it does seem an occasion for reflection and prayer rather than bonfires and marching bands.

"Lincoln must have known he was throwing down the gauntlet with his demand of troops from Virginia to join the North in putting down the seceding states. Nothing else would have made secessionists out of Governor Letcher and the other staunch Unionists." Narcissa saw Mirrie frown; she knew her friend was contemptuous of these men's supposed staunchness.

"But now," Professor Powers continued, "the die is cast. The time for reasoned debate is over, and those who have been most reluctant to dissolve the Union will now be the most eager to take up swords and rend it asunder."

Narcissa glanced at Mirrie but found her expression unreadable. Narcissa wondered if Professor Powers meant his words as a warning to his daughter that many of those who in the past had listened to her antislavery, pro-Union views with tolerance, if not sympathy, would do so no longer.

"Still, you ladies should go witness this historic event," continued the professor. "I will nominate Mr. Cohen to accompany you in my place; Stedman can send him an invitation if he hasn't already. Well, shall I accept on your behalf, or not?"

"Father, *what* are you talking about?" Mirrie said with a self-conscious giggle so unlike her usual hearty laugh that Narcissa looked at her, wondering.

"Oh, I beg your pardon, my dear. My thoughts outran my speech. This is an invitation to us from Stedman to view tonight's illumination from the balcony of his house on Clay Street."

"Oh, accept, by all means," Mirrie replied. "We *ladies* enjoy seeing the breadth to which human folly can sweep. Don't we, Narcissa?"

At dusk Narcissa and Mirrie, accompanied by a rather quiet Nat Cohen, set out for Dr. Stedman's home on Shockoe Hill. All along the streets, excited persons of both sexes and every degree rushed back and forth. Men and boys stacked wood for bonfires. Ladies wore little badges made from palmetto fronds, emblem of South Carolina as the first state to secede, on their bonnets or in their hair.

As the carriage took them past a sprawling building modeled on an Italian villa, Mirrie gazed up at it and remarked with a sigh, "The young ladies, with their hunger for battle, have won after all. Now it flies unmolested—the Stars and Bars."

At Narcissa's questioning look, Mirrie explained, "That's the Richmond Female Institute, a boarding school for the young ladies we are apparently educating by the old Spartan principle of urging our men on to fight or die."

Narcissa followed her gaze. In perhaps a dozen of the villa's windows hung the flags, designed with three broad stripes, red and white, and a canton of blue studded with seven white stars. Mirrie signaled her disapproval with an exasperated sigh. "The Institute girls claim to have been the first in Richmond to fly the Flag of Secession, or of 'States' Rights,' if you prefer. At first the Institute officials took the flags down, but the girls just made more. Now, I suppose . . ."

Mirrie's voice trailed off, and she looked down at her gloved hands, fingers interlaced tightly. Then she looked up at Narcissa. "Does the design look familiar? They make them by cutting up the Stars and Stripes and reassembling its elements."

Mirrie's obvious pain at the triumph of the secessionists reminded Narcissa of the question that had been puzzling her since Professor Powers's announcement of the invitation. "Mirrie, why did you want to come tonight?"

"Why," Mirrie replied, arching her eyebrows, her somber mood banished, "for you, of course. *Dr. Stedman* could be such a *useful* acquaintance. In fact, I must admit I suggested to Mrs. Stedman that we be invited, because I thought it might *cheer you up.*"

"Oh!" Narcissa said, to stem the flow of Mirrie's pointed

commentary. She glanced at Nat Cohen, who was looking out of the window, his attention tactfully withdrawn.

Dr. Stedman was the man Mirrie hoped could provide information about the medical college. But any questioning she did would have to be careful, Narcissa thought. Overt interest in such an unladylike subject as anatomical dissection would no doubt alarm the gentleman into silence. By "other people," Mirrie must mean Dr. Hughes and his wife. Cheer me up, indeed! The thought made Narcissa smile at its incongruity.

Mirrie, a wry smile on her own face, must have noticed the fleeting expression. "See," she said to Narcissa, "you look more cheerful already! And here we are."

Dr. Stedman and his wife welcomed them at the door. Dr. Stedman was short, plump, and pink of face. His wavy hair, extending down his cheeks in muttonchops, added to an impression of softness. Mrs. Stedman was a stout, ruddy woman in her fifties. Her gown, printed with pink, cabbage-sized roses, was unbecoming, but she had a broad, intelligent forehead, bright eyes, and a ready laugh.

The crowd was a cultivated one, but the air of near-hysteria prevailed here too. Both men and woman spoke more quickly and laughed more loudly than usual, and anyone who ventured a sober remark was shouted down. Narcissa noted that some of the men had donned their militia uniforms, while many of the women were wearing fashionable adornments *à la militaire:* tasseled epaulets, frog fastenings, Garibaldi blouses.

The Stedmans had caught the flame as well, it appeared. Blue bunting was draped over the doors, and tiny seccession flags were displayed in bunches among the silver urns and serving dishes. The polished silver reflected the sparkle of gaslights and candles.

While Nat Cohen went to fetch cups of punch, Mirrie took Narcissa to talk to Mrs. Stedman. After inquiring about the Stedman daughters and grandchildren, Mirrie turned to the subject of most concern to Narcissa. "I wonder that Dr. and Mrs. Hughes aren't here tonight," she remarked, scanning the room, then turning to Mrs. Stedman with a look of inquiry.

"Oh, we expect them any minute." Mrs. Stedman narrowed her eyes and shot Mirrie a significant look. Dropping her voice, she added, "Rachel Hughes is often unwell, you know. Her nerves. She takes a great deal of laudanum." It was tactless to criticize too loudly the taking of laudanum, since its use was widespread among women of their class.

Narcissa, hoping a neutral comment would prompt additional revelations, said, "How fortunate that her husband is a doctor, since she suffers so."

"Perhaps so. . . . Of course, Edgar Hughes might have gone farther in his career had he not had to cater to her."

Mrs. Stedman smiled a little as if preening herself on her own husband's success. "I will say Rachel does her part, sometimes bringing little treats for the students at the medical college and having them over to dinner at their house. Though just as often, when *I* visit, she is lying down with a sick headache."

Narcissa saw the gleam in Mrs. Stedman's eyes. She thinks Rachel is avoiding her, Narcissa thought, and she may be right. Mrs. Stedman's bustling energy and penetrating gaze might be too much for a woman who sought retreat from the demands of daily life in doses of laudanum.

Mrs. Stedman's smile faded, and she looked at Narcissa with sad eyes. "Rachel was very kind to your brother. I regretted that I was not able to visit him during his illness. My eldest daughter was confined with her first, down in Wakefield, and she wanted her *maman* in attendance. A healthy boy, thank God. Your brother Charley was a very dear boy. I would have been proud to have him as my son." She pressed Narcissa's hand for a moment. Then her mood lightened. "What was I saying? Oh, Dr. Hughes. Of course, his career never really recovered after the death of his first wife."

"Oh?" Narcissa was careful to express just the amount of interest that would keep Mrs. Stedman talking.

"There was an epidemic of puerperal fever at the time— almost twenty years ago now. Childbed fever, I mean; sometimes a doctor's wife comes to think like a doctor, and talk like one, I'm afraid!

"Anyway," she continued, "many of the poor souls in the hospital died. Dr. Hughes attended his own wife—she was an Archer, quite a good family. That marriage was the making of him, you know, his people not being from Virginia."

Narcissa struggled to maintain a blandly interested expression. "A relation of Dr. Cameron Archer?"

"Oh, yes," Mrs. Stedman replied. "Ellen was his older sister. Half-sister. There was quite a tidy bit of property come to Edgar Hughes with that marriage." She dropped her voice. "I believe Cameron Archer thought he should have had it.

"Anyway," Mrs. Stedman continued, "Ellen contracted the fever and died. The infant—it was a boy—died too. Edgar Hughes was devastated and left the area for some time. I believe he went back to his own home—Philadelphia, I think it was. Later he returned to Richmond and married Rachel Dawes. Of course, her family is quite wealthy, but not so socially prominent as the Archers.

"And as if there were not enough sadness in Dr. Hughes's life, there was another tragedy associated with Rachel's confinement. I believe there were twins who didn't survive the delivery. He stopped delivering babies after that, though I believe he had quite a good record other than those personal tragedies. And they never had any more children."

Mrs. Stedman broke off, glancing across the room; Narcissa, following her gaze, noticed a redheaded young man approaching through the crowd. He made his way toward them, a rather embarrassed-looking man in tow. The second man was a little older, perhaps in his mid-twenties, and very tall, with dark hair.

Both men greeted the ladies. Mirrie, who knew them both, introduced the redhead to Narcissa as Mr. Jamison, the darker man as Dr. McGuire. Mirrie introduced Narcissa as the sister of Charley Wilson. Both men expressed regret about Charley's death. Narcissa observed their faces. Did Jamison seem somewhat ill at ease?

Dropping his solemn expression after a few moments, Jamison spoke excitedly. "Mrs. Powers, as you are new in town, you may not know that this is *the* Dr. Hunter Holmes McGuire, the Moses of the medical set, who as you know brought more than two hundred Southern medical students from their 'captivity' in Philadelphia."

Narcissa did know of Dr. McGuire, who had been a hero of Charley's. McGuire, outraged by the Northern canonization of John Brown after his raid on Harpers Ferry, had incited the transfer of many of those Southern medical students to the Medical College of Virginia.

Narcissa read the doctor's physiognomy with interest. He had the figure still of a gawky adolescent, but his face was startlingly handsome, with raven's-wing brows, dark, flashing eyes, and, she thought, a rather discontented mouth. McGuire looked as if he might have lingered, but two other young men came up behind him and tugged on his arm. With a courteous, "Your servant, ma'am," McGuire took his leave.

Jamison moved closer to Narcissa and lowered his head

toward her as if to impart some special information. "I wish I had been there, in Philadelphia. Some of our Southern students went down to the depot to get John Brown's body, to perform an anatomy on it. But their plan was discovered, and some of the Abolishers went down too, and a fight broke out. I hear the police behaved in a very insulting manner. So our boys came back, on a special train the governor sent for them.

"They got a hero's welcome," he added with a sigh that expressed admiration and envy. "It does seem to me it would advance scientific knowledge to examine the brain of such a man—a lunatic, a murderer, and a traitor to his race.

"The Southern boys had the last laugh, though, on old John Brown," Jamison went on, baring his teeth in a wide grin. "Some of the boys from the medical college at Winchester had been to see the fight at Harpers Ferry. On the way back they found a body down by the river, dead. They thought, what luck! and had it sent back to the college for anatomy lessons. But when they got it back they found out it was Owen Brown, son of old Mad John himself! They preserved it for demonstration. I haven't seen it myself yet, but some of the boys have."

Jamison had entered on the very topic that consumed Narcissa's thoughts. She asked lightly, "Are cadavers for dissection really so difficult to come by, that students have to scavenge for them in the streets?"

Jamison laughed. "Well, it's the ideal to have one cadaver for each student. A good supply of anatomical material is an asset that a medical college in a city has over one in a small town like Winchester or Charlottesville. Why, the medical college here in Richmond features its abundance of cadavers in its advertisements!

"When McGuire brought the boys back south, the number

of students tripled. Now there's more than a hundred at a time wanting to do an anatomy. So you can imagine, demand has been high. Sometimes students have to share, or just watch the demonstrator and hope for a chance to try their hand. With summer coming on, of course we lose the chance. Once a body's sufficiently pickled to stand the heat, it's just too hard to work with.

"And now," he went on excitedly, "the boys are talking about joining up with their local regiments. I'm going to complete my training and go in for a field surgeon."

Narcissa, her mind filled with images, forced a smile in response. As they stood in silence for a moment, a second man came up and put his arm on Jamison's shoulder. The stranger was a little over middling height, athletic in build, dressed in a well-cut black frock coat. His brown hair fell in waves to his collar, and his Van Dyke beard was neatly trimmed, as if he had just come from the barber.

"Come along, Jamison. You're monopolizing the most charming lady in the room." As young Jamison blushed and stammered apologies, the man shot a long glance at Narcissa and nodded his head in a sort of abbreviated bow. Then he turned away, his arm still on Jamison's shoulder so that the young man perforce had to follow.

Impertinent gallantry, without an introduction, Narcissa thought, her cheeks burning. The stranger's drawl marked him as "old Richmond," it being the style of Richmond men from the best families to speak as if they were too indolent to form their words properly. But his manners marked him as someone a lady should be wary of.

Then her thoughts returned to what Jamison had been saying. A shortage of cadavers lent credence to the idea of a burking conspiracy. She couldn't wait to tell Mirrie. As she passed through the crowd to her friend, Narcissa caught sight of the man who had interrupted her conversation with Jamison. He was standing against the opposite wall, deep in conversation with Edgar Hughes.

"Mirrie," Narcissa whispered, taking hold of her friend's arm, "who is that talking with Dr. Hughes?"

Mirrie followed Narcissa's gaze. "Cameron Archer."

Archer seemed to feel their eyes on him. He glanced in their direction, looked away, then looked again. Narcissa bent her head toward Mirrie, whispering, "Hush, don't look! He's seen us!" She felt herself flush with anger as she continued to feel his gaze on her. He had known who she was when he interrupted her conversation with Jamison. "Most charming lady," indeed! Had he been concerned about what the young medical student might say to her?

By the time Narcissa had recovered herself to look back across the room, Archer had disappeared. She caught sight of Rachel Hughes, standing near her husband but looking around the room as if seeking more congenial company. She was dressed becomingly in dark green, her shoulders draped with a paisley shawl.

Rachel Hughes's eyes met hers. Narcissa thought Rachel hesitated a second before returning her smile; perhaps she was shortsighted. Narcissa made her excuses to Nat Cohen and drew Mirrie with her through the crowded room as Rachel, shepherding her wide skirts, came to meet them.

"I had no idea you had returned to town," Rachel said to Narcissa. She sounded displeased, Narcissa thought, as if she felt slighted that Narcissa had not called on her. Mirrie responded, speaking warmly of her sister-in-law's assistance in the Powers household. Rachel Hughes seemed to relax then, and urged the two to visit.

Just before eight o'clock, the guests were to assemble on the portico. The procession, which had formed hundreds strong in front of city hall, was to march up Twelfth Street to Clay, right past the Stedmans'. It would turn up Clay to Tenth, then to Broad, following a route designed to pay compliment to the young ladies of the Richmond Female Institute.

Nat Cohen, who had left the gathering to take in the commotion on the streets, returned, bringing with him Brit Wallace. The Englishman had an exhilarated air. "It's like the original Guy Fawkes Day," he joked, "with Fawkes himself to burn instead of a straw man!" When he caught sight of Mirrie and Narcissa, Wallace frowned and wagged his finger. "What a buffoon you made of me, Miss Powers, putting me on to that Southern Rights Ball to meet Hardie McDowell! I am only glad that I did not send to invite *him* for brandy and cigars! But I did invite *her* to dance, and she was kind enough to put me through my paces in the Virginia reel."

Mirrie grinned. "I never told you Miss McDowell was a man. If you are to be a success as a journalist, to say nothing of your success as a beau, you will have to learn our customs."

"Still," Brit protested, "you should have warned me that you Virginians choose names for your female children out of the front of the Bible, where the family names are written in, and not out of the text."

Mirrie laughed delightedly. "And how is our famous belle?"

"Very lovely," Brit responded with frank admiration. "Hair pale gold, complexion ripe peach—"

"Well, you must write about her in one of your dispatches," Mirrie responded, a touch of acid in her voice. "Then, when she is old and gray and withered, she will be able to say that, instead of Ronsard, 'Wallace *me célébrait, du temps que j'étais belle.*' " They all laughed, but Narcissa had caught Mirrie's glance at her. She wondered about the meaning of the glance, and her words. Mirrie had never minded hearing a beautiful woman praised. Then Narcissa's eyes widened as she realized: Mirrie had somehow cast Brit Wallace in the role of admirer for Narcissa. How funny!

Narcissa was still smiling to herself as she heard Wallace comment, "Miss McDowell is a fire-eater though, that's true enough, when it comes to that favorite theme of 'kill the Yankees.' Most of the ladies seem to want their men to return carrying their shields, or on them, don't you know."

Excited voices came from the portico. "They're coming!" Those at watch were giving word that the procession was in view. The crowd began to press toward the open doors to the portico. Narcissa found herself once again glancing around the room, seeking out Archer and Hughes, but without success.

Mirrie took Nat Cohen's arm, and Brit offered his to Narcissa. The men ushered them to places on the railing, where the ladies were standing in little islands created by the unyielding wire hoops of their skirts. The men stood behind them and carried on animated conversations, shouting into each other's ears.

From the back of the house, the guests looked down the hill to where Jefferson's Capitol, lit by a thousand torches, glowed amber. Thousands of men and youths were marching, roaring and whooping, carrying banners, flags, or torches. They formed a cascading river of yellow light that flowed through the streets of Richmond. Rockets and fireworks took the flames into the sky, overpowering the light from the pale moon. As far as the eye could see—up on Church Hill, down at Rocketts, and across the river in Manchester—bonfires glowed like fireflies. Between the whine and boom of fireworks, the strains of "Dixie" could be heard, played at a wild, foot-stomping speed.

Eyes dazzled and hearing dulled, Narcissa felt her elbow jogged. She turned to see Cameron Archer. He put his mouth close to her ear to speak under the tumult.

"It's enough to raise the dead, isn't it, Mrs. Powers?"

Chapter Six

RICHMOND
LATE APRIL

The following Sunday dawned viburnum-scented under a bright blue sky. The air was still. The roar of the James, swollen with April rains, was muted but audible up on Shockoe Hill and through the open windows of Second Presbyterian Church.

The dark wood and elevated Gothic design of the church were beautiful, the damask cushion comfortable, but Narcissa shifted in the pew, eager for the service to be over. Cameron Archer suspected, at least, that Charley had communicated his suspicions to her. That seemed to Narcissa the inescapable meaning of the words Archer had spoken at Stedman's the night of the illumination. *Enough to raise the dead*—he had phrased the remark close enough to the familiar "wake the dead" so that, had she not known about the resurrection men, she could have accepted the comment at face value. What had he learned from her reaction to his words? As she remembered it, her heart had stopped, her face frozen. She had given herself away to Archer, she thought with chagrin, and presumably, through him, to Hughes and any others who were involved.

What did they intend to do about her knowledge—or about her? That question, too, beat in her mind until her head ached. Was she in danger? She could not quite believe that she was, nor quite dismiss her fear. Hughes and Archer were physicians; they were gentlemen. So they seemed, at least, by their titles and their appearance, she thought wryly; suppose their actions proved them otherwise? If they were having people killed in order to dissect the bodies, what laws of chivalry would they break to keep their crimes hidden?

These dark musings were driven out of her head by the sudden clanging of a bell. Three deep bongs; then a pause; then three more. Mirrie grabbed Narcissa's hand. "The tocsin!" Mirrie exclaimed in an urgent whisper.

"The tocsin!" The words burst forth from a man behind them. The tocsin, Narcissa knew, was the city's warning for a slave uprising or other calamity, the call that would gather its men into armed regiments. But today war was on everyone's mind—had Mr. Lincoln called down an army upon Richmond?

In the pulpit Dr. McGrath was silent and seemed to withdraw into himself, listening or perhaps praying. As people began to rise from their seats and push into the aisles, Dr. McGrath called the elders to keep order. With an urgency just short of panic, the congregation jostled its way out the doors and into the street. Mirrie and Narcissa, giving way to those who seemed more in haste, were among the last to leave.

The two women stopped in front of the church and listened to the tolling of the big bell from Capitol Square four blocks west. Fifth Street was a stagnant river of mud. Slowly they made their way through milling crowds up the street toward St. Paul's Church by the Capitol.

It was a scene of chaos. All the churches had discharged their members, and the streets were crowded with people, but few seemed to move with any purpose. Some men, hurrying to join their regiments, were giving orders to their servants and valedictory kisses to their wives. Narcissa saw a young would-be soldier waving his hat and whooping. A little boy, still in the skirts of babyhood, howled and hid his face in his mother's dress; the ashen-faced mother bent to comfort him, heedless of the mud on her pale green silk.

Mirrie hailed a fiftyish man who was urging his horse through the crowd. "Mr. Frederickson! What is it?" The man pulled up and shouted to them, "It's the Federal steam sloop *Pawnee,* coming up the James!"

"What will it do?" Mirrie shouted back, hands cupping her mouth.

"A steam sloop of war with the run of the James? It'll knock the city of Richmond into kindling wood, that's what! Pardon me, Miss Powers, I must join up with the Howitzers." Waving a salute, he chirruped to his horse and continued down the hill.

"We must go to Father," Mirrie said, frowning.

Narcissa, touched by her look of concern, pressed her friend's hand. "He will be all right; the house is more than a mile from the James."

"Yes," Mirrie agreed, "we should be far enough away to be safe. But the trouble is," she added, her frown deepening, "we'll be too far away to watch!"

≫≪

Chimborazo Heights offered a panoramic view of the James down to Rocketts. There, with servants dispatched to fetch refreshments, a nervous hilarity took hold of the crowd.

Brit Wallace had ridden up the hill with an acquaintance from the Exchange Hotel. The fellow, a man named Barton, had just returned to the city after an absence of some years in hopes of gaining an appointment with the Confederate government now relocating in Richmond. Truth to tell, most of the visitors at the Exchange shared this hope. If it was to make the fortune of all these men, Wallace thought, the new government had better come up from Montgomery with a richly endowed exchequer.

Brit and Barton found their way to a good vantage point on the plateau atop the bluffs of Chimborazo from which to view the activity down along the river.

"Those are the Howitzers," Barton said, pointing. "See their guns? Six-pounders."

Brit scribbled in his notebook as Barton went on, noting the appearances of "the Fayette Artillery—the Greys—Company F—" He made a note to look up which comic opera might make the most telling comparison with the uniforms of these regiments, whose bright colors and lavish gold braid, tassels, and buttons seemed designed more for show than for use. With much gesticulation, the stage-soldiers were wheeling their guns—those not hopelessly mired in deep mud—into place.

Following the militias came a swarm of civilians who appeared to be armed with ancient muskets, shotguns, and pistols—weapons that could only reach their targets, Brit thought, if the Federals chose to abandon their ship's guns and swim to shore. The defense was as ready as it was going to be. Now all eyes strained for the first sight of the *Pawnee*.

It was easy to watch the drama being played out before him, Brit found; easy to coin amusing phrases that might win the admiration of his readers. (How many of them had ever seen an opera? he wondered; maybe best to change that to a music-hall reference.) And what was the phrase Miss Powers had used—eating run-mad mush? He could use that.

Virginians, so proud of their blood that was so easily brought to boil. Their fancy-dress soldiers came from the best families, eager to defend their rights and their honor. Their pride, their gold tassels, their mired guns, would make a good story. Yet it was impossible to believe that these enthusiastic but largely amateur soldiers could actually stand up to the hail of fire from a gunboat attack. The image of those fanciful uniforms soaked with blood was all too easy to conjure.

Fate had written a farce, or a tragedy, Brit thought, that was being acted out under his eyes. He could not write his own report until he learned which it was that she had written. Finally he closed his notebook, lit a cigar, and settled in to wait.

At last, word came: a false alarm, the result of a misread telegram. Now he could write his farce, Brit thought, and make his readers laugh at the antics of this city that thought it was ready to go to war because it was well supplied in hot blood and gold braid. But he could not escape the thought that what had for him been an afternoon at the theater had for others been a far more unsettling brush with fate. And some of those people—here, unaccountably, the face of Narcissa Powers appeared in his mind—were on the way to becoming his friends.

❧

The note from Brit Wallace announcing the time at which he would arrive to escort them to the slave auction provoked very different responses in the two women. Mirrie read it, then handed it without comment to Narcissa. When Narcissa finished reading, Mirrie said, "You don't want to go, do you?" There was an edge to her voice.

Narcissa sighed. What was in her mind was her dream about Charley, but she found she could not speak of it, even to Mirrie. At last she said, "I want to go, because I feel I may learn something about the woman who was killed. But I am not ashamed to say that I dread it. We are reared to avoid such things, to avert our eyes from them—as from a saloon, or something of that kind. Just as we are taught to speak of servants, not slaves—"

Mirrie shot back, as Narcissa had known she would, "So men go to slave auctions, and saloons, and women are supposed to pretend that neither exists! We *ladies* are set up as the defenders of morality on one hand, and forbidden to open our eyes on the other. How convenient! But I would prefer to *see*. We southerners complain that Mrs. Stowe never visited the South, never saw what she wrote about. We have an obligation to see, and to know."

Narcissa saw the stubborn set of her friend's jaw. Mirrie prided herself on being ruled by the head, not the heart. But in fact, though she may have arrived at her convictions through a rational process her commitment to them was as impassioned as any girl's for her lover. Narcissa knew that her own recent confusion about the institution of slavery— about so many things, come to that—would drive Mirrie wild, and she wished she had never let herself be drawn into the discussion. But, having entered it, she couldn't walk away from it without at least trying to express what was in her mind, however provoking Mirrie might find her muddled thoughts.

"Oh, Mirrie, I think maybe that's why I don't want to go. Many southerners oppose slavery, or at least want to see it come to an end. And many have freed their own slaves."

"Ha! Yes," Mirrie interjected, "in their wills, for the most part, after they themselves are dead."

Narcissa went on. "Don't be vexed with me. I don't want to defend slavery. It's just that my feelings are different from yours, not so clear-cut. You believe it is wrong and should be abolished right away. I . . . I fear it is not right, but yet I think of the servants I know, like my own Aunt Dodie. Should she be turned out of the only home she has ever known, by the act of a government who never asked her what *she* wanted?"

Narcissa could see that Mirrie was preparing an angry retort, so she rushed on. "And now, this war. We have been under attack for years, and now are under attack in truth, for our way of life by people who have not experienced it and do not understand it. We are sending our fathers and brothers and sons to fight—maybe not so much to defend that way of life as much as to defend our right to determine our own course. I don't know that I could bear, right now, to believe that slavery is so evil that it should be eradicated at any cost. How can I wish for our own defeat?"

The anger in Mirrie's face had softened into sadness, and she replied with a question. "But how long must Moses say, 'Let my people go!' And what plagues are we calling down on our own heads for refusing?"

It always seems, Narcissa thought, that time passes more quickly when you have something to dread. The appointed day was upon them, and she, Mirrie, and Brit Wallace were seated in a hired coach traveling west down Franklin Street.

It amused Narcissa to see how each of them had dressed for the occasion. Wallace wore brown tweeds and looked as if he were planning an afternoon's grouse shooting. If his choice was designed to evoke a sportsman's bonhomie among the men gathered for the slave auction, she thought that it would fail; he simply looked foreign, if not—in view of the warm day—downright eccentric. Mirrie's dress was maroon silk, bodice and skirts trimmed in dark-toned plaid. Combs and netting tamed her unruly hair, and a small straw hat was anchored on top with numerous pins. She looked like a young girl ready to call on an eagle-eyed and critical great aunt. Narcissa herself wore her accustomed black, made up in light polished cotton with a small crinoline, and a simple black bonnet—a choice designed to attract as little notice as possible.

They passed the Exchange Hotel, then the Farmers' Market, and crossed Shockoe Creek into an area of stables, dirty little shops, and dilapidated warehouses. Brit Wallace was twisting his mouth nervously and seemed to be trying to decide whether he should call off the expedition.

At last they reached the place—a long, low brick warehouse surrounded by a wide expanse of bare, reddish earth. A raised plank walk divided the yard from a tangle of overgrown bushes and vines that covered a slight rise to the west. A red flag flew at the open door, which was covered with printed bills. A light-skinned Negro man walked up and down with another flag, ringing a large bell. They could hear the man shouting, "O, yea! O, yea! O, yea! Walk up, gentlemen! The sale of a fine, likely lot of young niggers is about to begin!" Brit dismounted from the carriage and looked about him, then looked back at Narcissa and Mirrie as if wondering whether they would at last back down from the expedition.

There were, Narcissa saw, two distinct groups of white men in the small, dirty yard—the prosperous looking were undoubtedly serious customers, and they filed briskly into the building, puffing on cigars or spitting tobacco juice into the dirt. Another group of about a dozen, who seemed too poor to own slaves, were simply loafing.

Mirrie threw one questioning glance at Narcissa. There was so much of the challenge in her eyes that Narcissa felt she could not back down. She nodded. Before she could say a word, Mirrie was out of the carriage, and Brit Wallace was extending his hand to Narcissa.

Narcissa thought she had never been in such a squalid place. She had seen illness, death, and poverty, but always to some measure allayed by human bonds of loyalty. Here, those bonds were forcibly to be broken. There were rough wooden benches for the crowd of buyers and their agents. Directed by Mirrie, Brit Wallace led them along the dirt floor to stand at the back of the room. The floor was filthy with expecto-rated wads of tobacco, and many of the men were smoking. A couple of men shot doubtful glances at the two well-dressed women, but they continued to smoke. It was as if, Narcissa thought, she and Mirrie had given up their claims on the reverence for womanhood by entering this place.

Standing on a wooden box at the front of the hall, stripped to the waist and with an iron collar around his neck, stood a young black man. The auctioneer was proclaiming his vir-tues as a worker. Behind them were groups of slaves, men and women, of all ages. A young woman was watching the man on the block, her hands on the shoulders of a little girl about three years old. The child was restless, not understand-ing; the woman had an anxious expression. What was their relationship, Narcissa wondered, to each other and to that young man?

Were slaves just bodies to be bought and sold? To be sold even after death, if at last their bodies were worth more dead than alive? To be killed?

Her dream was again filling her head, as if she could hear Charley's voice calling her name. The pounding in her tem-ples was making her feel ill. She slipped away from Mirrie's side and walked out into the air. She stopped at the door where a dozen notices of runaway slaves, with descriptions of their appearance and rewards offered for their capture and return, were posted. She glanced at them. All were men, mostly young, many described as bearing the scars of beatings or branding.

The woman Charley had described had been near death— dying, or perhaps beginning to recover—from childbed fever. She could not have run away. Perhaps her owners had sold her to the resurrection men on the supposition that she would die. Perhaps—the possibilities were too horrible to contemplate.

Narcissa stepped out into the yard. She avoided looking at the group of men still congregated without apparent purpose about thirty yards from where she stood. A movement among the loiterers drew her gaze in spite of herself. She focused on it, then drew in a sharp breath as she heard the loud crack of a whip hitting flesh.

Over the heads of a half-dozen onlookers Narcissa could see a blond, red-faced man standing on the plank walk. His arm was already raised again, the whip poised. His object was a black girl who looked about fourteen. She was holding her blouse to cover herself in front. Her form looked womanly, but her face was still round and soft.

The lash fell. Though she winced, the girl seemed hardly aware of the beating. She was staring back toward the auction house, tears streaming from her eyes. The white man paused in his labor. "Crying for her mammy!" he called to the other white men who stood around, hands in pockets, viewing the scene with mild interest. "Cheer up, gal! You been sold down South to pick cotton. They'll have a handsome young buck for you there." As if stimulated by the thought, the man delivered another crack across the girl's back.

Into Narcissa's head rushed all the grief and rage she had been holding inside. As the man raised the whip to strike again, she shouted with all her might, so loud her ears rang with the sound of her own voice, "Stop it!" She took a half-dozen steps toward the man, then stopped, unsure of what it was she meant to do. She was acutely aware that, being where she was and unattended, she may indeed have forfeited the protection accorded her sex.

The man turned and threw down the whip. His eyes locked on Narcissa's. They were bright blue. In seconds, it seemed to Narcissa, he assessed her ability to cause him trouble and decided that it was not much. "Perhaps you would like to come over here and explain to me why I should not chastise this here slave," he said with exaggerated politeness, glancing around at his audience. The loungers were beginning to gawk; this was a new addition to the show.

Narcissa walked slowly toward the blond man, the blood hot in her face. She had told him to stop, and—for the moment at least—he had stopped. Now what could she do? The man closed the distance between them, swaggering. When he stood in front of her, close enough for her to smell his sweat and the pomade on his hair, he put his face near Narcissa's and whispered, "Whore."

Narcissa stared at him. She had heard the word spoken only once before, by a young friend eager to impart forbidden knowledge. Suddenly, irrelevantly, Narcissa wondered for the first time where the girl had heard it.

The man's face had the pinkish sheen of fair skin repeatedly burned by the sun. He wore his hair long and curled like a dandy. His light beard was stained around the mouth with tobacco juice. She saw his eyes shift away from her to a point over her right shoulder, widen, then narrow as the man grinned, revealing brown-stained teeth. She followed the man's gaze to see Brit Wallace behind her. Wallace had assumed the caricature pose of the boxer: fists raised, one leg forward and one back, knees bent. His brows were knotted; she saw a trickle of perspiration run past his ear.

"Look a'here, boys!" the man called to the onlookers. He shouldered past Narcissa, so close she had to step out of his way.

They responded with huzzahs and whistles. "Belt him, Jake!" one of them cried. The man they called Jake, still grinning, took a few steps forward and swung his fist hard across his body toward Brit Wallace's chest. Brit turned away from the blow and, quicker than Narcissa could see, delivered a punch straight to the face of his attacker. Jake sprawled flat on his back, his nose pouring blood. He put his hand up to his face, then screamed. "He broke my damn nose!"

Behind the fallen body of their champion, the loungers were scowling and gesturing. One man stepped toward Brit. A dozen more were behind him. The man called Jake held his nose with his left hand and, with his right, fumbled inside his jacket. Narcissa saw him draw out something that gleamed in the sun—a single-edged knife with a crosspiece, maybe a Bowie knife. Mirrie materialized at Narcissa's side, took her arm, and drew her a few steps back toward the street.

The scuffle attracted the attention of some inside the auction house. A well-dressed man with brown muttonchop whiskers and an air of authority stepped out and walked over to the fallen man. The blade that had been in Jake's hand was now hidden, Narcissa noted with relief, and he held his bleeding nose with both hands.

The prosperous-looking man surveyed the scene, taking in

the scored back of the black woman and the wounded face of the white man, then turned to Brit Wallace. "What happened here?" he demanded.

Brit answered him frostily. "This man was beating that slave unmercifully. I told him to stop. He was rude, and I hit him."

"No, I—I told him to stop," Narcissa stepped forward.

The man's gaze shifted to her, and his frown deepened. She wanted to say more, to tell him about the horror she had witnessed, but he spoke over her. "I don't hold with interference—not from a foreigner, not from a lady who seems to have forgotten herself. But, fact is, I just bought that slave, and I object even more to having my property damaged. Get along, Calder." He jabbed the toe of his boot into Jake's ribs. Still holding his nose, Jake heaved himself out of the dust and limped away, casting back an evil look. The other men were mumbling among themselves and seemed disinclined to welcome him as their hero.

"Ladies," the girl's owner said, "if it offends your sensibilities to see a slave disciplined, I suggest you avoid this part of town." He turned on his heel and headed back toward the auction house.

Brit was frowning, his face dark. "I'm sorry, Mrs. Powers. I will take you and Miss Powers away from this appalling place at once."

Narcissa shook her head distractedly. She hurried after the girl's owner and tapped him on the shoulder. "Sir, is it true she has been sold south?"

The man snapped his response. "My place is down in Midlothian, a few miles south of here. Not that it's any of your business," he added over his shoulder as he walked away. Narcissa turned away. Mirrie and Brit Wallace were watching her, concern on their faces. She looked past them to where the slave girl was standing, head bowed, eyes closed. From nowhere had appeared another black woman, older, whom Narcissa had not seen before. She was standing behind the young girl and seemed to be tending to her wounds. Was she the girl's mother? The woman's face was a mask. If she felt anything—pity, fear, or anger—it didn't show.

Jake Calder made another attempt to rally the men around him. "You there, Judah Daniel!" he called out to the woman. "Get away from that young heifer! You be wanting to fix her with your herbs and conjurations so she won't breed, I reckon. Her owner won't like that none!"

Now something showed in the woman's face. Just a contraction of muscles that lowered her thin brows and pinched her nostrils, but it was expressive of pure hatred. Narcissa held her breath, fully expecting the woman called Judah Daniel to spit in Calder's face. If she did—if she even raised her voice to him—the law would be on Calder's side.

Judah Daniel simply carried on with what she was doing, but her eyes never left Calder until the man turned away and said something to his companions that made them roar with laughter. Then Calder walked away, this time without looking back. As he did so, Judah Daniel shifted her gaze to Narcissa, and they exchanged a long look. It seemed to Narcissa that the woman was memorizing her face.

Mirrie and Brit Wallace came over to Narcissa, and Mirrie took her gently by the arm. Narcissa, not knowing what else to do, went along with them. "That cruel man, Calder," she said to them. "He lied just to torment the girl! Mirrie, isn't there anything we can do?"

Mirrie was quiet for a moment as they walked along. Then she said, "Even if we could buy the girl, and her family, what of all the rest? Richmond gets its money from trading slaves, more than from tobacco, flour, or any other *goods*. The only thing we can do is end it, all of it, forever." Mirrie's lips came together in a thin white line.

In the carriage, Narcissa twisted the velvet cords of her reticule and saw Jake Calder's face, heard the ugly words he had used, and imagined what she should have said to him. Mirrie scowled out the window. Brit crossed and recrossed his arms and legs, as if trying to keep his anger imprisoned in his body. At last he pulled out his ever-present notebook and pencil and began to make jottings.

Narcissa felt her face grow warm. It was uncomfortable to feel that an experience so disturbing to her was to be fodder for breakfast conversation in a country she had never even seen. She seethed for a moment. Then she put out her hand and gently closed the notebook. Brit Wallace looked up at her from under his brows. Then he replaced the notebook and pencil in his pocket. He seemed to be waiting for what she would say. Mirrie, too, looked up with curiosity.

"You have heard so many different opinions about slavery," Narcissa said quietly. "Today you have seen something of what it means. I am afraid we southerners will not be pleased to recognize ourselves in your dispatch."

"And," Mirrie broke in, "if we are not pleased, you can be sure we will hold it the author's fault and not our own."

Narcissa went on. "When you write your dispatch, you will come across as a Gulliver observing the Lilliputians. But you yourself have a heart and a mind. What do you believe, Mr. Wallace?"

Brit Wallace looked taken aback. "Mrs. Powers, the question is a new one for me since I arrived on these shores. Many people have been eager to assert that I must agree with their views, whatever they may be, but I do not think that is what you want."

Narcissa regarded him steadily. Beside Narcissa, Mirrie smiled encouragement.

"Let me first clarify that you are not requiring me to solve any problems that my answer may entail? It is one thing to ride the tiger, quite another to dismount."

Narcissa smiled a little in response. But still Brit Wallace was not ready to answer. He sat back, crossed his arms, stretched his legs, and looked down toward his boots.

"You must understand," he said at last, "that I am not impartial. I myself am a descendent of slaves."

Narcissa drew in her breath with surprise. Mirrie's mouth twitched up at the corners. They waited for him to continue.

"My family is thoroughly English now, but in fact we are Scots. My ancestors died at the Battle of Culloden, fighting for Bonnie Prince Charlie—fighting with a claymore against muskets. The Scots were not truly enslaved, perhaps, but enserfed. Our language was outlawed, our clan plaids were outlawed, playing the pipes was outlawed. Our lands were seized, and we were subdued and subjected to indignities by virtue of our Scottish blood."

"An answer by analogy," Mirrie said with quiet amusement.

"I read history at Oxford," Brit went on. "Virtually every race has at some time been branded inferior by another race. The Jews did it to the Samaritans, the Christians to the Jews, the Romans to the Saxons, the Saxons to the Celts—"

"So I suppose you view any such reasoning with a skeptical eye," Narcissa replied thoughtfully.

"Yes; I suppose I do," responded Brit Wallace with a smile.

They had come to the Exchange Hotel, where Wallace alighted.

Narcissa expected Mirrie to return to her arguments about the evils of slavery, and she was relieved when her friend was silent. But it wasn't long before Narcissa realized that her own mind, filled with memories of what she had seen, was making Mirrie's case better than any words could have done.

In the evening there were no callers, and Dr. Powers, Mirrie, and Narcissa made a quiet threesome, father and daughter reading, Narcissa mending a lace collar. After a time, the old gentleman relaxed his hold on the book. He was snoring softly.

Mirrie looked up at her father, then rose and reseated herself near Narcissa on the sofa. Narcissa sensed that Mirrie had been waiting to speak about some private subject.

"Narcissa," she began in a low, urgent tone, "we have received an invitation I feel we must accept." Mirrie flourished an envelope, and Narcissa recognized with a quick stab of pain the ivory paper and signet impressed in red wax— Mrs. Hughes had used the same paper and seal to write to her about her brother's illness.

Mirrie continued, "I believe if we are thoughtful we can use it to our advantage in investigating." Then she went on, in a more normal tone, "There is to be a party of ladies and gentlemen to tour the new hospital building that the medical college has just opened. The guests will gather about noon at the Egyptian building and then walk over to the new hospital. After the tour, we have been invited to dine at the Hugheses'. I know it might be hard for you to go back there," she added with a look of concern. "What do you think?"

Narcissa had known she would have to return to the Hugheses', to learn more about the various members of the household and find out, somehow, which of them had put Charley's letter in her Bible. She lifted her chin and said to Mirrie, "I agree. We must go." She thought again of what she had learned from Mrs. Stedman concerning the relationship between Hughes and Archer, based on Hughes's first marriage to Archer's sister, and the rumor that Archer had lost an inheritance to Hughes as a result of the marriage. Charley's letter mentioned angry words between the two men, yet for all she could see, they appeared more partners in crime than adversaries. The phrase "thick as thieves" came to mind. It would be helpful to see more of them together, and she hoped Archer would be one of the party.

The guests were gathering in the courtyard of the Egyptian building. The building at once drew and repulsed Narcissa, modeled as it was on an Egyptian temple—or a tomb. Its surface was smooth, sand-colored stucco, with two columns capped with a stylized palm-leaf design. The columns seemed curiously high and thick in proportion to the building, and the whole facade tapered upward, the effect being to dwarf the onlooker. Centered over the columns was a decoration in relief, a disk—were those two serpents curving up from below it?—and, fanning out on each side, massive wings like a buzzard's.

The ominous facade did not appear to affect the mood of the twenty or so people who had gathered in the courtyard to take the tour. The half-dozen ladies, Narcissa and Mirrie among them, had their parasols raised against the bright spring sun overhead. Rachel Hughes greeted them all, with an especially warm greeting and press of the hand for Narcissa. Narcissa thought that Rachel looked charming in a day dress of strawberry silk trimmed with deep ruffles of pale gray. Mirrie was likewise festive in peach and white, making Narcissa feel more crowlike than usual in black.

When Rachel turned away to speak to other guests, Mirrie detained Narcissa with a hand on her arm. "See that tall man over there, with the white beard?" Narcissa followed her eyes and saw a portly, smiling man of about sixty who stood with his hands on his comfortable stomach, enjoying the attention of two young women. "That's Carson Fielding, professor of chemistry and pharmacy." Narcissa and Mirrie looked at each other, and Mirrie gave a little shrug. It was difficult to imagine this jovial character involved in grave-robbing and murder.

Mirrie spoke again. "They say Dr. McPherson has gone back to South Carolina, something to do with the war. Although the medical college will continue to train students, many of them are returning to their homes or joining up with regiments here. I think you may as well concentrate on the doctors Charley named, Hughes and Archer, though you must keep in mind that no one involved with the medical college is in the clear."

The guests strolled in groups of two and three around the grounds, looking up at the palm-frond capitals of the columns and examining the low cast-iron fence that marked off the rise of land on which the building sat. On close inspection its posts proved to be three-foot-tall mummy cases, each with a plain, round knob at the "head" but footed with realistic bare toes.

Narcissa and Mirrie followed a group inside, passing between the columns beneath the forbidding disk with its buzzard's wings. The faint odor of rottenness increased the sensation of entering a tomb. But the chill Narcissa felt as she stepped inside the building was not a result of superstitious fear; its foot-thick walls made the building as cool as a root cellar.

The two women peeked into the lecture hall and peered into the glass cases lining the walls. In them were strange anatomical specimens. Most were unrecognizable to Narcissa. Then her eye fell on a jar in which was floating a newborn baby, covered with wrinkled gray skin. She recognized the head, but the limbs did not look human, curled up as they were, the internal organs hideously exposed. It had been born that way, she supposed, and died almost immediately. What had been the tragedy and shame of its mother was reduced to an object of curious interest to the young men who studied in the medical college—including her own brother.

What sea change took place in doctors' hearts, to make them able to see such things without revulsion? Suddenly another picture filled Narcissa's mind. When she was about fourteen, dogs had caught and mangled a kitten from the barn at Springfield. Charley had taken up the little animal, cleaned it, and assessed its wounds. "Don't be afraid to see suffering," he had told her, so serious for his thirteen years. "If you can't bear to see it, you can't help."

Narcissa shook her head to loosen the grip of horror and revulsion. Had Charley failed at last to bear the horror? Would she? She took Mirrie's arm and whispered, "Let's go back outside."

When they came out into the courtyard, Dr. Stedman was gathering the guests to walk over to the new hospital building nearby. In contrast to the Egyptian building, the new building was exceedingly plain—a three-story brick structure, narrow and deep, its facade relieved only by white-painted woodwork at the windows and doors.

"It's a shame to stay inside on a day like this," Rachel said. "I believe we shall have our dinner on the piazza—at least dessert." She then excused herself to return home and oversee the preparations.

They crossed over to the new building. Dr. Stedman, leading the group, beamed like a proud father. Dr. Hughes strode alongside Stedman, talking and gesturing with his nervous hands. Archer was nowhere in sight.

Their group paused in the entranceway, an unadorned space with doors opening on either side into little rooms. These rooms were plainly furnished with small desks and three or four chairs. Dr. Stedman explained that the rooms would be used as offices by whichever doctors were on duty at the time.

As they passed onto the first floor, Narcissa found herself at the back of the group. She half-listened as Dr. Stedman extolled the merits of the building, which housed eighty patient beds with water closets adjacent. Dr. Hughes, who had gone in with Dr. Stedman, was politely gesturing for the others to precede him. He had bowed in Narcissa's direction when he had first caught her eye, but had not spoken to her. Now she was aware that he seemed to be glancing in her direction.

As they prepared to mount the stairs, Dr. Hughes stood aside to let the others pass. Narcissa lingered so that she was the last to go up, and Dr. Hughes fell in beside her. He tried to smile—a movement of the cheek muscles only—then gave it up and composed his face in solemn lines.

"Ah, Mrs. Powers . . . I am sorry it has taken me so long to speak with you. I am pleased to see you have an interest . . ."

He seemed almost as uneasy as the first time they had met, when he had had to explain to Narcissa about her brother's injury and impending death. Narcissa nodded, wondering if this was simply the doctor's normal manner.

Dr. Hughes abandoned the attempt at polite conversation and took a businesslike tone. "I wanted to tell you that the students found some books that belonged to your brother. I have them for you in the office, over in the Egyptian building. It would be best to give the medical volumes to another student, who could use them, but I thought you should look through them first. I shall give them to you today if it is convenient for you to take them with you."

"I am much obliged to you," Narcissa replied. She felt only faintly the sting of Hughes's implication that she, a woman, could have no need of medical books. She was thinking of the letter Charley had written that had made its way to her. Suppose he had made some other notation concerning the grave-robbing or the crime he suspected, and placed it among his books? They reached the top of the stairs, and Dr. Hughes parted from her, edging through the group collecting at the near end of a long room lined with beds.

Narcissa's mind raced. Charley's books . . . perhaps another message was contained in them. She had to see those books right away. Abruptly, she turned and descended the steps to the first floor.

She quickly covered the hundred yards to the Egyptian building. A group of students was coming down the steps. Narcissa stopped one and asked, "Where is Dr. Hughes's office?"

"Down the left-hand staircase, first door on the right," the young man answered, "but there's nobody there right now. The lecture's just ended."

Narcissa acknowledged him with a nod and swept on, congratulating herself on her luck in arriving at a time when few people would be around. She should be able to look through the books without interruption. She walked quickly, not pausing to look around, hoping to discourage curiosity on the part of anyone she might meet. She did not want to be delayed by idle conversation.

The hall at the bottom of the stairs was dimly lit. Coming in from the bright daylight, Narcissa could see only a dark passageway, seemingly empty of people. The hall was lined with doors, closed or slightly ajar. It was unlikely she would be seen, Narcissa thought with relief. She made out which was the first door on the right, felt for the knob, and swung the door open. The smell of decay was strong, and she looked into the room, hesitating.

A reading lamp on the desk was lit. In the pool of light it cast, she saw a stack of thick books bound with twine. Charley's, surely.

Drawn by the sight, she stepped into the room. As she did so, something caught her eye. At her left, in shadow and invisible to anyone in the hall, stood a heavy wing chair. Someone was sitting in it, oddly slumped. Looking more closely, she saw a black man with grizzled hair, shabbily dressed, sleeves rolled back to reveal thin arms in which the veins and muscles were prominent. Two fingers of the left hand were missing below the knuckles. The man's head lolled, face toward the floor.

Narcissa froze, afraid to make a movement that would wake him. She wondered that anyone could sleep in such an uncomfortable position. Then she saw the strange, purplish cast of his flesh, the thin white cord that cut deep into his neck, and knew that he was dead.

Narcissa opened her mouth to scream. At that moment, she felt a disturbance of the air behind her. As she turned, sharp pain burst behind her left temple. Then all feeling left her.

Chapter Seven

RICHMOND
LATE APRIL

The first thing, for a while the only thing, Narcissa could sense was a single tone—like the highest note possible on a violin, drawn out by an endless bow. There was no light, no sense of time passing, no pain of any kind. Just the violin's haunting note, pure and unchanging.

Then the light came, and with it the throbbing in her temple. And next she saw faces. The face of a man peered at her. His mouth moved, but Narcissa heard nothing save the violin. She wanted to hear him, but she couldn't, and she hadn't the will to shake free of that high note.

She looked at the face with curiosity at first, wondering why it was there, and why she seemed to be lying on her back, looking up at it. Then she realized she knew the face. It was Dr. Hughes.

Then—as muffled voices began to register beneath the high note—fear seeped into Narcissa's consciousness. It was a vague discomfort at first. Presently, as details sorted themselves in her mind, Narcissa began to feel terror. She had been struck, she knew it now, and hovering over her was a man whom she suspected of unspeakable deeds.

The voices became more distinct, and the high note faded, leaving the pain and fear. Narcissa heard the muffled words "shock" and "cadaver." To the right stood Mirrie. Narcissa's hand shot out to grasp Mirrie's forearm with a suddenness and force that made her gasp.

"Lie still, Narcissa dear." Mirrie was bending over her, putting a cool hand on Narcissa's forehead. As Narcissa began to relax, she became aware that her bonnet had been removed and something soft but rough-textured—a wool blanket, a man's coat?—placed under her head. Some heavy fabric covered her skirts.

She saw that Dr. Hughes was in his shirtsleeves. His coat, she thought, under my head. Dr. Hughes . . .

Suddenly, memory came flooding back. In the office. A man, dead, strangled. She opened her eyes fully now, looking anxiously around her. She was lying on the floor in the same sparsely furnished office. The chair in which the dead man had been sprawled was empty. Narcissa tried to raise her head but could not. There was a sour taste in her mouth, and she swallowed, fighting nausea. Mirrie bent her face closer to Narcissa's. "Don't try to talk, dear," she said gently.

Dr. Hughes bent over them. His pale face looked bloodless. He was addressing Mirrie. "She must have fainted, then fell and hit her head. She has quite a nasty bump, and may be concussed. She should not try to get up or speak."

"There was . . . a dead man," Narcissa whispered to Mirrie.

"You were looking for my office"—Dr. Hughes spoke again, this time to Narcissa—"but you took the wrong staircase." He paused. "You must have walked right into the dissecting room. It's no sight for a lady. I am sorry; I feel I am to blame." He said the words with a cold formality.

Narcissa wanted to protest, to insist on what she had seen, but a wave of nausea took her strength away.

Dr. Hughes made a sweeping gesture around the room. "As you see—" he said, smiling slightly. "Of course, it is natural with a shock and an injury to the head that your memory would be confused. I found you at the door of the dissecting room, and I brought you back here to make you more comfortable."

Narcissa's throat closed. This man had carried her, unconscious, in his arms?

"How long . . . ?" Narcissa said faintly.

"Were you unconscious?" Hughes finished her question for her. "I've no idea. I left the tour a few minutes before the rest and found you here. Two minutes, or ten, no way to tell, unless of course we find someone who passed by at a certain time."

Mirrie looked up sharply. Narcissa turned her head away and pressed her fist to her mouth. "Just lie quiet, dear," Mirrie said again. This time Narcissa heard the words as a warning.

The decision was made to take Narcissa to the Hugheses' house nearby; later the doctor would look in on her and decide if she should take the return carriage ride to the Powerses' or stay longer.

Narcissa spoke only once, to ask for Charley's books. Dr. Hughes assured her they would be brought to her.

Dr. Hughes's manservant and Mirrie's driver, Will Whatley, bore her to the carriage for the short ride to the Hugheses', then up the steps to the same room in which she stayed on the night Charley died. Narcissa consented to be carried, saying nothing and trying very hard not to be sick.

Narcissa heard bits of what Hughes was saying to Mirrie about her injury. "If there was concussion, I believe it was slight. Nevertheless, it's quite likely she will never have a clear memory of the accident or the precipitating cause. Otherwise, there should be no harmful effects at all, and she should be fine in the morning, though you can never tell with head injuries. Sometimes the victim appears to recover, even goes about his business for a day or two, then suddenly drops dead. On autopsy, extensive lesions have been found. . . ." He continued in that vein, but Narcissa had ceased to listen.

I do remember what happened, Narcissa thought, although I cannot say it in front of you. She consoled herself with the thought that she should be fine in the morning.

As she had been before, Rachel Hughes was solicitous and, with Mirrie and a servant, helped Narcissa into bed. Then Rachel excused herself to see to her other guests; it had been decided the dinner party would go on as planned, since Narcissa's injury was not serious. Mirrie stayed with Narcissa.

When Narcissa felt well enough to prop herself up on a pillow, she touched the place where a knot had formed under her hair, just above her ear. Her hair was flecked with dried blood where the skin had been broken. "Listen to me, Mirrie. You have to believe me! I didn't walk into the dissecting room, faint, and hurt my head. A man was murdered, I found the body, and then somebody hit me!"

Mirrie looked at her friend in alarm. "Hit you! Tell me."

Narcissa gathered her thoughts, then spoke slowly. She told Mirrie what Dr. Hughes had said about having Charley's books in the office at the Egyptian building. "All I could think of was, what if Charley had left me another message, in those books? Perhaps Dr. Hughes had not found it yet. Or perhaps he put it there, I don't know," Narcissa added almost desperately. "I had to see those books before they went through another person's hands.

"I left the tour just after we reached the second floor. I went over to the Egyptian building and asked a student where the office was. I went into the foyer. You saw there are stairs on either side of the lecture hall that lead down to the lower level. I went down the left-hand staircase, as the student had said.

"It was very dark; I could hardly see. I found the first door on the right and opened it. I saw a packet of books on the table. But when I stepped into the room, I saw a man slumped in a chair. I thought he was asleep, but there was something odd about the way he was sitting. I looked at him for a long time before I realized that he was dead. Then I saw the cord around his neck, cutting into the flesh." Narcissa pressed her fingertips over her eyes as if to blot out the memory. "Then, before I could even think of what to do, someone hit me on the head."

"The dead man . . . what did he look like?" Mirrie asked.

"He was a black man. He looked old—sixty, maybe seventy. I didn't see his features clearly—Oh! He had two fingers that were just stubs."

"Cut off?" Mirrie asked.

"I suppose, but a long time ago. The skin had grown over. Don't you see? He must be another one they've killed to get a body for dissection."

Mirrie looked thoughtful. "Perhaps it was the body of an executed criminal, obtained legally," she said at last, but she was frowning.

"It's possible, I suppose," Narcissa responded doubtfully. Her eyelids drooped as she touched the tender swelling on her head. She was silent for a few seconds, then looked up at Mirrie. "But then, why hit me on the head?" Anger was gathering in her voice. "And why make up an absurd story about my opening the wrong door?"

Mirrie smiled grimly. "Dr. Hughes wants to make sure that, if you say anything about what you saw, you'll be taken for an addle-brained female.

"And," she continued, "I don't see any way that you can prove him a liar. I think it's best you appear to accept his version of what happened—at least for now. If he didn't strike you himself, he must be protecting the person who did. You must not let him suspect that you know about the dead man."

Mirrie paused, then went on, her tone more hesitant. "There is another possibility. . . . Hughes could be telling the truth, or what he thinks is the truth. Someone else could have attacked you, then carried you to the dissecting room, where Hughes says he found you."

Narcissa shuddered. Again she saw herself lying unconscious in the arms of some man whose hands were stained with crime. Cameron Archer? She thought aloud. "Dr. Hughes said he left the tour before it ended, but he gave no reason for going back to the Egyptian building rather than coming here, where his guests would soon be arriving. Dr. Archer, I didn't see; did you?"

Mirrie shook her head, then added with a thin-lipped smile, "Dr. Archer is here for dinner. Mrs. Hughes told me he asked that his regards be conveyed to you."

Narcissa put her hand to her temple, absentmindedly rubbing the sore spot. "I did not see him," she said again, "but he may have been in the building, perhaps in the dissecting room. And students were around, though I didn't see any whom I knew." Then her voice grew more urgent. "Mirrie. Do you have your little penknife with you?"

"Yes, but . . . if you want something written, can I—"

"No," Narcissa interrupted, her voice low but fierce, "I don't want to sharpen a quill. I want a *knife*."

Without a word, Mirrie picked up her reticule and fished out a tiny knife that folded into a silver case. She handed it to Narcissa, who tucked it into her waistband and lay back, cold under the blankets. The nausea was waning, but her head still hurt so that her body seemed to ache with it.

A few minutes later a servant entered the room with a sickroom tray of boiled egg and tea. Mirrie rose, thanked the servant, and asked her to put the tray on a nearby table. "I'm Miss Powers, Mrs. Powers's sister-in-law," she said to the servant. "What is your name?"

"Jane Scott," the servant replied in a low, pleasant voice.

"How strange that Mrs. Powers's brother should have been brought to this house in his illness," Mirrie said. "She came here to be with him—at his death, as it turned out."

Jane made a consoling murmur.

"And now she is here, injured."

"Is she hurt real bad?" asked the servant gently.

"No, I don't think so," Mirrie said. "Dr. Hughes says that by this time tomorrow, she should be able to travel."

"Did you attend Master Charley at all?" Mirrie continued. "What a sad loss that was!"

"Yes'm. He was a real nice boy. He had a gentle way about him. Didn't want to be no trouble."

From under her eyelashes Narcissa stole a glance at the servant. She recognized Jane Scott as the one who had helped her into bed after Charley's death. Jane was in her forties, softly plump of body and face, dressed in gray homespun with an apron and headscarf of spotless white.

"An illness like that must be quite a disruption to a household." Mirrie spoke with warm sympathy. "Was he simply far too ill to travel?"

Jane hesitated. "No, ma'am, not at first. It seemed like it was such a little thing it was a shame to send him home in the middle of his schooling. Mrs. Rachel had him brought here and tended him herself till I came. Then all of a sudden it did seem like he was too sick to be moved. Couldn't hold any food down. He got weak real fast."

"And of course Mrs. Powers came then," Mirrie said.

"Yes, ma'am. I was powerful glad when she got here."

"Did he say anything particular, that you heard?" Mirrie asked.

"No, ma'am. He was just raving mostly," the servant replied, a note of sadness in her voice.

Narcissa's thoughts seemed loosened, disconnected from one another. What if the things Charley had said weren't raving? She herself may have understood, especially if she had had the whole of Charley's letter. Frustration and anger were making the nausea return. Narcissa forced herself to calm her thoughts, to wait.

Mirrie continued her questioning. "Didn't it take you away from your regular duties to have to care for him?"

Jane answered readily enough. "Well, I was pretty new to the household then, been here just a week or two before he took sick. I lives over to Hanover Courthouse, but the Hugheses needed an extra servant quick and fixed it with my master."

"I thought the Hugheses had a large household?"

"Yes'm. There is just the four of us here in the house, but I heard tell they has about forty out at the plantation in Midlothian. They is Dr. Hughes's slaves that belonged to his first wife, and they is field hands mostly. She don't like to have them in town, and she don't go there much. The overseer, he come up here to make his reports."

"So," Mirrie persisted, "Mrs. Hughes has her own servant, who probably has been with her since she was a girl."

"Yes'm, that be Phebe."

"I assume Dr. Hughes has a manservant who has been with him for a long time—"

"Oh, yes, ma'am, Percy."

"—and a driver, of course."

Jane corrected her. "Percy, he drive the carriage too."

"And a cook?" Mirrie continued.

Jane nodded agreement.

"So, four of you," Mirrie concluded.

"Yes, ma'am."

There was a pause. "Would you be wanting anything else, Mrs. Powers?" Jane asked finally.

Narcissa smiled and said softly, "No, Jane. You may go. Thank you."

Narcissa heard the door close. Mirrie rose, then returned to perch on the bed. Narcissa opened her eyes. "Do you feel like eating?" Mirrie asked gently.

"No."

Mirrie paused, then said, "Would it be all right to talk?"

"Yes. I heard most of what you and Jane were saying. Do you think—"

That was enough encouragement for Mirrie. "I think I have solved one mystery for you! When you are feeling better, ask her yourself. Jane Scott is responsible for the paper in your Bible, I am certain of it."

"How can you be so sure?"

"Well," Mirrie replied, "first of all, since she is not the personal servant of one of the family, she would have been more likely to have been alone. So she would have had the most opportunity. And she has the slightest connection of personal loyalty to the family. A servant of longer standing would likely have taken what she found to her master or mistress, or more probably completed the destruction herself. I didn't ask if the cook had long ties with the household, because of course she's not likely to have been up here at all."

"But could not Mrs. Hughes have done it—hidden the paper in my Bible?"

"No," said Mirrie, shaking her head. "Leaving aside the question of loyalty to her husband. It was an indecisive action, the act of someone making a compromise with her conscience. Jane knew Charley wanted to communicate with you. She knew someone—her master or mistress, most likely—wanted the paper destroyed. Leaving it in the Bible may have been symbolic, in a way: if it was God's will that you find it, then you would."

Narcissa knew there must be objections to Mirrie's reasoning, but she could not summon them. She felt tired but calm, strangely remote from the subject they were discussing, as if her injured body had become a sort of cocoon.

Just after five o'clock that evening, Dr. Hughes came back to check on Narcissa. He had brought Charley's books with him, and he left them on the table next to the chair. He examined Narcissa by gently probing the knot on her head and asking general questions. Narcissa was careful to assure him that she remembered nothing of what had happened, feigning embarrassment and regret over her supposed faint. Then he left, turning down the gaslight.

Narcissa felt herself relax into the delicious sleep that comes when nausea and pain subside. It was about eight o'clock when Rachel Hughes brought a second tray with a boiled egg, toast, and tea. This time Narcissa felt she could eat a little. Mirrie left to go home, saying she would return the next day to fetch Narcissa.

"What a strange accident!" Rachel said wonderingly. "Do you remember anything of the sight that caused you to faint?"

"No," Narcissa said with what she hoped was convincing puzzlement. "Nothing."

"That is a blessing. It must have been truly awful, to see a human body . . . exposed like that. I am sure *I* would faint," Rachel said with a shudder.

Narcissa was puzzled. Rachel tended Charley, she thought, when, God help me, he was little more than a corpse. Can she really be so horrified by an anatomy? Narcissa framed a careful response. "Come upon unexpectedly, the sight would be a shock. But I have sometimes thought it would be wonderful to have medical training, to explore the secrets that foreordain so much of our human experience. Our experience as women, especially."

As if a veil had been lowered, all animation left Rachel Hughes's face. Narcissa wondered if the doctor's wife perceived a desire for medical training as unseemly in a woman. Or—Narcissa remembered the tragic history of Rachel Hughes's confinement—perhaps even an oblique reference to childbearing brought on a depression of spirits. Narcissa felt the familiar stab of pain and regretted her chance remark. There could be no grief equal to that of losing a child. She wanted to tell Rachel that she understood, that she herself had lost a child, but she could not. The two women sat in silence for a few moments, then turned to innocuous topics. Rachel Hughes took her leave soon afterward, wishing Narcissa a good sleep.

As members of the household retired one by one, familiar

daytime noises yielded to silence. Then the very silence gave voice to the curious creaks and sighs that bedevil the sleepless. Narcissa found herself starting at every sound. Once she sat up abruptly, sure that a shadow had passed by her door, blotting out the low light from the gas lamp left burning in the hall. She stared at the line of light beneath the door until her head ached.

Again and again she went through the sequence of events that ended in the blow to her head. She could recall nothing that gave a clue to the identity of her attacker. But she could not shake the conviction that Hughes and Archer were both involved, guilty of complicity if not of the actual deed. Had she been able to call witnesses, the body she had found might have been proof of burking. Hughes and Archer, or someone they were protecting, had killed that old man, and perhaps come very near to killing her. That being the case, she realized, it was as well she had not called out.

If they suspect I could remember what I saw, she thought, I am in danger here in this house.

Realizing she would sleep no more that night, Narcissa rose and turned up the lamp. She opened the penknife and placed it on the table, then sat in the chair to wait for morning.

❦

The great slab scraped as it shifted. Cyrus Roper did not look around to see if the noise had attracted notice—did not even wipe away the sweat that ran into his eyes. The tendons stood out in his neck as he exerted all his strength upon the iron rod he was using to lever the slab from its resting place flush with the street.

The slab rose a few more inches. Cyrus maneuvered it sideways, then lowered it onto the dirt. He stood, flexed his

[122]

shoulders, and looked around. The street was deserted and dark as a tomb. Even in the heart of a city swollen with would-be soldiers, and their would-be panders, whores, and robbers, no one stirred.

Where the stone had been pulled away, there was now an opening into the street wide enough to admit a man's body. Cyrus pulled a bandanna up to cover his nose and mouth, then lowered himself onto a ledge about two feet wide that rimmed a deeper hole. He reached back through the opening to fetch the bull's-eye lantern.

Crouching, he steadied himself. Then he slid the lantern open just enough to send a narrow beam of light down into the hole.

The pit was filled with body parts—severed arms and legs, some with ragged saw marks still visible, others soft and indistinct with corruption. These lay about four feet below him, in a round well perhaps ten feet across. Below them lay the bones, flesh eaten away by lime, the memento mori of a nightmare.

Cyrus shone his light on the far wall, then began to pass the beam slowly back and forth over the jumbled horror. He made a dozen passes back and forth, at each pass bringing the beam closer to where he crouched. Several times he stopped to take a longer look at something—a hand, some matted hair.

He spotted something that made him stop. It was a hand, severed at the wrist but flesh mostly intact, with two fingers missing below the knuckles. He could see that the wounds were old, healed over.

Cyrus stared at the hand for a long moment, his face expressionless. "Old Billy," he said at last. "I knowed you was here."

He continued to search the pit. At last, when the lantern

beam was pointing almost directly below him, he halted again. A few inches of white cloth were visible.

Cyrus reached inside his shirt and pulled out a roll of rough burlap sacking. Caught on it was the small leather bag on a leather cord that Cyrus wore around his neck. He took hold of the bag, rubbed it between his thumb and forefinger; his lips moved. Then he tucked the bag on its cord back inside his shirt. The roll of burlap he placed on the ledge beside him; then he unrolled it. Inside it lay a coil of stiff wire and a thick nail bent like a fishhook. He wound several inches of wire around the nail, then extended his arm and lowered the nail even with the cloth.

Cyrus maneuvered the wire until the nail snagged the cloth, then pulled. The cloth yielded a little, then slipped off the nail. Again he tried; again the cloth yielded, then slipped.

Cyrus was patient. At last the cloth was secured. Slowly, carefully, he pulled it free so that it dangled over the pit. The cloth looked to be more than two feet long, less than a foot wide, frayed or fringed at the ends. The portions not stained beyond recognition were white, with a slight sheen.

Cyrus reeled in his catch until the cloth was beside him. He took hold of the nail and shook it so that the cloth fell from it onto the sacking. He unhooked the nail, coiled the wire, and placed them on the cloth. Then he rolled up the sacking with the cloth inside and replaced it in his shirt.

Finally he shut off the beam from the dark lantern, lifted himself out into the street. He pulled down the bandanna and took a deep breath of the cool night air, then let it out with a shudder. He shoved the heavy slab back into place over the pit.

≽≼

As the dawn glowed behind the shutters, Narcissa felt the sense of safety that comes with the light. She closed the penknife and replaced it in her waistband, then lay on the bed and slept a little.

Soon there was a low knock on the door. "Come in!" Narcissa called, sitting up and fingering the little knife. The servant Jane came into the room with a breakfast tray. She set it on the table next to the bed, then opened the shutters. The expression on her face was as gentle as her voice had been. Narcissa released her hold on the knife, a little ashamed of giving in to nerves.

Mirrie's words of the day before came back to Narcissa. She wanted to question Jane about Charley, but would she be putting the servant in danger? Jane's untroubled answers to Mirrie's questions showed she had not been alarmed by the circumstances surrounding Charley's death. And, in any case, Narcissa thought, she would keep Jane's secret.

Jane was about to leave again when Narcissa asked her to close the door, then beckoned her to stand by the bed. "I heard a little of what you said yesterday evening to Miss Powers. I want to thank you for taking care of my brother."

Jane smiled. "It weren't no trouble."

Narcissa plunged on, feeling her heart beat faster but reassured by the woman's quiet manner. "I also wanted to ask you something. On the night I was here—the night Charley died—did you put a piece of paper in this Bible? Because if you did," Narcissa went on without pausing, "I want to thank you for that also." Narcissa looked into Jane's mild brown eyes, trying to put strength and reassurance into the look.

"Yes'm." The answer was a whisper. "Master Charley talked about you so much, I knowed he meant that letter to go to you. It didn't seem right to burn it."

"Were you asked to burn it?" Narcissa probed carefully.

"No'm, I found it in the ashes in Master Charley's room. That was after he was took so bad. I knowed it wasn't him that put it there. I reckon one of the servants was careless, didn't know what it was. I saved it out of the fire, and when you come I felt like you should have it."

Jane looked a little uneasy, Narcissa thought, but not fearful; her concern seemed to come from having done something beyond her appointed role—something the "white folks" might not approve of. But if Jane believed the act of burning to be a servant's mistake, why had she not given the paper to her mistress? Narcissa thought she could guess. She herself had seen mistresses berate their servants for some small deviation from routine. A question could have gotten another servant, or perhaps Jane herself, a tongue-lashing or worse.

"You did right, Jane. I think I was supposed to have it. Did you—know what it was about?" Narcissa tried to keep her tone light, but she could sense a slight withdrawal in Jane Scott.

"I can't read," the servant said simply.

Narcissa thought it would be unkind, and probably futile, to question her further. "You did the right thing by saving the paper for me. It was a letter he was trying to write to me in his illness. It makes me feel closer to him to have it, and I thank you."

Jane returned Narcissa's smile, then left the room. Narcissa settled down to eat her breakfast. More than ever she was eager to get out of the house. After a time she heard a soft knock, and Mirrie entered, Jane behind her. Jane had Narcissa's dress from the day before, brushed and spot-cleaned, and clean undergarments brought by Mirrie.

Mirrie stood near the window while Jane helped Narcissa dress and arrange her hair. The sound of voices reached them through the open window. Mirrie leaned down to look out into the narrow side yard below, then recoiled. Their attention drawn by the abrupt movement, Narcissa and Jane turned to look at her.

"Come here, Narcissa." Mirrie whispered. "Don't let yourself be seen."

Narcissa stood in shadow against the wall and leaned forward carefully until she could see the figures below. Then she too drew back. Almost directly below the window stood two men. One was a black man, Dr. Hughes's manservant, she thought—the one Jane had said was called Percy. The other—she thought she recognized the pomaded blond hair, and the bandaged nose made her certain.

"It's Jake Calder," Narcissa whispered. Mirrie nodded. "Do you know him?" Narcissa spoke in a low voice to Jane, who had come up behind her.

"Yes, ma'am," Jane answered, "I know him. He's the Hugheses' overseer down to their place in Midlothian. Like I said, he come up here most every week."

Narcissa felt her bruised temple throbbing. If that evil man is around here often, could he not be involved in the violence Charley had discovered, or suspected?

"Was he here when Charley was sick?"

The subject of Jake Calder seemed to make Jane uneasy. She looked down, frowning, and twisted her apron in her hands. "I . . . I ain't sure."

"Charley and that man had an argument," Narcissa invented, hoping the fabrication was not too obvious. "I know it would have upset Charley to see him . . . when he was ill."

Jane shook her head. "Jake Calder didn't visit Master Charley; at least not that I knowed of."

"It's all right," Narcissa said soothingly. "It's just that Charley didn't like the man, and I . . . I'd rather he not see me here."

Jane nodded. Narcissa felt sure that Jane could have said

much more about Jake Calder had she felt free to express herself. She thought again of the Negro woman who had defied Calder and come to the aid of the young girl at the slave auction. By sheer force of will that woman had driven Calder away, bested him in front of the other men. A brave thing to do, but also foolhardy. Such a man—full of pride, but without honor—would have his revenge by whatever means came to hand.

Back at the Powerses' home, Narcissa rested and walked in the garden during the daylight hours. After retiring early to her room that night, she lit the lamp, put on her nightgown, and settled herself in the most comfortable chair, with Shandy in her lap and Charley's books stacked on the table next to her. Five of the seven books were old schoolbooks, including a Latin grammar she recognized as a gift to Charley from Rives. Narcissa smiled sadly as she laid it aside.

She concentrated on the two books having to do with medicine. *The American Dispensatory* was a dog-eared old volume, published in 1814, that guided physicians in the preparation of their medicines. She leafed through it, but the book had been so thoroughly used over the years that it was hard to single out what Charley might have marked as important. After a few minutes she replaced it on the stack, eager to inspect the second medical volume. Shandy, roused by the movement, lifted his spaniel eyes to her face, then settled again with his chin on his paws.

The Dissector was a newer book, about eight inches high and four wide, bound in brown leather. Leafing through the pages, Narcissa saw that the book's purpose was to guide the process of dissection and aid the student in identifying the body parts—bones, muscles, tissues, down to the most min-ute—as they were exposed to view. The underlinings and notations were in Charley's hand, but she was soon disappointed to find that none had any obvious connection to the subject of the letter.

She then decided to go through the book from beginning to end. The introduction, entitled "On Dissecting, and On Anatomical Preparations," gave step-by-step instructions to the student, beginning with dress, which she read should be an apron, extending from the neck to halfway down the legs, and a pair of sleeves. Then the instruments were enumerated: at least four knives, one single hook, one double hook, one pair of forceps, one pair of scissors, one blow pipe, and two crooked needles. The sternum, she read, should be divided longitudinally through its middle. The chest cavity could then be opened to give access to the heart and other organs. It was remarkably like preparing a chicken or turkey for cooking, Narcissa thought irreverently.

The picture conjured by these words was so vivid it took her breath away: a shadowy figure, so dressed and fingering these instruments, standing over the body of a dead woman. The purpose of some of the instruments—knives, hooks, scissors—was so plain, it was almost as if she could see him taking them up and using them to undo the work of the Creator. But what could a blow pipe be used for?

Narcissa shuddered, then reminded herself that her mind's eye was envisioning the pursuit of knowledge in the cause of medicine. If it seemed to her the practice of some unholy art, it was her own ignorance that was painting the scene in lurid colors.

By turns fascinated and repelled, Narcissa read on through the various preparations used to preserve anatomical specimens to the section on "Precautionary Measures Against Dissecting Wounds." This brief section she read again and again, trying to understand. The writer cautioned students that, although they might wound themselves while performing a postmortem examination, such wounds were not necessarily more dangerous than the prick of a needle, of a briar, or of an oyster shell.

One exception seemed to be exposure of a wound or abrasion to the matter or fluids of corpses dead of disease "of an Erysipelatous character." In such a case, the dissector should immediately cleanse his wound by sucking or drawing the blood. If inflammation resulted, some simple treatments were suggested. But from what Dr. Hughes and the servant Jane had said, Charley's case had turned serious much more quickly than expected.

A corpse dead of erysipelas could, it seemed, transmit the disease to the student performing the anatomy. But how? The book seemed very hazy on that point. Had Charley received the treatments suggested? And if not, was it his own youthful carelessness—as Hughes had suggested—that was at fault? Or had Charley been allowed to die by men who feared him, feared his integrity?

The thought came to Narcissa not as a surprise but as a recognition. She realized she had been refusing to admit, even to herself, her suspicion that Hughes and Archer could have saved Charley's life. At the very least, they could have summoned her sooner. Instead, they had watched and waited. When they saw that Charley would not recover, that weakness and delirium had left him unable to speak to her, only then had she been sent for.

So she now believed, or half-believed. But was it true? Narcissa drew in her breath and let it out again with a sigh that was almost a sob. She simply didn't know enough to puzzle out whether malice or mischance had delayed the summons. But now the killing of an old black man had given a more tangible reality to the image of the murdered woman evoked by Charley's letter. The two were well suited to be victims of burking: one poor and uncared-for, by the state of his clothing, and old; the other rendered valueless to her owners by an illness from which she might not recover.

What could she do? She must somehow find another opportunity to talk with Dr. Stedman and his wife, to find out more about the medical school, its need for bodies, and the physicians whose oath to save lives might have been forgotten in their desire to unlock the secrets of life and death.

At last Narcissa rose from her seat. She hugged the sleeping Shandy and put her face down to his warm muzzle, seeking to banish for a moment her preoccupation with death. She carried the dog down the stairs and placed him gently on his cushion near the little hinged door into the backyard. Then she made her way back up the stairs and into bed.

Chapter Eight

RICHMOND
EARLY MAY

Judah Daniel stood at her door, looking out into the dark. The air was cooling around her, and she could hear the rush of the James. The moon had set, and the fateful comet sprayed its brightness in an arc at the horizon.

The comet meant a change was coming. Everyone knew it. And everyone had a different vision of what the change would be. But tonight the comet seemed to blaze inside her. She had dressed in dark clothes without a speck of white, so as not to be seen, and she had uncovered her hair and taken the braids out so that crisp curls—black, with just a few strands of silver—floated out from her head and brushed her shoulders. Her unbound hair gave her a feeling of release that brought a rare smile to her face.

Soon Cyrus would come, and together they would go up the hill and over the fence into Hollywood Cemetery. She took deep breaths, willing her heart to slow. She was not afraid, but she could not help thinking of what might happen if she were caught. She was risking the pain and humiliation of the lash, even a jail sentence, for being out after curfew—

plus whatever other charge the law would see fit to levy. And if Jake Calder was out riding with his ruffian friends, looking to pay her back by getting her in trouble with the law, the risk would be greater than usual.

But she could not turn back. She had felt the danger on Cyrus, even more so since the urgent message he had sent at dusk asking that the rites to pacify the spirit of the dead woman be performed tonight. Cyrus was in the web of a spider whose poison brought death. After we do the rites, she thought, I'll tell Cyrus he best get far away from here, maybe go up north. He needs to feel the spirit of the dead woman is at rest. But feeling that won't make him safe. If he gets to thinking about how those doctors knew where the body was buried—if he gets to worrying about how his father Old Billy is keeping secrets from him—

Then she shuddered. Old Billy hadn't seemed afraid of her, but if Cyrus ran away, Old Billy would suspect she had advised him. The spider would feel the break in its web and come at a run—toward her.

Judah Daniel heard a rustling in the bushes at the back of the yard. Cyrus was beside her in a moment. He moved quickly in the dark, and Judah Daniel remembered that he had had years of practice.

Cyrus met Judah Daniel with a rush of words. He panted them out, short of breath more from fear than from exertion, she thought.

"Old Billy didn't come home last night. I knowed the plateye got him. So I went to look for him. I found him. In the pit. I had a kind of a feeling he'd be there, with . . . her." Cyrus darted a look over his shoulder as if he expected to see some monstrous shape coming after him.

Hiding her shock, Judah Daniel reached out to take hold of his forearm. She had to reassure him, get him to trust her, so that he would follow her counsel. The danger was closing fast, though not in the form she'd expected.

A little of the tension eased out of him, and he went on. "I figured maybe nobody put the quicklime in, since we was supposed to do it. When I looked, I—" He broke off, swallowing and looking away. "He was there, like I thought. I knowed it was him because of the fingers. They rotted and he had to have them cut off, years ago."

Judah Daniel saw again those stumps of fingers. Old Billy himself was dead now, murdered and thrown into the pit. Didn't mean he hadn't killed the woman; just meant the doctors who had paid him to do it were trying to keep their secrets, cover their tracks. Cyrus was more in danger than ever. The quicker he got away from Richmond, the better.

Cyrus stepped closer, lowered his voice. "We got to do the rites tonight. He had her scarf with him in the pit. Like I told you, when we dug up the gal, there was a white cloth wrapped around her head. It'd bring a lot of money, Old Billy said. He said it was a silk scarf like a gentleman would wear. So he saved it. He hadn't ought to kept it, but the doctor said take her in her graveclothes, so I guess he figured that gave him leave.

"You told me to get the cloth to bury it with the rites. I never could find it in the house. But it was there with him in the pit. I reckon she was angry with him for taking it. I don't want to have it on me. We got to bury it now. I brought Old Billy's cup, too, to do the rites for him." He hoisted for her inspection a bag he had tucked under his arm.

Judah Daniel pulled her shawl tight around her and stepped forward. "Let's go."

Silently, swiftly, the two disappeared into the night.

• • •

In the darkness, inside the cemetery fence, Judah Daniel felt a wild elation. She could sense the spirit moving in her, but separate from her, like the feelings of another soul.

She was, she thought, a rational woman. She knew how to heal with herbs and medicines of all kinds, African, European, and Indian. Sometimes she felt as if the spiritual part of her healing was a costume she put on to inspire faith in those she was doctoring. But at other times, she knew her ability to heal came from a force outside of herself, and on this night she felt its power.

The cold white tombstones, vaults, and statues did not move her. But as she and Cyrus hurried up the hill toward the place overlooking the river where the black woman had been buried, and dug up, the darkness seemed to grow deeper and the chill more tangible. When at last they came to the place, it seemed to her that, among the dead white stones that crowded together in that space, the shadows were alive.

On Judah Daniel's instruction, Cyrus drew out a spade and began to dig. When he had a small trench about two feet deep and a little more in length, she put her hand on his arm. She pinched a bit of dirt from the hole, placed it in the bag with the herbs, and tied it. She gave the bag to Cyrus, who put it in his pocket.

He handed her the piece of silk. She turned it over in her hands. It was still silky in places not stiffened by blood and filth, and her fingers traced a letter *H*, embroidered in white thread on the white cloth. She folded it and placed it on a flat gravestone. Then she held her hands out for the pottery cup. She placed it on the cloth and broke it into pieces with the spade, then wrapped the cloth around the pieces and laid it in the hole.

"Say the words I told you," she whispered to Cyrus.

He was silent for a moment, then began to whisper into

the earth. "Dead woman, we done wrong by you to dig you up, but someone done worse. I brung these things to give ease to your soul. Don't follow me no more. If your soul can't find no rest, follow the ones that killed you."

He paused, then began again, "Old Billy, I break your cup to set your soul free from this earth."

Judah Daniel handed him the spade, and he refilled the hole. She stood reading the names on the monuments. Cyrus finished and wiped his hands on his pants.

It was Judah Daniel's turn to speak. She felt the air around her crowded, waiting. "Soul, I know you listening close here. You tied to this earth with anger and hate. I conjure you to let this man alone. He have it in mind to change his life, and he ain't going to trouble you no more."

She spoke to the dead woman. "Sister, I feel for you. You holding your anger, you holding your strength. Give them to me, and you rest with God."

They returned to Judah Daniel's house just as the sky began to lighten. She gave her parting instructions quickly. "Go to the Loyal Brethren's safe house. Wash yourself and burn all your clothes. They'll give you everything you need and put you on the road north." She gave him directions to the safe house. "Don't go back home," she said at last. "That's where the danger is for you. Believe me, you could walk into the armory carrying a rifle safer than you can walk into your house."

In the glimmer of the new morning, she watched his retreating back. He didn't turn around to wave at her. Damn, if he don't mean to go home despite all I said.

≥≤

With Mirrie's help, Narcissa had found it easy enough to arrange a dinner party at the Powers home, with the Stedmans, Nat Cohen, and Brit Wallace invited. She had even found herself enjoying the preparations. At Boisseux's shop on Main Street she had bought fresh fruit: Messina oranges, Palermo lemons. She had held an orange the size of a child's fist and inhaled the fragrance, picturing the glossy-leaved branches from which it was plucked under sunny Mediterranean skies. She had chosen lobsters and salmon fresh from cold northern waters. She and Beulah had made the lobster into a salad, using Narcissa's mother's recipe for mayonnaise. The salmon had been poached and served with a lemony sauce.

After a dessert of pound cake and fruit, as they sipped their wine in the parlor, Dr. Stedman talked about preparations for treatment of ill and wounded soldiers.

"How would medical students acquire the surgical proficiency to become field surgeons?" Mirrie asked, focusing on Stedman the flattering attention that, Narcissa knew, was a warning sign that her friend was after something.

"We offer excellent preparation in anatomy. As Mrs. Powers knows, to her sorrow!"

Narcissa felt stung by Dr. Stedman's jest at her supposed weakness in fainting at the sight of a cadaver. She accepted it silently, reminding herself that safety lay in appearing to remember nothing of the dead man she had seen.

"Of course," Stedman expanded, "our hospital has given us the care of such poor fellows as have a foot crushed by a wagon, say, or are injured in some similar way. Amputation is required, of course, in any case of compound fracture— that is, where the broken bone pierces the skin, if you will excuse such a description."

Narcissa decided that, rather than endure unending references to her supposed delicacy, she would be as direct as she could. "Dr. Stedman, I assure you my fainting was a momentary weakness. I believe I could stand the sight of—wounds quite well if prepared for it. The medical college advertises the availability of cadavers for dissection as an attraction for students. I know my brother was excited about the opportunity to explore these mysteries firsthand."

Stedman nodded sadly at this reference to Charley. Then his attention was distracted by Cohen, who was offering to refill his wineglass from the sparkling decanter. He sipped from the glass and smiled his appreciation.

Narcissa pressed on. "How are the cadavers procured?"

"Well, you know—" There was silence for a moment as Dr. Stedman sipped his wine. Narcissa felt the struggle between his professional zeal and his concern for her supposedly delicate feelings. At last, fortified with pride and wine, he exhibited the loquacity of the successful man when invited to talk about his profession. "There is no legal provision for obtaining cadavers for dissection. This despite the fact that careful, firsthand observation—or better yet, performance—of an anatomy has been the basis of medical schooling for a century now.

"I regret to say that this imposes a certain inevitable hypocrisy on the profession. At every medical school worthy of the name, cadavers are procured, either by the demonstrator of anatomy and his students, or by the janitors in some of the larger colleges. Of course, they are careful to avail themselves only of the most wretched residents of the potter's fields—those without friends and family to mourn them or visit the graves. It is the living, after all, whose feelings must be considered."

Mrs. Stedman overheard. " 'They?' You are unduly modest, my dear." She turned to Narcissa. "As a young man, my husband served as demonstrator of anatomy and oversaw the procuring of cadavers. He was quite good at it. The students used to call him 'Deadman' Stedman."

Dr. Stedman chuckled and glanced slyly at Narcissa, who gratified his expectations by raising her shoulders in a panto-mime shiver. An interesting bit of information, she thought; for all his white hair and innocent look, I should not assume that he is not involved. "And now," she asked, "does the demonstrator of anatomy fill this role?"

"Oh, Archer?" Stedman replied. "Ordinarily, he only accepts delivery, as it were, but by a singular happenstance . . . Well, of course, the warm weather will soon force a halt to all activities involving cadavers. But if it were not for that fact, Archer might find himself out performing the job. Our Old Billy—known to his black confreres as the 'sack-'em-up man'—has not been seen for several days. His son Cyrus, who helped him in the work, has disappeared also. Cyrus believes a lot of superstitious nonsense. For all that he was under Old Billy's thumb, I think he did the job with his knees knocking. Perhaps the old man is under the weather, and his son took the occasion to run away."

"They are slaves?" Narcissa asked.

"No, freedmen. They are paid for their work. Of course, handling corpses is not the healthiest occupation. There is an unwholesome miasma about the graveyard. Old Billy got quite sick years ago—gangrene. Had to have two fingers cut off."

Narcissa almost cried out. She saw in her mind the dead man she had found. The middle and index fingers of his left hand were stubs. A black man, old, but strong from physical labor. Old Billy. She looked across at Mirrie, who returned her look, eyebrows raised. She too had caught the significance of the description.

Narcissa began piecing together the information she had gained. Old Billy must have known about the murders, maybe even carried them out while Hughes and Archer stayed behind the scenes. Then something had happened. Perhaps it was Charley's becoming suspicious. The doctors felt their secret was no longer safe. They had killed their henchman Old Billy, and perhaps his son, too.

She had stumbled upon the body of Old Billy, and she had been attacked. Old Billy must not have been dead very long when she walked into the room and discovered his body. And his killer, or killers, must have been there in the room, or concealed somewhere close by. Had she walked in a moment sooner, they would have had to make sure she was dead, or risk discovery.

Hughes and Archer must feel threatened, she thought, her mind racing. All these deaths, and still the consequences of their evil were spreading like ripples in the water after the stone has disappeared. They should feel safer now, though, she reasoned. Even if she were to "remember" and tell what she saw, the body was no doubt disposed of so that it would never be found. So even if she remembered, even if she told, there was no proof. She would be dismissed as—what was the term Mirrie had used?—an addle-headed female.

Narcissa felt the blood rise into her face. She was so angry she could hardly keep her seat. These men were evil. She was more determined than ever that they should not escape the consequences of their crimes.

"Still," Dr. Stedman was saying in a querulous voice, "our resurrection men shouldn't just disappear. It imposes quite an inconvenience on the faculty." He frowned, twirling the wineglass's stem between his thumb and fingers. Then he sat back and took another sip of wine.

Brit Wallace—who had been listening intently, neglecting the brimful wineglass at his hand—leaned forward. "Can you tell me about those superstitions you mentioned?"

"Concerning the dead? Not so very different from the myths and superstitions of every country, including your own, Mr. Wallace," Mirrie broke in. "And, in fact, not so different from that model of enlightenment, ancient Greece."

Dr. Stedman nodded. "Yes, there is grave importance—ha, ha!—attached to the idea of a proper burial in every culture." He went on. "If the body is denied ritualistic burial, or disinterred after burial, the soul may be prevented from completing its journey to the afterlife.

"Such a person may thus be turned into a malevolent spirit called a plat-eye. This is far worse than the unhappy revenant so common in European ballads and folk tales. It is a shape-changing demi-devil that sets out to trap and destroy the unwary."

"How frightful!" Narcissa said with a shiver.

"Oh, you are in no danger," Dr. Stedman said, sitting back and lifting his glass. "The Negroes say you are only in danger from the plat-eyes if you believe in them."

"But isn't it true," Narcissa asked pointedly, "as with the ancient Greeks, that none of us is far from believing something of the sort?"

Wallace raised his glass in a salute and smiled over the rim at her. "*Touché*, Mrs. Powers."

After dinner, when the men joined the ladies in the drawing room, Brit Wallace picked up an album from a table and joined Narcissa on a sofa a little apart from the others. He opened the album on his knees and idly turned the pages as if merely passing the time, but Narcissa saw that his right knee was jogging up and down with suppressed excitement. After a few comments on the album's *cartes de visite*, he looked Narcissa in the face.

"Mrs. Powers, your questions about obtaining cadavers for medical study have given me an idea. I know my readers would enjoy the mysterious story of the vanished body snatchers, with all its elements of popular superstition. I could play up Richmond as a favorite, er, *haunt* of Edgar Allan Poe, and add colorful word portraits of the parties involved. . . ."

Narcissa was still for a moment while Brit looked at her, his smile slowly fading. "Do you find the idea so distasteful?" he asked.

"Mr. Wallace, I ask you in all earnestness not to pursue this idea until we can speak further." Narcissa fixed her eyes on his, determined to convince him that she was in earnest.

"My curiosity is whetted all the more, Mrs. Powers, since I cannot well imagine how your world would ever converge with that of two Negro body snatchers."

Narcissa hesitated. Her inclination was to share her suspicions only with Mirrie. But Wallace, being a foreigner, a journalist, and a man, could make a useful ally. He could go places a woman could not go and ask questions a native southerner would not ask. And it was clear he was going to ask questions anyway; better that he be told at least some of the story, enough to be warned.

Across the room, the piano struck up a tune popular just now in the South, the "Marseillaise." Narcissa looked around and saw Mrs. Stedman's head bobbing up and down as she struck the keys. Dr. Stedman, Nat Cohen, and Mirrie were singing at top volume, and even Professor Powers's quavering tones could be heard. The noise would cover her words, but she would have to be quick to finish before the singing ended.

Fixing her eyes on Wallace's face to read his reactions,

Narcissa began. "You know that my brother was a student at the medical college, and that he died. You may not know that he died of a wound complicated by erysipelas and gangrene."

Wallace nodded, a sympathetic but slightly puzzled expression on his face.

"I now believe," she went on, "that he may have died as a result of the doctors' not caring for his wound properly. I believe that his last days were clouded with suspicion about the men he worked with and trusted."

Wallace leaned forward and began to speak, then closed his mouth and settled himself back in the chair. Grateful for his willingness to listen, Narcissa told him about the fragment of Charley's letter she had found, with its revelation that a woman whose body had been procured for dissection had been murdered. When she finished speaking, Wallace leaned toward her again.

"So what do we know? A Negro woman is murdered, a woman who is already near death. Her body is dug up and dissected at the medical school. Some time afterward the student who performed the anatomy—your brother," he added with a glance at Narcissa that softened his words, "dies of a gangrenous wound. Two Negro men involved in the grave-robbing—and in fact this illegal activity is their accustomed trade—suddenly drop out of sight. Thus told, the facts indicate nothing more than a domestic tragedy of the quarters, revealed by chance, and complicated by coincidence.

"And yet, if that were so," Wallace continued, "why would it concern your brother? The woman is unknown to him, apparently? But—hold a minute—is it not likely that the resurrection men might have hastened the woman's death, so as to earn greater prizes from the medical college? Perhaps you have heard of the notorious Hare of Edinburgh, who turned King's evidence against his accomplice Burke and escaped punishment."

Narcissa nodded. He was confirming what she herself, prompted by Mirrie, had come to believe. Charley's anguish could be explained by his discovering such a terrible crime. Yet his reference to his own colleagues meant that Charley must have known, or at least feared, that someone close to him—Archer perhaps, or Hughes, not just the servants—had been involved in the crime.

Wallace went on. "If the missing men could be found and made to tell what they know, the mystery might be solved. But they cannot be found. Or rather, have not been found, by men whose activity in searching them out probably extended no further than looking for them in the usual place and at the usual time they were accustomed to appear!" Brit smiled sardonically. "Perhaps the resurrection men felt this would be a good time to find another line of work. It may be that, in the near future, Richmond will be a battleground that will feel no lack of corpses.

"Let me ask a few questions." His voice grew warm with enthusiasm. "I will see if I can turn up these fellows. I'm sure my father's old friend James Henry could be of help," he added, cocking an eye at Narcissa.

She shook her head emphatically. Dr. Stedman had now launched into a rather unsteady solo of "Believe Me, If All Those Endearing Young Charms," so she leaned closer to Brit and spoke in a low voice. "Come, you must promise me. My brother trusted none of the doctors. You must not mention what I have told you, to Dr. Henry or to anyone— and even more, promise me you will not write about it!"

Narcissa held his gaze until he placed his hand over his heart and said, "Upon my honor." The exaggerated solemnity of the gesture revealed a lack of seriousness, a nonchalance that could be dangerous both to him and to her, Narcissa thought. She had taken a risk by telling him as much as she had, but she had not succeeded in convincing him of the danger. Now she had to take a greater risk.

She leaned forward and put her hand on his sleeve. "You must be careful. I have not told you everything. Before I—lost consciousness—in the Egyptian building, I saw the body of a man. He had been murdered. When Dr. Stedman described him tonight, I realized it must have been the resurrection man, Old Billy. And I did not faint. Someone struck me on the head."

Wallace sat up straight, an angry look on his face. "Tell me who did that to you, Mrs. Powers, and he will answer to me!"

"I don't know," Narcissa said, her voice low and urgent. "Please, Mr. Wallace, you must not speak of this to anyone. If it were suspected that I remember what I saw, they would surely try to silence me. And I have no proof. Wait, and if you want to help me, be guided by me."

The struggle of Wallace's feelings showed on his face.

"Please understand," Narcissa urged again. "This trade in bodies has led to murder, and there are those who will kill to keep that a secret." She was quiet for a moment. "But you may be right in what you said, that Old Billy's son might be able to be found. If only we could speak to Cyrus!"

"Dr. Stedman referred to him as superstitious," Brit said thoughtfully. "If Cyrus is only playing dead, the local herb doctor or conjurer will know where he is, I'll wager."

Herbs, conjurations. Why did that sound familiar? Then she remembered the courageous woman at the slave auction. Jake Calder had used almost the same words to accuse her of doing something that would displease the girl's owner. What was the woman's name? She said it aloud—"Judah Daniel."

Wallace's eyes lit with interest. "Judah Daniel? Is he—"

"She." Narcissa answered. The woman's face was vivid in

her mind, and the look that had passed between them. Brit Wallace, for all his irritating self-assurance, had come up with a promising idea.

Wallace must have seen her hesitate. He pressed on. "Ah, then we must do as Saul did when he wanted to speak with the dead. We must go to the witch of Endor, or to this Judah Daniel, who is perhaps your local version."

The next day, when Narcissa relayed to Mirrie what Wallace had suggested, Mirrie protested that they could locate the woman without his help. But later that afternoon, Wallace called at the Powerses' house. Narcissa and Mirrie found him standing on the hearth rug, hands in pockets, whistling. He greeted them both, then looked at Narcissa. "About what we were discussing last night—" He darted a glance at Mirrie. "Is it all right . . . ?"

When Narcissa nodded, Wallace burst out, "I have found our witch!" He smiled broadly at their astonishment. "Judah Daniel," he said with a look at Narcissa, "the witch of Endor . . . or the witch of Richmond . . . or at least, the best-known conjure woman in these environs. If your superstitious grave robber is not drunk in a ditch somewhere, he may have sought her out."

"A conjure woman!" Mirrie exclaimed, smiling. "Can she put a spell on someone? Can she make love potions, punish straying husbands, heal the sick?"

"I hear that is the sort of thing she does," Brit Wallace said, returning her smile. "But we can go and see for ourselves, now."

"Now!" Mirrie and Narcissa exclaimed together.

"I was reminded—more than once in the course of my asking about—that it is against the law for a black healer to treat white people. We must be very circumspect. The blind pigs may come after us otherwise."

"Blind pigs? Is that a sort of ghost, like the plat-eye Dr. Stedman told us about?" Narcissa asked.

Mirrie laughed but let Brit explain. "No," he said, "that is the nickname for Richmond's Public Guard—being abbreviated as 'PG'—a pig without an eye is a 'blind pig,' do you see?

"But," he continued, "in case we are questioned, I have devised an acceptable excuse."

Wallace bent down behind the sofa and, with effort, lifted a basket that clinked with the motion. He rested it on the arm of the sofa and pulled back the checked cloth that covered it. Inside were perhaps a dozen glass jars and another half-dozen bottles, all filled with a dark brown substance.

"Beef tea and beef jelly," Wallace said proudly. "For the impoverished sick."

Mirrie burst out laughing. "Whoever did you find to prepare all those things? You must have an admirer among the hotel's kitchen staff!"

Narcissa frowned. "In your enthusiasm for finding things out, Mr. Wallace, I hope you have not forgotten your promise to me. This visit has a very serious purpose—deadly serious. If the grave robber can be found, we may make some progress toward unmasking a killer." She shivered, unconsciously lifting her hand to touch her hair where the blow had landed.

"I shall be a listener only," he assured her.

Should she resist his interference, refuse to go along, perhaps approach Judah Daniel in her own way? Narcissa hesitated. Wallace had eased the way by locating the conjure woman. And she could not deny that his presence had been helpful at the slave auction. All was prepared. Why not take the chance?

Chapter Nine

RICHMOND

MID-MAY

The Powerses' carriage, with Will Whatley driving, was juddering along narrow and rutted streets. Light was fading quickly.

The carriage slowed on a street of houses that, though small, their wood unpainted, looked decent and comfortable. Candles glowed behind shutters, and the twilight illuminated swept porches and tended yards. Will indicated to Mirrie that their destination was near at hand.

Soon the carriage halted. Brit Wallace climbed down, told Will to wait a little distance away, so as not to call attention to the place, and helped Narcissa down and then Mirrie. Together they crossed the road, stepping carefully over the deep ruts.

The house was tiny, its wood a worn and softened gray. The yard was crowded with strange, weedy-looking plants, but clustering around the path to the door were flowers— fragrant falls of purple iris, pungent lavender, soft lamb's ears. Narcissa smiled inwardly, gathering courage from the garden's serenity, and they stepped onto the stoop.

As they did so, the door opened a few inches, and a small girl peeked out. She was cradling something in her arms, protecting it from the white strangers—a yellow kitten, Narcissa saw. She smiled at the girl, who looked up at them with solemn eyes. Then she disappeared into the house, leaving the door ajar. From inside Narcissa could hear a piping voice answered by a low, husky one, but could not discern what was said.

In a moment a woman stepped from the house and stood before them, dark against the low light from the open door. Narcissa saw that the woman was tall, her skin very dark against the white kerchief that covered her hair. The woman stepped down beside Narcissa and looked her full in the face. She recognized Judah Daniel. Did the woman recognize her?

"Judah Daniel?" Brit Wallace asked in a low voice.

The dark eyes flicked toward Wallace and Mirrie for an instant, but she made no answer. She turned to look at Narcissa, and for several seconds the two women looked at each other.

Narcissa saw dark brown skin with a burnished copper glow on the high cheekbones; a strongly carved nose over a mouth that was well shaped but expressionless; large brown eyes that searched her face without giving any clue to what they read there.

Judah Daniel saw again the face of the woman she had seen at the slave market. Ivory-pale skin set off by dark hair and a black mourning bonnet, the nose small and straight, the lips curving. Dramatic against the skin were heavy, straight eyebrows and dark eyes that, seen close, had a spark of something—defiance? What had this young woman been doing in that place? Her face, now composed, had on that day exposed shock, anger, sorrow, confusion. It seemed as if she had interrupted Jake Calder in beating the woman, deflected the man's ugly anger from the slave girl to herself. A brave thing to do. Never mind that the white woman hadn't known what to do next. How to stop Jake Calder was a problem she herself hadn't solved.

The other two, the older woman and the man, Judah Daniel remembered as well. Tonight, as on that day, the older woman seemed concerned for her friend; the man was excited, curious, inclined to be protective of the younger woman.

Judah Daniel stepped back and gestured for them to come in. She had given no sign that she recognized them; nevertheless Narcissa was certain that she did. The house was one room, with a curtained-off portion at the back. A square table with three stools stood in the center of the room. Narcissa saw Brit Wallace step back to let her and Mirrie be seated. When Judah Daniel took the third stool, Narcissa flinched and looked up at Wallace. She saw with relief that his expression did not change. It struck her all at once that England must indeed be much different from Virginia, if a white man would stand while a black woman sat.

"Why do you come to see me?" Judah Daniel addressed Narcissa.

Brit stepped forward. "Perhaps I should explain. I am a journalist, and—"

Judah Daniel looked up at him. "You here for curiosity. She here for help."

Brit Wallace closed his mouth and stepped back into the shadows.

Again Judah Daniel fastened her eyes on Narcissa. Under that gaze, Narcissa found herself believing that this woman already knew why they had come, knew more than Narcissa had intended to tell.

Narcissa looked at Brit Wallace. He made a palm-up gesture with his right hand as if to say, It's up to you.

"I am hoping that you might help me"—Narcissa began hesitantly, choosing her words. Her hands, hidden under the table, twisted a handkerchief—"bring a murderer to justice and prevent more killing.

"My brother was a student at the medical college. He became involved in a grave-robbing—digging up a body for the medical students to dissect. It's an accepted practice," she added, not liking the defensive note in her voice.

Judah Daniel nodded. "I know the business of the resurrection men," she said.

Resurrection . . . that word again. Narcissa shuddered.

"Charley—my brother—stumbled upon something—something involving the doctors—that upset him terribly. Before he could tell me all that had happened, he died. His illness was erysipelas, and I believe that the worry he was under hastened his death. From a letter that he left for me, I learned that he accompanied one of the doctors when the body of a woman was dug up. When the doctors began the dissection, they found she had been killed, by a cloth forced down her throat."

Judah Daniel listened, quiet and calm, yet with an intent gaze that showed her comprehension. Narcissa felt herself relaxing despite the strangeness of the situation. "I think my brother found the doctors' reaction troubling. It was as if they knew something about the woman, about her death. I believe he came to suspect that one or more of the doctors was involved in"—Narcissa swallowed; it was hard to say—"murder. For the purpose of dissection."

Narcissa fell silent. Judah Daniel waited.

Finally Narcissa spoke again. "I don't think my brother knew who had done the murder. But the killing is still going on. I believe that the grave robber Old Billy was killed, and that whoever killed him tried to kill me too."

"Why you think Old Billy been killed?" Judah Daniel asked.

"I saw a dead man, in one of the doctors' offices at the medical college. It was an old black man. Two of his fingers were just stubs."

It was Old Billy, Judah Daniel thought; this woman happened on him just after he was murdered and before he was put into the pit. She watched Narcissa with increasing interest. God was revealing things to her through this white woman.

Narcissa hesitated. She hadn't planned to name the men she suspected. Was it because they were "respectable"—because they were white? She owed this woman more than that. By consulting Judah Daniel, she was drawing the conjure woman into the dangerous set of circumstances that had left Old Billy and the unknown woman dead, and herself injured. She spoke quickly.

"You must be on your guard. These men may be a danger to you. They are Cameron Archer and Edgar Hughes—and Hughes's overseer, Jake Calder."

Narcissa lowered her head, touched her hand to her temple.

Judah Daniel noted the gesture. Some pain, she thought, some injury there. She felt the reality of Narcissa's fear. "Tried to kill you, you say. Hit you on the head?"

Narcissa looked up at Judah Daniel, her eyes wide. Then she took her hand away from her temple and smiled a little. "That's right. You are very observant.

"If the dead man I saw was Old Billy," she continued, "then his son is in danger. And so am I. You may be able to help us both if you can find Cyrus and find out what he knows about the grave-robbing."

The white woman is being careful, Judah Daniel thought. She ain't sure it wasn't the resurrection men killed that woman, then maybe turned on each other. But she figures Cyrus might come to me, and what I find out from him might help her. I hope to God he's off away from here, safe.

Judah Daniel smiled inwardly. It would be an odd alliance, this white lady—daughter of a farmer by the look of her, not too highbred, but secure in the superiority granted by her skin color—and a man whom even his fellow blacks mostly avoided for the smell of his clothes and the taint of his occupation. The white man, Wallace, would think he could buy the help of Judah Daniel. Well, let him try. If the spider should turn its attention to these white folk, so much the better for Cyrus.

"What do you want me to do?" she asked Narcissa.

"I've heard that people come to you if they're sick or scared in their bodies or their souls. I've heard that Cyrus . . . believes in spirits, and I think that, if you sought him out, he might tell you what he knows, or suspects. Cyrus may have left town already, or he may be hiding. He may know who it was killed his father, Old Billy . . . and tried to kill me." Narcissa went on. "I need to find Cyrus, talk to him. My brother—"

Judah Daniel nodded slowly. "The fate of your brother's soul concerns you. He died troubled; maybe he don't lay easy in his grave. So you think if you find this Cyrus, you might find some answer to put your brother at rest."

Narcissa's face came up with fight back in it. "I am quite secure about the fate of my brother's soul. He was a doctor, and he cared about that woman, cared about her death, as he would any human being. He would not let her murder be covered up. Nor will I. I've come to you for help, which you can or cannot give me. That is," she said, remembering her supplicant position and softening her tone, "if you are willing to try."

Judah Daniel surveyed the young white woman across the rough wooden table, saw her eyes were bright with tears but her mouth firm. "I will see what I can do," she said at last.

She sat back, placing her hands palms-down on the table. Narcissa felt as if she were coming out of a trance. They all rose, and the visitors took their leave, Brit pressing some coins into Judah Daniel's hand.

In the street, night had fallen in earnest. This part of town lacked the gaslights common to more prosperous neighborhoods. The few lights from inside the homes did not reach the street.

Narcissa felt the hairs on the back of her neck prickle. She felt some fear for which she had no name.

Behind them, Judah Daniel closed the door and swung the bar in place to secure it. She turned toward the candle and stood for a moment looking into the flame. White folks brought trouble, and she avoided them if she could. But this time, thanks to her involvement with Cyrus, the trouble was already on her. And this woman, Narcissa Powers: she had stood up to Jake Calder, she was deserving of help.

Then her thoughts shifted to the woman whose body had been dug up, who had been torn from life so soon after giving birth. That woman had reopened some unhealed wound in Narcissa Powers—it had to do with a baby, a lost child—and had entered through that opening into her soul. Judah Daniel had seen them both there, the dead woman and the dead brother, looking out of Narcissa Powers's eyes.

She leaned over and pinched out the candle. The sting on her fingertips called her out of her reverie. She was drawn to help, but she had best be careful.

The three friends walked slowly, picking their way through the almost complete darkness. Narcissa regretted their negligence in not bringing a lantern to light their way to where the carriage waited out of sight. As they neared the corner, there came a sudden rustle, then a shout—"You there! Halt!"

They stopped, frozen. A shaft of light struck their faces. Wallace stepped in front of Narcissa and Mirrie.

Facing the glare from the bull's-eye lantern, Narcissa could tell only that there were three or four men, on foot.

"The Public Guard," said a rough, uncultured voice, "wants to know what you white folks are doing in the nigger section at this time of night. Up to no good, I'll be bound."

"I am a British citizen, and a journalist," said Brit Wallace in his huffiest John Bull voice. "What I am doing here is none of your affair. If you molest me or my companions in any way, I shall complain to the consulate."

"Oh, the consulate!" the voice said with mock alarm. Then it regained its sneering malevolence. "I ain't never heard tell that Richmond got any con-soo-late. The Public Guard don't answer to no con-soo-late, do we, boys?" Rude snickers arose in reply. "For all we know, you're a spy."

Narcissa drew in her breath, then whispered urgently to Brit Wallace, "It's Jake Calder!" Wallace made no reply, but Narcissa saw him brace his legs, readying himself to fight them off with his walking stick. It's useless, she thought. Calder would be angry, wanting revenge, and this time darkness would embolden his friends' desire for blood.

A thudding of hoofbeats arose suddenly from the direction

of Mirrie's carriage. Had Will seen, and driven the carriage to their aid? Narcissa wondered. No, the horse trotted light and quick. Was it just one more thug come to bully them?

The rider drew up his horse between Wallace and Calder. Over the creak of leather and clink of metal came a gentleman's drawling voice.

"What's the trouble, boys?"

"We was about to arrest these suspects what was found where they had no business to be."

"Never mind about that. Let them be released on parole to me."

There was grumbling from Calder and his cronies. The rider drew back his cape, revealing a pistol in his belt. The thugs fell silent.

Then one, not Calder, spoke. "All right, Captain. But the provost marshal is got to have a report," he added with a show of self-righteousness.

"Never mind the report, boys."

Narcissa heard the clink of coins, some muttered exclamations, footsteps receding. Then silence, broken by the drawling voice. She looked up to see hair curling under a wide-brimmed hat, a Van Dyke beard distinct enough in the near-darkness. It was Cameron Archer.

"Mr. Brit Wallace. I do apologize for any inconvenience to you, but I advise you to be careful—with the war on, suspicions abound, and there's a violent element abroad. You, too, Miss Powers, Mrs. Powers. Au revoir, ladies."

Narcissa heard him wheel his horse around and ride off. The night air struck cool on her burning cheeks.

When he spoke at last, Brit Wallace's voice was harsh with anger. "Mrs. Powers, Miss Powers, I must apologize. My technique for obtaining information appears to be less subtle than I imagined."

Wallace climbed into the carriage after Mirrie and Narcissa and seated himself opposite the women. In the light of the carriage lantern, his cheeks glowed red as if he had been slapped. Narcissa's blush had retreated, leaving her pale.

"That Calder and his friends almost had us." He spoke angrily. "Cameron Archer sent them away."

"Did Calder know who we were? Archer did," Narcissa said. "He called us by name."

"The Public Guard!" Mirrie repeated. "But what were they doing down here? They patrol the Armory and places like that."

"They had the caps," Brit Wallace said, his voice excited as he worked through the puzzle. "Of course, the protection of Richmond's white populace would be just a pretext for someone like Calder to terrorize slaves and free blacks with impunity. And yet . . . I would not be surprised if Cameron Archer stage-managed the entire encounter to frighten us! He won't succeed, I assure you."

Narcissa looked at Wallace, then at Mirrie. "You think Archer ar-ranged it? It is possible. Since Calder works for Hughes, it would have been easy for Archer to enlist his aid, for money, and for the pleasure of frightening us." She was silent for a moment. "Archer is ahead of me at every step, and he wants me to know it.

"We must be very careful."

❧

As Judah Daniel relaxed on her straw pallet, she asked for a dream that would guide her. It came. She was looking down onto a table where a woman was lying on her back, covered to the throat with a sheet that draped to outline the naked body underneath. The woman's skin was light brown. Her eyes were full of anguish and searched the darkness, seeming to pass over Judah Daniel without seeing her. The woman's lips worked, and Judah Daniel became aware of a low whisper that sighed, over and over, "Help me, sister."

Bending over the woman was a white man wearing a leather apron over his white shirt and dark pants. Black hair fell over his eyes and shadowed his face. He was holding a knife poised above the woman's throat. Its short, sharp blade was the brightest thing she could see.

Judah Daniel knew that, in a moment, she would see the knife thrust down into the flesh, see the blood spurt over the white sheet. She tried to hurl herself at the man, but she couldn't move. It felt as if she had no body to move. She could only watch. Then the man raised his head. She saw dark eyes under heavy brows, and the eyes were weeping. He looked straight at her. She knew it was Charley Wilson. She saw his lips moving, and the whispered words grew louder. "Help me, sister." You don't want me, she thought, and tried to break away from his gaze.

Judah Daniel sat up in bed and wiped the tears from her cheeks with the backs of her hands. For a long time she sat hunched in the dark, her arms encircling her bent knees, listening to the subtle night sounds riding the breeze up from the river.

The next day, Judah Daniel found that the nightmare weighed on her mind, making her forgetful. She'd burned the blue flag root she'd been boiling into a syrup used to treat dropsy. Now she would have to make another visit to the marshes to collect the plant. As she scraped at the sticky mass in the bottom of the pot, she had recognized the message her mistake was sending her: there was something else she ought to have her mind on. She'd seated herself at the table and rested her head between her hands, waiting.

It hadn't been long before Darcy slipped in through the

back door and came up to stand beside her. The child was trembling. Judah Daniel took her two hands in her own. "They say Cyrus is dead," Darcy said in a whisper. "Killed."

It seemed no one would lay out the body until the doctoress arrived. When she did, the few neighbors congregated on the Ropers' front porch had had little to say. One man admitted to finding the body. He had heard noises the night before, horses' hooves—whether one or more horses he couldn't say—angry talk, a scream, followed by the horses' hooves again, riding away. No, he hadn't looked out the window to see who was causing the commotion. It had been late that morning before he'd gotten the nerve to go onto the porch and look through the window. The isolation that had surrounded the sack-'em-up men in life was only growing deeper now that both men were dead.

Judah Daniel pushed open the door into the one-room house. The smell that assaulted her was that of a days-old corpse, but it was only the usual stench of the resurrection men. Cyrus was lying sprawled on his back across a mattress on the floor. His throat was cut, and blood soaked the wads of cotton batting and shreds of ticking that lay strewn on the floor. She looked more closely and saw the remains of another mattress, also ripped apart. Nothing else looked to have been touched. He, or they, must have found what they wanted—those gold coins that Old Billy was said to have hoarded—but they had killed Cyrus anyway.

Was gold the motive for this killing? People had feared the old man but despised the son; had his father's death left Cyrus open to attack?

Surely this killing meant more than that. She had fully expected that the doctors, or their henchmen, would kill Cyrus if he returned to this house. The lure of his daddy's gold had been too much for him.

She looked down at Cyrus, sorrow pulling at the lines of her face. Then anger drove out sorrow. Now that there was no need to protect Cyrus, she was more inclined to help Narcissa Powers. Meanwhile, she had to see to it that Cyrus was buried quickly. His death would be reported to the authorities as heart failure, which it surely was. Nothing like a cut throat to bring it on, she thought wryly. They wouldn't investigate. That would be up to her.

※

For Narcissa, the passing days clouded the excursion to Judah Daniel's with a sense of unreality. In the daylight, preoccupied with familiar things, she could hardly believe that it had taken place at all. After dark, in dreams, she would see a shadowy figure taunting her, beckoning her to an open grave.

At last the young girl she had seen at Judah Daniel's brought a message asking her to meet the conjure woman at the public market in Shockoe Bottom, a place where whites and blacks could converse with relative ease.

It was bright and hot by late morning, the time set by Judah Daniel. The streets around the big brick building were crowded with soldiers, hangers-on, and ruffians. There was little produce so late in the day, but Narcissa lingered, passing the time, until Judah Daniel found her, moving slowly down the narrow aisle to stand next to Narcissa. Both women kept their faces carefully neutral as they examined bunches of fragrant onions, the dirt still clinging to them.

Judah Daniel spoke softly, not looking at Narcissa. "Cyrus had no hand in the death of that woman, Mrs. Powers. I know to my soul he told me the truth about that. But maybe what I found out can help you."

Judah Daniel turned away. As she brushed past Narcissa, she pressed a folded sheet of paper into her hand.

Narcissa tucked the paper into her reticule, played the dawdling shopper a moment longer, then walked up the hill to the Capitol grounds, where she could find a bench to sit and read. The paper was torn from a newspaper and written along the margin in faint pencil. Holding it close to her face, Narcissa read the word "Hollywood," and below that a name—"Ellen Archer Hughes."

She rose and walked, crumpling the paper as she turned over the words in her mind. First the two names together— Archer and Hughes. She recalled what Mrs. Stedman had said. Ellen was of course Cameron Archer's sister. Doctor Hughes's first wife. But she had been dead for years, Narcissa thought, puzzled. What could she have to do with this?

Hollywood Cemetery must be the place where the body had been dug up. That was what Charley had meant by "the incongruity of the site"—a black woman dug up from among the resting places of the wealthiest and most important Virginians.

Cameron Archer had brought Charley to the cemetery, had known the body would be there. Hughes had been angry, perhaps because the cloth that had been forced down the woman's throat had not been removed, thus exposing an apparently natural death as murder. Both doctors, it seemed, must have known who the woman was, or at least what had been done to her. They had either killed her themselves or arranged the burking to be carried out by Cyrus and Old Billy, or perhaps—a thought occurred to Narcissa—by Jake Calder. They had gone to a fair amount of trouble to make it seem like an ordinary grave-robbing, had even buried the body.

Was she a servant? Narcissa wondered. The Hugheses' servant Jane told Mirrie she had come to the Hughes household shortly before Charley's death. Had Jane come to take the place of another servant, one who had died? Whose imminent death from childbed fever had been hurried along because the medical school needed bodies for dissection?

The servant had been buried near the grave of Hughes's first wife, Archer's half-sister, a site to which both men, and Calder for that matter, would have easy access. Old Billy and Cyrus may have come along to dig up the body, but they need not have known anything about the murder. But a mistake had been made: the cloth that killed the woman had been left in place. Without it, no one would have known that murder had been done.

Perhaps Old Billy and Cyrus found out, and their knowledge had put the doctors in danger. Old Billy had been killed, and Cyrus had disappeared. It all seemed so simple; it was as if she had seen it with her own eyes. It only wanted a trip to Hollywood Cemetery to fill in the outline.

Chapter Ten

Narcissa, Mirrie, and Brit Wallace stepped down from Mirrie's carriage at the entrance to Hollywood Cemetery, on Cherry Street, a few minutes' ride from the Powers home west of Richmond. Wallace had brought along a huge basket equipped for a picnic, and Narcissa found she was enjoying herself despite the serious purpose of their visit.

The friends stopped to examine the stone tower at the cemetery entrance. It had an appearance of great antiquity, its top broken and jagged as if gradually fallen into disrepair, although in fact it had been constructed as a ruin less than a decade before. Brit Wallace surveyed the tower with a serious expression, then turned to Narcissa and Mirrie. He spoke in a dreamy voice, his hand over his heart. " 'Who was he that piled these stones?' " Then he laughed. "I would think twice before I gave him further employment as a stonemason."

Mirrie responded, laughing. "Or, who was he that stoned this pile?"

Narcissa, now rather embarrassed for her admiration of the structure, protested. "It *is* more picturesque this way, don't you think, than if they had simply finished it and put the roof on?"

"Your admiration sanctifies it, Mrs. Powers," Wallace replied with a bow. He hoisted the picnic basket. "Bring on your storied urns. Perhaps then I may earn a story."

They set out to find the family burying ground of the Archers, in the oldest part of the cemetery. They entered through an iron gate in the stone wall and followed a series of serpentine walks that rose and fell gently through the undulating grounds. They were heading generally southwest, toward the river. It was quite warm already, a May day that could be mistaken for June, but the lanes were shaded by the towering oaks and hollies that had been preserved from the original woodlands. Weeping willow, yew, and cypress, the traditional plantings of cemeteries, had been added more recently and had yet to reach impressive height.

They passed groups of well-dressed pleasure seekers, some in carriages and some on foot. Boys fished in the little ponds and played in the creeks that wound through the grounds. As Narcissa, Mirrie, and Brit neared the oldest section, there were more grave markers and fewer revelers.

They paused to look at the tomb of President Monroe with its monument, a whimsical wrought-iron birdcage twice the height of a man.

"Were they afraid he would escape?" Brit Wallace jested. "Sorry," he added, catching Narcissa's eye.

They could hear the low roar of the river. They were close now.

They walked the few yards to the farthest corner of Hollywood, where its highest hill rose to a bluff that ended abruptly in a precipitous drop. They stood at the brick wall that bordered the bluff and looked down. "That's the Kanawa Canal," Mirrie said, pointing to a narrow band of water about thirty yards below them. They could see beyond it the tow path, and then the James. The river ran swift in its course, foaming white around boulders. "And that's Belle Isle," Mirrie added, indicating a low, wooded strip of land almost directly in front of them, around which the current parted. Gazing along the course of the James to the east, they could see the land curve back toward them in a crescent as the river turned south. The city swept upward from the water to the white-columned Capitol and the steeples of Shockoe Hill and Church Hill.

At last they turned away from the prospect. They set down the picnic things and began to wander among the gravestones. Many plots were enclosed with iron railings, but they either opened with gates or were low enough to step over, speaking more of family pride than of any attempt to keep out the curious.

Mirrie found the spot they were seeking and called to the others. The Archer family plot was one of the oldest there, predating the creation of the park-cemetery by many years, as its tall yews and cypress trees testified. A low iron fence enclosed a collection of stones and memorial sculptures in a mixture of ages and styles. At the center was a mausoleum of white marble, its entrance flanked by cypress sentinels.

Narcissa thought of the grief of the living who had erected these monuments to their loved ones, lost to them on earth. She hesitated, her hand on the gate. At last she took a deep breath, raised the latch, and went in.

Moving around the perimeter of the Archer plot, circling closer to the mausoleum at the center, she scanned the writing engraved on the stones. Some was almost obliterated with age, some recent; none of the stones looked new.

At last she found herself in a secluded spot behind the

mausoleum. Her attention was drawn to a small sculpted lamb, its legs tucked under. The grave of a child. There was writing on it: a name, *McCollum Archer Hughes*, and the dates *March 4–March 11, 1843*. The child had died only a few days after its birth. And the name—surely this was Edgar Hughes's son by his first wife, Cameron Archer's sister Ellen. There were more words carved in the base of the sculpture. She bent down to read them. *I shall go to him, but he shall not return to me:* the words spoken by King David when God took the life of the infant son born from David's sinful union with Bathsheba. The words conveyed the grief that Dr. Hughes, the mourning father, had shared with David. Did Hughes also share David's guilt for causing the death of his son?

Behind the lamb and looking down on it stood a marble angel, a little less than Narcissa's own height but raised about two feet by the base on which it stood. Narcissa looked up into the face—a woman's face, she thought, with delicate features and wavy hair drawn back from a center part. It was a woman's figure, too, though purified of fashionable exaggeration and rendered almost sexless by a simple robe carved into deep folds at its borders. Her feet were bare, and her hands were clasped at her waist, fingers interlaced. Her wings, each stylized feather carefully carved, were furled and folded against her back. Her eyes were downcast or closed, as if she were in prayer—or rather, Narcissa thought, in submission, as if her prayer had been answered and the answer was, Wait.

It's a corpse, Narcissa thought, a dead woman in her shroud, given wings that she cannot use until the day of Resurrection.

She looked down at the base of the statue. In the marble was incised the name *Ellen Archer Hughes*. The dates of her birth and death were carved there, too: *May 11, 1821–March 11, 1843.* She had died on the same day as her son.

Narcissa stepped back to look for any sign of ground recently disturbed. There it was, between the mausoleum and the angel monument, screened by statuary so as to be virtually invisible to any who were not seeking just such a sign. Grass grew thin in this shaded spot, and its growth was sparest on a patch of ground where runners of fast-growing ground ivy crisscrossed the dark earth. This patch formed an oblong shape about six feet long and half as wide.

Suddenly it was real. Charley had stood near this spot, Narcissa thought with pain—had witnessed the opening of the ground and the raising of the dead woman who had lain there. Soon afterward, he too had been buried.

Brit Wallace came up to stand beside Narcissa. She gestured toward the place, then walked slowly back to where Mirrie was waiting. When Brit returned, Mirrie took her turn examining the place. Then the three of them seated themselves and unpacked the picnic. Mirrie passed out plates, napkins, and fried chicken, and Brit poured cold tea into pewter cups. Narcissa took a few small bites from a drumstick, wishing she could be alone with her thoughts. For a while, no one broke the silence.

"The location is ideal for hiding a body," Mirrie said at last. "It is not a spot that would likely be discovered by chance."

"Yes," Narcissa responded slowly. "And yet after the body was placed there, it must have been dug up almost immediately, soon enough for the body to be used for dissection. Hughes and Archer *must* have arranged it between them."

"But what happened?" Brit asked eagerly. "How did it all go wrong?"

Narcissa's face was solemn. "Maybe Charley's conscience was the cause of all of it. Maybe he asked questions, maybe Old Billy told him more than he should have. Then, later, something must have happened to make Hughes and Archer feel Old Billy couldn't be trusted, so they killed him."

"Perhaps"—Brit Wallace held up his hand for quiet as he worked through his thought—"Old Billy was threatening to tell the authorities what he knew, and Hughes and Archer killed him. Your brother need not have been involved, Mrs. Powers."

Mirrie frowned. "It's possible, but who would believe the word of a Negro grave robber over two doctors? The 'authorities' would have laughed. You may not know, Mr. Wallace, that here in Virginia, blacks cannot testify against whites in a court of law."

Wallace's face fell. "Damnable system," he muttered under his breath. "Still," he asserted, "They might not have wanted to risk the stain on their reputation. If the story was bad enough, it could have endangered their positions."

Mirrie made her wry face. "True enough. The imputation of having people killed in order to rummage through their corpses would be a social and professional handicap to any-one, I should think."

"In Edinburgh," Brit Wallace said, stretching his legs out on the ground and leaning back on his elbows, "if someone is about to die—especially from some interesting disease—the resurrection men stand watch outside the house. They want to get the body while it's fresh. And of course there is rivalry as to who will be first to claim the prize. Families go to great lengths to protect their loved ones. They post guards, and some have even installed iron grilles over the gravestones. But there is bribery, and apparently the resurrection men are rarely cheated of a choice corpse."

Narcissa thought again of the words inscribed on the memorial to Hughes's infant son. "Mrs. Stedman mentioned that Dr. Hughes's first wife and their baby died as a result of childbed fever—puerperal fever, the doctors call it. The murdered woman had been suffering from the same affliction. Perhaps it is of special interest to medical students, and that is why they went to so much trouble?"

Wallace sat up, took his ever-present notebook and pencil out of his breast pocket, and scribbled a few words. He tucked them away again and sat with his chin on his knees, looking out toward the river. "It seems as if the rather tasteless jest I made to you, Mrs. Powers, may come to pass. Now that Union troops have set foot on Virginia soil, Richmond's medical students may soon have more subjects to practice upon than they ever dreamed of. I have been meeting some of the leaders of your new government, and your army. They fear a battle with no holds barred will be necessary to convince the Federals to 'let the erring sisters depart in peace,' as the saying goes."

"Then you will have much to say in your next set of dispatches," Mirrie remarked.

"Yes!" Brit seized eagerly on Mirrie's opening. "As a matter of fact, Brigadier General Beauregard has taken rooms in the Exchange Hotel. I have scheduled an audience with him this evening."

"How will you describe the hero of Fort Sumter for your readers?" Mirrie asked.

Brit leaned back again and looked up toward the canopy of leaves that shaded them from the hot sun. "Pierre Gustave Toutant Beauregard—" he began. "Of course, comparison with Napoleon is inevitable. He is French, or Creole rather, and he is short. He wears his black hair close-trimmed, as did the emperor, but in deference to current fashion he sports a natty mustache, waxed to points, and a little beard like a smudge of bootblack on his chin. He wears fine-looking uniforms. They arrived before him at the hotel, an advance army of trunks."

"So you have been working up your word-portrait," Mirrie said. "What of the man as a soldier?"

"Time will tell. Unfortunately, I was not at Fort Sumter." Brit pulled a clover blossom from the grass and sniffed it. Then he threw it down and gave his listeners a serious look. "I hope not to lose the next opportunity. They say the once-and-for-all battle will likely be fought on Virginia soil."

They were silent for a moment, thinking what that might mean. Then Mirrie spoke, smiling to invite more witticisms. "And Virginia's General Lee—what do you think of him?"

"I have seen him only once," Brit replied, "and not as yet had conversation with him. Among Richmonders, feeling is divided as to whether Lee more closely resembles God the Father or God the Son. Though his command is of a desk, thus far."

Narcissa felt Brit Wallace's eyes on her as he said this, looking for her to admire his wit or protest his irreverence. She did not meet his gaze. The talk of war seemed to blow around her like an icy wind, but she could not feel it. She was back with Charley, standing over that pathetic grave, feeling the anger she knew he must have felt.

Brit Wallace had stopped short of expressing a possibility that did fit the facts—whether he had not thought of it, or merely wished to spare her pain, she did not know. Had Charley been urging Old Billy to tell the truth, promising to take the stand himself against his teachers? With Charley to introduce Old Billy's testimony, the black man would have been listened to.

For Hughes and Archer, the murder of Old Billy was tidying up. It was Charley's death that was their deliverance.

≫≪

In the kitchen of the luxurious house where Cameron Archer had his rooms, Judah Daniel sat back comfortably in the rubbed oak settle and lifted a cup of steaming coffee to her mouth. What luck that the cook, Tildie Grant, had come to her to have a boil lanced only last winter. Tildie was a smiling, good-natured woman, comfortably plump over muscles gained from lifting heavy iron pots onto pothooks, pounding dough, and sawing through hambones. Tildie had fussed over her, made her feel at home, and returned to her baking.

The rolling pin slapped down on the dough with a gentle rhythm as Tildie's voice rose and fell. "I always heard tell Doc Archer was supposed to come into money, but that it went somewhere else. Taking rooms with the Widow Jennings make an economy for him. They is related in some degree. The Archers got a lots of folks around here."

Judah Daniel knew it was not Widow Jennings's charms that drew the doctor here. The dowager owner of Tildie, and numerous other servants that harder-worked slaves would consider pampered, was eighty if she was a day. Maybe the doctor even hoped to inherit this house and its human property some day.

"Having a gentleman in the house always make for more work," Judah Daniel commented.

Tildie dipped her head in agreement as she attacked the dough again. "He mighty particular in his habits. Has to have his linen snowy and his boots shined just so. Course his own man, Gideon, see to his boots. He don't raise his voice to us none."

Judah Daniel decided to steer the conversation toward her interest. "I reckon Doc Archer be getting married some day before too long."

Tildie smiled, pumping her elbows in and out to work the rolling pin. "Reckon he might. He ain't here much, but Gideon don't gossip. That man as closemouthed as the tomb. Course, now this war's got everybody's heads turned. The widow's great-nephews called the other day, and they—"

Tildie went on, but Judah Daniel, swirling the remains of the coffee in the mug, lost the thread of her remarks. Tildie didn't know anything about Archer's personal life, or was too sweet-natured to say. Bad news that Gideon wasn't a gossip. Judah Daniel would have to leave open the possibility suggested by Old Billy, however unlikely she thought it was, that Archer was courting in the cemetery and saw the murdered woman buried there.

≫≃

"Our old friends the Frogs will croak again tonight," Mirrie remarked at breakfast. "But I suspect that they are spring peepers after all, and that their season is almost done."

The words were spoken lightly, but Narcissa detected a note of sadness. The war was breaking up the little circle that had so often gathered at the Powerses' house. Mirrie looked away, buttering a piece of toast as if the act required all her attention. She took one bite, then pushed the plate away and sat, chin in hand, gazing at nothing. Shandy sat unregarded, looking up with sad eyes at his mistress.

In letters from her sisters, Narcissa learned that their husbands were volunteering as soldiers for the Confederacy. Her brother John was delaying only until after Mary's confinement. All the familiar young men from western Hanover were going for soldiers. Narcissa had heard that General Lee called his decision to leave the Union the hardest of his life. How could that be? Narcissa wondered. Hard to leave, yes, but hard to decide? The river doesn't stop to think which way to flow, and a tug as deep as nature commanded loyalty to home.

Narcissa fretted about Mirrie's silence. Was she ill, or had her father's health grown worse? But Narcissa's concern seemed to have an irritating effect on Mirrie. She would snap at Narcissa, apologize, then retreat again into silence. Perhaps the Frogs would coax Mirrie into speech with their eagerness to hear her witty opinions. As Narcissa mused on the evening to come, she suddenly had a thought so surprising that she set her teacup down with a clatter: Mirrie was silent because she could not think which way to go.

Among the first to arrive in the evening was Brit Wallace. He bore the news that Dr. Henry, who had been Wallace's introduction to the Powers household, was preparing to leave Richmond, to offer his services to the Union cause. Narcissa was watching for Mirrie's reaction: interest flickered in her face, but it was momentary.

Narcissa's eyes turned to Mirrie again when the Stedmans arrived. As usual, Mrs. Stedman scanned the room with a regard so acute that Narcissa felt she must be able to tell the silver from the silver plate on the table across the room. Dr. Stedman was standing ramrod-straight in his brand-new medical officer's uniform: a tunic of grey cloth, belted over his comfortable belly with a green silk sash, and dark blue trousers with a black stripe. His cloud of white hair and his whiskers were newly trimmed.

Narcissa joined the circle around Stedman. He greeted her so warmly that she felt with embarrassment that perhaps he misunderstood her interest in him. He was explaining that the Confederate Congress in Montgomery had authorized an increase in the army's medical department, bringing the number to ten surgeons and twenty assistant surgeons. As one of the ten surgeons, he had the rank of major. "The Confederate government," he went on, "is preparing its directives for the medical service—not only for the field but for hospitals."

Brit Wallace, who had joined the group, turned to smile at Narcissa. "You admire Florence Nightingale," he said jovially. "Now is your chance to become the Florence Nightingale of the Confederacy."

Before Narcissa had time to form a reply, Stedman spoke. "Our southern *ladies*"—he drew out the word—"most certainly do not belong in hospitals, much less in the public eye, clamoring for reform." Then he gave the younger man a forgiving smile, as if to indicate that a foreigner could be excused from such a lapse in taste.

Narcissa spoke up. "Florence Nightingale proved in the Crimea how much women can do, not that it should have needed proving, since women have been the nurses all along for their families." Stedman was looking at her, eyebrows raised in as much astonishment as if Shandy had suddenly spoken. Piqued even further by this reaction on the part of the complacent doctor, Narcissa continued. "And nuns care for the poor who have no families. Do you not honor them for that?"

Stedman, red in the face, was glancing around as if in search of someone to rescue him from this conversation. "Nuns are not ladies," he finally said, bowed, and walked away.

Brit Wallace's face was red, too, but with suppressed

laughter. His back to Stedman, he silently clapped his hands together. "Bravo, Mrs. Powers!"

Narcissa barely nodded acknowledgment. She was gripped by an idea taking shape in her mind. She turned to look for Mirrie and caught her friend standing quite still, looking toward the door. Narcissa turned to see what Mirrie was staring at—Nat Cohen, dressed in a gray uniform trimmed with gold.

Mirrie walked over to Cohen but did not take his proffered hand. He reached out and touched her forearm. He was speaking, but Mirrie interrupted in an edgy voice loud enough to be heard across the room. "Well, Mr. Cohen, or I suppose it is Colonel? So you have decided to join the boys in dressing up and shooting rifles. Could not the Glorious Cause make better use of the skills you have learned as a businessman?"

Mirrie's sarcasm brought a blush to Cohen's face. Narcissa wondered if she should go over and rescue him, but she hesitated. She suspected he cared deeply for her friend. In fact, the very depth of Mirrie's anger made her wonder if Mirrie's own feelings were not more deeply engaged than she would like to admit. But to Mirrie, ideals took precedence over people, and she would not soon forgive Cohen for taking a stand that ran counter to what she herself believed.

Nat Cohen was still holding onto Mirrie's arm, speaking into her ear. Mirrie pulled away and said, "Your minds are as uniform as your clothing. It's all 'do my *devoir*' and the 'tented field.' "

Then Brit Wallace joined Mirrie and Cohen. Mirrie excused herself and went over to where Stedman and his wife had seated themselves. "Mrs. Stedman," Mirrie said, a trifle too loudly, "would you play for us? A martial air, something suitable for the occasion?"

The other guests moved over to the piano, and Narcissa joined them. Mrs. Stedman's choice of music was the lugubrious song "Lorena," a favorite of soldiers. Narcissa saw that Cohen's usually jovial face was somber, and Mirrie, who had called for a song, stood silent, mouth set in a line.

After the guests had gone and Narcissa was ready for bed, she went to Mirrie's room. Mirrie was standing, bent at the waist, brushing her hair with hard, angry strokes. She was ignoring Shandy, who was dancing around her feet, eager to make a game of it.

Narcissa sat in the slipper chair near the bed. She soon found that Mirrie was ready to talk—and eager to condemn the decision Nat Cohen had made. "The foolishness of it!" Mirrie's forehead wrinkled as she looked up at Narcissa. "He talked about being a Jew. I said, tosh! Who cares for that. He could go out for an administrative position like Attorney General Benjamin—*he* does not feel the need to lead troops in the field."

"I'm sure many Jewish men and boys are enlisting," Narcissa ventured.

Mirrie's tone grew sharper still. "If they have nothing better to offer than their bodies as cannon fodder, well and good. Mr. Cohen has run that store for years. He could take a responsible role in obtaining supplies—God knows the South will need them! Tredegar is the only foundry in the South that can produce the bigger artillery pieces. But Mr. Cohen does not want to involve himself with the troublesome facts."

"What does being a Jew have to do with his decision?" Narcissa queried.

Mirrie threw back her head to shake her hair out of her face. The white-streaked red curls fell around her shoulders and down her back to her waist. Narcissa thought how vulnerable Mirrie looked in her high-necked white nightgown. "He has told me before that, over and over again, wherever they settle, Jews are forced to prove that they can belong—that their differences in faith and practice do not cut them off from the rights of citizens, or from the responsibilities. Of course, he does not observe many of the traditional practices of Judaism. He will not refuse to fight on the Sabbath. He should refuse to fight at all!" Mirrie looked away and began to braid her hair.

"That may be what you would do, Mirrie," Narcissa replied, "but that is not what he has chosen. Your beliefs can dictate only your behavior, not his. Even if you were his wife—"

Mirrie's head came up with a jerk. "I do not wish to discuss the matter any further," she said coldly.

Narcissa, eager to unburden her own mind, accepted the assertion at face value. She waited for a moment, then began. "Mr. Wallace asked me if I intended to be the Florence Nightingale of the Confederacy. He was joking, of course, but—"

Mirrie looked at Narcissa, eyebrows raised. "Of course! You have been looking for a way to find out more about the doctors who treated Charley. This is ideal!"

"And," Narcissa said, "serving as a nurse would give me a chance to do some good . . . for the 'Glorious Cause,' as you put it," she added with a touch of defiance.

Mirrie sighed. "Don't misunderstand me," she said at last. "The South is my home, and I would not have it come to harm, much less any of our friends or neighbors or family who put on the uniform. And nursing is itself a glorious cause."

Narcissa went on. "I will go to Dr. Stedman and offer to serve in the hospital at the medical college. If I can assure him I'm no firebrand Florence Nightingale, I believe I can convince him to take me. And, as you say, if I can enter that charmed circle, I may be able to discover the secrets they are hiding."

"He will certainly warn you of the gore and horror of a military hospital such as Florence Nightingale experienced at Scutari," Mirrie replied. "Although of course we are not to that point yet and, pray God, never will be. And Stedman will not be the only one to tell you that a lady's delicacy could be compromised in such a place. Although I would argue with him on the matter of 'a lady's delicacy' until Judgment Day, I fear for you just the same. Hospitals are places of contagion. Even though no major battle has been engaged, the armies are already sick with those diseases that lurk in swamps and fester in the heat and damp. And I am even more fearful for your possibly working in close quarters with Archer and Hughes. If you come too close, they may try another attack on you. Perhaps—"

"I do not wish to discuss the matter any further," Narcissa said, a smile softening her mimicry of Mirrie's own words. Mirrie raised her eyebrows, but smiled back, and at last rewarded Shandy's attentions by taking him into her arms and letting him lick her face. The little dog squirmed with delight.

Narcissa sat watching them, trying to think through the arguments she could use with Dr. Stedman. But Mirrie's mention of Hughes and Archer brought images to her mind that scattered her rational thoughts. Hughes repelled her, linked as he was to Charley's hideous death, but also in his person. It was strange how the man's fingers revealed thoughts and feelings that left no sign on his sagging, unhealthy face. The life that was in him was too little to animate a whole man, only enough to vivify his hands, as if mice had gotten into a mummy's wrappings and made it appear to move.

But if Hughes made her flesh creep, Dr. Cameron Archer had managed—in a series of encounters in which she had not even been able to respond—to make her feel both angry and afraid. She burned at the memory of his remark on her charm. But hadn't she been taken in, just a little, by the compliment, followed as it was by an admiring glance that swept over her, head to toe? Wasn't at least some of her anger directed at herself, for the split second of disappointment she had felt when she had found out who he was and seen the true purpose of his gallantry?

His remark later that evening—*raising the dead*—what had it been, a taunt, a threat, a warning? His sudden appearance in the street outside Judah Daniel's house was likewise chilling in effect, ambiguous in meaning.

Once she had some sort of normal dealings with Archer at the hospital, would his strange hold over her imagination be broken; would he be reduced to mere humanity? She wondered.

❧

The Franklin House, on Sixth Street between Marshall and Broad, had become a favorite place for Brit Wallace to dine when no social engagement offered itself. He liked the unpretentious low-beamed rooms, which reminded him of British taverns. He liked the bachelor fare of oysters, beef, and lager beer, with stronger stuff for those who wanted it, flavored by the rich tobacco smoke that hung heavy in the air.

He had finished dining and was leaning against the high-backed bench, puffing out his own contribution to the sweet, heavy air. He was listening.

The Franklin House was full of talkers, men who "had it on the highest authority" that Union General McDowell of the Union would attack in such a place, or that General

Beauregard planned this or that feint to draw the Northern army. Brit fancied he could tell in less than a minute if their words were worth his attention. He could tell by watching the men who never spoke, but who knew—the war clerks, especially, whose shoulders stiffened with wariness whenever the truth was touched on too close.

He would listen and look, and form his theories, among the good fellows at the Franklin House. The formal interviews with government officials then became a fine game, a game of pursuit, like foxhunting, but also a game of jabs and feints, like boxing or fencing. Not that it much mattered if his guesses concerning Confederate battle plans were right or not. The weeks that would pass while his dispatches crossed to England and then back in published form—if indeed they ever made it through the blockades—made the point moot. To see a battle, that was what his career needed.

Among the excited men who contested for vocal supremacy around him, Brit detected a drawling voice that seemed familiar—someone he knew in a different context than the Franklin House, he thought, cutting his eyes around to locate the speaker. The face was in profile, the brow large, with wavy brown hair brushed back, the nose arched—Archer, that's it, Cameron Archer. Brit could see the high collar of his gray tunic, bearing the black band of the medical service.

Brit sat up and looked at the man who had so thoroughly pulled his nose in the company of Mrs. Powers and Miss Powers, under the pretext of "saving" them from harassment by the Public Guard. Brit had made up his mind that the whole episode had been stage managed by Archer himself, to scare the three of them away from asking questions. He had seen Archer say something to Mrs. Powers on the night of the illumination, too, something that upset her, but she had never told him what it was.

Archer turned to meet Brit's gaze. The two men exchanged a long look.

I will have to speak to him, Brit thought, rising to his feet, or look a coward for backing down. He walked through the crowd of men toward Archer, holding his gaze, trying frantically to think of what he must not say. It would be ungentlemanly to mention Mrs. Powers's name, and he could not risk putting her in greater danger.

When he came up next to Archer, Brit turned away from the men that were standing around, signaling his desire that they not be overheard. Archer did the same.

"Mr. Wallace," Archer said. His tone was expressionless, his eyes alert.

Brit glanced at the insignia and guessed the rank. "Captain Archer. I gather you did not expect to see me here, for you have not donned your highwayman's mask and cape."

Archer's expression was stony. "You are young, Mr. Wallace, and you are a foreigner. If that were not the case—"

"You would call me out?" Brit asked, smiling a little. "Quaint custom."

Archer frowned and seemed about to give an angry answer. But he composed his features and said again, with exaggerated patience, "You are a young man, and you are a foreigner. The things that concern us in Virginia do not concern you. If you gave your lifetime to the study, perhaps you could learn. I doubt it."

"I have heard," Brit said with a thin-lipped smile, "that it is wise never to ask a man whether he comes from Virginia. If he does, he will be insulted that you had to ask. If he does not, he will be insulted that you suspected it of him."

Archer frowned and moved a step closer to Wallace, who steeled himself not to step back. The two men stared at each other for several seconds. "I regret," Archer said coldly, "that more important duties prevent me from teaching you a lesson. But in any case I fear your time among us will soon be coming to an end."

"Is that a threat?"

"Call it a prophecy. Good evening to you, sir," Archer concluded, inclining his head with minimal politeness and turning away.

Brit went back to his table and pulled some crisp Virginia banknotes from his pocket. A servant appeared and took them. Then he walked out into the warm, still night, wondering what he should have said or done to bring the confrontation to a more satisfactory conclusion.

≽∈

Judah Daniel stood on the little porch of the Hughes house and shifted the basket on her arm. Good thing I ain't standing here with a broken arm needing fixing, she thought, long as it's taking them to get to the door.

At last the door swung open, and a brown-skinned, gentle-faced woman, clad in the gray dress of a house servant, looked out. "Morning, sister," Judah Daniel said quickly, stepping close to the door and pulling back the white napkin to reveal the brown eggs nestled in the basket. "I got fresh eggs here to sell."

The woman looked down, then up into Judah Daniel's face, then down at the basket, then up again, frowning, "I ain't sure—" she said doubtfully. "Cook's out."

"These are *country* eggs, brought in on the wagon this morning from—" As Judah Daniel had hoped, the servant filled her silence with what was in her own mind.

"From up in Hanover? That's where I'm from. Oh, I do miss the country."

Judah Daniel guessed "up in Hanover" would be Ashland,

or Hanover Courthouse. The phrase would be "over to" Montpelier in western Hanover. She chose one, pursued the game—"Up around the Courthouse?"—and was rewarded with an answering smile that transformed the woman's face.

Judah Daniel played her next card with delicacy. "I ain't from there, but I know some folks. Who's your people? Listen, honey, do you mind if we go on back to the kitchen? My feet could use the rest."

Again the woman hesitated, looking back over her shoulder. Judah Daniel saw the smile vanish from her face so quickly that she herself took a startled step backward. Pushing aside the sweet-faced woman was another servant whose dark brown skin had a grayish tinge and whose expression would curdle milk. She glanced down at the eggs, her mouth pursed as if she smelled something bad.

"Jane Scott, I done told you not to gossip with strangers. We ain't that kind of a household, we got a reputation to keep up."

"Yes, Phebe," Jane replied meekly, casting an apologetic glance at Judah Daniel before disappearing into the house.

The woman then turned her attention to Judah Daniel. "What you doing, hanging around here trying to gossip with the servants? We got no call for your kind of doctoring."

So this woman, Phebe, recognized her, Judah Daniel thought. Bad luck. And worse luck that Phebe was one of those slaves who identified with their masters so completely that she referred to her fellow slaves as "the servants"!

The sharp-featured woman pulled the door shut.

Judah Daniel stood there a moment, smiling a thin smile. If she could get to Jane Scott, away from Phebe, she might learn whatever it was that Phebe was trying so hard to keep shut up inside that door.

Chapter Eleven

RICHMOND
EARLY JUNE

Dr. Stedman received Narcissa and Mirrie in the medical office at his home. They exchanged news of the war for a few minutes before Narcissa introduced the subject on which they had come. "Dr. Stedman, it appears that the opposing sides in this conflict are determined to come to blows. When major battles are engaged, every man who is able will be called to fight. The young physicians you have trained will be called as well to tend the wounded on the battlefield. I am sure you have given much thought to the role of the medical college."

Dr. Stedman nodded. "We intend to continue training physicians and surgeons. That role will become even more important now that training in the North is no longer an option. And of course the college's hospital facilities will be devoted to care of the wounded. If we find the war lasts more than a few weeks, we will act on construction of a hospital in the pavilion style similar to that erected at Scutari in the Crimea."

"I want to help," Narcissa stated simply. Dr. Stedman sat back and peered at her over his pince-nez.

"Of course, Mrs. Powers, all the ladies of Richmond will be much involved in preparing bandages and the like. I don't quite see—"

Narcissa pressed on. "All our able-bodied men are enlisting as soldiers. Many of your students are choosing to go into the cavalry rather than do the less glamorous work of surgeons. The slaves who have helped with hospital work will also be called on to labor for the war effort, I shouldn't wonder. I know you feel that nursing is not appropriate employment for a lady. I am not suggesting that I—we—can do the work of physicians or of servants. Still, we can help with administrative duties, see that things run smoothly— just as a lady does in her own household. And there are special needs for a military hospital. We can help write letters home, and provide those little touches—a kind word, a gentle hand—that may make a difference in recovery. I am volunteering to serve in that capacity."

Narcissa saw by the softening of his expression that her self-effacing approach had had the desired effect. Dr. Stedman removed his pince-nez and looked at her thoughtfully for a moment. Then he stood and leaned over the desk toward her, placing his hand on a six-inch stack of papers that lay on the blotter. "Mrs. Powers, let me consider what you have said. We are setting up a new government, a new medical system, and entering into potentially bloody conflict at the same time. You can well imagine that I have much on my mind. I promise to give your offer most serious consideration. Now, ladies, if you will excuse me, I must attend to matters that await my attention."

Narcissa was soothing and deferential in leave-taking, sure

that, if they had not won the point, they had pushed it as far as possible for this day.

Two days later Narcissa and Mirrie received a note asking them to come to the medical college hospital. Their carriage set out through an early summer rainstorm to keep the appointed meeting. At the hospital, Stedman ushered them into a sparsely furnished office and launched in upon the matter, striding back and forth across the floor. "You know that I was resistant to your offer when it was made, and I apologize for any apparent lack of gratitude. I only wanted to be sure that you understood the consequences of what you were asking."

He stopped, hands clasped behind his back, looking for their response. They nodded; satisfied, he resumed pacing. "I have thought it over, and consulted with my colleagues. After some discussion, we have agreed to let you assist in the hospital. On a trial basis, of course."

He halted again and shot her a glance.

"Mrs. Powers—have you had the measles?"

"Yes, in childhood," she replied, and he went on.

"An outbreak has occurred in a regiment from the Tennessee hill country. Fifty of their sickest men are here. The hospital was already filled beyond capacity. We've had to set up cots in the lecture hall. Trouble is, just as our medical men are dispersing to their regiments, a half-dozen of our students show signs of coming down with measles."

"I can start now, Doctor," Narcissa said, leaning forward in her eagerness.

"Very good," Dr. Stedman smiled. "Let me have a servant take your things and show you where you will be working. I'm sure you will make yourself very useful. By the way," he added, "there may be some resentment among the medical staff. If they express themselves in an ungentlemanly way, you must inform me at once."

Narcissa thanked him and said a hurried good-bye to Mirrie. Then she followed a manservant down the hall to a room a little bigger than a closet, where she hung her shawl and bonnet on pegs in a cupboard. She hesitated, then removed her gloves and tucked them inside her bonnet. She was a lady no longer, but a nurse. She thought of Charley and smiled to herself. She knew he would have been proud of her.

On her previous visit to the college hospital, the layout had seemed spacious, tidy, and efficient. Now the rooms were crammed with cots and filled with men, a dozen or more in a room planned for four. Most appeared to have little in the way of a uniform; they wore rough, hand-woven and hand-dyed pants and open-collared shirts.

The profusion of spots was everywhere, but the level of illness differed. The sickest tossed on their cots in evident discomfort or lay doubled up and shivering under blankets, though the room was stiflingly hot. Others were sitting up, talking and laughing with one another, and even playing cards. Some of these eyed Narcissa warily and fell silent, while those in pain seemed to her to greet her arrival with kindling hope.

She caught sight of Dr. Hughes taking a patient's pulse. He saw her and crossed the room to where she stood. "Mrs. Powers, your offer is very welcome. These fellows here have had their dosing, but they need some water; in this heat, a cool cloth or a fan for a few minutes might bring some relief."

Narcissa was struck by the difference in Dr. Hughes from when she had seen him on previous occasions. He spoke with confidence, and he moved with energy and decision, the grace of his gesturing hands now commanding his whole body. Students followed him, listening attentively to his observations, eager for his approval. The man was in his element here among the sick.

"Benjy will help you get what you need." Dr. Hughes gestured to a black boy about ten years old, who was hanging back, shifting his weight from one foot to the other, uneasy as to what would be expected of him. Dr. Hughes sketched a bow in Narcissa's direction, then set off down the hall.

Narcissa stepped close to the youngster and bent her head near his. "Benjy, could you get me some cool water in a basin, and some clean towels?"

"Yes'm," he replied, darting out the door and returning almost instantly with the things she had requested.

Facing the scruffy bunch of soldiers who were now her patients, Narcissa found a stool and placed it by the head of the first bed. Its occupant, a young man with a tangled mass of blond hair over a beardless, thickly spotted face, eyed her warily.

"So you are from Tennessee?" she said conversationally as she dipped a towel in the basin and wrung it out. "I'm sure it is much cooler there in the mountains. But we will do what we can." She began to daub his face gently with the towel and saw him exhale with relief as the cool cloth touched his temples.

"Yes'm," he mumbled. "I sure wish I was there right now. But I got to whip me some Yankees before I can go back."

Narcissa had gone through one room and started on another, keeping Benjy busy with fetching water and clean cloths, when the youngster came up to her and whispered, "Soup."

As he said it, she became aware of a new smell discernible through that of unwashed bodies and damp wool. Her job now, it seemed, was to help the two servants whose task it was to carry bowls of soup and bread to the patients and to help those too sick to eat on their own. The soup was a thin gruel, and those patients strong enough to speak were quick to lament its lack of flavor.

"I wish I had some of my ma's soup," the complaint would rise from one to be echoed by others throughout the room.

"Soak the bread in it!" cried a voice. "That way, you don't notice the taste so much, and it softens up the bread so's you can chew it!" Before long, the healthier patients were mopping the bowls with the last crusts. Narcissa was proffering spoonfuls to a skinny youth, pale beneath his spots. He had managed a couple when suddenly he bent double. A foul smell arose from beneath the blanket. She looked around for Benjy, but he was not to be seen, so she went out into the hall.

"Is there a doctor here?" Narcissa asked one of the servants, who was stacking the soup bowls on a tray. He gestured toward a room down the hall. Almost running, she found Dr. Fielding, the college's professor of chemistry and pharmacy, who was doling out medications. Seeing the worried look on her face, he stood up and followed her out. She told him what she feared.

"We've had a couple of cases like this," Fielding said, after he had examined the patient and summoned a servant to tend him. "Measles itself isn't a serious illness, but the sequelae—the illness and infection that attack the weakened patient—can be fatal. Dysentery is one. And of course some of these fellows in the camps don't know any better than to piss upstream and fill their canteens downstream—er, begging your pardon, Mrs. Powers.

"This man will have to be moved. We can dose him with

blue mass or calomel—mercury's the important ingredient in both. And the other patients should be watched closely. An outbreak of dysentery in a situation like this can decimate a population in close quarters."

Narcissa watched him making notes in a small notebook. "Do you make notes like that on every patient?" she asked.

"Oh, yes," Fielding replied, filling a page with jottings and then cramming the notebook and pencil into his pocket. "I try to take a few notes on the spot, then of course write it up afterward. That's crucial, not only to trace the treatment of the individual patient but to have a record of all patients to compare, to see what works and what doesn't. That's the basis of medical advancement," he added rather pontifically.

A picture came into Narcissa's mind: Edgar Hughes, standing in the doorway of the room in which Charley lay dying, making notes on a folded piece of paper. It was likely Hughes had written up the entire course of Charley's illness and treatment. If she could look it over, and perhaps compare it to other accounts, there was a possibility of finding out whether Charley was treated promptly and appropriately.

Responding to a hail from one of the students, Fielding hurried away. Halfway down the hall, he called back to Narcissa, "Bring clean dressings!" Her speculations retreated, driven back by the needs of the moment.

Over a few weeks, Narcissa fell in step with the routine of hospital life. Most of the men recovered enough to be discharged back to their units. A few died, and some were invalided home. The young measles victim she'd met on her first day had died; Narcissa came in the next morning to find his place taken by another sick soldier, and the routine went on as before. Never was the saying "There is nothing made by grieving" taken more to heart.

Breakfast was at seven, with coffee, tea, milk, bread, butter or molasses, and any meats left over from the previous day's dinner. Whatever was available was divided equally, with the delicacies reserved to tempt the appetites of the sickest. If any man wished for a particular dish, and the doctor in charge determined it would do him no harm, every effort was made to procure it for him.

After breakfast the assistant surgeon visited the patients, filling in the printed menu forms with the invalid's name, the number of his bed, and whether his diet was light, half, or full. The quantity of whiskey to be given—two to four ounces per dose—was also specified. At two o'clock a dinner of poultry, beef, ham, or fish and vegetables was distributed. Supper, a lighter meal of the same components, was served at six. For those deemed too debilitated to eat these foods, the doctors insisted upon a starchy and tasteless concoction in which arrowroot was a major ingredient.

Narcissa developed a sort of uniform for herself. Each day she wore one of her black dresses with a fresh white collar and undersleeves. Covering the skirt was a lightweight black overskirt with deep pockets into which she would put her handkerchief, a few coins, a small Bible, and other necessities. Over this she could put a white apron should more protection be required.

She arrived at the hospital just before breakfast was served to help make sure the weakest and the most rebellious invalids received some nourishment. When all were fed, she bathed foreheads, wrote letters home, and otherwise eased the feelings of the sufferers. For many, this was their first time away from home, and the pangs of homesickness overpowered those of illness or injury. Then the round of feeding would begin again, and so on, until she left exhausted just as dusk darkened the sky.

As she grew to accept the routine of the hospital, she was also accepted by it. Her womanhood was no longer remarked on. Her initial welcome by Hughes had eased the way for her, and she was grateful, though she had not set aside her suspicions of him. The notes Hughes made on his patients, she realized as she came to know every inch of the hospital, must be kept in his office at home, and she stayed alert for the chance to look there for the record of his treatment of Charley.

But she had not encountered Cameron Archer, who she heard was spending most of his time working with the field surgeons up north of Richmond, where a major battle was expected. Coming face-to-face with Archer again was a hurdle left to clear.

One day in late June, the hospital received its first gunshot wound: a young sergeant named Cope, accidentally shot in the arm during drill ten days earlier. Cameron Archer came in with the stretcher, accompanied by the young student Tyler Jamison.

"Mrs. Powers! Please be so good as to come here," Archer called to Narcissa, then disappeared into the room where the surgery would take place.

Narcissa stood looking after him. So this at last was her meeting with Cameron Archer. She might have known that he would be thoroughly in control of the moment. She could give no thought now to Charley, to the murders of the unknown woman and of Old Billy, to the attack on her. The life of a wounded soldier was now the connection—and the barrier—between her and Archer. And Archer himself seemed like a different person, the gentleman's pose of languor replaced by an energy that sharpened his speech and quickened his stride. He was ready for surgery, white oversleeves gartered above his elbows and a leather apron covering a none-too-white shirt and gray trousers tucked into high black boots.

When Narcissa came into the room, Sergeant Cope was lying with his face toward her, eyes open. His dark brown hair and beard were matted, his face pale and beaded with sweat. He saw her and made a tight-lipped smile, then winced and closed his eyes. He was shirtless, his torso covered with a sheet; his lower body was clad in filthy trousers, and his feet were bare. Archer and Jamison were standing over him, their backs to her, examining the wounded arm.

She came up to the sergeant's head, picked up the cloth from the bowl set nearby, wrung it out, and wiped his forehead with firm, gentle strokes. The patient's eyelids flickered, and he reached up with his left hand. Narcissa grasped it in her own. She could feel him relax a little. As he breathed out, she could smell the biting sweetness of brandy on his breath.

Then she looked at the wound. The middle section of the upper arm had been eaten away; white bone showed through flesh that was dark red and pulpy like the meat of an over-ripe plum.

Archer was talking to Jamison, gesturing with his index finger at the wound. "The ball went cleanly through the muscle, no bone involvement, but his luck was bad; gangrene set in. You can see the muscles and tissues on the anterior and lateral portions of the arm are gone. The bones and arteries are visible. There is healthy flesh posteriorly—a small portion." Archer lifted Cope's arm, and the student looked underneath.

The stench of rotting flesh took Narcissa back to Charley's deathbed, and for a moment she was there again, watching death consume her brother. She squeezed her eyes shut to dispel the vision, then looked at the wound again, trying to see it as a doctor would see it, as Charley himself would have seen it, making death not a mysterious power to be feared but an enemy to be fought with all the weapons of the human mind and heart.

Narcissa's eyes met Archer's for a second. Then he went on.

"We will amputate four inches down from the shoulder joint. I have little hope that he will survive the operation itself, but without it, he will surely die. He has been well stimulated with brandy.

"Mrs. Powers, you will administer the chloroform."

Narcissa could not believe her ears. This was a far more exacting procedure than she had ever expected to undertake. Was there no other doctor or student around to administer the anesthetic? She stood immobile, ready to follow Archer's orders, afraid that he would change his mind.

"Take you that funnel," he said, "and place the cotton wool inside it, then invert it over the nose and mouth. Drip the chloroform slowly until the patient loses consciousness— as if in a deep sleep. If there is any sound or movement from the patient, do the same again. And don't worry," he added with a glance into her eyes. "The entire procedure, to save his life or end his suffering, will be over in five minutes."

Narcissa disengaged her fingers from Cope's grip to pick up the funnel and the chloroform bottle. She saw the wounded man lower his uninjured arm to his side and make a fist. As she dripped the chloroform into the funnel, she saw the fist relax and unclench. She used the flat of her hand to raise Cope's eyelid gently. No response. She looked up and nodded to Archer.

The surgeon, with an even, almost conversational tone, continued to instruct Jamison. "Tie the tourniquet here. . . . You see I isolate the blood vessel with the arterial forceps here. . . . I take this thread to ligate. . . . I divide the muscle here, well above the gangrenous flesh. . . . Mr. Jamison, you have experience in using the capital saw, I believe?"

"On cadavers, sir," Jamison replied. Narcissa, her eyes fixed on Cope, heard the quaver in his voice. "And a cow once."

Intent as she was that Cope not wake up, Narcissa was more aware of his shallow breaths than the rasp of the metal sawteeth against the bone. She watched the sergeant's eyelids, occasionally darting a glance at his hand, as if he were all in the world to her, her husband, her precious newborn child. All the while she tried to observe what the doctors were doing, keeping in mind that Charley's infected wound might have been similar to Cope's.

Suddenly the breaths sounded louder. The sawing had stopped. Narcissa heard the severed arm fall with a thud into the basket beside the table.

"Now the rongeurs," she heard Archer murmur. ". . . the bone file . . . we leave the ligatures long. . . ."

At last Archer straightened and waved his hand toward Narcissa. "No more chloroform, Mrs. Powers; allow the sergeant to revive."

Narcissa set the bottle and funnel down on the table. She picked up the cloth again, wrung it out almost dry, and wiped Cope's face. He was still breathing, thank God, lying as if in a deep sleep. The thought of what he would feel when he awakened made Narcissa shudder. But the dead thing, death-bearing, that had been his arm was safely removed now. If God willed it, he would recover.

Archer and Jamison wiped their bloody hands on their aprons. Then Archer reached over to shake the student's hand. "Congratulations, *Doctor* Jamison," Archer said with warmth in his voice. Jamison flushed with pleasure and looked over to where Narcissa was standing. Archer's gaze followed.

"I'm sure we have saved him!" the young man said happily. But Narcissa saw Archer's look turn dark, saw him turn away. She felt they were thinking the same thing, she and Archer: Charley should not have died. Did the darkness of Archer's expression indicate his guilt?

The joy she felt for Cope's having survived the amputation drained away, leaving her heavyhearted.

As she entered the cloakroom to collect her things for the ride home, Narcissa felt more tired than she had ever been in her life. She had called up all her strength to save Cope's life; now there was none left.

Yet Cameron Archer—who had disappeared as soon as he had pronounced the operation on Cope a success—presumably had hours of this labor ahead of him. It was no wonder the doctors considered themselves a breed apart. But their strength involved a kind of hardness, a callusing of emotion. Archer had to be rationing the intensity of feeling he brought to Cope and to the dozens of others like him.

Narcissa was deep in thought as she reached into the cupboard to take her bonnet from the peg. Her fingers touched an unfamiliar fabric, coarse and with a sticky dampness that made her draw back her hand. Gingerly she lifted the bonnet by its black ruched trim and held it at arm's length.

Around the black bonnet was tied a filthy rag resembling, she thought with a shudder, a soiled bandage. It was tied so tight that the bonnet was crushed. Wedged into the bonnet above the knotted rag was a piece of paper. Carefully she drew it out and placed it on the desk.

In block capital letters, printed in pencil, was written, "Be careful your curiosity does not choke you."

Narcissa recoiled, remembering the cloth that Charley described as choking the dead woman. Logically, she knew that this could not be the same cloth, but it might have looked much the same as this one.

Narcissa looked around her, though she knew she was alone: the wooden floors would give warning of the lightest, most cushioned tread. Still, she was overwhelmed with the feeling that someone was watching her, enjoying her discomfiture. She shook off the feeling and composed herself. Then she carefully removed her apron and bundled into it the bonnet, rag, and paper. She would not touch them again, if she could help it; once she had shown them to Mirrie, she would burn the lot.

Be careful your curiosity does not choke you. Archer had threatened her before; this had the mark of his technique. Like the words he had spoken to her at the illumination— *enough to raise the dead*—the import was clear only to her. This time the reference was to the way in which the woman had been killed, choked by a cloth shoved down her throat. But, once again, the phrasing was careful. Dr. Stedman had warned her about possible ungentlemanly expressions of resentment, and this letter would be dismissed as nothing more than that. If she complained, Stedman would feel justified in his belief that ladies should not serve in the hospital. She fumed as she headed out the door and to the carriage where Will waited to drive her home. Even though the words were clearly threatening, they were nothing she could use to prove a crime. But Archer's threat might have one effect he didn't intend: it had made her more determined than ever to find Hughes's notes on his treatment of Charley.

≫≪

Judah Daniel was examining the wares at the farmer's market in Shockoe Bottom, moving slowly in the heat. The basket over her arm was lined with layers of velvety mullein leaves she had picked along the road. They would cushion any tender wares she might purchase, such as eggs or ripe peaches. Then she would use the leaves themselves: whole, to make a poultice, or dried and brewed as a tea to treat colds, or cooked down into a syrup that would head a boil or ease swelling feet.

Judah Daniel looked over at the woman beside her. She saw the open, friendly face without a hint of reserve or suspicion. This would be easy, she thought; Jane Scott would never suspect the planning that had gone into this apparently chance encounter.

"You work up at the Hugheses', don't you? My niece used to help out there wash days. Told me there was a death some months back," Judah Daniel said casually.

"Oh yes," Jane Scott said, nodding, scanning Judah Daniel's face as if trying to remember where they had met before. "It was a sad thing. That young medical student got blood poisoning and died in the house. Yes, it sure was sad."

"Oh?" Judah Daniel's voice held only the mildest interest. "What I heard of was a servant . . . seem like it was a woman or a girl."

"Oh, you mean Aster Jacks. I weren't there then. Seem like she died of the childbed fever. Phebe—that's Mrs. Hughes's maid—don't like them talking about Aster."

"You ever heard who the baby's father was?" Judah Daniel kept the same offhand tone.

"No . . . but I did hear tell the baby look real light-skinned, lighter than the mother, and she was bright-complected."

"Where that baby now?"

"The field servants is caring for it over to the plantation, in Midlothian."

"How that Jake Calder feel about that?"

The meaning of her question was clear, and Jane Scott responded as if it had been spoken. "I reckon she be safe enough for ten, twelve years. Then I doubt it matter if she his own daughter. Some men ain't worth spit." Jane Scott said this with sorrow in her mild brown eyes.

"Ain't that the truth," replied Judah Daniel, shaking her head.

The two women parted as casually as they seemed to have met, but Judah Daniel was smiling inside. So much for the uppity Phebe and her pursed-up hush-mouth. Let's pull this thread and see what ravels.

Chapter Twelve

RICHMOND
LATE JUNE

Narcissa had decided against informing Stedman about the rag and note. It could result in his turning her away from the hospital—for her own protection, as he would see it. At any rate, she reminded herself, the extent of Stedman's own involvement in the grave-robbing and burking was not at all clear. But she refused to be scared away.

One hot morning, about two weeks after the incident, Narcissa had just arrived at the front door of the hospital when hurrying footsteps on the steps behind her caused her to turn around. It was Brit Wallace, almost running in his haste to catch up to her.

Behind him she could see a hack in which Mirrie sat looking out at them. Mirrie must have set out with Brit soon after Narcissa had left for the hospital in the Powerses' own carriage, with Will driving. Narcissa felt a jolt of alarm.

Brit drew level with Narcissa. He was far from the natty figure he usually cut. His stock was tied crooked, and he looked as if he had not shaved that morning. His face was red and wet with perspiration, and she could see what his exertion, in the sultry heat of Richmond's summer, had cost him.

"Mrs. Powers, I apologize—" He panted the words out. "Judah Daniel has been arrested."

"Arrested! Why? By whom?"

"The provost marshal's men have put her in McDaniel's Negro jail down in Shockoe Bottom." Narcissa shuddered. The Negro jail incarcerated free blacks and slaves whose crimes would likely result in execution—and those considered dangerously insane. "I don't know the charge," he continued. "A black man who says he is a friend of hers sought me out last night. How he knew where to find me, I don't know.

"I've been there this morning, but they won't let me see her. In fact, I have been instructed to leave town—I'm told I am suspected of being a spy!"

Narcissa could tell that Brit Wallace's trust in the impervious armor of his British citizenship and his journalistic passepartout was shaken. With his rumpled curls and downturned mouth, he seemed very young, and she thought she detected, along with anger and disbelief, a touch of embarrassment.

"What has happened?" she asked.

"I wrote a dispatch describing the events of *Pawnee* Sunday."

Narcissa thought back to that day, with its repercussions of shame and renewed effort to organize the city's defenses.

Brit had collected himself enough to recover some of his vanity. "The dispatch was very well received in England, I understand. But now that copies of the *Weekly Argus* have made it back across the ocean, I find the Richmond readers about as unwilling to accept a satire on themselves as I should have expected them to be." He gave a shrug.

"I am persona non grata here, and it's best that I leave,

at least for a few weeks until this internecine squabble is settled. I shall pay a visit to Dr. Henry, who is in Washington helping to set up a sanitary commission to assist the Union soldiers and their families.

"But you have to help Judah Daniel." Wallace's voice grew more urgent. "The worst thing is, I am responsible. I know that our visit to her has raised the alarm with Calder and his cohorts, and this is the result."

"If you are responsible, I am more so." The steadiness of her voice surprised Narcissa. That's what my life is like now, she thought. If there is something that must be done, feelings have to wait. "I will go now with Mirrie. I will just go tell them in there"—Narcissa nodded toward the hospital—"and then I can leave."

"Good-bye," Brit Wallace said, holding out his hand. "I hope it is only for a little while."

Narcissa took his hand briefly. "Good-bye."

The Negro jail was a small brick building with shuttered windows. From the outside, there was little to mark it as a place of horror. As they reached the doorway, angry shouting reached their ears, together with an unearthly keening that sounded like a soul in torment.

Narcissa and Mirrie were admitted to see the warden. George Griffin was a big man, well over six feet, with gun-metal-gray hair, a darker beard, and heavy black brows. Narcissa felt his was a figure to inspire fear—no doubt viewed by many as a useful qualification for his position.

"We are here to see Judah Daniel," Narcissa said after the introductions.

"Nobody here by that name," Griffin responded flatly. A glint in his eye told her there would be more to come. She held his gaze, waiting. "We got a Judith Daniels here," he said at last. "Got a complaint she was doctoring white folks." He turned aside to spit into a brass spittoon.

"Who brought the charge?"

"Public Guard," he replied. "They keep an eye on those free blacks; one day we'll get enough on her to take her to trial. She's an abortionist." He was waiting for their reaction. They stared back at him, trying to understand what they had heard.

"Oh, I'm sure you're wrong," Mirrie said. "Judah Daniel does so much good among the free blacks. Those of us who are concerned with the health and welfare of the free black population in Richmond often go through her to see that the neediest will be helped."

Narcissa, while admiring Mirrie's high moral tone, wondered if this argument would be likely to carry any weight with Griffin.

"We would like to talk with her," Mirrie pressed on. "Perhaps we can help to resolve this misunderstanding. Meanwhile, I would appreciate it if you could discover the specifics of the charge against her, so that we can help her to refute it."

The warden's scowl was deeper than ever, but he called out to an attendant, "Bring Judith Daniels down here so these ladies can talk to her." He then excused himself, and the two friends waited.

At last Judah Daniel came into the room. Her hands were manacled in front; judging by her gait, her feet were likewise bound under her skirts. A fat black woman, wearing a gray dress stained under the arms, was with her, and a skinny white youth in a Public Guard uniform stood behind them. Judah Daniel's eyes took in the room and its occupants, but any reaction she may have had did not show on her face.

"Please leave us," Mirrie said with quiet authority to the guards. The youth shrugged and moved across the hall, where he leaned against the wall and folded his arms to wait. The fat woman looked huffy, but Mirrie's quiet firmness won out. She also left the room and disappeared down the hall.

Narcissa and Mirrie helped Judah Daniel to a seat. She was moving slowly, and her face looked gray and creased. Her clothes were the same Narcissa had seen her in before—brown homespun skirt, white bodice, white band concealing her hair—but they were stained now, and the clothing hung limp on her spare frame.

"I feel this is my fault. My seeking you out attracted their notice," Narcissa said quietly. "But I am here—and my sister-in-law, Mirrie Powers—to satisfy them that you've done no wrong."

"They watch me. They watch all the free blacks. They're so afraid of us." A bitter smile twisted Judah Daniel's mouth. "Freedom makes us dangerous. If we go around the slaves, the slaves might catch freedom. They don't want us around the whites neither. Maybe they're afraid of us catching whiteness."

"Where did they come up with this charge against you—that you do abortions?" Mirrie asked in a gentle voice. Judah Daniel shot her a glance as if to read her thoughts. Mirrie met her eyes with a calm gaze. Judah Daniel relaxed then and, turning her eyes on some invisible scene beyond the jailhouse walls, began to speak.

"Judith Daniels was my name in slavery. When I got my freedom, I gave myself a new name, Judah, for the blessed kingdom. And I changed Daniels to Daniel to show I don't belong to no one." She pronounced the words slowly and carefully, as if she had memorized them and was recalling them exactly. Her manacled hands lay still in her lap. "I've had my freedom seven years now—be eight years on the ninth of September. I am a good conjure woman and a good doctor. I can deliver a baby alive after the doctors done give up. And I can make a baby come before term.

"I was born in Georgia, in Savannah. When I was twenty-eight, I went with my mistress to her son's home in Chesapeake. She died there the next year. Her husband been a doctor. Her son had a plantation and lots of slaves, more than a hundred.

"I was a house servant in Savannah, and I learned to read. I read the doctor's medical books when I could. I put that learning together with what I learned from an old conjure woman come to Savannah from Jamaica. Her mother was from Africa. I learned to birth babies and heal the sick and ease the dying.

"One day, after my mistress died, a young girl came to me. She told me the master raped her, and she was carrying his child. She asked me to get rid of the baby. She cried and begged. She didn't want to have a child in slavery, a child that might grow strong and tall to be sold away by its own daddy.

"I told her I couldn't do it. That very night they pulled her out of the river. She drowned herself rather than have that baby. I cried and I prayed over that girl's body. She weren't but fourteen years old. Then I let it be known that no woman would be forced to bear a child in slavery—that she could come to me. The slave doctoresses know how to make medicines, even make one from the roots of the cotton plant, to keep babies from being born into slavery. But most women want their babies. They won't stop hoping things will turn out different for them.

"The master suspected me. He would come around and ask questions. But I was careful, and he didn't push it with me. I think he was afraid of me. He was right to be afraid of me. I knew how to kill him or drive him blind and crazy. But I didn't do it.

"Things had been going on this way for more than a year when another girl came to me desperate and scared—only this one was white. The master's own daughter was in the family way. She was so afraid she couldn't hardly talk. Would I do for her like I did for the slave girls, she said, 'cause she couldn't have this baby. Her daddy would kill her, she said. I tell you the truth, she so pale and shaking, I thought if I said no she'd pick up the knife I'd been using to scrape the corn and kill herself right there.

"I said no. I figured maybe it could still come out all right, she could marry the boy who got her in trouble. But to tell the truth, I was afraid. I could be tried and hanged, or most likely hanged without a trial, for doing what she asked. Then one night the master came to me himself. Do for his daughter like I did for the slave girls. He begged me with tears in his eyes. I had to wonder what could get him so upset. I could think of only two reasons. I never tried to find out which it was. He promised to give me my freedom and enough money to set myself up away from there. I didn't have no family to keep me there. Finally I said yes. I gave that young girl the medicine, and I helped her through it. She was so sick. But as soon as she could get up out of bed, they sent her away. I never did see her again.

"I went to the master for my freedom. He was cold. Likely he wanted to forget he ever seen my face. He told me, 'Judith, you already free. My mama freed you in her will.' Two years I wasted to his greed and evil. But now he wanted to get rid of me. I made him pay.

"I walked away from there with my freedom, and one hundred dollars of his money—money that us slaves made for him and never saw a penny of up until that time—and the medical books that belonged to the old doctor. And I ain't never made another woman lose a baby, nor done no doctoring for white folks."

Judah Daniel looked at Narcissa and Mirrie in turn. She was angry that she had to rely on these white women for help, but she forced herself to be practical. If they would speak for her, knowing who she was and what she had done, she was willing to accept them as allies against the white men who had entrapped her.

"Don't worry," Narcissa said to her, leaning forward to touch her hand. "You will be free again soon. I have an idea that may help speed your release."

When the warden returned, he had Judah Daniel led away again, then settled into the chair behind his desk with a sigh, as if he anticipated having his time wasted by these interfering ladies.

"Tell us the specifics of the charge against her." Narcissa kept her voice even.

Griffin picked up a piece of paper from his desk and held it at arm's length. "About nine o'clock on the night of May 16, two white women and a man visited Judith Daniels. The man and one woman went into her house while the other woman waited in the carriage."

Narcissa could feel Mirrie stiffen next to her, while she herself struggled to conceal her shock. They were those women! But both of them had gone into the house. Was he trying to trick them into a reaction?

"The man and the woman were approached by the Public Guard as they left the house. The Guardsmen stated that they saw no reason to make further inquiries at that time. Nor did they determine the identities of the man and the two women."

Narcissa remembered the sound of the coins Cameron Archer had poured into the guardsmen's hands. The bribe had been generous enough, apparently, to cloud their memory, but not enough to erase it.

The warden went on. "We later received information that Judith Daniels was performing abortions, and we believe the unknown white persons were coming to her for that purpose. This charge has been alleged before, when she first came to Richmond seven years ago."

Narcissa chose her words carefully. "But it has never been substantiated, has it? And there is only hearsay to link an abortion—or any sort of medical treatment—to the visit by those unknown parties. This charge is worthless in a court of law, and I believe you know it.

"I suggest you parole Judah Daniel to us. We will help to see that she is employed in a useful capacity as a servant in the medical college hospital."

Griffin knit his brows. He looked at Narcissa and Mirrie in turn, as if weighing how much trouble these ladies could cause him. Finally he said, "Where your interest in this matter comes from, I don't know. Frankly, it does you no credit. We will let Judith Daniels go, but I assure you we will continue to watch her." He stopped short of saying that they, too, would be watched, but the unspoken threat hung in the air.

❧❧

Judah Daniel walked the few miles home. She had refused the white women's offer of a ride in their carriage. She wanted to be alone, the way no one in jail is ever alone. She wanted to shuck off those false selves that had overgrown her skin— what those people saw when they looked at her, the sound of her own voice explaining herself to them. She wanted to clean herself down to the bones.

When the Guard come for her, surprising her in the street near the Farmers' Market, she'd thought at once of Cyrus. Had they discovered his throat had been cut, and his house robbed, and linked her with the crime? It had almost made her laugh to hear the trumped-up charge against her. But a spell in McDaniel's jail was nothing to laugh about. She'd sent word to John Chapman's bake shop for someone to find Darcy and give her shelter. The Chapmans would have taken care of the girl as long as was needed. Thank the Lord, though, it hadn't been long.

The sun dropped low in the sky as she walked into its slanting light. The shadows were long and black. She was near home now. She kept her eyes down. Between the glare and the shadows, she didn't see anyone; didn't want to talk if she did.

The riders came toward her out of the low sun. They seemed about to ride past her without notice. Public Guard. Trouble for somebody, she thought automatically, no wonder there's nobody out on the street.

Then one of the riders called out to the others. They all—there were three of them—turned their horses and reined to a halt in front of her, blocking her path.

Judah Daniel felt the heat coming off the horses' skin and breathed in the dust they had stirred up in the road. She shaded her eyes with her hand. She couldn't see the faces of the men, but she recognized the shiny yellow hair of Jake Calder, astride a skittish chestnut. It was only three days ago she had had his name on her lips, questioning the Hugheses' servant Jane Scott. Now here he was. A sour taste filled her mouth, and she wanted to spit.

"Judith Daniels," he called out. "Jail weren't to your liking, I reckon, since I see you got out mighty fast. Your white ladies help you? What'd you do for them to make 'em so grateful?"

Judah Daniel squinted, trying to make out the expression on Calder's face. Why was he talking to her like this? He was digging at her, trying to provoke a response. She put her answer in her face: she'd see him in hell before she'd tell him anything.

They stared at each other for a long moment. The other two men were grinning at each other, sharing some private joke. Calder was on the outside, the way she would have to pass. She saw he kept the horse on edge—jabbing with his spurs, pulling back on the reins when the horse started forward. She edged to her right, preparing to move around Calder, but he moved to block her path.

Calder spoke again. "Guess you're mighty eager to get to that shanty of yours." He turned his head toward the other two men. "Guess you're looking forward to sitting by the fire . . ." He let the sentence trail off. The other two laughed.

Tingling numbness took hold of Judah Daniel—her lips, her hands and feet. She felt so weak that it was all she could do not to sit down in the road. At that moment—at the exact moment that the men spurred their horses and rode off—she smelled smoke.

She gathered her skirts in her hands and took off running. She could see her house. Its wooden frame stood silhouetted against orange flames. The fire sucked in the air with a low roar, exhaled it again in dark smoke pouring into the sky. As she ran, she saw people running out from the neighboring houses. She saw a man, hunched over, running under the smoke away from the door. He had a bundle—was it rags?— thrown over his shoulder, and he was running back to where a little crowd was gathered. Strong arms caught her as she ran, pulled her back from the flames, held her. She saw the faces of her neighbors, eyes filled with love and concern. Then the crowd parted. She saw the face of John Chapman. She looked down at the bundle he carried. It was Darcy.

The hands pulled Judah Daniel to sit on the ground. Chapman knelt in front of her with Darcy, placing the girl so that Judah Daniel could cradle her upper body.

There was no apparent injury, thank the Lord; her clothes weren't even singed. A blanket someone had brought was put over the girl. Darcy seemed in a kind of fitful sleep, taking quick, shallow breaths. Judah Daniel felt Darcy's neck for the pulse and found it weak and rapid.

She looked up to where John Chapman was still kneeling. She felt surprised he hadn't rushed off to superintend the men who, using hand-fashioned hoes, rakes, and shovels, were working to stop the fire from spreading to neighboring houses. It was in the man's nature to take charge of things.

Then Chapman raised his eyes. They were red-rimmed, and they flicked away from her face. "Darcy came to us like you told her to when you was taken away. But she couldn't find that little cat she carries around with her."

"Princess, she named it," Judah Daniel said softly.

Chapman nodded. "She was upset about it. Then this afternoon we heard the Public Guard was at your house. When we couldn't find Darcy, we was afraid she came back here. We—" He broke off and wiped his sleeve across his eyes.

Then he looked Judah Daniel in the face. "They ordered us to get off the streets. They said they'd shoot any nigger who put a head out of the door." Tears were running down his face, but he seemed unaware of them as he looked into her eyes. She felt his strength, and his caring.

"Thank God you came," Judah Daniel said softly, taking

her hand from Darcy's head to grasp his hand. "She'll be all right. Just got to get her spirit back. She's mortal afraid of fire."

Chapman nodded his understanding. Judah Daniel had taken the young girl, burned in a fire at the age of three and unwanted by her owners, and nursed her back to health. The scar Darcy bore on her face was a reminder of that fire, and a reminder of the invisible wound that had left her for several years unable to speak.

Chapman straightened his shoulders. "You know you and Darcy got a place to stay with us as long as you want it."

Judah Daniel watched John Chapman get up and trot over to where the men were working. You don't get to be what he is by giving in to humiliation, she thought, admiring his strength. "And I don't give in," she said softly, as she looked down at Darcy, "and neither do you."

❧❧

With Narcissa seated across the room embroidering a tea towel, Mirrie and Nat Cohen were engaged in the nearest thing to a private conversation possible between a gentleman and a lady who were not married to each other. Narcissa kept her eyes on her embroidery, but her mind was busily wondering what they could be discussing so quietly for so long. In the big back parlor, with its clutter of books and objects, she could not see the pair unless she turned to look across the room—which she was resolutely trying not to do.

A maiden lady like Mirrie was presumed by society not to know about certain things. Yet, although Mirrie had never been married, she had traveled and read widely in the literature of less constrained times and places. Mirrie was, if anything, rather too bold in her speech, Narcissa thought, so as to show people she was not a prude. If Narcissa had ever doubted her friend's open-mindedness, Mirrie's quiet sympathy for Judah Daniel's shocking history would have convinced her that it was real.

Yet this openness did not extend to Mirrie's private emotions, which were as safely guarded as those of the most prudish old maid. Narcissa was afire to learn the nature of her friend's feelings for Nat Cohen. But she had little hope that Mirrie would reveal them to her, and she despaired of her own ability simply to put the question and risk a withering rebuke.

Tomorrow Nat Cohen would be riding off to join his regiment. Based on his success as a businessman and the wealth he could contribute to raising the regiment, he had been given the rank of colonel. He looked like a different man in the gray, gold-braided uniform, Narcissa thought—no longer a man of the world, but a soldier of the Confederacy.

Then Mirrie spoke in a tone Narcissa could not help but hear. "I would not have expected this of you!"

Narcissa stared at the handiwork in her lap and willed herself not to look over toward the pair. She could guess what Mirrie looked like, face flushed redder than her hair, but what of dignified, urbane Nat Cohen? Was he taking this second helping of scorn from Mirrie on the subject of his enlistment as humbly as he had the first?

Cohen replied sharply, but with more humor than anger in his voice. "I wasn't aware there was any shame attached to an honorable proposal of marriage."

Narcissa's eyes widened. Now it was Mirrie's face she wanted to see.

Mirrie's response came with icy distinctness. "It is customary, in enlightened societies, to be acquainted with the person you propose to marry. The very fact of your . . . intention shows that you do not know me at all. Although, someone very like

you has been my friend for years, and has listened with understanding on his features when I talked of the evils of marriage,
and how the institution demeans women, making them mere
appendages of men. Were you aware, Mr. Cohen, that you had
a doppelgänger? A most agreeable fellow, who will smile at
anything while his soul remains untouched."

Narcissa could imagine the shrug of Cohen's shoulders as
he said, still with a laugh in his voice, "Your idealism is one
of the things I love about you."

There was a "hmph!" of outrage from Mirrie, then, "You
value my convictions, so you seek to dismiss them! It's this
war, sending all you men to your sweethearts, and then to
your encampments, like lemmings off a cliff! If you ever
heeded—" Mirrie's voice dropped.

Cohen's voice, low-pitched but firm, was the next Narcissa
heard. "We live in the only world we have. The choices we
have are given to us. We are tied—"

Mirrie broke in. "Tied! If we cannot break our ties, how can
the world progress? Human beings are meant to cast off old
forms that retard progress, just as higher forms of life evolve
from lower. If we reverenced all our *ties*, Mr. Cohen, we would
have no need of your store. We would be living in caves and
tearing the flesh off the bones with our teeth! But no—we have
progressed. We eat off fine china, we cut our meat with silver.
Yet look around the table. We are still savages, the powerful
tyrannizing over the weak, the male over the female, enacting
the old forms that were set in the primeval jungle when we
gathered around the fire. What would we find if we broke those
ties? Would we find that we could all be free?" Mirrie's words
rang out, thrilling Narcissa with the vision of a world remolded
nearer to the heart's desire.

"Away from that fire . . . your world is cold, Miss Powers.
But I know the warmth that is in you, and I want it to

warm me." Emotion roughened Nat Cohen's voice. Then the lightness returned. "I own, I am not so far from a savage myself. My blood is red. I may soon see it, more of it on the outside of me than I would like. But do you think that, if I became a husband, my forehead would flatten and my jaw thrust forth, like an ape-man?" Cohen paused, then went on. "I believe I know you. Do you not know me? Do you not believe that we could be the same he and she, if we were—"

"Don't say any more!" Mirrie broke in, almost sobbing. "I want us to remain friends. Don't say anything that will force a breach between us."

Some moments passed. Narcissa heard Cohen sigh. "Very well. I will write to your father. Whether you read the letters . . . well, I hope that you will."

Mirrie and Cohen moved toward the door. Narcissa kept her eyes down, willing herself to be invisible. She was relieved when Cohen left without crossing the room to take leave of her. Indeed, she thought, one tie I would willingly break is that of chaperone!

Mirrie walked past Narcissa and out of the room, her back straight and her face bright with anger. Narcissa stood for a moment. Nat Cohen must have gone for years accepting Mirrie's vestal repudiation of marriage. But something—perhaps the threat of death, the knowledge that there was not so much time after all—had wrought a change in his feelings. When Mirrie had spoken of a new world in which women could be free, Narcissa had felt it would be worth sacrificing the security of convention to make that dream a reality. But Nat Cohen, with his warmth and wit—what would Mirrie lose if he went out of her life, never to return?

Then she went to follow Mirrie, to offer comfort she felt sure would be rejected.

Chapter Thirteen

RICHMOND

EARLY JULY

Judah Daniel and Darcy had gone to stay in the sprawling house that was home to the four generations of Chapmans. Rebuilding her own house, small as it had been, was out of the question for now, with all the building materials in the city devoted to the war effort. They had only the clothes they were wearing and the coins she had kept buried behind the house. But replacing their few belongings had not concerned Judah Daniel.

Darcy's quiet sadness had concerned her, and she had not been able to find the cure until John Chapman discovered the yellow cat Princess hiding under a tangle of sweetshrub and forsythia at the back of the burned house. Grinning like a boy, he had pulled the kitten out of his jacket and put her in Darcy's arms. He had had to turn away at the sight of her smile.

As soon as she was easy in her mind about Darcy's health, Judah Daniel had gone to the Powerses' house, where Mirrie had welcomed her kindly, then left her and Narcissa to speak in private.

"You helped me," Judah Daniel said to Narcissa. "Now I'm going to help you. Cyrus is dead. And you—whoever killed Old Billy and Cyrus likely come for you next. You ever seen a spider eat its web? It's getting ready to string up another one."

She saw Narcissa's shudder.

"When he come to me, Cyrus had a scarf. It was a silk scarf, cost a lot of money. He told me it was wrapped around the face of the woman. Someone put it on her before she was buried. Then, when they dug her up, Old Billy saved the scarf. Whoever killed Old Billy put the scarf with his body, where he thought it would never be found—in the pit at the medical college where they puts the body parts."

Judah Daniel drew a breath, then went on. "It was their job to put in the quicklime that eats the flesh off the bones. But Cyrus had a feeling when his daddy didn't come home. Instead of throwing in the quicklime, Cyrus went down into the pit and found Old Billy's body and the scarf. He brought the scarf back out."

Narcissa turned her head away. The vision was nauseating.

"I saw it," Judah Daniel continued. "It had a letter *H* embroidered on it."

"Hughes!" Narcissa exclaimed. Then a doubt came to her. "He must have known there was a chance Cyrus might find it. Why would he take the risk?" Narcissa asked.

"Didn't care, would be my guess." Judah Daniel shrugged. "How could Cyrus prove how that scarf got in there, and who would listen to a half-crazy Negro? Cyrus didn't count for much even with the black folks."

"How was he killed?" Narcissa asked, lines of pain in her face.

"His throat was cut."

Narcissa put her hand to her throat.

Judah Daniel went on. "There was a servant at the Hugheses' house who had a baby and died about the same time the grave was robbed—died of the childbed fever, is what they said. A slave, name of Aster Jacks. Stand to reason it was her body they dug up. They got her baby over to the Hugheses' place across the river."

Narcissa repeated the words to herself. Aster Jacks. Named, the ghost seemed to dwindle. It was strange how death had given the slave woman a power she surely never had in life.

"What else did Cyrus tell you about . . . her?" Narcissa asked.

Judah Daniel frowned. "Not much. He heard from the doctors she was real sick with childbed fever and would have died anyway, if she hadn't been killed. But don't none of this explain why somebody stuffed a rag down her throat, and then wrapped a costly scarf around her face."

Judah Daniel had an idea about that, but it wouldn't do to say just yet, not until she had more proof. Now that she would be working in the hospital to satisfy the terms of her parole, she would have a better chance to get at that proof. But white folks was white folks, after all, even though this young woman didn't seem nearly as bad as some.

Narcissa looked at her. "If the baby is alive, we must see that no harm comes to it." She looked away, hesitating. "My brother would have wanted it that way," she said at last. "You had better not come here any more," she added. "But I will see you at the hospital. I am glad to have your help."

Judah Daniel nodded in acknowledgment of Narcissa's compliment, then took her leave.

Returning to Springfield for the birth of Mary's baby had been the last thing on Narcissa's mind, as events were moving toward the battle that would decide Richmond's future and likely fill its hospitals with more seriously wounded men than they had seen thus far. A letter from her sister Lydia had changed her mind.

Dear Sister,

The time for Mary's confinement has come. I am fearful for her health. She writes she cannot keep down any food, and the heat is oppressive to her. Mary's spirits are very low. She remembers her mother's difficulty with her last confinement.

There are no doctors left near Springfield, they have all gone to wear the uniform of field surgeons. Her kinfolk cannot come from Ford Junction—they say soldiers are everywhere, and they fear getting caught up in the battle that all are awaiting. Lelia expects to be confined next month and dare not make the trip. I have promised Mary I will come, but I must ask you to come as well, for if Genia or Clayton were to fall sick, I would have to return home at once. I know you and Mary are not close, but at a time like this, all women are sisters.

Narcissa's first reaction had been irritation. She'd never attended at a confinement; having given birth herself no more qualified her to help with the process than having a leg amputated qualified a soldier to be a surgeon.

That thought called to mind the amputation performed on Sergeant Cope, when Cameron Archer ordered her to administer the chloroform. She had not been asked to do so again, and never expected to be. Archer had called on her for some private reason of his own, she had decided: to test her, to frighten her, perhaps to provoke a reaction from her, by showing her an amputation similar to the one Charley had had before he died. She did not know the reason. But she knew she could perform the procedure again.

The use of the anesthetic to ease childbirth pains was disputed. Many doctors believed it went against God's word—"in sorrow thou shalt bring forth children"—but those doctors were men. That was something she could do for Mary, if it was needed.

Soon she had paced it out in her mind: she would walk to the little closet where the drugs were stored, extract the bottle of chloroform, then, feigning a call of nature, go to the cloakroom to empty half its contents into a vial that she would conceal in her reticule. The room had been empty; the need for haste had emboldened her. Feeling like an actress performing a role, Narcissa had crossed the room and entered the closet, picked up the bottle, and crossed her arms to conceal it in her oversleeve.

In the cloakroom, Narcissa felt surprise that her hands were steady as she poured the fluid and carefully resealed both the large bottle and the small vial. The chloroform was a tangible sign of her initiation into a world of secrets. She had only stepped over the threshold, but she was on the other side.

Still, what if the baby was turned the wrong way? Neither she nor Lydia would know what to do. She remembered hearing her mother talk about a granny midwife, an old slave woman, but she would have been dead for years now. . . .

Judah Daniel had been a midwife. She had offered her help to Narcissa in finding out the reasons for the killings. Perhaps she would help with this, too. She would ask Judah Daniel.

HANOVER COUNTY
EARLY JULY

At Springfield, Aunt Dodie met Narcissa with outstretched arms, calling over her shoulder to Dru to bring the bags. Narcissa introduced Judah Daniel as an experienced midwife from Richmond, to which Aunt Dodie made a respectful nod. Then she asked, "How is Mary?"

"Oh, she moaning and fussing. She lay back and moan, then she set up and fuss." Aunt Dodie smiled indulgently, and Narcissa could see that her sister-in-law's condition had won the old servant's sympathy, at least for the time being. "Just like all womenfolks with their first."

"Where is John?"

"He gone to the barn, and there he'll stay. I seen the look on his face." The three women shared a laugh. Narcissa realized it was the first time she had seen Judah Daniel smile with simple amusement. The doctoress was in her element, sure of her ability, Narcissa thought, and she felt a warm rush of gratitude.

"Go on up and see how things progressing," Aunt Dodie said.

The door to John and Mary's bedroom was open to encourage a breeze, but the heat of July was thick in the room. Narcissa tapped on the open door, then stepped into the room, followed by Judah Daniel. Lydia sat in a chair next to the bed, patting Mary's forehead with a cool cloth. Narcissa introduced Judah Daniel, and the midwife stepped quickly to the far side of the bed, pulled the sheet up like a tent, and began examining the patient. Mary seemed hardly aware of their presence; she had all her attention, all her strength, centered on the alien presence that was occupying her body.

The contrast between Lydia and Mary struck Narcissa. Lydia's hair was smooth, her face serene, though with a little frown of concern on her brow. Her figure, despite the thickening of her waist with the births of her children, was tidy, and her gray calico dress fit smoothly.

Mary's face was mottled, red spots on skin as white as the sheets that covered her swollen belly. She looked both angry and apprehensive, like a bully that has picked a fight and is getting the worst of it. Narcissa kissed her cheek; her skin was hot and damp.

Judah Daniel murmured a few words to Mary, who closed her eyes and seemed fractionally to relax, then walked over to Lydia and Narcissa. She drew them a few steps away from the bed and spoke in a low tone. "How long she been like this?"

"Two days," Lydia answered, a worried frown on her face.

"Tell her I brought something to ease her pains," Narcissa replied, "if you think it will relieve her fear. Chloroform," she added in response to Lydia's questioning look.

"Did you!" Lydia smiled. "You are clever! But Mary's not afraid of the pain just now. She's afraid she will be enceinte forever. In truth, if her pains do not begin soon, I fear for the child."

Judah Daniel nodded. "I can give her something that will purge her and then bring on her pains. Aunt Dodie can help me get it ready in the kitchen."

"What is it?" Narcissa asked.

Judah Daniel looked at her through half-shut eyelids, as

though anticipating her reaction. "Just a weed grows wild in the fields. You know it as a poison."

"Poison!" Narcissa and Lydia said together. Narcissa glanced over at Mary, who made no sign of having heard.

Judah Daniel nodded quickly. "If she was to take too much of it, it would make her real sick, maybe kill her. But if I give her just enough, it will act just like I said. Is her husband a big man?"

Narcissa and Lydia stared, shocked by the non sequitur. Then Narcissa spoke. "Yes, he is tall."

Judah Daniel nodded again. "And she's small, look like she'd stand just over five feet tall. One problem is, the baby's big like the daddy. Other problem is, sometimes with first babies the momma's body don't know what to do, how to get started. You brought me here to help," she addressed Narcissa. "Are you going to let me do what I know how to do?"

Narcissa thought of what she knew about Judah Daniel. The conjure woman. Was this poisonous concoction a bit of super-stitious nonsense that could endanger Mary and her baby? Yet it seemed to her she knew Judah Daniel, had known her since that first glimpse of her at the slave auction. It was something about her face, serious but somehow more alive than other people's, her strong and capable hands. She was a healer.

Lydia was looking at Narcissa, a tight little smile on her face. "A granny midwife, Narcissa? Have the doctors aban-doned us women so completely?"

Narcissa answered both her sister's and Judah Daniel's questions with one word: "Yes."

Narcissa had watched Judah Daniel prepare the dose and give it to Mary. The purgative had taken effect quickly; now they were waiting for Mary's labor to begin in earnest.

Around five o'clock Aunt Dodie came to the door. "Them

old biddies from Vontay is sitting in the parlor. Said they heard the midwife was here. I sat them down and served them something to eat, but now they's wanting to come up and see Mary."

"Narcissa!" Lydia's voice was sharp. "Go talk to them, chloroform them, do whatever you have to do, just keep them out of this room." She shuddered. "I still get the shivers from the tales they told me when I was confined with Clayton."

Narcissa remembered with wry amusement that, as a young girl, she had listened outside the door to hear these same ladies reveal the secret horrors of childbirth. Now she avoided them, and deplored the effects of their stories on women nearing confinement. She pushed down her sleeves, smoothed her hair, and went down the stairs. When she entered the parlor, startled looks from Mrs. Wiley and Mrs. Mays gave Narcissa the distinct impression that she had been the subject of their gossip. She forced herself to welcome the "old biddies" with a peck on the cheek.

Mrs. Mays nodded coolly, then pursed her whiskery lips to sip at her glass of scuppernong wine. Mrs. Wiley, the rowboat to Mrs. Mays's frigate, looked down rather guiltily at the half-eaten cookie in her hand, popped it into her mouth, and simpered at Narcissa, dislodging crumbs.

"I brought along some fried chicken for John," Mrs. Mays remarked, looking around as if she expected him to come out of hiding. "Your Dodie took it into the kitchen. I expect the servants will get it all before the poor man even gets a piece."

"I'm sure John won't starve," Narcissa said lightly. "Perhaps you would like some yourselves."

Mrs. Wiley brightened for a moment, but Mrs. Mays frowned and responded, "I had my dinner hours ago." Mrs.

Wiley's eyes returned to the cookie plate, and her hands fidgeted like the paws of a mouse wondering if it dare test the cat.

"We wanted to go up to see Mary. Aunt Dodie told us the midwife said Mary could not be disturbed," Mrs. Mays continued in the same disapproving tone.

"Yes, she wants her to rest." Narcissa was careful not to raise any specific objections for the harpies to counter.

"Oh, we wouldn't tire her out," Mrs. Mays replied. "We've been at many confinements, haven't we, Sarah?"

Mrs. Wiley's spectacles made her pale blue eyes huge. Once again Narcissa thought of a small, timid animal.

"Of course, your dear mother was with Lydia for her first confinement—we understood we weren't needed—but after she died, when Lydia was confined with that boy of hers, you can be sure we were here to help her out. Unless there are some ladies present with experience in these things, a woman is just at the mercy of the doctor. Why, many's the time I've seen them try to use forceps when a woman had just begun to get her pains hard. That's foolishness! I soon set them straight, didn't I, Sarah?"

Mrs. Wiley looked up at her friend and nodded in admiration. Her hand began to steal toward the plate of cookies.

"A little knowledge is a dangerous thing," Mrs. Mays continued, "and that's what these doctors have, most of 'em. I say go with a midwife any time, though they aren't what they used to be when my own mother, rest her soul, was alive. Why, she could reach right in and turn the baby—any good midwife could. Nowadays, if the baby don't present right, it's the forceps or worse."

Here it comes, thought Narcissa.

"Poor Arabelle Carter. She was confined with twins. Now, you know, folks used to say two babies, two fathers, but I don't believe that. My own cousin Mary Green had two sets of twins, and both of 'em lived to grow up, and the boys was both the spit and image of their father. The girls favored Great-Grandma Green.

"Anyway, Arabelle Carter's twins were cut to pieces right out of her body. A midwife don't even bring those cutting tools with her to the bed. Many's the woman faints dead away when the doctor comes clanking in, and it's a mercy if they do. The doctor said it was kill the babies or kill the mother, and maybe it was true—but Arabelle was never the same after that, and I blame that doctor. I do."

Narcissa broke into the flow of words to offer more wine.

"That was the saddest funeral, those two little coffins," Mrs. Mays added, holding out her glass. Mrs. Wiley, whose glass had been empty for some time, handed it to Narcissa as well.

Narcissa turned away quickly and stood with her back to them at the sideboard, pouring the wine with exaggerated care. Why must they bring up these horrors at every delivery? She remembered Arabelle Carter as a quiet, sad woman. What had Mrs. Stedman said about Rachel Hughes's loss of her babies and her addiction to laudanum? Perhaps Rachel, like Arabelle Carter, had never been the same.

When Mary's cry came, Narcissa almost dropped the decanter, but recovered and set both glasses in front of the guests before running upstairs. Looking back, she saw the harpies exchange a glance in which she could read satisfied anticipation. The curtain was rising on the last act.

After that scream, things happened quickly. Labor pains convulsed Mary's body. Each would leave her limp, so that Narcissa wondered if Mary could survive another. Then the next would come, even stronger. There was no time to employ the chloroform. Narcissa stood near Mary's head on one side, Lydia at the other; they grasped her arms and helped to support her when the pains were on her. At last Judah Daniel said, "Not much longer, Mrs. Wilson. Give me a big push—now!"

A climactic convulsion forced Mary down onto the bed. Now there was a new life in the room. Judah Daniel held up the slippery shape, supporting it under its two arms, for the mother and aunts to see. Narcissa could see it was a girl, beautiful, perfect, delicate and strong, mouth squared in a wail of protest. Through her own tears, she saw the look of amazement on Mary's face as she held out her arms to her daughter.

Judah Daniel smiled with satisfaction. The baby was fine, the mother was fine. Then she glanced at Narcissa. There was grief in the girl's face, so strong it was like her baby had been taken from her all over again. Odd how she'd brought chloroform for Mrs. Wilson's labor. Maybe she'd been hoping it would put a distance between her and the birth, blot out her own feelings along with the childbirth pains.

Judah Daniel was about to reach her hand out to her, but turned away to the baby instead. Over the gulf of the differences that divided them, what healing did she have to offer Narcissa Powers?

WASHINGTON CITY

"It is as if I have crossed to the other side of the chessboard," Brit Wallace wrote. "On the short acquaintance of one day within its confines, Washington seems no more than a reflection of Richmond reversed in a looking-glass.

"Here the soldiers are in blue, mostly, though many appear interchangeable with their sworn foes to the south. Here, as in the South, are companies of fez-capped Zouaves, named and costumed to emulate those who so distinguished themselves in the Crimea: what will happen should they ever encounter each other in battle? Here, at the heart of the government that is going to war at least in part to put slavery in check, there are still slaves.

"As regards the cities themselves, the capitals resemble one another, at once callow and quaint, adorned with pearls of neoclassical architecture cast among the literal swine of a pioneer village."

Brit frowned and rested his pencil. He was doing his best to preserve the disinterestedness appropriate to a journalist. Yet the fact was, he was eager to return to Richmond. His few weeks' sojourn in the Union capital had given him time to think over the sequence of events in Richmond. He now believed that the uniformed youth who had come to his room at the Exchange Hotel and demanded that he leave the city had been simply a friend or hireling of Cameron Archer. It had been Archer's way of making true his "prophecy" that Wallace would not be around much longer, and may not have had any official validity at all. Wallace could have kicked himself for being so gullible.

In a half-hour he would tighten his cravat and go to dine with Dr. Henry. He knew he would hear all about the newly created Sanitary Commission, and would possibly pick up some useful information about the Union plans for war.

But his mind kept returning to Narcissa Powers, to the mystery they were engaged in investigating back in Richmond. He would have to sound out Henry on the subject of puerperal fever—but carefully. He had given Mrs. Powers his word to keep the chain of suspicious events a secret. Having left Richmond did not mean that Henry himself was in the clear, after all; and today's rift was no proof against yesterday's complicity, nor yet tomorrow's.

RICHMOND

Richmond is home now, Narcissa mused as she lay in darkness looking up at the ceiling of the now-familiar bedroom in the Powerses' house. Her life at Springfield seemed to belong to the remote past. It had been strange, returning there with a bottle of chloroform in her reticule and with the conjure woman Judah Daniel at her side. Strange how the black doctoress had come to seem more a part of her world than did her own kin. I could learn from her, she thought; but still society's division ruled their interactions. Judah Daniel had ridden to Springfield and back to Richmond sitting on the driver's box next to Dru. Narcissa thought again of what Mirrie had said about ties that had to be broken.

Still, it was a relief to be back here, gliding toward sleep, away from the cries of Mary's baby—cries that more than once had brought her out of bed and to her feet before she remembered they were not for her.

Her mind drifted, and she found herself remembering, almost reliving, those cries, muffled by her sleep-fogged state. Suddenly another cry—this time it was no memory—pierced the haze and jarred her to wakefulness. Someone was whimpering; the sound seemed to be coming through the open window. Narcissa pulled aside the bed's net draping and ran to look. The moon was bright, casting long shadows across the yard. She thought she saw a man's shape, there, at the far end of the yard.

Narcissa screamed. As if in a dream, she saw the figure

turn slowly. Something fell to the ground, something light-colored, and lay there, still. The man vanished. How could he move so quickly? Had there really been someone there?

Narcissa thrust her feet into her slippers and ran down the stairs, toward the back of the house, and out the door. She knew she was doing a stupid thing—what if the man was still there, hiding in the shadows?—but anger overpowered caution. She wanted to close on him, to frighten him as he had frightened her. As he had been frightening her, it seemed, ever since Charley's death.

"Stop!" she shouted as loud as she could. "You! Stop!"

She came to the spot by the rose bushes where the man, real or imagined, had stood. The light-colored thing was still lying on the ground, but a shadow was spreading across it, darkening it. There was a smell, too, familiar from the hospital. Not a shadow, but a stain. Blood. She bent down to stare at the thing. It was—had been—Shandy. The dog lay on his back, slit open from the underside of the muzzle down the length of his belly. Blood soaked his fur, soaked the ground around him. He didn't move. She silently thanked God that the little animal's death had come quickly.

Something glinted in the grass near Shandy's body. Narcissa bent down to look at it. It was a knife, like a Bowie knife but smaller, the blade about five inches long. Jake Calder, she thought.

Mirrie came up to stand beside her. Narcissa heard her draw in her breath, then let it out in a sob. She turned to Mirrie and held her as they knelt together. Mirrie touched the silky head once. Then they stood up. Mirrie's eyes were glistening with tears.

Narcissa took Mirrie's hands in hers. "I think I know who did this. But I want to look at the wound. You need not—"

"I want to see."

Mirrie took off her wrapper and bundled it gently around Shandy's body, and they went back to the house. In the kitchen, they placed oilcloth and old newspapers on the table, then pulled away the wrapper. They lit the gas lamps along with two lanterns to illumine the body as much as possible. Narcissa blotted the wet blood with a towel and steeled herself, thinking of the wounds she had seen examined in the hospital and the signs the doctors pointed out to the students.

What did this double cut, forming a cross on the little dog's belly, remind her of? Narcissa wondered, and thought of Charley's medical book describing dissection. She looked at Mirrie. "I think whoever did this was imitating the cuts that are made to open up the cadaver for dissection. But it's not a very good job. For one thing, the knife cut down to more than an inch deep in some places. The organs are . . . damaged." She had started to say, ripped apart.

Pale and frowning, Mirrie peered down through her spectacles.

Again Narcissa thought of the knife lying out in the grass, remembered having seen Calder's hand reach for a knife under his coat that day at the slave market. In her mind's eye she could see the sharp edge, the crosspiece. She had believed at the time it was a Bowie knife, but now she wondered. A smaller knife would have been easier to conceal under a coat. A knife like this one, dropped by Shandy's killer when she had startled him with her scream.

Having the knife in her possession gave her power. At last she had evidence of a crime. If she could prove the knife belonged to Jake Calder . . .

"Can you be sure?" Mirrie asked doubtfully.

"Sure enough. The man is cruel. This—" She felt revulsion choking her throat. "This was done by someone who enjoys causing pain." She thought of the slave girl Jake Calder had whipped, and lied to. It was not enough for the man to cause physical pain; he wanted to break the spirit. Maybe Calder had thought Shandy was her own pet rather than Mirrie's, or maybe Shandy had simply been a convenient form in which to send his message to her.

A chained slave, a little dog. Calder liked his victims helpless. Could it have been Calder who attacked her in the Egyptian building? She shuddered at the thought. Then another thought occurred to her: Aster Jacks's baby, supposedly safe among the servants at the Hugheses' plantation in Midlothian, yet ultimately at the mercy of Jake Calder. The thought made her heart sink.

Chapter Fourteen

"Cannot you hire me a horse? I will give you twice the going rate."

Immediately, Brit Wallace wanted to bite his tongue. Now that he had betrayed his eagerness, he may as well prepare to empty his pockets.

But what was the point of feigning indifference? Everyone in Washington was excited to fever pitch over tomorrow's expected battle, thirty miles away, which would finally bring the contesting armies face to face. Those who could were going to watch as the fate of the Union was decided. Although it was not his country, his cause, the battle could be the making of his career, and Brit was determined to see it.

The livery stablekeeper smiled until his red-veined gray eyes disappeared in a crosshatch of wrinkles. He turned away and spat tobacco juice into a puddle under the eaves, then looked at Brit a long moment before replying. "Senator Ely offered three times my regular price for a buggy and two horses. I told him the same thing I'm telling you. I ain't got 'em. There ain't a buggy left in town."

But the man made no move to go about his business. He either enjoyed the game of refusing custom, Brit surmised, or he was hiding some nag by which he hoped to make his fortune.

Brit was thinking of his own fortune to be made. He had studied the events leading up to this moment. The theater of war was raising its curtains on Manassas Junction, whose very name proclaimed its importance: connecting railroad lines, by which—according to who controlled them—the defenders or invaders of Virginia could receive fresh troops and supplies from the north and west.

Brit took a deep breath, exhaled, and replied, "I do not need a buggy, nor a driver, nor a boy, nor anything whatsoever but a horse, saddle, and bridle for one day. I am prepared to pay you twenty dollars. If you have the animal, tell me so now. If not—" Brit shrugged, but he had already seen the gleam of avarice light in those watery eyes.

"Well, now, sir, seeing as it's so important to you, I do have one horse I can let you have in the morning. But I'll need a fifty-dollar deposit, in case you don't make it back," McClintock said, smiling. "And it's no use coming before dawn. Come at first light, and we'll have everything fixed up for you."

Having no choice, Brit agreed to the arrangement. He would be leaving later than he had hoped, but it could not be helped.

RICHMOND

Narcissa had been disappointed that the knife she'd found near Shandy's body bore no mark identifying its owner. By itself the knife did not prove that the Hugheses' overseer had been the killer of Shandy, though Narcissa believed it to be true. And even if Calder had killed the dog, he might have been doing the bidding of Archer or Hughes, or both. Calder's other deeds—the warning to her and Mr. Wallace outside Judah Daniel's house, followed soon after by Calder's setting fire to the house—could not be mentioned. If Calder learned Judah Daniel had named him, he would find a way to punish her.

Still, she reasoned, if someone recognized the knife as being like the one carried by Jake Calder, she would know more. But how to find out, whom to ask, without alarming those she suspected of complicity in the crime?

She thought of Rachel Hughes. If Rachel recognized the knife, she might at least call her overseer to Richmond to question him about it, if not banish him from her service. If they could be certain that Calder would not be at the Hugheses' place in Midlothian, she and Judah Daniel could go there and reassure themselves that Aster Jacks's baby was safe.

Now Narcissa and Mirrie were sitting in Rachel Hughes's elegant formal parlor, a cobalt-and-gold tea service sitting on the polished wood table before them.

While Narcissa was thinking how best to proceed, Mirrie opened the attack. "Your overseer, Jake Calder, is an evil man. I want to ask that you discontinue his employment immediately, and send him away, preferably out of the state. I think he may intend harm to my friend." Mirrie looked at Narcissa. Rachel Hughes looked too, her eyebrows raised, then turned back to Mirrie.

"Why ever do you think Jake Calder would harm Mrs. Powers? Why do you think he even knows who she is? They have never met in this house, to my knowledge." Narcissa thought Rachel showed admirable self-control in responding to an accusation that must have seemed like a madwoman's fantasy. When Mirrie had spoken her piece, would Rachel stand up and demand that they leave, or simply laugh?

Mirrie countered. "Mrs. Powers and our friend Mr. Wallace saw Jake Calder one day at a slave auction. He was beating a slave. Mrs. Powers and Mr. Wallace asked him to stop, and . . . words were exchanged, and Mr. Wallace hit Calder and knocked him down."

Rachel frowned a little. "Mr. Wallace hit Jake Calder and knocked him down? Then I should think Mr. Wallace would be the one in danger, should Calder be seeking revenge."

We are going about it the wrong way, Narcissa thought, we should have showed her the knife before we told her our suspicions.

Mirrie persisted. "Late last week, someone came into our yard at night and killed my dog. Whoever did the deed used a large knife, the kind Calder wears."

With Mirrie watching her expectantly, Narcissa picked up a parcel she had set at her feet and unwrapped it. In these cultivated, feminine surroundings, the long, sharp blade looked brutal, even with the blood washed off.

Rachel shuddered. "What a truly terrible thing to do," she said, looking at the knife. For a moment there was color in her face and warmth in her expression. Then both drained away. When she spoke again, her voice was cold. "Calder has a knife. So does every other *southern* man, I dare say. Let me propose another explanation, Miss Powers. Your abolitionist views are well known in this city. There was a time not long ago when such views were tolerated, even indulged. But now we are fighting a war to preserve our way of life. This very day, this very hour, they say the battle may be fought that will put an end to this painful state of suspense we all are in.

"It was a terrible thing to kill your dog, and I condemn anyone who would do such a thing. You are a lady, after all, and deserve protection, even if you have been perhaps too . . . public in expressing your opinions."

Rachel Hughes and Mirrie stared at each other as Narcissa looked on. Mirrie's face had grown red with anger. At last she spoke, very quietly. "So you will do nothing about Calder?"

Rachel shrugged. "Calder is an overseer, employed to discipline slaves and enforce their respect. As such, he is of necessity an unrefined person. But you are suggesting that, based on the . . . story you have told me here, and a knife that may belong to anyone, my husband and I should take away the man's employment and banish him from his home? And this at a time when every man between sixteen and sixty is putting on the uniform?" Her voice was rising now, and her lower lip trembled. "What do you suggest that I do? Go live in the country and discipline the slaves myself? Why do you not turn Yankee outright?"

Rachel put her hands to her temples. Then she gripped the arm of the sofa, pushed herself to her feet, and went to tug the bell pull that would summon her servant. Narcissa bundled the knife back into its wrappings, and she and Mirrie rose as well.

Rachel Hughes leaned on the back of the sofa. "My nerves are so weak," she said in a low, sad voice. "Had I known the purpose of your visit, I would have asked that you talk to my husband instead. Any excitement affects me very badly.

"I am sorry," she went on, "if I have failed adequately to express my sympathy for the death of your pet. A lady should be protected," she said again, looking at Mirrie, "whatever her thoughts about politics may be. What does it matter what we think? Little can we do, whatever we may believe . . . whatever we may suffer."

"Miss Rachel?" The servant Phebe had come into the room. She held a stoppered bottle in her left hand. She placed her right hand under Rachel's elbow and led her back to the sofa. Narcissa saw Rachel's eyes follow the bottle. There was a hunger in them. Laudanum, Narcissa was sure. Rachel would not take any action against Jake Calder. She depended on his brutality as she did on laudanum, to keep the world at bay.

Phebe led them to the door and closed it behind them.

Mirrie motioned to Will Whatley to bring up the carriage, then turned to Narcissa. Mirrie's face was pale, Narcissa saw, except for two spots of color on her cheeks, which were as red as if she had been slapped.

"She speaks of her suffering!" Mirrie spoke through clenched teeth. "The pampered wife of a doctor! Little she knows or cares about the suffering of her slaves under Jake Calder."

Narcissa spoke quietly. "You remember, Mrs. Stedman told us she lost her children. She takes it very much to her heart."

Mirrie whirled around to face Narcissa. "What is that compared to the thousands of slave mothers who raise their children only to have them sold away, who give birth to children that are never really their own?"

Narcissa felt tears well up in her eyes. Mirrie's anger at once faded at the reminder of Narcissa's own grief at the death of her infant child. "Narcissa, please forgive me," she said, taking her hand. "I let my anger overrule my heart. I know that no one person's suffering is diminished in comparison to another's, or to a thousand others."

Mirrie broke off, then began again. "Rachel has a terrible reason for grief. But did grief make her selfish, unable to feel for the victims of Jake Calder's cruelty? She will allow him to hurt anyone as long as she is protected! I will not back down from my beliefs. But I will try not to lose sympathy for her, though she may have lost it for others."

Narcissa sighed a little. She shared Mirrie's sorrow and anger over the brutal killing of Shandy. But she saw that Mirrie had taken Rachel Hughes's insinuations that Mirrie's own abolitionist opinions were to blame for Shandy's death very much to heart—perhaps even believed this explanation. Mirrie now saw her dog's death as an attempt to silence her. What would she do in response? Not back down from her beliefs, Narcissa was certain of that. If only Nat Cohen were around to listen, sympathize, and in his quiet way bring Mirrie around to a calmer view of things. But he had not called at the house or, as far as she knew, written since Mirrie's rejection of his suit.

Narcissa's own belief about the meaning of Shandy's mutilation had not changed, despite her inability to prove ownership of the knife. Jake Calder had cut up the little dog to look as if it had been dissected, to frighten her from any further investigation. And he may have succeeded, although indirectly, Narcissa mused. She had hoped to find a pretext to visit the Hugheses' home, then find a chance to look in Dr. Hughes's office for some record of Charley's illness. Now Rachel Hughes would be suspicious of her, would think she was looking for information to discredit Jake Calder. Narcissa could not help but feel a little guilty. Rachel had been kind to Charley, after all. Mirrie's impetuous behavior, her insistence on always knowing what was best, had not helped curtail Jake Calder's actions. Pray God it had not increased the danger for Judah Daniel, or for Aster Jacks's baby.

First light found Brit astride a sturdy, hard-mouthed gray gelding he dubbed Greyfriars. His preparations were few: water in a military-style canteen slung on the saddle, brandy in a flask in his chest pocket, field glasses, slabs of bread and cheese bulging both pockets of his lightweight sack coat. He had chosen a pale linen coat, which besides being cool—a necessity in mid-July—had the advantage of clearly marking him a noncombatant. He had his papers and passes in readiness, and was called upon to present them a half dozen times before he was well under way.

As he headed southwest, his heart lifted. The day was fair, though a white haze promised intense heat by midmorning. The deeply rutted road ran through rolling farmland partitioned by woods, which at midsummer appeared impassable. Behind such woods as these, he surmised, lurked the Confederates' "masked batteries" so dreaded by the Federals.

Perhaps William Howard Russell was even now traveling down this same road. Since arriving in Washington, Brit had found himself always a step behind the correspondent for the *Times* of London. Russell, Brit thought with admiration and not a little envy, was like Job's warhorse; he smelleth the battle afar off, the thunder of the captains, and the shouting.

The captains . . . Old Henry and the friends he had made through the Sanitary Commission had been helpful there. Brit now knew a good deal about the Northern generals, as well as the Southern. The Union's Brigadier General Irvin McDowell commanded the troops that, in order to protect Washington City and establish a base for invading Virginia, had crossed the Potomac and occupied the heights of Arlington and the town of Alexandria.

The cautious McDowell had been urged on by everyone from his president to the loungers in the street—and especially by the newspaperman Horace Greeley—to force his green army "on to Richmond." Crucial to the attempt would be the success of Brigadier General Patterson in holding off potential Confederate reinforcements near Winchester, about fifty miles northwest of Manassas Junction. Commanding the Confederate force at Bull Run would be Brigadier General Beauregard, once a classmate of McDowell's at West Point. Brit was pleased at Beauregard's playing this crucial role, since the general had been the subject of one of his dispatches for the *Weekly Argus*.

Dr. Henry had also provided information Brit hoped would be helpful concerning puerperal fever, the affliction mentioned by Narcissa as a link between the deaths of Dr. Hughes's first wife and the murdered slave woman. Brit had kept his promise to Narcissa by phrasing his questions carefully: it seemed that the patients of "a certain doctor" were believed to have suffered to a disproportionate extent from puerperal fever; could Henry shed any light on the matter? Eager to go on with his monologue concerning plans for the Sanitary Commission, Henry had been uncharacteristically brief. He mentioned a couple of names, dates, and theories, and let it go at that.

Brit was eager to convey the information to Narcissa and to find out what it might mean. A plan had suggested itself to him, though the details were as yet hazy; after the battle, he would present himself to some high-ranking officer in the Confederate army—perhaps Beauregard himself—and obtain a pass to proceed on to Richmond.

It was almost ten o'clock when Brit took the road leading to Fairfax Court House and then on to Centreville. He heard for the first time—from how far away? he wondered—the booming of cannon whose balls were meant to kill. He strained his eyes to peer down the road and saw, walking toward him, a body of men in dusty blue uniforms.

Brit pulled his horse to a halt and watched the men approach. They had their rifles over their shoulders but could hardly be said to be marching. The lines straggled down the road as far as he could see. Some stopped to pick blackberries off the vines that grew near the road. As an invading force in enemy country, they were behaving quite strangely. Were it not for the uniforms and weapons, he thought, they could be farm laborers coming home after a day in the fields. Perhaps the battle is already over, Brit thought with a sinking heart.

Hailing an officer who was among the leaders, Brit called out, "Where are your men going, sir?"

"Well, we're going home, sir, I reckon—to Pennsylvania."

Just then Brit heard the cannon boom again. "Is not the battle still engaged?"

"I reckon it is," the officer agreed pleasantly. Then he added, "We're going home, because the men's time is up. We're three-months' men, you see; we've had our share of this work."

The erstwhile soldiers filed past, some smiling at Brit with berry-stained mouths. He stared at them for a few moments, then turned Greyfriars into the field to ride past them. The line went on for three or four miles. Three-months' men, indeed, he thought, and began composing his dispatch.

It was early afternoon when Brit turned toward Centreville. Along this road he at last met with some traffic going *toward* the battle: the store cars of the troops, plus the buggies and wagons of civilians who had come down from Washington.

Beyond Centreville rose the hill on which these were converging. Brit gathered up the reins and chirruped. "Come on, Greyfriars, old boy. We'll see action yet!" At the top of the hill, he dismounted and procured water for himself and the horse. He refilled his own canteen, wrung out his handkerchief in the bucket, and wrapped it around his neck. Then he tethered the horse to a sapling while he observed the action in the field.

The prospect lay open to view as far as the blue humps of the Alleghenies. But all eyes were gazing down onto a low, rounded rise of ground formed by the confluence of several ridges. The rise, which he heard called Henry Hill, was fringed with woods, and it was from these woods that the firing came, marked by a hazy, light blue smoke punctuated by puffs of white. In the open, clouds of dust obscured the identities of the antagonists, and Brit could only hope the combatants could distinguish each other better at ground level than the spectators could from above.

He ambled over and introduced himself to a man who proved to be an aide of one of the senators. "Oh, we've whipped them," the man said lightly. "We've taken their batteries. It will all be over soon."

Were the fire-eating Rebels themselves only three-months' men, after all? Again Brit was spurred by the fear that he had missed the battle that would decide the future of this youthful nation. He hurried back to Greyfriars, swung himself into the saddle, and set off for the road that would take him to the front.

The little road was choked with supply wagons, and consequently with dust. The movement of the wagons led credence to what Brit had heard; apparently the Federals were on the move south. "On to Richmond"? For a moment, Brit wondered what that would mean for his friends in the city. Then he had to pull up short—in front of him was a bottleneck of sorts at a small bridge. The drivers of a set of wagons were forcing their horses north, toward Centreville, and against the tide of wagons, horses, and men headed toward the battle.

"Turn back!" shouted these men who had come from the fight, sweat streaking the dust that covered their faces. "Retreat! We're whipped! God damn you, turn back!" Their frenzy brought those at the head of the line to a halt, but behind, the forward momentum continued. Brit pulled Greyfriars out of the road to safety as drivers jumped down from the wagons, grabbed their horses' heads, and tried to pull them by main force through the crowd. The cry went down the line, "Turn back—turn your horses!" Backing, plunging, rearing, and kicking, the horses turned in the road to go back the way they came.

Brit took Greyfriars through the field parallel to the road. Soldiers were running through the corn, not stopping to call out or even to look up at his approach. The sides of the road were littered with cooking tins, knapsacks, and greatcoats, swords, pistols, and bayonets, while uniformed men fled past in supply wagons and ambulances, on cavalry horses and mules. Their faces, blackened by gunpowder, were contorted into grimaces of fear and rage.

Brit had ridden, he thought, about three miles from the hill when he came to an open piece of ground, beyond and circling which was forest. Two field pieces guarded the road, and the soldiers manning the guns looked exhausted and grim. Shots sounded close by in the woods, but the guns on the left no longer maintained their fire.

Suddenly a sputtering fire sounded from the right, and out of the forest rushed a number of soldiers. Their uniforms were blue. Their flag, which had wound around its pole, showed red, white, and blue through the haze, but was it the Stars and Stripes or the Stars and Bars?

The gunners labored to wheel the piece around to return fire, but someone shouted, "Don't fire! They're our own men!" In a moment Brit was engulfed by what seemed to be an entire regiment, fleeing in disorder. "Cavalry!" one man called out. "They've cut us to bits! Hurry—they're behind us!"

The firing seemed to encircle him now, sputtering volleys and the sharp, whistling flight of shells that burst with a roar that shook the earth. Brit used all his strength to steady Greyfriars, hoping to guide the horse to safety rather than give him his head and risk his running into the guns.

But it was useless to try to find safety. The air was thick with smoke that made Brit's eyes water and concealed the landmarks that had been visible from higher ground. The woods offered no protection, for the trees themselves were exploding into spears and daggers of wood. It was as if nature had taken up the battle, dwarfing the puny men, whose screams could not even be heard.

Then, suddenly, the tide of battle turned away. The noise of the guns moved off. Maybe there was a chance to get away before it returned.

Holding the reins in his right hand, Brit reached down with his left to give Greyfriars a reassuring pat on the shoulder. He felt his forearm seized, and a violent jerk pulled him out of the saddle.

Half-crouching on the ground, so surprised that his fear was driven out of him, Brit looked up into the barrel of a long pistol. He said not a word; nor did the blue-jacketed bearer of the pistol, who swung himself into the saddle and spurred Greyfriars away.

Brit then took his bearings the simplest way possible: he fixed the noise of the battle, and walked the opposite way.

As he approached a line of trees, he saw ten or a dozen figures lying scattered on the ground. Most were blue-coated, a few gray, but all were preternaturally silent. They could not all be dead—could they? Some of the wounds were terrible, heads and trunks and limbs exploded and shattered and pierced. Some had obviously been dead for hours, their flesh swollen and blackened in the heat. Their comrades must have dragged away those who had life left in them.

As he stared, the flesh on his neck prickling with horror, a movement caught his eye. He turned toward it. That man, legs blown away at mid-thigh. He had moved his hand. His eyes were slightly open. Just a twitching of the nerves after death, Brit thought. Then he saw the hand move again. There was a little light left in the eyes, and they were focused on him.

To force himself to move toward what was left of the soldier was the hardest thing Brit Wallace had ever had to do.

He was little more than a boy in the uniform of a Federal foot soldier. His head was bare, his face very pale under its mask of dirt and soot. The mouth worked around the swollen tongue. "Water."

Brit brought out his canteen. He took the boy's chin in his hand and poured water between the cracked lips. This he followed with brandy from his flask, which he poured in sips until it was gone.

The soldier swallowed, and a little more life came into his eyes. "Help me straighten out my legs," he whispered.

"Just rest. Don't try to move. I'll go for help. You'll be all right." Brit spoke urgently, rising to his feet as he said the words. He left the canteen tucked into the soldier's hand, though he doubted the man had the strength to raise it to his own lips.

Brit looked back the way he had come. The noise had changed. The gunfire was farther off now, and he could hear men shouting. Again Brit turned in his tracks, this time to the sounds of the living.

The young gray-clad captain who took him prisoner was polite, almost courtly. He relayed Brit's information about the wounded soldier to a boy who was running past. Then he asked Brit, along with three Federal officers also captured, to accompany him to be delivered up to Colonel Owens.

Brit felt weak-kneed with relief. It was as if he had returned to earth from some strange, dreadful place—the moon, perhaps, or hell.

Colonel Owens was sitting on a canvas camp stool, arms resting on knees. He received the Federal prisoners tersely. "Hold them with the others, Captain," was his sole comment.

"And this is Mr. William Wallace, Colonel, a British journalist come down from Washington to observe the action. He was not armed, just had these things on his person." He held out Brit's field glasses, flask, and notebook. "Do you wish me to let him go?"

The colonel's gaze lighted on Brit. He looked into his face, then down at his light linen jacket and pants, then at the objects the captain was holding out for his inspection. Brit saw the man gather himself as if the guns were sounding again, then rise to his feet, draw his pistol from its holster, and bring the barrel to a spot two inches from the center of Brit's forehead. "God damn your white-livered soul! I'll blow your brains out on the spot!"

Though the man's voice shook, his pistol hand did not

waver. If I move, Brit thought, he will shoot me. So he did not move.

Slowly the pistol was lowered. "God damn you," the colonel said again, with quiet sincerity this time. "You came here to see the battle. You came here to make a story out of my men dying." His voice was rising again. "There's a place in hell for such as you, for those who can see without feeling. By God, I ought to—"

At last the captain interceded. "Colonel, he is a British subject. The goodwill of Britain mustn't be put in jeopardy. It may be we can make a good trade for him."

The colonel let his breath out in a sigh, then turned away. Brit breathed again. The moment was past. He would be allowed to live.

RICHMOND
JULY 24

At the tobacco warehouse turned impromptu prison, the line moved quickly, for the most part. Each man concluded his business in short order and was then herded into one or another of the waiting groups, to be either imprisoned or paroled.

Brit Wallace looked about, noted details, estimated numbers, and tried not to think about how hungry he was. He wanted to memorize it all, fearing to take out his notebook lest he attract attention. He observed his captors. He saw faces he knew he had seen before, but none claimed acquaintance. Some avoided eye contact, faces set in a cold rigidity that denied a human bond with their Federal captives. Others laughed and joked with the prisoners, perhaps feeling how easily their places could have been changed.

Their uniforms at least could, in many cases, have been swapped. There were some gray uniforms among the captured Federals, and even more blue uniforms among the Confederates. With those who affected outlandish costumes, such as the Zouaves, there was no apparent way to distinguish which side they were on. On the long train ride to Richmond, Wallace had heard rumors of tragedies caused by confusion—friends fired on, and "hold your fire" orders given for friends who turned out to be enemies.

Perhaps one in twenty of the captives, including Wallace, wore civilian clothes. Spectators had come from Washington in carriages, packing picnic lunches. When the Federals broke ranks and retreat became rout, many civilians had been captured. Some, including a few United States senators, had been sent to Richmond for imprisonment.

Where would they all be housed? Wallace wondered. The building he was standing in now was a tobacco factory, emptied to its bare boards to serve a more sinister purpose. Richmond was already overcrowded from the influx of government functionaries, hangers-on, soldiers, and refugees. Now there appeared to be thousands of captives, as well as thousands of wounded from both sides, who would have to be housed and fed. He thought of Narcissa and her work at the medical college hospital. That structure, once thought so spacious, was now a tiny island in a sea of wounded men.

Narcissa—he had something to tell her. It had seemed important once. He tried to trace in his mind's eye the clean curves of her face.

His mind drifted to the women he had felt something for in his life. There were a few for whom he had felt more than bodily hunger, a few whose memory seemed sweet to him and filled with promise. He had never felt any urgency to choose one woman over the others, to marry. He was young, and there would be time. Yet for so many men he had seen lying dead on the field, time had stopped. Some of them left wives, children. Some of them had not yet begun to love, or to live. None had been safe.

He felt that life was very much different from what he had thought. If time were given to him, he would try to understand it.

His turn to step forward and give his name. Keeping his voice low, Wallace said, "My name is William Grandison Wallace. I request my immediate release. I am a British subject, a journalist. I took no part in the fighting, and I take no side whatsoever in this conflict."

The officer did not lift his eyes until he had written the full name in the ledger that lay open before him. Then he looked up with studied indifference and said, "I believe you came down from Washington, did you not, William Wallace?"

"That is correct. But I was planning to return to Richmond. I have a wide acquaintance here."

"Don't know about wide," replied the officer. "It's high acquaintance you'll be wanting now. Meanwhile, empty your pockets."

Brit placed his purse of money, notebook, and mechanical pencil on the table. The officer spread out the purse's contents, counted it, noted the amount in the ledger, and handed the purse to an attendant. He pushed Brit's notebook and pencil back across the table and gestured with a pointing finger to one of the groups. Wallace scooped up the returned belongings, stuffed them in his pocket, and joined those bound for prison.

After washing his face and hands for the first time in three days, Brit Wallace ate greedily from a communal bowl of corn bread and watery soup. He was one of forty-seven men confined in a space of about a hundred square feet on the third floor of the tobacco warehouse. There were many such spaces in several such warehouses overlooking the James River. They knew their prison overlooked the river, though they were not allowed to look out. Word was, two prisoners had been seen through windows by the guards below, and had been shot to death where they stood.

The prisoners had quickly established the rough camaraderie of men under difficult, but not desperate, circumstances. All expected a more-or-less speedy release. Now most were writing to their loved ones, eager to dispel fears and, if possible, enlist aid.

Brit Wallace took out his pencil and paper and jotted several quick notes to various acquaintances in the city in hopes of obtaining their help toward parole. Then he began to compose a letter that, though in the interest of propriety addressed to Professor Powers, would convey to Narcissa the interesting information he had found.

A short time later he read over the result.

Dear Professor Powers,

It is with some embarrassment that I tell you I am being held as a captive of war in Richmond. I fear my friends in this city may believe that I am deserving of this fate by some action undertaken by me against your state and country.

Let me assure you this is not the case. I was present at the battle near Manassas in my capacity as a journalist and had the misfortune to be taken. Through some inexplicable enmity, my captors were unwilling to exchange me. But let me ask you not to trouble yourself about it, as I feel sure my friends will come to my aid as soon as they are able.

In my mind at the time of this unfortunate incident was an item of possible interest to Mrs. Narcissa Powers concerning a discussion we had in happier times. I ask you to direct her attention to the New England Quarterly Journal of Medicine *of 1843,* for a most interesting glimpse into the matter.

Please express my cordial good wishes to Miss Powers and to Mrs. Powers. I hope to be at liberty to visit you soon.

Wallace signed and folded the letters, addressed them, and placed them in his pocket until he could find someone to undertake their delivery.

Chapter Fifteen

RICHMOND
LATE JULY

Brit Wallace walked the length of the hall with a jaunty tread, composing a witticism that would cloak the overwhelming sense of relief he felt. Only a day since his requests for help had gone out. It was gratifying to think his friends had rallied to his aid so quickly. Had Mrs. Powers been concerned for him? Would she be waiting in the room to which he had been directed, on the ground floor of his warehouse-prison, with Miss Powers and the old professor? Would he see worry melt into affection in her warm brown eyes?

He rubbed his hand over the stubble on his chin. Well, no harm done that a shave, a bath, and some fresh clothes could not repair. Yet something had changed inside as well. Would she see it?

He reached the door and had opened his mouth to speak when his elation fled. Cameron Archer stood before him, dressed in his Medical Service uniform, a pistol holstered on his belt. The doctor's face was sallow. A half-grown beard covered his jaws, blurring the trim lines of the Van

Dyke. His tunic bore dark red stains, blood or Virginia clay. Only the high cavalry-style boots had their customary polish.

"You were told to leave Richmond and not to return!" Archer barked.

"I did intend to return. Though, practically speaking," Wallace answered, "I had no choice in the time or the manner of my arrival."

"A great victory." Archer smiled a little. "But won at such a cost. We needed more surgeons, orderlies, ambulances, supplies—"

Archer seemed to forget where he was for a moment. Brit felt sure he was remembering those fields filled with dying and dead men. Then Archer turned his eyes, gray-green and cold as coins, on Brit's face. "I could have saved you from an unpleasant experience if I had called you out and shot you instead of sending you packing."

"I suspected my exile was the result of your interference," Wallace retorted.

"Call it an attempt to save you from the consequences of your meddling. But it seems my effort was in vain. You're interfering in matters that don't concern you, and that touch very close upon my honor and the honor of my family. I don't expect you to understand that—"

Wallace looked over his shoulder toward the door before responding, assuring himself that no one could overhear. He felt sure that, should anyone hear what he was about to say, Archer would most certainly kill him. He stepped close to Archer and spoke in a voice as low, and as chilling, as the sound of a sword being drawn from its sheath. "Oh, yes, I do, don't you know. I understand that you have been involved in the sordid occupation of obtaining corpses by grave-robbing and probably by murder. That you are morally responsible for the death of young Charley Powers. That you attacked Mrs. Powers when she found evidence of your crimes and may have been kept from killing her only by the unwholesome tendresse you are cherishing for her."

Wallace's heart was racing, muscles tensed to defend himself or, since he had no weapon to counter Archer's pistol, to run. But Archer's reaction was not what he expected. "Attacked? Mrs. Powers?" Shock had driven out anger on Archer's face.

Wallace looked at him in disbelief. If that was how the doctor wanted to play it, very well; he would comply. "She pretended to believe that preposterous story that she fainted and was injured by her fall. But she knew she had been struck by a blow to the head, and she remembered what she had seen—the grave robber, your chief henchman, murdered. You knew she suspected you, and you were dogging her steps. How can you pretend to deny it?"

"I deny it," Archer said. "And yet, I fear I am to blame."

The stunned and rueful expression on the face of Cameron Archer took some of the heat out of Wallace. But, having gone so far, he had no choice but to press on, to provoke some decisive reaction from Archer. "The key that will decode your crimes is already in Mrs. Powers's hands, or soon will be, in a letter I wrote from this prison. It was all laid out twenty years ago by Dr. Oliver Wendell Holmes. You drew her brother into league with you, and it was by graverobbing that he received the taint that killed him. When she reads the essay, she will have the proof."

Archer seemed lost in his own thoughts. Suddenly he looked up.

"You fool!" There was a note of anguish in Archer's voice. "Don't you realize you've put her in very great danger?"

It was midmorning. The doctors had done their rounds. Two patients had died in the early hours, and their beds were now filled by men whose battlefield amputations would have to be redone. Both were feverish, their wounds inflamed: only the sickest were sent here to the medical college. It was unlikely they would survive many days. When they died, or recovered, their places would be taken in turn. All over the city, public and private buildings had been turned into hospitals for the wounded of Manassas. All over the city, wending from hospital or private home to the burying grounds at Oakwood, Hollywood, and Shockoe, came the military funerals. The empty saddle—the led warhorse—the wailing of the Dead March in *Saul*.

The hardest duties of nursing in abeyance for a moment, Narcissa was writing letters for soldiers whose wounds or weakness made them unable to hold the pen, or who did not know how to write. No service meant more to the soldiers, since her pen and paper represented the only connection they might have with their families for many months—or, indeed, the last they would have with them in this world. It moved her to awe to see men search for the words of love, solace, and counsel that would send their wives, children, mothers, and fathers into a long and unknown future.

Narcissa was finishing a letter from Fred Jordan, a private from the western part of the state, to his wife. Jordan had received a wound in the shoulder and lain ill for two days. Now his fever was gone, and his wound was healing. In a few days he would be discharged to his battalion.

But with healing had come a longing for home and family so intense that it was tormenting him like a fever. Narcissa had spent a long time with him on the letter, getting him past the conventional. "How are you? I am fine" by asking questions about his wife, their child, and their home. At last he was speaking from his heart, eyes closed, and Narcissa was writing as fast as she could.

I miss you and our little Ruth. I hold to the memory of her tiny hand in the hollow of my neck. I want to be as strong as she feels I am and as you believe me to be.

I have seen the elephant now; that's what the boys call the first fight with the Yankees. We whipped them. They turned tail and ran back across the line, and I hope they never set foot on Virginia soil again. If they do come back, we will whip them again. But I cannot tell you the horrors I have seen.

I was wounded in the shoulder. The force of the ball knocked me down, and I lay there for a while, wondering how bad I was hit. Then I started to think of the Twin Falls, and how we used to sit and look at the water thundering down. You said the East Fall looked like the lace of a bride's veil and the North Fall was like a strong man rushing to her. We called them the Bride and the Bridegroom.

Narcissa noticed Benjy hovering at her elbow, eager to attract her attention yet not wanting to interrupt. She acknowledged him with a smile but kept writing, unwilling to break the flow of Jordan's words.

When I remembered that, it was like I felt the strength coming into me. Wherever this war takes me, I will be your Bridegroom, rushing to come back to you.

Jordan fell silent. Narcissa let him rest in his memories a moment, then said briskly, "There now! A very nice letter that your wife will treasure. It will go out this afternoon."

Jordan smiled his thanks. Narcissa folded the paper in preparation for mailing, saying a silent prayer that if it be God's will this young man would survive the war. Then she rose and went into the hall, where Benjy had been pressed into service bundling foul linens for the wash.

Seeing Narcissa, Benjy stuck his hand into his shirt and drew out a somewhat crumpled packet of paper. "From Will Whatley"—Mirrie's driver was well known to the boy—"He told me to put it in your hand myself."

Narcissa fished a coin from her pocket and gave it to the boy, receiving a gap-toothed grin in return. Then she stepped into a corner of the hall out of the way of traffic and unfolded the packet.

Her own name was written cross the front in Mirrie's bold script. Inside was an envelope addressed to Professor Powers, for delivery by hand. It was unsealed. Opening that, she found a short note, written in pencil, with the scrawled signature "William Grandison Wallace." She was shocked to read that Brit was being held in a Richmond prison, but a note at the bottom of the page, in Mirrie's writing, assured her that Mirrie and her father would exert their influence to obtain a speedy release for their friend.

Then she read again, puzzled, Brit's message to her. "A discussion in happier times"? By his tone, he could have been referring to a parlor game, or the newest installment of a serial by Dickens. But the reference to the medical journal made her feel sure that the casual tone was feigned, and that the information he wanted her to have referred to the crime he had been helping her investigate.

A twenty-year-old issue of a medical journal from New

England may not come quickly to hand, Narcissa mused as she shoved the letter deep in her pocket. Then she thought again of Hughes's office at his home, its walls lined with row upon row of volumes, bound to match in colored leather and stamped in gold. She had been longing to get inside that office, to search through Hughes's records of his medical cases for some account of his treatment of Charley. Now that she and Mirrie had angered Mrs. Hughes with their accusation against Jake Calder, it would be difficult for her to wander in the house away from the eyes of Mrs. Hughes or her servants. Still, Narcissa resolved to go at once, and put her mind to thinking of a pretext under which she could look for both the notes and the volume.

≫≪

Cameron Archer put out his hand to brush Brit Wallace out of his path to the door. Wallace caught Archer's forearm in a tight grip and forced the other man to face him.

"You do not wish her harm—word of honor?" Wallace said in a low voice, staring into Archer's eyes.

In Archer, surprise and confusion seemed to have overcome anger. "Of course not," he replied, also in a low and urgent tone.

"But there are those who do," Wallace persisted, "and you know who they are."

Archer broke his gaze at last and glanced toward the door, then back at Wallace. "I fear I do. God knows, I tried to warn her—"

"As you are a man of honor, let me come with you," Wallace urged. Sensing resistance, he renewed his grip on Archer's arm. "Or fight me now."

"Come on then." Archer's voice was rough. "You'll go out of here as my prisoner; it will save time." Wallace acquiesced, allowing Archer to take hold of his arm and pull him out the door and down the hall. Archer's air of authority waved away inquiries. Wallace realized that none of those looking on knew whether he was being taken off to be freed or to be shot, nor did they care.

>=<

Narcissa gathered her bonnet, gloves, and reticule, then waited, watching as Dr. Hughes removed a soldier's amputated stump up to the thigh, above the line to which gangrene had spread. As he finished, the patient began to moan. Hughes's assistant, a brand-new student, sloshed chloroform onto a pad of cotton wool and pressed it over the patient's nose and mouth until the moaning ceased. Hughes straightened and turned away, shoulders sagging with fatigue as he wiped his instruments on a towel, turning the bloody cloth to find a dry spot.

Judah Daniel stood nearby, rewinding the silk thread left over from the student's tying off the severed arteries. Narcissa wondered at Hughes's choice of Judah Daniel to work with him. It was menial duty, cleaning and replenishing supplies, carrying off amputated limbs; and it was sometimes physically demanding—holding resistant patients until the anesthesia could take effect. Most of the doctors used male slaves for this work. Judah Daniel, whose service in the hospital was part of her parole, was as strong as any of them, but Narcissa wondered if Hughes did not see the fire in the woman's eyes, or did not care . . . or perhaps sought to subdue it.

Narcissa stopped a few feet from Hughes and addressed his back. Her heart was pounding, and she spoke quickly, not from the urgency of her errand—though she hoped it seemed so—but from the boldness of her lie. "We have nearly run out of bandages. I know the ladies met at your house yesterday to scrape more lint. I will just step across and get it."

She called the last words over her shoulder. She was eager to get away before Hughes could protest that the storage closets on the lower floors were full of bandages. Most likely, she thought, he doesn't know; doctors merely assume the supplies will be there, and give the nearest person a tongue-lashing if they are not.

Narcissa felt that luck was with her when her knock on the Hugheses' door was answered by Jane Scott. She told the servant her made-up errand and added, "I must return to the hospital as quickly as possible. You need not announce me to Mrs. Hughes. I will wait in the doctor's office."

The door to Hughes's office was closed, but the knob turned in Narcissa's hand. She went in and closed it behind her. Her heartbeat sounded loud in her ears as she opened and closed the drawers of the big mahogany desk.

The third drawer she opened held a stack of papers several inches thick, laid flat but still creased from Hughes's folding. She scanned the top page eagerly—pencil scribbles, mostly abbreviations and symbols. Then she saw at the top of the page a clearer notation: *26 Jul.* Just two days past.

She looked more closely at the writing. There was a name she recognized, Douglas—the man whose gangrenous stump Hughes had amputated this morning. There was Jordan, whose letter to his wife had touched her so, and other names as well. She could decipher little else, but she felt sure it was all here. Perhaps another doctor could make sense of it. But she had to find the month of March, find the name Charley Wilson.

She turned to the second page. No date. About a half-dozen pages down she found the next: *25 Jul.* It looked as if Hughes's habit was to take his notes from his pocket and place them here in his desk, each on top of the last. She turned to the bottom of the stack and read, *1 Jan. 1861*. The whole year was here.

She felt along the edge of the stack with her thumb. About halfway down, where March should be, she again looked for a date: *3 May*. Of course, the numbers of patients had increased since the declaration of war. She turned back more pages: *2 Feb*. Good; work forward from there: *4 Feb., 6 Feb.*— Hughes had had a day off—*1 Apr*. It can't be true, she thought, knowing that it was. She went back and looked at the pages again. Then she riffled through the whole stack. Nowhere among them were the pages dated between the sixth of February and the first of April. The missing pages went back further than Charley's illness. Then she thought of Aster Jacks. Would her confinement not have been around that time?

Trembling with anger and frustration, Narcissa closed the desk drawer and turned to look at the shelves. She forced herself to breathe deeply and slowly; scanning the shelves top to bottom, left to right, she began a slow circuit of the room.

Narcissa felt buoyed when she saw the words *New England Quarterly*, with the years 1842-1843, printed on a spine bound in green leather. It was a two-inch-thick volume, the only one of that name, its duller gold out of place among the newer bindings. She pulled it out and riffled the pages to find the contents. Her eye was caught by the words printed at the top of the page, like a chapter heading: "On the Contagiousness of Puerperal Fever." Childbed fever, the disease that had killed Archer's first wife and would most likely have killed Aster Jacks, had her murderer been willing to wait.

The click of the doorknob brought Narcissa's head up with a guilty start. Jane Scott put down the tea tray—Narcissa recognized the cobalt-blue-and-gold pattern she had seen on the day she and Mirrie had called on Mrs. Hughes. With a nod, Jane left the room. "I'll be right back with those bandages, Mrs. Powers," she called softly on her way out.

Narcissa eagerly scanned the pages. The elegantly worded sentences of the author, Dr. Oliver Wendell Holmes, did not lend themselves to quick perusal, but in the first sentence, this phrase stood out: "Puerperal fever is sometimes communicated from one person to another, both directly and indirectly." A few pages later, in italics: *The disease known as puerperal fever is so far contagious as to be frequently carried from patient to patient by physicians and nurses.* And further, in quotation marks, "'Every person who had been with a patient in the puerperal fever became charged with an atmosphere of infection.'"

There were stories of doctors for whom one case of puerperal fever led to the deaths of four new mothers, six, a dozen: "Sixteen caught the disease and all died. . . . Some have lost ten, twelve, or a greater number . . . lost sixteen patients . . . five fatal cases . . ." It appeared the infection could be carried on the hands, clothes, or instruments of the physician or midwife—even on laundered bedclothes.

Her eye lit on the word *erysipelas*. One physician attributed the first case in an outbreak of puerperal fever to his clothes and gloves being embued with the effluvia from a patient suffering from erysipelas. Then again and again: *gangrene, erysipelas, peritonitis.* It seemed these afflictions—capable of infecting living flesh with rottenness—were able to change their forms back and forth. Doctors attending victims of puerperal fever contracted peritonitis and erysipelas. The taint of erysipelas traveled to sicken and kill new mothers in the form of puerperal fever.

In the final paragraph of the essay Narcissa read these words: "The time has come when the existence of a *private pestilence* in the sphere of a single physician should be looked upon not as a misfortune, but as a crime."

The words seemed to throb with the blood pulsing in Narcissa's temples. They were heavy with omen, but their meaning was elusive. The fever that had killed Dr. Hughes's first wife so long ago was somehow linked to the recent death of his servant. A murder. And these deaths had somehow tainted Charley. The "atmosphere of infection," the "private pestilence," was centered in this house. The man in whose office she was standing, whose book she was holding, whose acts of supposed mercy she watched every day, carried with him contagion and death.

When the doorknob turned again, Narcissa wanted to run and hide. She knew that the hand turning the knob belonged to Edgar Hughes, drawn to her fear of him as a vulture is drawn to decay.

It was not the doctor, but Rachel Hughes who opened the door. Narcissa knew Rachel would not likely welcome her in the house, after the accusations she and Mirrie had made against Jake Calder. Yet Narcissa found that any discomfort she might have expected to feel around Rachel was driven out by a terrible pity for this woman who had herself lost so much to her husband's incompetence. Had Rachel's twin sons died of puerperal fever, too? Could another doctor have saved them?

Rachel Hughes paused inside the door, perhaps—Narcissa imagined—made ill at ease by the naked distress on Narcissa's face. As Rachel watched, Narcissa closed the volume and replaced it on the shelf, then went over to Rachel.

"I've come for the bandages," Narcissa said quietly. "I apologize if I startled you. Jane let me in."

Rachel Hughes smiled. "I will forgive you if you will take tea with me. I see you have not touched this, and it will be cold by now. I have sent Jane on with the bandages. A few moments' rest will do you good. You cannot be so busy as all that." Rachel's words were friendly, but Narcissa felt a chill of reproach. It seemed as if Rachel had divined that Narcissa was lingering in her husband's office on a pretext. Was she familiar enough with hospital routine to know the bandages weren't needed?

Rachel picked up the tea tray. Why did she not leave it for the servants? Narcissa wondered. She felt she had no choice but follow Rachel into the hall, though she wondered if they would both wind up in the kitchen. It seemed an improbable action for the ladylike Rachel Hughes.

Suddenly, Rachel seemed to stumble, and dropped the tray onto the marble floor. The beautiful teapot, cup, and saucer lay shattered. Rachel's mouth formed an *O* of distress and, looking as if she would cry, she bent down to pick up the glittering pieces. Then she staggered and put out her hand to Narcissa.

Narcissa gripped Rachel's hand with both of hers to keep her from falling, but the older woman had lost her balance. Rachel slumped, her entire weight pressing into Narcissa's hands. A jagged shard of broken china that Rachel had been holding slashed into the flesh of Narcissa's palms. Narcissa gave an involuntary cry of pain, then tried to reassure Rachel. "It's nothing," she said, picking up a napkin to stanch the blood.

Rachel stood up and dropped the shard. She seemed to compose herself with effort. "Oh, my dear," she said quietly, "I was so concerned about the broken china that now I've done a far worse injury. Come—we'll fix that up. We still have a few bandages left!" Rachel swept down the hall and up the stairs with Narcissa following, bustled her into a room that was plainly her own boudoir, and seated her on a low sofa. Narcissa noticed that her first act was to cross to a little table next to the high, canopied bed, pour a small amount of liquid into a glass, and drink it down. The accident must have shaken Rachel enough to seek immediate relief in laudanum. The delay was momentary, and Narcissa did not begrudge her taking the soothing medicine.

Rachel then went to fetch a little wooden chest filled with medical supplies. Seating herself next to Narcissa, Rachel turned back her own cuffs and dabbed at the cuts. They continued to bleed profusely. She applied an ointment to each cut in turn. Her movements were practiced. Narcissa remembered what Mrs. Stedman had said about doctors' wives coming to talk and think like doctors. And Rachel had tended to Charley, perhaps bandaged his wounds until gangrene made them too offensive.

Rachel covered the anointed cuts with pads of soft lint, then wrapped strips of cloth across the palms from the fingertips to the wrists, strapping down the thumbs. Narcissa almost laughed despite the pain; her hands had become two useless and ungainly paws. "Now," Rachel said, rising from her seat, "perhaps some brandy instead of tea. I'm sure the pain must be excruciating." She left the room, closing the door behind her.

Left alone, Narcissa shivered despite the day's oppressive heat. A strand of hair tickled her nose. She reached her hand up to tuck it away, but the clumsy mitt could not do the task.

I'm helpless here. As Charley was, she thought, remembering with a shudder the sight of his maimed body beneath the blanket.

She felt the blood drain from her face—felt the knowledge before her brain could form the thought. Charley, helpless in this house, tended by Rachel Hughes. Rachel, who knew all too well the meaning of the medical volume Narcissa had been reading. Rachel had killed Charley by applying tainted dressings. And now, the same "private pestilence" was poisoning Narcissa's own body through the bandages wrapped around her wounded hands.

A floorboard creaked in the hall. Rachel Hughes was returning. Narcissa bit her lips to bring some color to them. Rachel must not see how frightened I am.

Rachel came in with a decanter and two cordial glasses and reclosed the door behind her. Narcissa avoided her eyes, frantic to get away, yet wanting to hide her fear from Rachel. The older woman sat next to Narcissa again and placed the decanter and glasses on the long, low table in front of them. She filled the two dainty glasses and set one before Narcissa. The other she drained in one draught.

"Oh, how foolish of me," Rachel said with a titter. "You won't be able to drink it . . . unless I help you." She made no move to do so, however.

Narcissa did not want to look at her. If Rachel saw the fear on her face, it would put the end of the game out of doubt. Rachel could not let her live, could not even let her die this slow way, as Charley had, taking weeks for the infection to do its work. Rachel Hughes could not let her leave this room alive.

They sat in silence for a few minutes, Rachel seeming almost to have forgotten Narcissa's presence. Rachel poured herself another glass of brandy and drank it in quick sips but did not renew her offer to Narcissa.

When Rachel began to speak, her voice was slurred. Narcissa, drawn to look at her, saw that her gaze was unfocused, fixed on objects that had long ago vanished from sight. "He killed my babies. Did you know that? He killed his first wife, her baby, my lovely babies. He killed his black whore. She had to die for what he did. But he did not kill me. He killed everything he loved—but me.

"Why could he not have killed me?" Rachel Hughes's voice rose in a wail. "He brought the taint of death to me from the corpse he had been dissecting. He came straight from there to deliver our babies. I held them in my arms the first day. They were healthy and beautiful. I was so happy. Then I came down with the fever and spent days out of my head with agony. When I came out of it, my babies were dead and buried, poisoned by the putrid matter that was on their father's hands when he took them out of my body. He wouldn't let me see them, but I know how they died. I read about it, and then I tried it out, on Aster Jacks and on your brother. They rotted to death.

"I never again subjected myself to his attentions. It would be for him as if I were dead. As if he were dead, too, I thought. Until he got his whore with child. He denied it, but she told me. I told her I would kill her if she did not tell me.

"You know what I planned to do, don't you? I know you were reading the Holmes essay. It all seems so clear, doesn't it? The doctors themselves carry the fever that destroys so many women. The babies die with their mothers, or live without them.

"The doctors deny it. Even my husband denied it. 'A gentleman's hands are clean.' Fool! We are all flesh and blood, and rottenness. I guess he knows it now."

She is proud of what she has done, Narcissa thought, disbelieving.

Rachel went on. "I read Holmes over and over, and I noticed the connection between puerperal fever, erysipelas, and gangrene. I decided my husband's whore would die as his first wife had done, and their baby, and my babies. Then at last I would see what my husband had hidden from me, the horrible way they died.

"The granny midwife out at the plantation attended her confinement, then I had Aster brought here. I told her the baby was dead. There were no cases of puerperal fever at the hospital, so I prepared my bandages with tainted matter from an amputation. The whore developed the fever. She started to rot, just like my babies. She lay there smelling the stink of her own decaying body. I should be famous." Rachel Hughes's little smile made Narcissa shiver. "But she didn't die; she began to recover, to moan and cry out. I had to shut her up. I tied a rag around her mouth, but she wouldn't be quiet. Then I put the rag in her mouth. I pushed it with my hands as far as I could down her throat, and then I used the poker to push it out of sight."

A creak from the loose board in the hall made Narcissa start. Rachel Hughes must have heard it too, for she leaned forward and fumbled in the box of medicines, then drew out an ivory-handled surgical knife with a short, razor-sharp blade. Knife in hand, she put her arm around Narcissa's shoulder, draping her shawl over the hand that held the knife. Narcissa could feel its blade cold against the vein in her throat. "Don't speak," Rachel hissed. Rachel's hand was trembling so that the knife threatened to pierce the skin.

If there had been anyone in the hall, nothing more was heard. Finally Rachel lowered her arm. "No one's coming. I sent them all away."

Narcissa spoke to Rachel in a low voice, not looking her in the face. "You are very distressed. Perhaps you should take some of your . . . medicine."

"Laudanum. For my nerves," Rachel said. She got up unsteadily and crossed again to the little table, poured the remaining contents of the vial into the glass, and drank it down. Then she returned, still holding the knife, and resumed her seat next to Narcissa, looking uncertain of what to do next.

Narcissa spoke again, keeping her tone conversational so as not to upset Rachel. "My brother never hurt you. Why did he have to die?"

Rachel glanced at Narcissa, then looked away. She smoothed her skirt with her hands, holding the sharp knife so awkwardly that Narcissa wondered if she had forgotten it was there. Then the flame started up in Rachel's eyes again. "Edgar was horrified when he saw his whore laid out on the dissecting-room table. That was Cameron Archer's doing; he found out where she was buried, from one of his old family servants, and had her dug up as a rebuke to Edgar. When they found the rag I pushed down her throat, Archer thought Edgar had killed her, and Edgar let him think so. But he knew I infected her with the fever, then killed her.

"I told him I did it to relieve her suffering. I don't suppose he believed me, but it didn't matter. He would never expose me. He was too ashamed of what he had done to me and to his first wife and to our babies. Anyway he knew Archer would never bring an accusation of murdering a slave against a man who was connected to him, to the high-and-mighty Archer family.

"Edgar told me that Charles had done the anatomy and was asking questions, talking to the hospital servants. I thought, how fortunate if that young man should contract erysipelas, as Dr. Holmes describes. Then he would die and be out of the way. The more I thought about it, the more it seemed the perfect solution. Except that he stayed healthy. So I had to fix it so that he would be cut on the arm when he was here at dinner one night. I spilled wine on his coat and took it away to be cleaned. Then I left a pin in the sleeve. It was just a scratch, really, but it was enough. I bandaged it, and when it became infected, I insisted he stay here so I could change the dressing every day. From your reading, I'm sure you know what happened."

Rachel looked down at Narcissa's hands.

"What of . . . Aster Jacks's . . . baby?" Narcissa said. She had to force out the words; her throat seemed to have rusted shut.

"I told Jake Calder to take care of it." Rachel smiled a little. "He has been very helpful to me. He deserves a reward."

Narcissa pulled away so violently that Rachel brought up the knife. Rachel spoke again, rambling, as if her thoughts were outrunning her ability to form the words. "Calder killed that old darkie who tried to blackmail me—"

Old Billy, Narcissa thought.

"—and killed his son, too. Calder will be disappointed to be cheated of you, and not for the first time. He tried to kill you when you found Old Billy. He didn't hit you hard enough. Then he tried to scare you off by that silly business with the dog. I guess he would have caught you sooner or later, but I can't wait for him."

Rachel was holding the knife out in front of her with both hands. Narcissa could see that Rachel was losing control of her hands; they were going lax, so that she had to pull them back up with a jerk. Rachel would soon be unconscious from the laudanum and brandy she had taken, but would it be soon enough? Rachel worked her mouth, then spoke slowly, as if her lips and tongue were numb. "I had better kill you now."

She lunged toward Narcissa. But the draughts had made her clumsy, and Narcissa evaded her, leaping sideways away from the sofa, half-falling against the high tester bed. She put up her bandaged hands to defend herself, but Rachel lay twisted, her upper body slumped across the sofa. As Narcissa watched, the malevolent gleam in Rachel's eyes went dark. Her hands relaxed. The knife dropped from her fingers and slid to the floor.

Narcissa ran to the door, pounded it with her useless hands, and screamed with all her might.

Footsteps pelted up the stairs. The door flew open. It was Jane Scott.

"Thank God," Narcissa exclaimed, then stopped. She would have to speak carefully, lest the servant think that she was the dangerous lunatic.

"Mrs. Powers, what's the matter? What's wrong with the mistress? She told me not to come back, but I—"

Jane looked past Narcissa to where Rachel Hughes was lying, sprawled sideways on the sofa, unmoving. The servant's eyes widened with fear.

Narcissa forced herself to speak calmly. "I believe Mrs. Hughes has taken too much of her medicine. You must go get someone, get a doctor. Don't worry. You can't do anything here. Mrs. Hughes will know you did the right thing, and so will Dr. Hughes.

"But first, get these bandages off my hands, and bring me the brandy."

It seemed to take forever, but Jane finally had the bandages torn off. Narcissa grabbed the decanter and poured the brandy over first one hand and then the other. The burning pain was like a cleansing with fire, and Narcissa was glad of it.

Chapter Sixteen

RICHMOND

Hughes drew himself up and frowned at his colleague. "Don't be absurd, Archer. I haven't harmed that young woman. She left a little while ago to fetch more bandages from my house. She should be back at any moment."

Archer frowned back. "I don't know what to believe anymore." He shot a glance at Brit. "Wallace, step across to Hughes's house and see if Mrs. Powers is there. Remember, you have given your word not to run away."

"*My* word you may count upon. Though by God, I don't know why I should believe either of *you*," Wallace responded. He strode out the door, slamming it behind him.

Judah Daniel heard the door slam downstairs. She had been on edge all morning. The air was heavy with secrets. First Archer, at the hospital very early, had received a message that had sent him storming out. Hughes had been distracted ever since. She'd watched him to make sure he didn't amputate a healthy limb by mistake.

Then Narcissa Powers had made an excuse to leave her nursing duties—to walk the short distance over to the

Hugheses' house and pick up bandages that could easily have been fetched by a servant. It wasn't like the young woman, who seemed to value her time with her patients as much as they valued her attention. Judah Daniel had come to respect Narcissa, even to regret the fact that her white skin, her ladyness, bound her like a whalebone corset. In the moments when Narcissa seemed to shake free of those bonds, it seemed to Judah Daniel that they could learn from each other.

After Narcissa left, Judah Daniel wondered if Hughes would try to follow her. But that hadn't happened. Instead, Archer had returned with the young Englishman, Wallace, and demanded a private interview with Hughes. Just a few moments before, they had entered the office downstairs.

Judah Daniel picked up an armload of bandages from a table at the top of the stairs—a servant walking around with empty arms drew suspicion—and went down the steps to the first floor where the door had slammed. The young Englishman was standing in the hall, hand still on the doorknob, a frown on his face.

Seeing her, Wallace spoke abruptly. "Mrs. Powers—is it true she's gone over to Hughes's?"

"I would not doubt they are lying to me," he added under his breath.

Judah Daniel answered him as bluntly. "I believe so. You go on over there. Leave it to me to keep an eye on things here." She gestured toward the closed door.

Wallace looked doubtful. "I think Hughes—"

Judah Daniel spoke quickly. "Mrs. Powers may need your help."

Her words brought a swift response from Wallace, who released the doorknob and turned toward the door into the street, pausing only long enough to smile his thanks.

• • •

Archer and Hughes faced each other. Hughes had squared his shoulders in a show of defiance, but his face was white, the lines sharply drawn.

There was little furniture in the room: a small desk with paper, pen, and inkwell, a chair behind it, and a chair facing it—the hierarchical arrangement of doctor and patient or teacher and pupil. Archer took the seat behind the desk and waved Hughes into the chair opposite. Hughes sat down, hands gripping the seat, back not touching.

"I have tried to preserve the honor of our family and our profession by not exposing you," Archer began without preamble. "I will give you the chance to resolve this matter in a way that preserves the dignity of your name."

Hughes's voice was rough. "What do you believe me to have done?"

"I know that you killed Aster Jacks. As you've probably guessed, some of my sister's old servants remain loyal to me. They told me she had died, and that you intended to bury her in secret—at Hollywood Cemetery. Near the grave of my own sister, dishonored by your crimes!" Archer's hands clenched into fists. "Aster was her servant, come under your power by your marriage. Her mother was our servant, and her grandmother." Archer drew a breath, then spoke more calmly.

"You have always been cold as a corpse yourself, Hughes, but I was determined to make you feel something. If not pity, then shame, regret—anything! So I got Old Billy and Cyrus, and poor young Charley Powers, and dug her up out of the ground. We brought her back to the dissecting room. I made sure that you would see her and know that your shameful acts were known—at least to me.

"But I didn't know until then the extent of your guilt. You hadn't waited for her to die of the fever that was killing her, you hastened her death by stuffing a rag down her throat. It's a horrible way to kill. You are a doctor. You could have given her a more merciful death."

Hughes covered his face with his hands, but made no sound.

"Charley grew ill, and he died. A stroke of luck for you, I suppose. But you killed Old Billy, I know that now—or paid someone to do it. Then his son Cyrus died suddenly. Did you kill him, too?"

No movement, no sound, came from Hughes.

"And I know now, too, about the attack on Mrs. Powers. I blame myself that it went so far. If I had induced her to trust me, instead of trying to scare her away, far less damage would have been done."

Archer stood up slowly and walked the few paces to where Hughes sat, hunched in his chair, hands covering his face. Archer drew his pistol from its holster and held it in his palm.

"You have not lived the life of a gentleman, Hughes, but I offer you the chance to die like one. Take my pistol. I will stand outside the room. If the deed is not done in one minute, I will do it myself."

Hughes lifted his head from his hands. His pale face was splotched with red where his fingers had dug into the skin. His eyes were red-rimmed but dry. He put his left hand on the back of the chair and rose shakily to a standing position. He extended his right hand for the gun.

Archer placed it in his hand, then turned away.

"Stop," Hughes rasped. Archer heard the hammer being drawn back. He turned slowly.

Hughes held the pistol aimed at Archer's chest. "If I have killed so many, what is to prevent me from killing you?"

"Don't be a fool," Archer said. "You can't expect to get away with it."

"It might be worth it," the older man replied, "just to see the fear in your eyes. Just to see the contempt in them die at last."

"Go behind the desk." Hughes waved the pistol. Archer obeyed. "Now take a piece of paper and write what I tell you."

The doorknob clicked as it turned. Hughes jerked the pistol in the direction of the noise, then trained it on Archer again.

The door opened and Judah Daniel stepped into the room, halting a few feet from Hughes. She looked from him to Archer, then back at Hughes, her face expressive of mild interest, as if the two men were actors in a *tableau vivant*.

"If you kill him," she said to Hughes in her low, husky voice, "you will have to kill me too."

Hughes looked at her for a moment, glanced back at Archer, then looked again at Judah Daniel. "Why shouldn't I?"

"And if you kill me," she said, taking a step closer to Hughes, "you will have to kill your man Percy. Your housemaid Phebe. Your housemaid Jane. The servants at your plantation—you would have to kill them too.

"I am a branch of the vine that bears fruit to you—that has made you rich, given you dignity and power. The vine holds up your house, and it wraps all around you. Can you chop it down? And dig out the roots? And the one fruit of your manhood, got on a slave woman—can you kill your child?

"They know the truth. Did you think they were deaf and blind? Every hidden thing will be revealed."

Hughes stared at Judah Daniel. At last he spoke. "The child—she told me the child was dead."

Archer stepped up behind Hughes and, in one movement, seized the gun and the arm that held it. Hughes released his grip and stood, head bowed.

≫⧀

Narcissa looked down at her hands. The skin was puckered and white around the jagged cuts that ran across both palms. The blood had clotted. If she were careful, the bleeding might not start again. She was aware of throbbing pain, but she could not attend to it. She expected every moment to see Rachel rise with an angry scream and come at her again, her fingernails digging, tearing . . .

The chloroform! Narcissa remembered her reticule down in Hughes's office. With the contents of that vial, she could subdue Rachel until help arrived.

Narcissa ran down the stairs, her heart in her throat. If Rachel should regain her senses in the moments in which Narcissa was out of the room, if the madwoman should launch herself at her . . .

Narcissa threw open the connecting door and ran down the hall. She found her reticule where she had left it on the floor of Hughes's office, concealed by the carved foot of the desk. She snatched it up. Her fingers almost refused to work, but finally she pulled open the strings, reached in, and drew out the vial. The glass felt cool against her wounded palm, and she smiled to herself. She would need a cloth . . . her handkerchief, just the thing! She let the vial slip into the deep pocket of her overskirt, the right-hand pocket, where she kept her handkerchief. Now to run upstairs again. Pray God Rachel Hughes had not regained consciousness. Narcissa would sit near her head, cloth ready in her left hand and the vial of chloroform in the right, with the stopper loosened. If

Rachel made a sound or a movement, the drug would quiet her reviving madness until help should come.

Narcissa walked quickly down the hall, through the connecting door into the house, and down the entrance hall toward the staircase. The curve of the staircase took its top steps out of her sight, and she hesitated. Had there been a noise?

She froze. There it was, a pressure on the creaking step near the top that she had heard during the night she spent sleepless in the bedroom at the top of the stairs. Should she run past Rachel to the front door, only a few yards away, or back to the office and out its door?

In the split second in which Narcissa hesitated, she saw through the stair rails a narrow column of dark cloth. A man's trousers. She let out her breath in a sigh of relief. Jane had brought help already. She rushed to the foot of the stairs and turned to look up.

Standing just above her on the third step, his hand on the curved banister, was Jake Calder.

Narcissa stepped back, staring, then turned to run to the door. Calder came down the three steps at once, his heavy boots loud as they hit the marble floor. He closed the distance between them in two strides. As Narcissa reached out for the door knob, Calder put his boot down hard on the hem of her wide skirt. As she struggled to pull away, he grabbed her right arm, slid his grip down to her wrist, and twisted her arm up behind her back. Narcissa gasped with pain. Her breath came in quick pants, and her heart thumped painfully. Jake Calder stood behind her, so close she could feel the heat coming from his body, could smell the sickening sweetness of hair oil mixed with sweat. If only she could get free of him, get to the door. But the pain in her shoulder from his wrenching grasp was so intense that she could not move.

For a long moment, Calder neither moved nor spoke. At last Narcissa felt a ripple of movement that rose from his chest and into his throat. Calder was laughing. "I thought that crazy woman done got drunk and passed out. But now I find you here, Narcissa Powers. So I reckon you had a hand in it. She wasn't no nigger lover like you. Although her husband sure was." Calder's body was shaking with laughter. "Yep, old Hughes is a nigger lover sure enough, and I got the proof of it outside in the wagon."

Narcissa was silent, forcing herself to be still, to breathe slowly. She had to think. Calder clearly meant his words to have meaning for her. Had he found the autopsied body of Aster Jacks, brought her corrupted flesh to light?

Calder's hand squeezed her wrist and brought her arm up along her back, sending a stab of pain through her shoulder. "Didn't you hear me, whore? I got Hughes's bastard baby out in the wagon. That crazy Rachel Hughes give it to me to get rid of, didn't you know that?

"That ain't nothing," he went on, whispering, his mouth close to her ear. "But you, now—" She felt him laugh again, his body shaking against her own. "Yes sir, I reckon I ought to thank her for putting you into my hands."

Narcissa turned her head away from his foul words in her ear. Calder straightened then. "Here's what you're gonna do. You're gonna come take a little ride with me, just you and me and the doc's brat. You're gonna sit up with me, next to me, real close. If you see anybody knows you, you're gonna smile at 'em, say a pleasant word, look like you're having a real good time. Cause my boot heel's gonna be on that baby."

Narcissa turned to look in Calder's face. The bridge of his nose bulged where Brit Wallace's fist had broken it, and a bruise across it was fading in purple and yellow. He was smiling, but his eyes were cold.

Calder spoke again. "Accidents happen to slave babies, ain't it sad. If you call for help, maybe they'll believe you. Maybe they'll believe me. But that baby will be dead. Ain't nobody even knows it's alive but the slaves, and they can't testify in court. You understand what I'm saying to you?"

Narcissa nodded. Then she wet her lips with her tongue and said, "Yes. I understand. I will come with you."

Calder released his hold on her wrist. He stood looking down at her, his expression unreadable. Then he offered her his arm.

To hang on a man's arm in broad daylight implied an engagement. If any acquaintances saw her, Narcissa knew, this gesture would signal to them that something was wrong. She fought down her revulsion and put her arm through his. They walked out the door together, and he handed her up into the rough-boarded farm wagon, drawn by two strong horses.

There on the floor, concealed and mercifully shaded from the slanting rays of the sun, was a bundle of rags. The baby. Forgetting Jake Calder, Narcissa knelt on the rough floorboard. So still—was the baby already dead? She pulled the ragged wrapping away from the tiny face. The eyes were closed. She stroked the baby's cheek and down her shoulder to her arm. She felt the blood beating there. Alive.

Aster Jacks's baby was alive. Aster—star. In her mind, Narcissa named the baby Star.

She was beautiful. What would she be now, five months old? Yes, her size was right for that. She had been cared for, even if she was now wrapped in rags and thrust into a shallow wooden box against the footboard of an open wagon. Her head was covered with downy curls just a shade brighter than the golden hue of her skin.

Narcissa felt along the baby's forehead, her face and lips. The heartbeat was quick and shallow, the skin hot and dry to the touch. Narcissa knew the signs from so many of the young men who had been treated in the hospital. The baby was becoming dehydrated. She needed to take nourishment, to nurse, or at least to have some water.

Jake Calder swung up to sit on the plank seat of the wagon. He pulled Narcissa up next to him, took her left hand in his, and pulled it under his right arm, pausing for a moment to glance at the cut across her palm. He pinned her arm between his arm and side and pressed the fingers of her hand around the rough tan fabric of his sleeve. They would look to all the world like an affectionate couple, Narcissa thought distractedly. Calder leered at her, then jerked the reins to move the horses forward.

"The baby needs water," Narcissa said.

"I ain't concerned with that now," Calder replied, looking at her with mild amusement. "Maybe you can find some water where we're going." He looked away to drive the horses. A little smile was turning up the corners of his mouth, a smile that chilled Narcissa more than any threat could do.

Narcissa looked down. Calder's boot rested on the baby's temple.

Should she show him that she was afraid? It would excite him, she knew. She remembered the look on his face when he whipped the slave, and taunted as he whipped. He would want her to cry. What means would he use to make her do it?

The baby was safe enough for now, she thought, if Calder got the cooperation he wanted. But soon—when they arrived at whatever destination he had in mind—she would be able to keep the baby from injury only for so long as her own pain and shame amused him.

It would soon be dusk, then dark. He would take them

to some secluded spot. He would get down from the wagon, or make her get down first. She had to take him by surprise. She would have only one chance.

≫≪

Brit Wallace was puzzled that no servant answered his knock at the Hugheses' house. He tried at both doors of the double house. He thought about going back to the hospital—perhaps he and Narcissa had just missed each other in the few moments that he had pulled Judah Daniel aside and told her to keep an eye on Hughes and Archer. It was too absurd to go back there and risk their missing each other again. From the vantage point of the Hugheses' front porch, he could look down Marshall Street to see most of the traffic that passed the medical college and its hospital. He sat on the steps to wait. The granite step was hard but pleasantly cool.

A familiar smell reached him. Fresh dung. He looked along the street in front of the house. Judging by the droppings, a carriage or wagon had stood there for a few minutes at least, and recently.

Brit looked up and down the street again, this time at the houses. Across the street about two doors down a servant was polishing a brass door knocker. Brit jumped up and dashed across the street. The woman looked up and took a step back. Brit thought of the picture he must make, still grubby and unshaven from his days in prison. He slowed to a walk and put on his most ingratiating smile.

"Good day to you! I seem to have missed a meeting with my, er, sister over at Dr. Hughes's house. Did you see her leave? She's a young woman, dark hair, dressed in black." He hoped Narcissa had not put off her widow's weeds during the weeks of his exile from Richmond.

The woman looked at him, suspicion in her eyes. "Yes,

sir, I believe I saw her. She left about fifteen, twenty minutes ago, with the Hugheses' overseer. They was in that old farm wagon."

"With Jake Calder!" Brit could not hide his alarm. The woman nodded. "Which way did they go?" She inclined her head to his left. West.

Brit thanked her and turned away. His first impulse was to find a hack, try to follow them. But besides looking like a derelict, he had no money, no weapon, and no insight into where Calder might be headed. He had to get back to the hospital, find Hughes and Archer, and Judah Daniel.

Edgar Hughes pushed open the door of his house and closed it again behind him. The house was empty and quiet as a grave. Jane Scott he had left at the hospital. Phebe and Percy had been sent away, days ago now, down to the house in Midlothian.

That old crone Phebe had looked about to cry when Rachel told her to go. Who knew what secrets of Rachel's she'd been keeping? Maybe Rachel had cared about her old servant after all, rewarded her loyalty by sending her away. After all, Phebe was still alive.

And so was he. Rachel had not killed him. Why not? He had fathered the hatred that she had given birth to and nursed like a baby, that now tyrannized over her like a spoiled child. Perhaps that was why she allowed him to live: to keep her hatred strong. Or perhaps it was because her contempt for him was so profound that she had feared the others—Charley Wilson and his sister, Old Billy, even dull-witted Cyrus—more than her own husband.

Odd about Cameron Archer. Rachel hadn't touched him, apparently, or sent the madman Jake Calder to kill him. Why? Perhaps she was a little in awe of the Archer name. If so, family pride worked both ways: Archer, still believing that Hughes was guilty of the killings, had nevertheless let him leave the hospital, unwilling to bring infamy upon the man who'd once been related by marriage to the Archer family. That was one reason. The other he could read in Archer's eyes. The man regarded him as a wounded animal that would crawl away to its lair and die.

And maybe he would. But he had to do one thing first, one act of courage and decision that would give him the peace to die.

He put his hand to the banister and mounted the stairs, stepping softly as he had learned to do when Rachel had one of her headaches. From Jane Scott's rather garbled recounting, he knew more or less what he would find.

As he expected, Rachel was still lying on the sofa. He crouched down beside her, sitting on his heels, and felt her wrist and throat. Her pulse was weak, her respiration slow and shallow. She could go either way, slip into death or struggle back to life.

Despite the heat of the day, she looked cold. Though he knew the pallor of her skin and the blue tinge of her lips were the effects of a too-heavy dose of laudanum mixed with brandy, he draped a soft cashmere shawl over her, placed a pillow beneath her head. Then he reached into his pocket, took out a small bottle, and opened it. With his right arm under her shoulder, he drew her upright, then put the bottle to her lips. A few drops spilled from the corner of her mouth, then she swallowed.

After a few moments, he gently eased his arm out from under his wife and lowered her head onto the pillow. He corked the bottle and put it back in his pocket, then walked softly out of the room.

Down in his study, Hughes seated himself at his desk and

placed the bottle in front of him. Then he pulled several blank sheets of paper from a drawer, dipped his pen, and started to write.

Jake Calder drove the wagon west down Marshall Street about a dozen blocks, then turned down Adams, heading south toward the river. They passed stores and homes, and the streets were crowded with carriages, wagons, and people on horseback and on foot. At first Narcissa scanned their faces eagerly, but all seemed intent on their own errands, and she saw no one she knew. Could she call out, then push Calder away quickly enough so that he could not hurt the baby? His grip on her arm was strong, holding her down. He would feel her muscles gather to make a move before she could make it.

They crossed the line of the Richmond, Fredericksburg & Potomac Railroad and continued several more blocks, turning south or west at every corner. They were coming close to Monroe Square, where Narcissa knew soldiers would be drilling. She wondered if she could hail them—surely they would come to the aid of any woman, she thought. But Calder turned the wagon south, avoiding the square.

When Calder turned the horses south on to Cherry Street to double back toward the river, Narcissa realized where he must be taking them. Hollywood.

The shadows were long now. "They'll have locked the gates," Narcissa mused, hardly aware that she spoke out loud.

Jake Calder turned to smile at her. "Ain't no problem. I know another way in." He went on, showing off his knowledge. "The Archers used to own all the land around here. Their family burying ground was on the land that was bought for the cemetery. The Archers kept the right-of-way for the old trace that runs up the hill right next to the river.

"It's a rough ride, for you, ma'am," he said mockingly, turning to exhale his foul breath into her face, "but you just hang on to me."

After a few minutes, Calder proved his words by turning the horses into a road that was little more than a rut worn into the side of the steep hill. Thickets entwined with honeysuckle rose up on each side. Narcissa saw Calder move his booted foot off the baby onto the edge of the box to keep it from sliding. But the box was thin wood. If he wanted to, Calder could crush it and the baby under his foot.

Narcissa's breath was coming faster. She could hear the rumble of the river's waters over the boulders in its path. They would soon come to the Archer plot at the crest of the hill overlooking the James. The Archer graves must be Calder's destination, she thought, her mind racing. The graves, with their pure and silent monuments—something else he could defile. He had brought Aster Jacks's body here, although it may have been the doctor's idea to bury his slave mistress in his own family plot.

It must be now, Narcissa thought. God help me.

"I think I'm going to be sick," Narcissa said in a broken voice. She bent her head away from Calder and doubled over, her right arm over her stomach.

"Don't try any tricks," Calder warned, but he relaxed his hold on her left arm.

Narcissa wrapped both her arms around her waist and bent double. As she retched, near to gagging in earnest, she thrust her right hand deep into the pockets of her overskirt. She brought out her handkerchief, transferred it to her left hand, and pressed it against her mouth. Then she thrust her right hand into the pocket again. Her fingers closed around the vial of chloroform.

She would have to work the stopper loose with her

wounded right hand so that it would be ready when she got the chance to pour its contents on the handkerchief and clap it over Calder's nose and mouth. But if she loosened it too much, she risked spilling the precious chloroform.

She sat up, still pressing the handkerchief to her lips, and glanced over at Calder. He was scowling, his face drenched with sweat. He was leaning forward now, his feet braced on the floorboards, steadying himself as he drove the horses hard up the rough path.

At last they reached the crest of the hill. The tops of the tall oaks and hollies still held the sun, but the monuments were in shadow. Calder pulled the horses to a stop. The wagon lurched with the sudden movement, and the baby let out a weak cry.

Jake started as if he had forgotten the baby's existence.

Narcissa moved sideways along the bench, turning toward Calder. The motion caught his eye, and he looked around. He was half-standing, his left hand holding the reins. He put his right hand palm-down on the bench to keep his balance.

Narcissa pushed up from the bench and launched herself at Calder. She drove her right fist, the vial of chloroform clutched in it, up into Calder's nose. She felt the bone give way, and he fell back with a hoarse scream of rage and anguish into the back of the wagon.

She was on him at once, holding him down with her body. She pushed the handkerchief over his nose and mouth, then doused it with the entire contents of the vial. For once, the wire cage of her hoops and the heavy crinolines were a help; he could not get his hands up to defend himself. Calder struggled briefly, then went limp. It was over sooner than she had believed possible. She wondered if he had fainted from the shock of the blow to his nose. She used both her hands to press the cloth over his nose and mouth until she was sure he could not be feigning unconsciousness.

At last, Narcissa dared to sit up. She clambered into the front of the wagon, looking for something to hit him with, to ensure that he would not come around right away. She gently picked up the baby, little Star, whose faint cries sounded like the mews of a kitten, and put her on the seat. Then she picked up the box in which the baby had been confined and hit Calder with all her might on the side of the head.

The thin wooden slats of the box came apart in her hands and she threw it down. Calder hadn't made a sound. She leaned over to feel the pulse at his throat. He was alive.

As she straightened, she saw a gleam of metal where his coat had fallen open. It was the hilt of a knife stuck into a sheath on his belt. She drew it out and held it in her hand. The blade was more than an inch wide at the hilt and above five inches long, sharp-edged and tapering to a point. I could kill him, she thought. I could take this knife and slit his throat.

"God, tell me what to do," she prayed aloud. Then she heard again, as if in answer, Star's mewing cry. Narcissa stretched tall, drew back her arm, and threw the knife as far as she could into the tangle of honeysuckle. Then she climbed down from the wagon, gathered up the baby in her bundle of rags, and began to run.

She hurried back down the trace, running where she could but afraid to fall and injure her tender burden. Once she came to Cherry Street, she could cut up away from the river to one of the houses there. They were near where Judah Daniel had lived, before her house was burned. Judah Daniel would know what to do to help Star, but she was staying in the Chapman house in another part of town. Still, someone . . . anyone.

Suddenly Narcissa saw a light flickering in the dusk. It was below her, down at the bottom of the hill where the trace led out from the cemetery onto Cherry Street. She pushed forward, intent on that light.

"Mrs. Powers!" It was Judah Daniel's voice. Could it really be that Judah Daniel was here? Then she saw other forms, and faces—Brit Wallace, Cameron Archer. They were running to meet her. She ran past Wallace and Archer to Judah Daniel, who reached out with her strong and gentle hands and took the baby. She cradled it in one arm, put the other around Narcissa. The baby is safe, Narcissa thought. Relief burst through the walls that for so long had been holding back her tears, and she wept.

>≈<

They had gone to the Powerses' house. Cameron Archer and Judah Daniel had examined the baby Star and summoned a wet nurse. Narcissa had been surprised when the arrogant Archer called Judah Daniel into consultation over the baby—until she learned the startling news that the doctoress had used her intuition to save the doctor's life. Now the baby slept peacefully in a darkened corner of the front parlor. Narcissa relaxed in the presence of familiar things.

Judah Daniel was speaking. "I didn't know for sure Dr. Hughes was the father of Aster Jacks's baby. I just figured that saying so would upset him one way or another, get his mind off of killing you." She nodded at Archer, who smiled in response, and went on. "I been watching both of you. He looked like a man had his last hope snatched from him. That made him dangerous."

Cameron Archer's smile turned rueful. "And what did I look like?"

Judah Daniel thought a moment. "Like a man who'd take whatever life give him like it was handed to him on a silver platter. That's a different kind of dangerous."

Archer's eyes widened, then he nodded slowly.

Mirrie leaned over to Narcissa. "And while Judah Daniel was saving Dr. Archer's life, Mr. Wallace was finding out you were in the clutches of Jake Calder," Mirrie explained, beaming her thanks to Brit. "He was certain you would not have left the Hugheses' without some word to the hospital. He knocked on all the doors on the street until he found a servant who had seen you leave with that—monster. Mr. Wallace found Dr. Archer and Judah Daniel, who were on their way to the house with Hughes, and Dr. Archer guessed where you were being taken."

This time the looks of gratitude were for Cameron Archer.

"That dreadful Jake Calder." Mirrie shuddered. "I can't bear to think. If it hadn't been for your quick thinking, Narcissa, there would have been two new graves in Hollywood. Calder is in custody now, thank God," she added.

"What about . . . Rachel Hughes?" Narcissa asked, afraid to hear the answer. Given Rachel's social position and the lack of evidence that she had killed anyone, it would likely be left up to Hughes himself whether his wife would be restrained or continue to move about in society, disguising her madness.

"She's dead," Archer said, an unaccustomed gentleness in his voice.

Narcissa's shock showed on her face. Had the laudanum and brandy she'd encouraged Rachel to drink resulted in her death?

Archer read her face and responded. "No, Mrs. Powers,

you did not kill her. After you left the house with Calder, Hughes returned there. His wife . . . well, you may read the letter yourself," he said, drawing a folded paper from the inside pocket of his uniform coat. "He killed her, and then himself, with massive drafts of laudanum mixed with alcohol.

"Here, Miss Powers," Archer said, holding out the letter to Mirrie. "Please read it aloud that we may all hear it."

Mirrie read in a calm, clear voice.

Do not judge her too harshly. She has been tried beyond the endurance of woman.

After puerperal fever killed my first wife and our child, I feared there might be truth in the argument of Dr. Oliver Wendell Holmes—that doctors carry the disease themselves. I could not rid myself of the fear that I had killed what I loved best in the world. I resolved never to be present at another confinement. Despair came near to destroying me.

Would that it had destroyed me utterly!

When I met Rachel, she redeemed me with the precious gift of her love and trust. I ceased to blame myself for my first wife's death, taking comfort that the vast majority of my colleagues disputed Holmes's arguments. Rachel convinced me that I should attend her at her own confinement, and thus should be made whole again.

You have heard, no doubt, of what happened then. Our twin sons died a terrible death. With them died her love for me.

When she heard that our servant Aster Jacks was to be confined—the child is mine, I admit it—the knowledge overpowered the fragile balance of her sanity. After the birth, Rachel had Aster brought to our house.

*She told Aster the baby had died, and she let me
believe it as well, but she tended Aster with seeming
concern. Then, to my horror, Aster contracted the fever.
Rachel continued to attend her, and Aster began to
recover. Then, suddenly, she died.*

*When I saw poor Aster's body opened in the dissecting-
room, I knew that my wife had killed her by suffocation.
It was only later—after the death of young Charles
Wilson—that I began to suspect Rachel had done more.
She had put to shame some of the greatest medical minds
of our day by proving the observation of Oliver Wendell
Holmes. Not only can puerperal fever be passed between
doctor and patient, but the fever can be passed in
different forms—gangrene, erysipelas, puerperal fever, may
all be forms of the same hideous contagion. What had
been done by me in ignorance, by carrying the infection
on my hands and clothes, she did deliberately by tainting
bandages with the effluvia of disease.*

*When you find us, we will have been released to our
eternal punishment. By the provisions of the will of my first
wife's father, McCollum Archer, and of my own will,
Cameron Archer inherits all our property. I leave it to his
honor to see that Aster Jacks's child is freed from her servile
condition, given an appropriate inheritance, and sent to be
raised by my family in Philadelphia. I would like her to be
called Stella Hughes.*

Pray for us.

The silence was broken by Judah Daniel. " 'In Rama was
there a voice heard, lamentation, and weeping, and great
mourning. Rachel weeping for her children—' "

" '—And would not be comforted,' " Narcissa joined in, " 'because they are not.' " The two women exchanged a look of understanding.

"I thought that he had killed Aster, of course." Cameron Archer spoke stiffly. His face was pale. "At first, I blamed him only for seducing her. I wanted to see his face when he saw her body exhumed and knew that I had discovered his secret shame. . . . But when I found out she had been killed, I figured he had done it to rid himself of an inconvenience.

"I watched him. Then I sensed that you were suspicious as well," he said to Narcissa. "I decided to scare you off. The trick with the bonnet was mine, though I blush to admit it." Narcissa saw the corners of Judah Daniel's mouth twitch in a smile that vanished as quickly as it had come.

Brit Wallace broke in. "Is that why you paid those thugs to accost Mrs. Powers and me in the street?"

If he expected a fight from Archer, Wallace reckoned wrong. The doctor looked subdued, even embarrassed. "I didn't set them on you. I had heard you were asking about Judah Daniel"—he glanced at the woman as he said her name—"and I followed you there. I saw them harassing you, and paid them to take off, but I failed to pay them enough, apparently. I apologize to you, Judah Daniel."

"And to Mrs. Powers, and to me?" Brit Wallace demanded testily.

A slight smile lightened Archer's face. "And to Mrs. Powers."

Narcissa looked back at Archer but did not return his smile. "Of course, I could not tell you I found the body and was attacked. Everything you said to me, everything you did, spoke of your guilt! But you might have guessed, when I passed your little test by assisting at the amputation, that I did not faint at the sight of a dissected body. Had you not dismissed me as a mere *lady,*" she went on, "there could have been a much earlier end to this horror."

Archer acknowledged her words with a bow of his head. For once, Narcissa thought, it's been *I* who've left *him* speechless.

Epilogue

RICHMOND
THE END OF JULY

Early the next morning, Judah Daniel stood at the door of the Chapman house, sipping coffee from a mug and looking out into the yard where Darcy was playing with John Chapman's young granddaughters. The girls were teaching Darcy a game of intricate hand-clapping. The words of their song came to her: *Possum up the 'simmon tree, raccoon on the ground, Possum up the 'simmon tree, shake those 'simmons down.*

She was tired and more unsettled in her mind than she had been in years. But she had done the right thing, as it turned out, helping Narcissa Powers. The baby Stella had been saved, her mother's spirit released to its rest. God works in mysterious ways, she thought, and through people who never suspect they do His will. But those of us who meditate on it can sometimes feel His hand.

≫≪

After breakfast, Narcissa and Mirrie went to sit on the wrought-iron bench in the garden behind the Powerses' house. Mirrie refolded a letter that had come that morning and placed it in her pocket.

"Mr., or rather, *Colonel* Cohen sends his regards," she said to Narcissa. "He complains of not having been in any 'action' so far. Little does he know that you have been in peril of your life, not once, but twice."

Narcissa patted Mirrie's hand but looked past her to the velvety rose blossoms at the end of the garden path. "Stella is on her way to a new life. Dr. Archer is carrying out Dr. Hughes's instructions and giving her a generous inheritance. How strange that I should have thought of her as 'Star.' Some merciful angel was looking over her. Perhaps, after this war, I can see her again." Then she focused her gaze on Mirrie. "Won't you think about Mr. Cohen's proposal, Mirrie? You are still young enough . . . you could have a child."

"And what of you, Narcissa?" Mirrie responded, gently deflecting the question. "You will have your choice of admirers, I think, in Mr. Wallace and Dr. Archer."

"You know, Mirrie," Narcissa replied, laughing, "I am not sure that either of those gentlemen is quite grown up himself!"

Then Narcissa's smile grew pensive. It is too soon, she thought. Perhaps, some day. But for now, we have things we must do, all of us—Cameron Archer and Brit Wallace, Mirrie, Judah Daniel, me. We were unlikely allies. Whether we will meet again as allies or as enemies, only time will tell.

The unlikely pair of crime solvers, Narcissa Powers and Judah Daniel, return in Angel Trumpet, *the second novel in Ann McMillan's Civil War mystery series. The following is a sneak peek at the elegant and haunting sequel.*

Prologue

MANAKIN PLANTATION,
GOOCHLAND COUNTY, VIRGINIA
OCTOBER 1861

Colonel John Berton rode into the slanting sun. Powdered red-clay dust filmed his gray wool uniform and tanned face. He wore his slouch hat pulled low, shading his eyes. His horse knew the way and pursued it at a steady walk.

When he came to a narrow drive, lined with ancient cedars, that branched off the main road, he pulled up, wet his lips from his canteen, and looked down the drive into the deep, fragrant cedar shade.

Berton was thirty years old, brown haired and bearded, of medium height and build. His colonel's insignia, as well as some things less tangible—the way he carried himself, the way he sat his horse—showed his aristocrat's blood. It was the invisible properties of blood, passed down from father to son, that made Berton heir to this plantation home, its thousand acres, its fifty slaves.

Berton's chestnut gelding pawed the dirt, scenting home. Berton tightened his thigh muscles, urging the horse onto the drive. They covered its mile length at an easy pace. Now and then, a break in the line of cedars afforded a glimpse of brown plowed earth and stubbled fields, then, farther, of dark green forests. The field hands would be plowing and ashing the acres from which the wheat had been cut, plowing and sowing winter wheat on acres where corn had been harvested, planting potatoes, felling oak, walnut, sycamore, and pine.

At last the drive met the brick walkway and curved away on either side. Berton held the reins in a gloved hand and stared at the two-story white frame house, classically symmetrical, with chimneys at each end and paired sets of windows spreading out from an unpretentious one-story portico. All was quiet inside the house and around it. Where was the servant who would meet a guest and see to his horse? He looked around, frowning. At length he dismounted and walked forward, holding the chestnut's reins.

Now he could see a figure that had been hidden in shadow: a brown-skinned girl sitting on an overturned box near the door. Her mouth hung open. She was grabbing at something in front of her face, and she took no notice of him.

Berton dropped his reins and walked up the steps, staring at the girl. She did not look up or pause in her repeated gesture: first one hand, then the other, clutched at the empty air in front of her eyes. The sound of his boots on the wooden porch seemed to rouse her. Her hands stopped their clutching motion, and she raised her eyes toward his looming form. Her eyes were deep black, their color swallowed up in darkness.

Berton took a step backward. As he continued to stare, he saw her gaze shift away from him, the clutching gesture resume.

Berton took off his hat, ran his fingers through his hair, and pushed open the door. He crossed the great hall to the river portico, swung open the heavy door, and walked halfway down the flight of low stone steps, held together with iron bands whose rust had left stains like old blood. He looked down the terraced slope to where the James ran reddish brown. He saw no one. Then he looked up at the house. sunlight glanced off the tall, many-paned windows, repelling his gaze.

Berton trotted back up the steps into the hall and entered through the door on the right. Here, in the southeast corner of the house, was the room his family used most. A half-finished piece of embroidery in its hoop lay on a chair, the threaded needle stuck into the linen as a sign of its owner's intention to return. Berton frowned, opened his mouth to call out, then closed it again.

He crossed to the room opposite, glanced in. No one. This strange silence quickened his heartbeat; he was beginning to feel lightheaded. He shrugged it off and walked back across the grand hall into the north wing. This time he looked into the library—no one—then into the dining room. Here he paused. The long mahogany table that could seat ten was laid for four. The silver was polished, the stemware sparkling, the linen spotless white. A bowl of late roses sat in the center of the table. One fallen petal glowed red against the white cloth.

He walked over to the mahogany sideboard under the far window. He looked out to where sunlight struck sparks on the river, threw long shadows on the lawn. Then where it angled through the ancient panes, revealing names and dates—*Mary Anna Barbour, Col. Berton, March 20, 1780; Louisa Berton, J. Selden, 1854*—etched into the thick, wavy glass by the diamonds of newly engaged belles.

He turned away and walked the few paces to the south

staircase. He put his booted foot on the bottom step, hesitated just a moment, and mounted the stairs.

Then he noticed the smell. Long before Manassas, he had known—as every countryman knows who has seen a hog butchered or carved up a deer—the smell of blood.

Chapter 1

CHAMPS-ELYSÉES PLANTATION, NORTHERN VIRGINIA

"Oh, I don't believe in ghosts," Narcissa Powers said, then wondered why she'd made the statement. It wasn't that she wanted to stop the old woman from telling the tale she had offered up. A distraction from musing on this fool's errand, and on the high-handed doctor who had requested it, would be welcome. Anyway, saying *I don't believe in ghosts* was like saying, *You can't scare me.* The very need to make the assertion called its veracity into questions. Narcissa smiled at her own naïveté.

Auntie Lora smiled in return, revealing soft gums where a few teeth leaned like ancient gravestones. Three women—the young white widow Narcissa, the old slave Auntie Lora, and the free black doctoress Judah Daniel—sat snapping the ends off beans and tossing them into one pot for the day's meal, the ends into another pot for the hogs. The clearing where they sat held a dozen slave cabins made of boards rough-hewn from the huge oaks and chestnuts that had grown there once. Now the forest was returning, sending out onto the bare dirt a tangle of knee-high trees and honeysuckle from which crickets sang their maddening one-note song.

"That is," Narcissa added, her expression growing thoughtful, "I do believe that the souls of the dead are interested in us. Even that they may linger on earth to right some wrong." She thought of her brother Charley, who had died in the spring, and of how, after his death, his spirit had seemed to guide her through the frightening events that followed. "But I believe they wish to help us, not to hurt us."

The old woman nodded. "Well, miss," she said at last, "supposing *they* hurt. Suppose their suffering in life was so bad that they died wanting nothing more than to hurt back." She stopped and looked at Narcissa with a humoring condescension. "Nice lady such as you be, I reckon you can't understand how people could be so hate-filled. But maybe you understand this better: supposing they love. They love a thing here on earth so much that they can't stand to leave it when they die, even to get to the heavenly kingdom."

Auntie Lora paused to let the thought settle, her gap-toothed smile widening. "But the dead and their feelings don't belong here amongst the living. Gets things all jangled up. Folks say that's what cause a place to be haunted. Like Champs-Elysées."

Auntie Lora's eyes shifted over Narcissa's head. Narcissa turned, following her gaze to the top of the hill, about a quarter-mile distant, where the magnificent plantation house called Champs-Elysées stood overlooking the Potomac. The house had been built more than a century before of brick brought over from England, built as the fashionable new dwelling for a son whose name was one of the most ancient in the colony. On this side was visible the shallow portico whose four columns rose almost the height of the house, surmounted by an elegant pediment. Sinuous vines of wisteria as old as the house softened the severity of its perfection.

Narcissa and Judah Daniel had come to Champs-Elysées at the request of Dr. Cameron Archer to meet his cousin Jordan Archer. She was expected this day, returning at last from the Maryland boarding school where illness had detained her through the summer. Narcissa and Judah Daniel were to bring her back to Richmond. It was an extension, to say the least, of both women's duties at the medical college hospital supervised by Dr. Archer. But the surgeon had a way of giving orders that made it easier to acquiesce than to refuse, however good the reason for refusal.

As the plantation was close to the Potomac, and to the armies camped on either side, its portable treasures had been removed to Richmond months before. But the Federal army that had been driven back at Manassas could march against any moment and engulf Champs-Elysées. So the house remained deserted, guarded most nights by one or another of the soldiers from the Confederate encampment about ten miles away. Today—drawn no doubt by the news of Jordan Archer's expected arrival—the pickets were at their post earlier and in greater numbers than usual.

Narcissa turned back to find the old woman's eyes on her. Narcissa smiled inwardly. *The ladies of Champs-Elysées no doubt stay aloof from this kind of work. So what does she see when she looks at me?* She selected a bean from the pile in her apron. *I'm not quite a lady, but not a servant.* Snap! The stem was off. *A widow, by my clothes.* Snap! with the help of her thumbnail, the blossom end was off. Drop the bean into the iron pot on the left, the ends into the pot on the right. Select another bean. *In straitened circumstances, perhaps, but young enough to marry again, pretty enough. Death, danger, loss of hope, have come close to me, but they haven't marked me. Have they?*

"You, now, Judah Daniel." Auntie Lora's gaze shifted to the third woman. "You understand about them lost souls well enough, I'll be bound."

"I do that, Auntie Lora. I do that," was Judah Daniel's reply.

Narcissa watched the two exchange a look and felt oddly excluded. The talk about ghosts had taken her back to a time only a few months past—a time when buried evil and living madness had combined to threaten both Narcissa and Judah Daniel. She had come to think of Judah Daniel as an ally. Now she was reminded of the gap that remained between them. Judah Daniel and Auntie Lora, within moments of their meeting, seemed to read each other's thoughts. Yet apart from their brown skin, the two could hardly be more different. Judah Daniel was lean, sharp-eyed, with a perceptible power that ran through her even when she held herself quiet and still. Auntie Lora's eyes were clouded, and she slumped as if bone-weary. Her ankles, visible where she sat with her slippered feet propped up on a pile of feed sacks, were swollen to elephantine size—the result, Narcissa assumed, of some dropsical condition.

What would be best to treat it? Narcissa's nursing experience now included every conceivable injury of war, as well as those plagues endemic to the campgrounds—measles, mumps, dysentery, fevers—but not dropsy. Her brother Charley's medical books might have something about it. But no doubt Judah Daniel had already made her diagnosis and thought out whatever bark, roots, or berries she would need to help the old woman with the time-honored arts of the herb doctor. Narcissa resolved to ask her about it later.

The sun was getting high, and it was hot. Narcissa looked

over at the foot-high pile of snap beans still waiting their preparation and sighed a little. "Tell us about the ghosts of Champs-Elysées," she said to Auntie Lora.

The old woman was drawing her breath to begin the story when a whoop rang out up at the house. The women's hands fell still as they peered up toward the source of the commotion. Was the long-awaited battle at last engaged? Narcissa wondered for a moment, then dismissed the thought. She had heard no shots, no alarums. She rose, shaking the beans from her apron back onto the pile, and started running toward the house. She glanced back to see Judah Daniel close behind her. Even Auntie Lora was making surprisingly quick progress, walking in a fast, hitching stride.

At the top of the rise she could see four young soldiers fairly jumping up and down with excitement, could see coming along the road a cloud of dust that swirled around a figure bent low over the horse's mane, cloak streaming in the wind. As Narcissa came up, one of the boys turned to her and shouted, "It's her! It's Miss Archer!" Narcissa looked again. Yes, she could see that the figure rode sidesaddle.

With a drumroll of hooves and an ever more frenzied outcry from the soldiers—whose number had somehow swelled to a half-dozen—Jordan Archer rode up to the wide verandah with which Champs-Elysées fronted the river. The boys rushed forward, each offering his hand to her, but she slipped from the saddle unaided and swept through them, acknowledging their clamorous welcome with an elated smile. Jordan's heavy blond hair—which Narcissa had taken for a wideblown cape—had come loose from its netting and streamed down her back almost to the hem of her emerald-hued riding jacket. Her triangular smile dimpled her cheeks and spoke of mischief. As she tugged off her pearl-colored kid gloves finger by finger, she looked around her, thin brows drawn down over her bright blue eyes. Then the frown vanished and her smile burst wide. She rushed past the others into the arms of Auntie Lora. Narcissa wondered what it must feel like to the young soldiers, to wish for a moment to change places with an old slave woman.

After a bit, Auntie Lora held Jordan away and frowned up into her beaming face. "Don't you be telling me you done rode all this way with no escort."

Jordan laughed. "No, Auntie, beat them here, is all. There's a slow old wagon with all my trunks should be here in a half-hour or so. Is there anything to drink? I'm parched!" Jordan pulled out the pins that anchored the little straw hat, tore it off, and began to fan herself with it.

Arm in arm with Auntie Lora, Jordan mounted the wide stairs of Champs-Elysées, Narcissa and Judah Daniel following behind. At the top of the stairs, she looked back over her shoulder and called to the young men gathered below, "I want you all to come for supper this evening, as many of you as can. I'll send a letter to your commanding officer." Jordan turned to Auntie Lora but spoke loudly enough so the young men could hear. "I saw some chickens in the yard. Better we feed them to our boys than let the Yankees get them." The soldiers hollered approval. Jordan glanced at them over her shoulder and went on. "This will be the last gathering at Champs-Elysées, until we drive the Yankees out once and for all!"